CONVICTION

A New World, Book Two

M.D. Neu

A NineStar Press Publication

Published by NineStar Press
P.O. Box 91792,
Albuquerque, New Mexico, 87199 USA.
www.ninestarpress.com

Conviction

Printed in the USA
First Edition
March, 2019

Print ISBN: 978-1-950412-37-2

Also available in eBook, ISBN: 978-1-950412-35-8

Warning: This book contains graphic violence.

A little blue world, the third planet from the sun. It's home to 7 billion people with all manner of faiths, beliefs and customs, divided by bigotry and misunderstanding, who will soon be told they are not alone in the universe. Anyone watching from the outside would pass by this fractured and tumultuous world, unless they had no other choice.

Todd Landon is one of these people, living and working in a section of the world called the United States of America. His life is similar to those around him: home, family, work, friends and a husband.

After the attack on San Jose, Todd is appointed to Special Envoy for Terran Affairs by the nentraee, a position many world leaders question. Undeterred Todd wants to build bridges between both people. However, this new position brings with it a new set of problems that not only he, but his new allies Mi'ko and Mirtoff must overcome. Will the humans and nentraee learn to work together despite mistrust and threats of more attacks by a new global terrorist group, or will the terrorists win? Will this bring an end to an already shaky alliance between nentraee and humans?

For Eric

One: A New Life

"I BELIEVE THIS should be adequate." Mi'ko checked his datapad to ensure all the proper requisitions had been finalized. He glanced around the room again with a pleased smile.

"Do you think he'll enjoy living here?" Mi'cin asked.

They were here to inspect the quarters he had selected for Todd in the secured area of the speaker's ship. He could have left it up to Vi-Narm or one of his other aides, but this was important and he needed to handle these details personally. Todd was important, and he wanted to make sure everything was perfect. Plus, it was an opportunity to spend more time with Mi'cin.

"Mister Todd Landon was adamant about staying in his own home and commuting, but it's not practical." Mi'ko ran a hand over the desk, then checked his fingers for dust. "And with the rise in protest against us across the planet, it's not safe. Even though his government insists it is."

"If you say so," Mi'cin said. "He didn't strike me as very logical after our brief meeting." He went to one of the windows and opened it. "It would be nice to have quarters like this for myself. Does he need all this space? He's one male." He inhaled deeply and viewed the park below. "It smells like home. But it's a replica, not the real place." His nose crinkled.

"Mi'cin, don't sulk. Our living situation isn't that bad, and you are not a child." Mi'ko put a hand on his son's arm and squeezed. "I know you hurt. We all ache for our home, but these ships are our home, for now. It's a pain we all share. By working with the humans, especially Todd, that pain and the loss of our home will lessen."

Mi'cin's expression fell. "Assuming the humans will work with us."

"Please be supportive." Mi'ko frowned. "I understand you have your misgivings, but please." He inhaled, smelling the damp trees. "And since when have you not enjoyed the ship's gardens?" He looked out to the woodland where several tall trees, paths, and waterways ran in countless directions.

The grounds were replicas of some of the famous parks on Benzee and her satellites. The ship's builders gave as much space as feasible to allow people the chance to enjoy the open space. The artificial light that mimicked the day-night cycle of Benzee had gradually been adjusted to the length of Earth's day.

"He does, indeed, have a better view than us, but that's all right." Mi'ko grinned and thought.

This new position for Mi'cin will help focus him. Give him a chance to interact with the humans and learn about them.

"A view of space would have been equally nice," Mi'cin said, "but I doubt he'd be used to such a thing." He turned back to the window. "Such a waste."

"I assure you it's not a waste." Mi'ko ran a hand over the soft fabric of the chair. "Considering the nature of this position. Plus, I thought a view of nature and all the fresh scents would make him feel more at home. It will give him a sense of what Mentra Park was like."

Mi'cin clucked his tongue.

"What?" Mi'ko questioned. "That was one of your favorite parks on Mentra. You made me take you there whenever we went to visit my parents. You loved the views of Benzee."

Mi'cin said nothing.

"Mi'cin, please."

"As you wish, Father."

"I'd like to ask you to assist Mister Todd Landon to help him acclimate," Mi'ko said. "It's going to be hard for him at first. Even though he's been studying our language and culture—"

Mi'cin's sigh muted his father. "Of course. I'll do my best. You have my word. Besides, isn't that what your aide is supposed to do?"

"True, but this is the first time I've had an aide who's my son."

"Well, Vi-Narm can't do it all, and your other aides are busy," Mi'cin said. "I can use the experience, as you and Mother both keep telling me."

"I can think of no one better to support me." Mi'ko focused on his son. "You know, you're both very quizzical, so you will be good for each other. I hope you can become friends." He reached out and gently touched Mi'cin on the cheek.

A soft chirp came from the door. It opened to reveal Vi-Narm. Her tightly braided hair had a few wisps out of place; her breathing was heavy.

"Vice speaker, there is a problem with the Envoy position. General Gahumed, with the support of General Fanion, is calling for a special session in the council chamber."

"What now?" The muscles around Mi'ko's eyes twitched and the tips of his ears started to warm. It had been like this for several weeks. These continued issues with his own people were taking far too much of his time.

"THANK YOU FOR picking me up." Todd glanced over at Mi'cin, who sat in the black sedan with him. He was jealous at how everything Mi'cin wore seemed to fit him perfectly. Particularly with his bright green eyes and his perfect soft brown hair.

He looks a lot like his mom.

"You are welcome," Mi'cin said.

"I'm a little nervous."

"It is understandable." Mi'cin focused on his datapad. "You race has inferior space travel, but I can assure you it is as safe as flying in one of you antiquated airships."

Todd clasped his hands in front of him, resting them on his padfolio. The news of Mi'cin now being one of Mi'ko's junior aides made him personally uncomfortable, especially after the questions Mi'cin asked at the White House dinner. Professionally, it was a good opportunity. They would both be learning, which meant he wouldn't be the only one screwing up.

"How do you like the new job?" Todd asked.

"The position is a challenge. However, it is putting some of my knowledge to use. I, like you, have much to learn." Mi'cin spared a glance at Todd.

Todd sighed.

"What's wrong?"

"You mean, more than getting on one of your shuttles?" He continued with a forced smile. "My cat, Bianca. I'm leaving her behind, and I'm going to miss her."

Mi'cin was quiet a moment. "You are close with your animal companion?"

Todd nodded.

"As I'm sure Vi-Narm informed you. We do not yet know how you feline will react to our closed environment and what feline-carried bacterium could do to our cádo and other animals. It is too much of a risk."

Todd stared at his hands and his padfolio.

"Interesting. It is clear this conversation make you unhappy and is not something you wish to continue." Mi'cin tapped his fingers over his datapad. "You personal belongings will be sent to you new quarters. I am glad we reached a satisfactory solution with you living accommodations and maintaining you residence on Earth." He slipped the datapad away and tapped his hand on his leg.

"Well, it's home, you know? There're a lot of ghosts there." Todd rubbed his hands on his legs. "It's hard to just pack up and move, especially since I can't bring Bianca."

"Ghosts? You mean nayus, spirit energy?" Mi'cin leaned in.

Todd chuckled.

Wow. A part of human culture that actually interests him.

"No, it's just a human—well, English...American—saying. It means a lot of memories."

"Memories of you husband? Of the life you had?" Mi'cin asked.

"Yes, that's all part of it." He glanced out the car window, not wanting to talk about it. He hoped Mi'cin wouldn't pry. Was it prying, or was he trying to make conversation? The Nentraee, and Mi'cin in particular, were so formal and stiff it was hard to read his body language.

"I will have to check into that. American English colloquialisms are difficult to understand." Mi'cin pulled out his datapad.

"You'll want to add researching the differences on when to use 'you' and 'your,'" Todd said.

Mi'cin made notes on his datapad. "Thank you, Mister Todd Landon."

Once the sedan pulled up to the Nentraee checkpoint, they got out. The Nentraee security watched them. Mi'cin withdrew a plastic card that looked like a credit card, and the security person scanned it. They spoke quiet enough Todd missed what they said, but he still picked up on musical qualities in their accent.

Sadly, they speak better English than I do Nentraee even with their missteps and incorect word choices.

"Welcome, Special Envoy Mister Todd Landon," the security guard said with a thick, lyrical Nentraee tone. He was a tall male with fair features. He had blue eyes and dirty-blond hair.

Mi'cin stopped and turned to Todd. With pursed lips, he quickly returned to the sedan, shaking his head, the tips of his ears seemed a bit swollon and they definitely had hinks of blue. Mi'cin pulled out an envelope. He immediately headed back to Todd.

"Forgive me." He handed the envelope over. "Mister Todd Landon, these are the diplomatic papers and identification you will need."

Grinning, Todd opened the envelope. The papers were mostly written in the Nentraee language, but some of it was in English.

"Do you need my passport?"

The guard processed the question. "No need, but please keep...Nentraee badge at all times. The other papers are...records."

Todd found the card in the envelope and handed it to the guard.

"The card is encrypted with"—he pointed at Todd—"DNA," the guard added.

That explained the physical exam. Both groups, human and Nentraee, wanted to monitor his physical reaction to the Nentraee environment. He pocketed the ID badge, placing it with his passport and pocket watch. The two items that reminded him of who he was. One a government-issued identifcation and the second a gift from Varick, his former boss. He was also the man who, if not for him, Todd really wouldn't be here.

It was because of that first meeting with the Nentraee that Todd was here today. It was also because of Varick Jerry died. No, not Varick per se, but because of the terrorist who blew up all those people and destroyed parts of San Jose. Varick, like Todd, was an innocent victim. He sighed at the memories, feeling the slight tick of the watch. It was now his anchor to home. He put the rest of the paperwork in his padfolio as they walked over to the shuttle.

Wow! So, that's a Nentraee shuttle. I wonder what makes it fly? I wish Jerry were here to see this.

From the outside, the shuttle seemed more like a large private jet. However, the design was organic and smooth. Everything was seamless—even the windows didn't appear to have a starting or stopping point. It seemed to be one solid piece.

Mi'cin vanished through the access port, but Todd stopped, for a nervous second, before following him.

I can't believe this. I'm getting on a spaceship. A real live spaceship with a real live alien. So freaking cool.

"Please, have a seat, Mister Todd Landon." Mi'cin sat as well.

Todd examined the interior. His stomach flipped with excitement, or was it worry? He wasn't sure which. The inside of the shuttle was much like a private jet or what he thought one would be like. Various seats swiveled with retractable tables and workstations. He ran his hand along one of the windows.

"It's not glass?"

"No. We use a transparent metal. There is no human word for it," Mi'cin said.

Todd nodded as he continued his examination. On one side of the cabin was a couch and, across from that, a large screen displaying the Nentraee government seal. There was a smaller gray panel next to it. The cabin door in the back was emblazoned with the same seal as the large monitor. By the ship's front entry was what Todd thought must be the flight-deck door.

"This is the vice speaker's private shuttle. You and I, as well as the rest of his staff, will travel in this ship. It is equipped for diplomats to travel, and it is relatively comfortable. It can even be used for small meetings, should there be a need." Mi'cin pointed to the back. "There is a private compartment, which is for the vice speaker's use only. He and Vi-Narm are coded to open the cabin door."

Todd nodded.

"We will also use this shuttle for ship-to-ship travel," Mi'cin explained, starting to swipe information from his datapad to the terminal in front of him.

One of the security personnel entered the main entry port, placing his whole hand on a panel next to it, which closed the door. If they end up working with CRiNE, they wouldn't need to use their whole hand, just their finger, assuming the deal was approved.

I hope that all works out. It would be good for Varick.

"We leave shortly," the guard said, moving to the front of the ship. The flight-deck door closed behind him.

"How long will the flight take?" Todd ran his hand over the chair. The material was soft and cool to the touch—like leather, but silkier. They were cream with touches of dark blues throughout. The chairs and couches were embroidered with a Nentraee symbol.

"Not long. Two and half standard hours, perhaps less. Travel is longer in the atmosphere. Our ship's engines have to counter gravity, and the Federal Aviation Administration rules, but once we are in space and beyond the satellites, we will move faster. Much like the human space station and rockets, outside of gravity, travel becomes much easier and faster."

"I see."

This is how the uber-rich must travel when they fly.

Mi'cin focused on his datapad.

Todd stopped watching what Mi'cin was doing and gazed out the window in silence. He wasn't sure what to expect, but it amazed him when they lifted off and there was no noise. The airport grew smaller as they ascended. This was nothing like air travel. It was smooth and quiet, with no large engines and no pressurization, nothing clued him into their liftoff.

As Todd continued to check out the cabin, he thought Mi'cin observed him. Todd even thought he saw the alien smile.

When the shuttle transitioned to space just beyond Earth's atmosphere, there was a contrast between the dark of space and the blue of the planet below. The curve of the blue world had a hard edge with a few white clouds breaking it up.

Todd gasped and dug his fingers into the seat. "Dear God."

"Are you all right?" Mi'cin's voice was tight and loud.

"I've never... I mean, we're in space. That's Earth. We're really in space. I wasn't expecting. I mean...this...wow."

"I assure you, we are perfectly safe," Mi'cin said. "I was never impressed with space travel, not even when we went to Mentra or one of the other satellites or stations around our world. It was routine. I do not even remember hearing of accidents."

"How can you not be impressed? This is absolutely incredible. I should have taken a shuttle ride before this. I need my phone to take some pictures." The lump in his stomach started to lessen. He felt his pockets, but, of course, he didn't find his phone. It would have to be modified to work with the Nentraee systems anyway.

"Why don't you enjoy the view? We will reach the fleet soon. I assure you, there will be plenty of opportunities for you to take photos." Mi'cin grinned at him. "It only gets more interesting from here."

"I wish Brad could see this."

"You, or is it your?"

"Your"

Mi'cin tapped on his datapad. "Your brother?" Mi'cin questioned.

"Yep. Man, he would love this. He's very much chomping at the bit to see one of your ships. His trip to the cultural ship only made him want to see more. He's always been into the idea of space travel. I guess that's why he's working for NASA." Todd's cheeks were getting sore from the smile.

"Well, as soon as all the details are worked out, he and your"—he glanced over to Todd and Todd nodded—"friends will be able to come visit you as often as you would like." Mi'cin's eyes narrowed and his face became more serious as he checked the datapad. "Ah, the files on ghosts and American colloquialisms have loaded."

Todd ignored him as he enjoyed the view from the window. The rest of the trip was silent while Mi'cin reviewed his device and Todd took in the sights of Earth and all the Nentraee ships. The alien ships made the International Space Station look like a child's homemade space project using toilet paper rolls and tinfoil.

How backward we must seem to them.

Todd leaned forward to see out the window.

These ships are huge. No wonder some of them are visible from Earth. Man, look at all those smaller ships rushing about.

Todd wasn't sure what he had expected, even with the photos provided by NASA and the Nentraee. Perhaps boxy, clunky ships that had no style, built solely to evacuate as many people as possible. But these ships, much like the shuttle, had an organic appearance. They showed wear and tear, and various small pod-type vehicles attached to the larger craft, providing maintenance. Quick flashes of light sparked from the areas where repairs had to be made. Even so, everything about them appeared seamless, as if made of a single piece of metal.

"My God, the Ràdo," Todd mumbled, opening his padfolio and pulling out the photo of the battle cruiser.

The Ràdo's design was nothing like the civilian ships. Blocky armor plating covered the hull. No clear grand domes or view ports showed themselves. Instead, a smattering of small pinholes, like portholes, at the bottom of a ship, where light emitted from the inside. The only things larger than the huge cannons, breaking from the hull, were the oversized drives—one on each side—meant for intercepting and outmaneuvering. What appeared to be sensor arrays broke from different points of the ship, all varying sizes of spiky masts. Smaller plasma, or laser, gun turrets popped out like mushrooms all over the vessel. Several large communication dishes towered near the top of the beastly ship. The utilitarian crafts attending it were like ants caring for their queen; nothing compared to this monster.

He shuddered.

We would never stand a chance against them if they decided to attack.

The shuttle turned. The battleship disappeared from view, while the speaker general's ship came into sight.

"Wow," Todd whispered.

Larger than the Ràdo, the speaker general's ship had sleek lines with huge windows and clear domes, a beautiful ship unlike the battle cruiser. Todd could see plants and what looked like blue sky inside. A floating city in space with smaller ships, shuttles, and pods dancing around it.

"You must have an impressive flight-control system to keep the ships from running into one another," Todd said toward the window. When no response came, he turned. Mi'cin was busy, his head buried behind his terminal. Todd sat in silence as the outside crafts went about their business. Their shuttle reached the docking bay and came to a soft landing.

At the soft chirp of his device, Mi'cin lifted his head. "Welcome to the speaker general's ship, the center of the Nentraee government, and your new home, Mister Todd Landon." He stood as the door to the ship opened and he gestured to the docking bay. "Are you ready?"

Todd got up from his chair.

I'm gonna need a map.

Todd held his breath as they made their way past security and all the their ships coming and going. The docking bay was like an airport—there were all kinds of

Nentraee rushing about. They rushed by faster than he could take it all in before they left the docking bay.

The small corridor opened up into a grand gallery with murals of different Nentraee and what had to be their home world. Some showed battles, others pointed to space with their planet behind. Another had a native female addressing a large crowd in a domed city with their home world behind them. One of the largest murals showed several Nentraee under a domed floating spaceship in between the Nentraee home world and their moons.

"What is that?" Todd stopped and pointed.

"That was Calda," Mic'in stopped. "One of our largest orbiting cities. I believe it was home to twenty thousand Nentraee." He sighed and his lips turned into a frown. "We were unable to save it during the evacuation of our world."

"I'm sorry."

Mi'cin was quiet and continued walking.

The passageway was filled with bright light and all manner of Nentraee rushing about. In addition to the pounding sounds of a crowd, Todd's head filled with a symphony of Nentraee voices.

Mi'cin moved them along so quickly that Todd didn't have a chance to appreciate the beauty of the ship. He passed through a giant arch that led to open spaces two or three football fields deep. When they finally reached the door to his new quarters, Mi'cin stopped.

"So this is it?" Todd asked.

"Yes. The door has been programmed for you."

The wide corridor had soft flooring in neutral colors. Doors and a few windows lined both walls, all the way down to the end of the hall where a large glass opening provided a view of open space. Embedded in the walls, lighting filled the area, making it welcoming and secure.

This looks like one of those high-end luxury apartment buildings.

He moved closer to the door, and it slid open. "Neat trick."

"You have automatic doors on...your planet." Mi'cin's head tilted.

Todd grinned and walked in.

"We tried to make things as familiar for you as possible," Mi'cin said. "You will see you have a kitchen similar to what you have on Earth. In the study there"—Mi'cin pointed—"you have you...no your terminal that has been coded directly for you to use. You will be able to communicate with Earth from there as well. It has secure links to your planet's antiquated datanet; I believe you refer to it as the internet."

Man, Jerry would have loved that and been able to explain how they were able to do it.

Todd sighed.

Mi'cin ran his hand over several small devices. "There are various datapads for you to use. They should be familiar to what you have on Earth. Of course, ours are faster with additional features, such as three-dimensional imaging, bio scanners, multiholographic interfaces as well as other advances. You should find them easier to use." He picked one up and tapped the device, causing it to activate. "They interface with any computer terminal on the ship that you have access to. There are also virtual visual interfaces you can use, should you be without a datapad or not near a terminal." He put the datapad back on the desk. "We've equipped everything to work with you personal tablet device, phone, and the bulky portible computer device you own."

"You mean my laptop?" Todd's eyes narrowed.

"Laptop. Yes. That is what I meant. Thank you."

"Great. That'll be nice. I do hope your systems are in English, though. I'm still having trouble with your language."

"We've modified them, yes. It will directly translate our language to yous..." Mi'cin stopped. "Yours?" he questioned, and Todd nodded. "And the other way around. We also enabled it to translate other human languages to English for you. The translation matrix is almost perfect; however, if you find a mistake, please report it. As you have already done with my use of *your*. The rest should be easy to figure out."

Todd went to the window. "Wow! It's beautiful. Is this what we passed on our way here?" The trees would make the redwoods of Muir Woods seem like saplings. The air had hints of what he thought might be pine, but that didn't seem quite right because it also smelled sweet. Streams gurgled and waterfalls splashed. The sounds of nature amazed him.

"Yes." Mi'cin joined him. "This is one of the many gardens on the ship. This park is a smaller replica of the one on Mentra, the second satellite that orbited our home world."

"So beautiful. Thank you so much." Todd's face brightened into a grin. "I've always wanted a house with a view. I can't imagine the work that went into all this."

"The original park was almost ten times the size." Mi'cin pointed. "I went there as a child. It was a favorite place." He turned from the window, changing the topic. "Your...sleeping quarters are through there."

Todd broke from gazing out the window and turned to Mi'cin.

Mi'cin gestured to one of the closed doors. "Along with a bathing room. If you would like to change the internal environment, that will be up to you. This is now...your home, and we want you to be comfortable here." He ran a hand over the furniture. "I understand how humans like to leave their mark on things."

Todd nodded and turned back to the window.

There was a soft *bing* and Mi'cin pulled out his datapad. "Your personal effects should be here in a couple of hours, once they are scanned and cleared."

Todd wasn't giving Mi'cin his full attention; he continued to check out the view of the park.

"You miss your home, don't you?" Todd asked as the trees drifted back and forth and the water splashed.

"This has been my home for a long time." Mi'cin stood a little taller, crossing his arms over his chest.

"It's not the same." He faced Mi'cin. Todd's expression remained flat.

"No, it is not, but it is what we have left, and we have to make do." Mi'cin shifted his stance, a blueish tinge at his neck.

Todd's lips pinched together.

"As part of my duties, I will have Earth delicacies brought here once a week to stock the kitchen."

He opened a cabinet door in the kitchen, revealing dishes, mugs, and cups. Todd would have to inspect them later.

"If there are special needs you require, you can compile a list, and I will do what I can to get them for you. The costs will be adjusted in your compensation, similar to that of your nonbusiness transport back to Earth. Our hope is that you will want to try our food." He closed the cabinet door. "Our doctors assure us that our bodies have a similar digestion, so there should be no physiological issues."

"Mi'cin, I can't imagine how difficult this all must be. This place..." Todd looked around the apartment. "I'm sure this space was meant for more than just one person."

He met Mi'cin's eyes and could sense Mi'cin's sadness.

"Your words are appreciated." Mi'cin bowed.

"Thank you. Thank you for everything." He walked around the space that was now his new home.

Mi'cin bowed again and moved to the door. "Mister Todd Landon. Would you like to see the rest of the ship? I am sure there are several of my people who would like to meet you. They have only seen humans from the broadcasts and the media or on the cultural ships. You might find it interesting."

"That would be great." Todd shook out his hands and bit his lower lip. "Mi'cin, can you and the others please call me Todd? We don't use our full names. It's a little awkward to hear my full name all the time."

"Of course, Todd." Mi'cin pulled out his datapad and made a note. "This time will give us a chance to get to know each other better, and I can share more about my home world with you, and you will be able to practice our language. I can also show you where you can shop and buy items for your life here."

IT HAD BEEN a long day. Todd looked around the study as he got comfortable in the chair.

"I hope you enjoyed the tour of our ship and the company of my son," Mi'ko inquired. "I hope he did not overwork you...no I believe Mi'cin said it would be *your*...recovering leg?"

"My leg is fine, almost completely forgotten. I'm supposed to exercise it, so the walk did me good, and Mi'cin didn't go too fast." Todd shifted his position on the chair as his leg tingled.

It was fine until we started talking about it. Now, not so much.

Mi'ko's family apartment had more space than Todd's. A big living room and kitchen with separate dining area. A hall off the kitchen led to what he assumed were bedrooms. On the opposite side of the general living space, a guest bathroom and a study could be found. Even with all the extra space, the apartment had a tight feel for the number of people who lived there. They seemed, however, to make it home. Plants and books, as well as different trinkets of what he thought to be art or decorative pieces occupied the space. Warm, but neat, furniture and an enjoyable woodsy scent completed the comfortable feel.

Mi'cin had brought him home for his first meal on the ship. It seemed like some kind of fish with rice and a vegetable dish. It was good, despite him being leery about not knowing what it all was.

I'm going to have a lot of research tonight.

The family dynamics fascinated him. Even though the older boys lived elsewhere, they were expected to enjoy dinner together. It would remain that way until they had families of their own. After dinner, they were excused by Laina. It was nice seeing them in this light.

We're so much alike.

"This whole day has been amazing. The ship, the people, the food, everything's remarkable. I can't get over your technology. I'm sure every government has been after you to share it. You must be hundreds of years more advanced than us."

"Actually you—your?" Todd nodded and Mi'ko continued, "Your space technology in this area isn't that much farther behind ours. Of course, there are some differences: gravitational fields, resource reclamation, and our drive technology. But yes, they have asked about it." He put his drink on the table. "We are considering it."

"My brother would love to see all your ships. He sent me a text again last night, reminding me about it."

Mi'ko sipped his drink.

Todd wasn't sure what the name of the drink was, even though he had asked a couple of times. *A'cen or A'xen, something like that.* It had a fruity chocolate kind of flavor.

"Mi'ko, Mister Vice Speaker, may I ask a quesiton?" Todd sat back in his seat.

"Of course." Mi'ko put down his glass.

"I don't want to offend you, but why am I here?" Todd touched his chest with both hands. "I'm not a diplomat. I'm not a scholar, and I'm certainly not one of the great minds of my people."

Mi'ko nodded with a polite smile.

"Not to mention, no one wants me here except for you and maybe the speaker general," Todd said. "Hell, not even my own people want me here. Sure, everyone is pleasant enough and helpful when need be, but..." He frowned. "Even Mi'cin and Vi-Narm don't want me here."

The tips of Mi'ko's ears turned blue and almost seemed to get bigger. He hadn't seen this bodily reaction before on the vice speaker.

Maybe I offended him.

"It could be me. I don't know." Todd tried to backstep, seeing Mi'ko's reaction. "They are nice enough, and Mi'cin did take me around today, but it all seemed forced. Like I'm an obligation, a task to be tolerated." He took a breath. "I'm sorry. I mean no disrespect, but none of this makes any sense. Even my own government has..."

"Your government has concerns about our choice." Mi'ko rubbed the tips of his ears, and the color and swelling started to fade.

"Putting it delicately, yes." He laughed, sitting back, feeling absorbed by the same softness as the furniture in the shuttle.

"My son and Vi-Narm have also made their opinions clear on the matter. I apologize if it has made you uncomfortable."

"I'm sorry if I sound like I'm whining. Mi'cin is fine and Vi-Narm..." Todd raked his hand through his hair. "We'll figure out a way to work together, but that doesn't explain why I'm here."

So many people were heroes the day of the attack. What makes me so special?

Mi'ko turned to the bookshelf. "There is a book—" He pointed to a shelf. "—Laina pulled down for me to review. It was the night I wrote the declaration that allowed you to come here and possibly stopped an armed conflict with your people."

It was Todd's turn to nod; the government people had told him this in a briefing. He didn't need to be told to keep it quiet. He wasn't dumb. Still, he was sure people had found out, and it was probably why people were down there protesting.

Idiots.

"Todd, our two cultures are very different," Mi'ko said. "Even among your world with so many different cultures, we find ourselves with very little to compare it to." He stopped. "I didn't lie to you when we talked of this at the hospital. It is a challenge to find the correct words."

"I've done hours of research on this position," Todd started. "I haven't found anything about it." He leaned in a bit more.

"Nor would you. It wasn't part of our cultural information we provided your people. This honor predates the Clan War and many of our current laws; it is, as you would say, outdated."

"So, before your world's great war?" Todd said. He had learned that the clans were basically the various Nentraee races; however, prior to the Clan War, they rarely mixed. It was because of that isolationist ideology the clans went to war.

A global race war.

"Very good. You have done your research. Before the war, in order to try to build peace among our people, and within the clans themselves, we would have a special envoy from different warring factions. Our clans were small, not like what we have now. There were subgroups within the clans. The envoy would live and work within the group to understand them." Mi'ko stopped and stared at his hands before continuing.

"How they lived. How they raised their families. How they worshiped. Learn what it was to be part of that clan. What made them special." He turned to Todd. "With the purpose to avoid another war. As times changed, and the clans merged, these positions became rarer and more prestigious. They ranked higher than any diplomat and were extremely important to the group, and later to the clans. The goal was a simple one: peace."

"So I'm kind of like a peace offering?"

"I do not think I understand the reference."

Todd shook his head. "Um, it's a gift you give in order to avoid war or a fight. Anyway, I think I understand what you mean."

"All right." Mi'ko continued. "We haven't used this position in hundreds of years. After the Clan Wars, there was no reason. We were at peace, and we had to rebuild our world. But now, after the attack and the fear that more conflict was to come, we thought it might help."

"So, why not have a person from each country? And more importantly, why me?"

"I would have thought that would be clear by now, Todd. You represent everything we value in a being." Mi'ko's face grew bright. "Just like with the envoys of old, they were selected not by their own people, but by the other group or clan they had been at war with. How else do you learn? How else do you gain peace?" He leaned in. "If you are given a diplomat, one trained by the government, they only have the interest of that government at heart." His lips split into a smile. "As it should be, but that is why these people were so valued; they were normal everyday people. What set them apart was that the individual acted in an extraordinary manner and their action gained the trust of the other group." He reached back to check on his tieback. "It was a deed that caught their eye; a kind gesture, a brave act, an act of gentleness, it could have been anything. No one knew, so no one could plan for it, because it could have been anything that caught the leader's attention."

"Like saving the life of the vice speaker."

I guess that does make me a bigger hero than I thought I was.

"Your act of bravery was beyond anything we could have known would have happened here." Mi'ko adjusted in his seat, his voice becoming softer. "Now I ask you, how better to learn of a people than by a male who would sacrifice himself for a stranger, an alien, a potential monster?" His brows raised and the smile grew bigger. "That is a person worth knowing, and that is a person worth having learn about us. Who we are." Mi'ko found his drink again and sipped it. "That is why you are here, and that is why you are my special envoy, reporting only to me."

"I had no idea how special this appointment is." Todd picked up his drink and took another taste. "This is very good, by the way. It's like a chocolate-covered strawberry." He took another sip and felt the ticking of his timepiece.

Remember, be the man you want to be. The one everyone thinks you are.

"I'm glad you are enjoying it." Mi'ko finished his drink. "I hope you will enjoy many things here with us. You know, sometimes, we do not get to pick what we want. Sometimes, what is really needed gets picked for us by some higher power. Its meaning not fully understood until everything plays out; keep that in mind when you question why you are here."

Two: Faa

MIRTOFF RUBBED THE top of Faa's head as he rested on her legs. "The tree-lighting ceremony in London on four December will be an enjoyable event. It shows friendship between the nations of Norway and Britain and how, with that support, they were able to overcome a horrendous evil."

"I agree." Mi'ko called up requests for all the planned events and their dates. "It'll be an excellent event for you to be seen at, and the humans are eager to have you in attendance."

"Have the concerns about another terrorist attack been addressed?" Mirtoff asked.

"Yes," Mi'ko said. "Vi-Narm has worked with Danu and Downing Street, as well as the White House to ensure all necessary safety measures have been addressed. They will have a no-fly zone in place, and all the surveillance systems are being updated. The location will have both members from the British intelligence agencies and plainclothed human security. There should be no problems."

"Excellent."

"How's Todd adapting to his new life here?"

"I'm keeping him busy with all these requests," Mi'ko said. "There is much for him to learn and go over." He stood and adjusted his suit, then crossed to the window and looked out at Earth. "His world is even more confusing to him than ours. He's had to research the Tree Lighting. He hadn't heard of it before."

"Really?"

Mi'ko nodded.

"I suppose we'll all be learning a lot," Mirtoff said. "How is Mi'cin working out? Are he and Todd getting along?"

"I believe so," Mi'ko said with a chuckle. "Mi'cin's attitude has changed dramatically. I think he's becoming fascinated with Todd and the human culture."

Mirtoff leaned back. Faa shifted at the movement. "Is Todd going to be ready to stand in the Council Chamber in front of the full Speaker's House?"

This latest development didn't please Mirtoff, but the Speaker's House had a right to make such a request.

Gahumed is only doing this to make a point. Poor Todd is going to be caught in the middle of this. I wish I could have stopped it.

"As busy as I've been, I've tasked Vi-Narm with his preparations," Mi'ko said. "She understands General Gahumed and General Fanion well. I'm sure she'll have Todd ready. He hasn't mentioned it to me, which is encouraging."

"Very good news indeed."

"It's disappointing the Speaker's House waited this long. They should have done it before Todd started. It's already been two standard weeks," Mi'ko said. "I suppose they had to research the legality so we couldn't challenge it."

Mirtoff frowned.

Gahumed and Fanion had made their argument well. There was nothing she could do. She hated having to spend time on such pettiness.

"I have no doubt Todd will be fine." Mi'ko returned to his seat.

"Excellent." Mirtoff scratched Faa's head again, then picked up her datapad. A photo of the Chinese leader was on her screen.

"You know, I can understand Mi'cin's fascination. Humans and their culture are interesting; China, for example, has regional history that goes back thousands of years, not to mention the different celebrations." The dates for several Chinese events appeared for her to review.

"I can't possible go to all these," Mirtoff said. She stopped the dataflow and checked the month of December. "Many, including China and India, seem to celebrate Christmas." She felt a hint of a smile on her lips. "I wonder if Todd will want to do an event here?"

"He has mentioned it might be nice for our people to see how this holiday is celebrated."

Mirtoff felt more relaxed about Earth now. Mi'ko was right—this envoy position was a good idea.

Now it would be up to Todd to convince the Speaker's House that he is the right person for the job. I pray to J'Veesa he can do it. The alternative could be a tragedy for both our people and the humans.

"Well, if nothing else, we've learned the humans love a *party*," Mirtoff said.

"Party?" Faa struggled to make the correct sounds. "Provider, what a party?" He shook to fluff the fur on his head back out.

"It's a human word. It's like *A'Zan* or *A'da Magina*."

"A'da Magina. Day of Hope." He jumped off the sofa with a happy murmur and pranced over to Mi'ko.

"Yes, Faa, like that." Mi'ko reached down and rubbed his head between the ears.

"Faa like A'da Magina. Human have Day of Hope?" His foot thumped as Mi'ko scratched.

"In a way," Mi'ko said. "They call it Christmas."

"It might not be a bad idea to recognize it," Mirtoff said. "It holds religious meaning for several and family meanings for others. It may be interesting for our people."

"Todd would also like to introduce our holidays to the humans, a cultural exchange." Mi'ko rubbed Faa's back. "He thinks it would be a good way to learn about one another. He thought *Den A'Tae* would be nice. That would please the Dentraee and hopefully General Gahumed." He left Faa alone and returned to his terminal display. "But I'm not sure they would understand our ceremonies. Most of our holidays are not times to celebrate."

"A'da Magina is, and what of A'Zan or *A'Godá Faoo*?" Mirtoff swiped it over to Mi'ko's main viewer. "And it would be good for them to see a less-guarded side to us, show them our *fun side.*"

Mi'ko raised his brows.

"An expression I heard from an Earther." She waved her hand as if swatting the words away.

"I see." Mi'ko faced the large screen. "A'Zan could be interesting; however, it is more of a Zan'entra celebration. You and your clan could put on quite the spectacle." He grinned at her. "A'Godá Faoo would be good, but I've completed my rights of fatherhood long ago, and none of my sons have children. What of Ecra?"

"No. He and Ra'pia have not been joined yet, assuming she ever asks him." She sighed through her nose. "Besides, it's much more an Ultween or Martween celebration. Is there anyone you know from your clan? We could check with Speaker Syde if he knows of anyone from the Martween clan."

"I'll check."

"We can discuss it later." Mirtoff adjusted her shoulders allowing for small pops of comfort from the joints. "I would, currently, like to get through the next six weeks." She called up additional information on her schedule. "There is much to learn about human traditions. It's exhausting."

"About Thanks for Giving?" Mi'ko said. "You will be expected to go to the state dinner with the president. Todd says it's an important holiday for his nation, so he is pleased you're going."

"At least, I missed the Canadian Thanks for Giving in October, but I'll have to go next year." Mirtoff leaned back. "I suppose."

"Perhaps. It's almost a year away," Mi'ko said.

"Danu has been working on the American Thanks for Giving, and he should have everything taken care of." Mirtoff stretched her arms. She had been sitting far too long. "If you don't mind, I may ask Danu to work with Todd to ensure I am fully versed on the etiquette for the holiday."

"Of course. That shouldn't be a problem. It'll be good for him to work with more of our people."

"Excellent."

The door chirped, and Mi'ko stood, went to his monitor, and pushed the panel on the desk, allowing the door to slide open.

"Hello, Todd," Mi'ko said, speaking English.

"Good afternoon, Mister Vice Speaker. You wanted to see me?" Todd turned to Mirtoff. "Oh, Madam Speaker, hello." He bowed.

Todd hadn't spent a lot of time with the speaker general. However, during his interactions with her, she seemed remarkably intelligent and professional. Unlike those times, today, she didn't have a cup of tuma. As always, her auburn hair was braided up into a bun with a few wisps running along the side of her face. Her brilliant dark brown eyes, which Todd had learned were rare for the Nentraee, always seemed to sparkle, giving her a kind appearance.

"Todd, a pleasure," Mirtoff said.

Faa trotted over next to her and sat down as she spoke.

"I should go." Todd adjusted the cuffs of his shirt. "I didn't mean to interrupt you."

"No sense, Todd." Mi'ko waved him over. "We are finishing up, and I requested your presence, so there is nothing for you to interrupt."

"It is I who should go." Mirtoff dusted off her pants. "I need to get Faa back for his lunch."

"A cádo." Todd knelt to look at Faa. "I didn't know you had one, Madam Speaker."

Todd hadn't seen one this close. From what he understood about them, they were akin to dogs or, maybe, cats. Bigger than Bianca for sure, Faa seemed to be about the size of a cocker spaniel, if not a little bigger.

"Oh, he's beautiful. I love his eyes," Todd said. "Hello, little guy." He stuck his hand out for Faa to sniff. "I'm not gonna hurt you."

"Provider, this human Todd?" Faa asked, tilting his head toward Mirtoff.

"Jesus H. Christ!" Todd shouted and dropped on his butt.

Both Mi'ko and Mirtoff shared confused expressions as Faa jumped on the chair behind Mirtoff. A small whimper came from his mouth.

"It talks. I didn't know it could talk. How in the holy hell does it talk?" Todd picked himself up off the floor and knelt. "I'm...I'm sorry. He startled me. I didn't mean to scare him." He gestured to Faa. "You never said they talked."

"You have animals that speak on your planet, don't you?" Mi'ko questioned.

The cádo shook and his eyes were double their normal size.

"Well..." Todd tried to calm his voice. "Parrots or some other birds, but that—not like that. I thought he would mimic words like them, but he's smart. He knows what he's saying, doesn't he?"

Mirtoff's hand gently rubbed Faa's back and his head.

"Human scared Faa."

The Nentraee words came out slow and deliberate so Todd could understand.

Mirtoff sat. Faa climbed onto her lap and nuzzled her arm.

"It's all right, little one. He won't hurt you."

Todd recognized the words. "I'm sorry."

"Faa, this is Todd Landon," Mirtoff said. "Todd, this is the cádo who selected me, Faa."

"Hello," Todd said and waved.

Faa turned to Mirtoff and then to Todd. His muzzle shifted around, and then he finally said, "Todd." He swished his tail.

"How?" Todd asked.

"They communicate at a lower level than we do, but they have intelligence. However, they are totally dependent on us."

"But the language? The intelligence?" Todd asked.

Faa murmured as Mirtoff rubbed his head. He had stopped trembling.

"The best comparison is they are similar to small children," Mi'ko said. "We assumed since humans have animals that talked and are smart it wouldn't be so shocking. You said yourself you talk to your cat all the time."

"But Bianca doesn't talk back." Todd paused. Well, she did, in a way, and they understood each other, but not like this. "I just...that is an animal trait that we'll need to let people know."

Faa sniffed the air and got up. He jumped off Mirtoff and sauntered to Todd. He sniffed the air again. "Todd Landon." He seemed to struggle to pronounce the words.

"Just let him come to you," Mirtoff said.

The three watched Faa move closer, each step cautious. Todd remained kneeling on the floor.

"They don't eat meat, right?" Todd asked.

"Correct." Mirtoff kept her eyes on Faa.

Faa sniffed and moved closer, his tail swishing. With a nimble movement, he jumped and landed on Todd's lap. Faa pushed his front paws into Todd's chest and stared at him. "Todd Landon."

Todd's heart skipped a beat as Faa looked him in the eyes.

Faa was gray and had a short muzzle, dwarfed by his large green eyes and his floppy ears.

"Faa." Mirtoff snapped her fingers and pointed to the floor, addressing Faa in Nentraee words that Todd didn't recognize.

Faa mentioned Todd's name twice, along with other words, but Todd couldn't focus, his heart starting to pound. He wasn't fearful of animals, but he had never run across an animal that looked him in the eyes as if sizing him up for a meal.

Relax. It's fine. He's just like a big dog. He's not going to hurt you. Look at those big, beautiful eyes. I'm sure he's more scared of you than you are of him.

Faa continued speaking and used Todd's name again.

Todd turned to Mirtoff and Mi'ko for some hint of what the creature said. He couldn't read their expressions.

"He likes you and wants to be friends," Mi'ko said.

Faa nudged against Todd's legs and started to murmur happily.

"Okay, by far this is the oddest thing I've experienced since I started." Todd paused and sat so Faa could sit more on his lap instead of knocking him over. "He's adorable and beautiful. Don't get me wrong." His voice cracked as he forced a small chuckle. He wasn't sure what to do with the cádo resting happily on his lap.

Faa is a heavy little beast.

Mirtoff called to Faa in Nentraee and clicked her fingers.

Faa's muzzle shifted.

"I'm sorry, Todd," Mirtoff said. "I didn't expect him to act that way. He's normally not that curious. It's good information so we can address this with our population. I should have had you and Faa meet sooner."

Faa jumped off and walked to Mirtoff's side.

Todd's shoulders and neck relaxed now that Faa was off him.

Faa nudged the back of Mirtoff's leg and addressed her in Nentraee.

"He hopes to see you again, and he wants to be your friend," Mirtoff said.

Mirtoff and Faa moved to the door. She knelt next to Faa and whispered in his big floppy ear.

Faa giggled and then padded over to Todd, glancing up with his big doe eyes. "Bye Bye, Todd," he said in English, then padded back to the door, and Mirtoff and he walked out.

"Bye, Faa." Todd waved.

Amazing. That was incredible.

Todd took a moment, not sure if he'd managed to breathe the entire time Faa was there. He stood and dusted off his pants.

"You handled that well." Mi'ko took a seat at his desk.

"They're incredible," Todd said. "I can't imagine having a pet like that. What is their language capacity? Do they all talk? Do you think they will learn my language? Clearly he already knows a few words." He took a breath. "Wow! How do you get them? Can anyone have one?"

Todd made his way to the small conference table.

"Their capacity for our language varies from cádo to cádo, and as for learning your language, I don't see why not. Provided they have interest in learning it," Mi'ko said. "Animals such as Faa can be very picky. As for the rest of the history of the cádo, that will have to wait for another time." He stood and poured both he and Todd a glass of water. "However, Faa liked you, which is a good thing. Cádo are known to be good judges of character."

"Well, he's amazing. And those eyes, not to mention his fur; it's so soft, like silk." Todd opened his padfolio, ready for their meeting. Next to the notepad was a datapad.

Mi'ko glanced down at the pen in Todd's hand. "You will need to learn to use our datapads and our other devices. They will only make your job easier, I assure you. We don't waste resources on such things as paper. I will have Mi'cin tutor you further."

It wasn't that Todd didn't want to use a datapad or the visual links. They were similar to a smartphone. But he liked taking handwritten notes and not relying on technology. So many things broke, data got lost, and with paper, he wouldn't have to worry about it.

"Of course, Mister Vice Speaker." Todd sipped his water, feeling his face warm slightly.

"I would like you to review the nations I have direct dealings with and pick the cultural events I should attend," Mi'ko instructed. "I want to make sure I do not offend anyone. Also, I cannot attend everything, so you will help in forming an appropriate response to the ones I cannot attend."

"What about sending one of your aides?" Todd suggested. "It's not uncommon on Earth, and we can make sure people understand that you can't be everywhere." He made notes on his datapad as well as jotting a few things down on the paper he brought.

"As special envoy, I will trust your opinion and your guidance on this," Mi'ko said.

"Not a problem. Anything else you need done?"

"We will be opening our cultural ships and our government ships to more humans, and I would like you to help with that." Mi'ko reached back and checked his tieback. "Please talk to Vi-Narm or Mi'cin so they can assist you." He took a drink of water. "We will need to pay attention and ensure we safeguard our cádo. More than ever after your encounter with Faa."

Todd made a few notes. He would work with Mi'cin. Vi-Narm always scowled at him and was short with him. If he asked a question, she would make him feel stupid for asking it.

"I know much of this is out of your area of expertise, so please use whatever resources you need," Mi'ko said. "Also, the speaker asked if you could assist Danu with some of the engagements she has upcoming."

"Of course, I'll do what I can."

"Thank you," Mi'ko said. "I cannot stress how important it is that your people see us as friends."

"I understand, Mister Vice Speaker," Todd said. "If you check out the social media pages we created for you, along with the videos we've posted, you have hundreds of millions of followers. It's impressive. Anything Nentraee-related is always in the top-ten 'trending now' sections."

"I am glad." Mi'ko stood. "See you tomorrow at the ceremony. Both myself and the speaker general are anxious to get this finished."

Todd stood.

"I'm pleased to see you so at ease," Mi'ko said.

"Of course, Mister Vice Speaker." Todd bowed. "It'll be fine." With a smile, he walked out of the office. Once he heard the door close behind him, he sighed. He would have to check again to review the ceremony. It was odd that Mi'ko seemed worried about it. Normally it was Todd who worried.

I have to pull out the Kap'erin for tomorrow. I'm sure I'll be expected to wear it.

Three: Ceremony

TODD FINISHED REVIEWING the details on the ceremony before leaving his quarters.

Ceremony. Bullshit! It's not a ceremony but an interview in front of the full Speaker's House. Why didn't Vi-Narm tell me? She made it out to be no big deal.

He rushed down the hall, his cloak, the Kap'erin, billowed out behind him. Several Nentraee stopped and bowed as he passed. He turned the corner and checked his datapad for directions. His palms were damp. His heart pounded, and not from rushing.

Vi-Narm waited for him outside large ornate doors decorated with carvings of gold and silver. The surrounding light bounced off the metals, creating shimmering circles of light on the floor.

"Todd." Vi-Narm offered a stiff bow, her cloak shifting about her shoulders.

Damn it.

He should have been more diligent, not assuming that all the reports she gave him were the only ones.

We'll learn to work together. If I survive this.

"Hello, Vi-Narm," Todd said as he searched for a hint of a friendly greeting, but her face was stern and her lips a straight line.

"We will go in the council chamber where the Speaker's House will be in session." She eyed him coolly. "Once they address us, you will present yourself and answer their questions to the best of your ability. The interview process is simple, so you should have no trouble. But, do not be fooled. This will also decide if they will accept you."

"Wait. Accept me?" Todd tried to process while catching his breath. "What happens if they don't approve of me? Mi'ko didn't say anything about that."

What happens if I can't understand their broken English and answer the question wrong? God, I hope it's in English.

"Then he must believe you will be fine and not want to worry you." The slightest suggestion of a smile reached her lips.

Sweat broke out on his forehead. Vi-Narm had sent him file after file last night for review. "There was so much information to review, and some of it made no sense until I researched it further, taking more time." He frowned. "It didn't help that you've been sending me a ton of information. I haven't been able to sort through it all."

"It's not my job to help you sort through what I send." Vi-Narm's voice was calm. Cold. "I send the document that are required for all your different tasks. It is your responsibility to organize them and go through them and be prepared."

Todd shook his head and stared at the floor. He inhaled deeply and met her eyes. "I would've appreciated you pointing out the information that was important for today's events. I could've focused on it."

"Perhaps you should organize your time better, or is that a failing of your character?"

"But I—"

"It was in the report I send to you this morning," she interrupted. "You did read it? Did you not?"

"Today? This morning? As in, while I was still in bed, or while I was getting ready for this interview?"

Or when I was on the toilet?

Trying not to sound as pissed as he felt, he checked his pocket watch. Since getting it, he kept it with him as a good-luck piece. Now, more than ever, he needed the luck.

"Vi-Narm, how could you send it this morning? I didn't have a chance—you made it sound like this was only my welcome ceremony. That was my impression from... I didn't have a chance to..."

She hates me. That's why she's doing this. She hates me and is determined for me to fail.

He saw a hint of a smile, and he was sure there was a brief twinkle in her eyes.

God, she's a total bitch. With luck, she'll trip and fall on her way into the chamber. That might loosen the stick up her ass.

He took a breath and held back the frown that was stalking his face. "I'll do my best."

She watched the chamber doors open. "Let us hope Mi'ko's faith in you is well placed."

The soft ticking of his watch reminded him why he was here.

I can do this.

They walked in, with Todd keeping pace. Even though he had been rushing and his leg was hurting, he would be damned if he was going to fall behind.

The chamber was breathtaking. The walls displayed murals of past events that were important to the Nentraee, each painting displayed in a gold and silver frame. They walked deeper into the great hall. Every arch was meticulously carved, and the surfaces were all highly polished. The photos he had seen didn't do the space justice.

Mirtoff stood in the center of a crescent table with Mi'ko to her left and several other members off on either side, one from each clan. Seeing the members of the Speaker's House this way, Todd noticed just how different they all were. Taller and shorter, darker and lighter skin, different-colored hair and eyes. Noting them all here like this, it was obvious how alien they were. Yes, they had pointed ears, but they also had larger foreheads with varying degrees of ridges in them. Some were more pronounced like the U'Ztraee. Mi'ko and his clan, the Ultween, had the softest ridges. And Mirtoff and her clan, the Za'entra, seemed to be somewhere in the middle.

So alien. So strange.

The crescent-shaped table was constructed of wood similar to walnut, with inlays of dark granite slabs, accented with more gold and silver. Todd shifted his gaze so the light bouncing off the table didn't blind him. Above the table, seven large panels of heavy fabric each had a distinct emblem embroidered on it, corresponding to a different clan. Each member stood in front of their clan's matching panel.

As he and Vi-Narm approached, everyone focused on him. In addition to the seven speakers standing at the table, staff stood off to the sides at what seemed to be workstations. Out of the way but near enough should one of the council need assistance. Some of the aides milling about were either members of the military, security, or support, indicated by the color of their cloaks.

As for the council members, the colors of the ceremonial cloaks represented their specific area—purple for the speaker general, deep blue for the vice speaker, ruby red for the military, and emerald for the other members of the Speaker's House.

They definitely have style.

Todd and Vi-Narm stopped halfway between the entrance and the table. Their cloaks rustled as they moved. The members of the Speaker's House all sat, and the floor started to shimmer around them. The area where the council stood shifted, raising the seven members several feet off the floor. Two sets of stairs appeared, leading from the platform back to the main level. It was all seamless, but the room filled with a soft hum as it happened.

As everything rose into place, Vi-Narm spoke, "As requested by this honorable Speaker's House, I bring forward Mister Todd Landon, Special Envoy to Mi'ko Soemu for Terran Affairs." She bowed and moved off to the side, leaving him alone.

The lights of the hall dimmed. Surrounding him and the members of the Speaker's House was a soft, warm glow. He felt naked. Being so exposed and unprepared was overwhelming. What would he do if they didn't accept him? He bowed.

Dammit, I should have focused on this more. I shouldn't have waited until last night to dig into this ceremony, but why didn't Mi'ko tell me about it? Was he relying on Vi-Narm to prepare me? No. This is my fault. It was my responsibility, and I screwed up.

He rocked on his heels.

Before the silence became overly uncomfortable, Mi'ko stood to speak. Minor stress lines creased the corners of his mouth and around his eyes. "I welcome you, Special Envoy. You honor me and my clan with your presence. I greet you with the Arm of peace." He reached out his arm, bowed to Todd, and continued. "As in the time of our ancestors, I present the male I chose as my special envoy to teach us about our similarities and help us to understand our differences. All in the hope of one day becoming one." He looked around the room, his eyes meeting each member as he spoke. "I wish to remind this Speaker's House of his selfless deed in saving my life. Granting me more time with my family as well as allowing me to continue my work. If not for him, I would not be here. It is for this debt, a debt which I cannot repay, that on behalf of my clan, the Ultween, and my family, I now ask you to accept my choice for special envoy, and to welcome him as I have."

Even with the warm greeting and kind words from Mi'ko, Todd would have loved nothing more than to find the nearest door to duck out. This was nothing like what he had expected. He thought it would be a kind of welcoming ceremony, not a full-on "royal court" type of event. His hand moved to his pocket watch, and he took a small breath. It was silly how such a small object could help him relax.

Mirtoff spoke, "As you all know, I was not in favor of this, at first. However, after much debate and personal reflection, I have come to be pleased with bringing in Special Envoy Landon. I, too, share in the gratitude of Special Envoy Landon actions. We will learn a great deal from him, and I am pleased to have gotten to know him, and I look forward to knowing him more as the time ahead will provide. On behalf of my clan, the Za'entra, I, too, welcome him with the arm of peace, with no questions or recourse."

She stared at Todd, stood with her arms outstretched and presented to Todd, then bowed in respect. She lifted her gaze. "I would also like to add my personal hope that we, along with him, will build a lasting foundation worthy of this great hall and worthy of our two worlds."

Mi'ko and Mirtoff now stood there, waiting for the others to take action. He wasn't completely sure what would happen next, but he tried not to fidget as he stood there, bathed in the warm light.

All he heard was the tick of his watch.

An older Nentraee woman stood. She studied him a moment with dull, blue eyes, her thin, dark-blonde hair arranged ornately on her head in a tight braid. She adjusted her cloak and spoke directly to him.

"Mister Todd Landon, you the first human to be give this honor, not to mention the first give such an honor bestowed upon them in many long year. You actions speak of you character and I, too, am grateful, however, unlike our speaker general and vice speaker, I have yet speak with you. Or any human." She turned from him to Mirtoff and Mi'ko. "I would ask one question. Because of the circumstance that bring you before us today, actions cause by monstrous events of you own people—people not captured, I would like to add. Their behavior almost cost us the life of vice speaker and did, in fact, cost the lives of several of our Nentraee, four of which were from my clan. So, Todd Landon, my question, do you believe human and Nentraee can learn and live in peace?"

He processed the weight of each of her words. Her English had been hard and heavy, but he understood it easily enough. He scanned the room, the paintings on the wall hidden in shadow. He focused back on the woman, desperately trying to remember her name—then it hit him.

"Speaker Rosta Gonu," he said, as respectfully as possible. "The actions of the people who killed so many and caused so much damage are horrible and unforgivable. They are evil cowards." He took a breath. "They do not represent me, nor do they represent the majority of my people. We have a great many things to learn from one another. It won't always be easy, and we'll make mistakes along the way. I can assure you I will make several of these mistakes myself, but that is how we learn. It will be a challenge but also an opportunity for us, and I have to believe in the end it will all be worth it."

Todd stepped forward and the light moved with him. "As for living in peace." His shoulders fell, and he shook his head softly. "I wish I could say that there will never be any violence, but to be honest"—his mouth turned down in a frown—"I don't know if there'll be more attacks. We humans are flawed, and as you realize, we haven't even stopped killing our own people."

He was sure his being ashamed of his home and his people showed on his face as he spoke. His eyes set on her and he straightened his shoulders. "It's my hope that I'll help bridge the gap and lessen the fears of everyone. Perhaps, someday, with the steps we take here, there will be peace for all of us. It's asking a lot to have faith in my people, but I hope you do." There was so much more he should say, but it was best to stop there. He bowed to signify his answer was complete.

Rosta Gonu gazed at him a moment longer before turning to the other members. She lifted an arm and bowed. "The clan Caleen welcomes Todd Landon as special envoy, and it, too, is hope that you will help lessen the fears of both our people, bringing peace to all. No easy task, but nothing worth have ever is. Welcome, Special Envoy." Her arm lowered, but she continued to stand.

He let out a breath, watching the three Nentraee before him.

Several moments passed. Todd glanced at the vice speaker and the speaker general as two more members stood: General Yee Awon of the U'Xtraee clan—an older male, the darkest-brown skinned of all the members. Speaker Syde Badrah stood for the Martween clan and was head of health and education—a younger male, short in stature with delicate features.

"The clan Martween welcome Special Envoy Todd Landon with no questions and no recourse, and we thank him for save our vice speaker." Syde extended an arm and bowed.

Thank God. That was quick and easy. And his English wasn't bad.

"The U'Xtraee welcome Todd Landon with no questions and no recourse," General Awon said. "The bravery you show even now to be here so far from home is to be respected and welcomed. You are a...strong ship for humans to ride on." His voice was gruff and his accent was rich but understandable. After he spoke, he extended an arm and bowed.

Todd bowed to each member. His breathing relaxed.

There were two more left; General Vi-Kamu Fanion, who oversaw the ground forces, and General Gahumed La-Enn, who was in charge of the space forces.

What's taking so long? Why don't you just ask your questions? Why sit there examining me like a show pony?

They were the heads of the military and, from what Todd understood, both culturally and religiously conservative for Nentraee.

The ticking from Todd's pocket watch beat like a drum he was sure the others could hear, but in reality, it was only in his imagination.

General Gahumed tapped on the table console and narrowed her aqua eyes on Todd. She waited for an aide to appear and hand her a datapad. The general checked the presented information before speaking. She remained seated.

Todd peeked over to Mi'ko for a hint of what was coming, but he was focused on General Gahumed.

Everyone is watching her. Are they afraid of her?

"You country does no speak kind of you," General Gahumed said.

Todd's heart skipped a beat as he shifted on his feet.

"They say you not a fit choice for posting. They point to you lack of train and lack of education. They also point that you loss of mate in attack might affect you judgment. They point that you were distant from you family for many year and only reconcile prior to us arrival." Her eyes narrowed on him.

She's as bad as the secretary of state. What does this have to do with anything?

"They say you do no thing extraordinary in you life. You lack conviction. That you no thing than an average male of average intelligent." Her head tilted.

Todd kept his hands from forming a fist.

"They suggest several other who might be more fit for honor. Why is this, Mister Landon? Why you no address this with them? They suggest you weak. May it be you race no approve of matings of same sexes?"

Todd was sweating and his face and neck burned.

Why the hell does it always come down to who I sleep with? Why the fuck does it matter? Why hide the truth? Why not just let it all hang out there? Not like I can run and hide or avoid any of this now.

"It might be for many reasons." Todd shifted on his stance. This was all new to him. "It's true I don't have an advanced degree. I'm certainly no diplomat. I'm not a military person, and I've had no formal training." He forced himself to quit moving. "I don't fit with the ideal of who should be here, and I'm sure there are a million people more qualified on Earth than me." He chuckled nervously. "I realize I've got a lot of baggage..."

The confused expression on the Nentraee faces made Todd stop. They didn't understand the reference. "Um...I know I've had a lot of personal trouble in my past. To be honest, I'm not even sure I would pick me for this post, but that's not important."

General Vi-Kamu held up a hand. Her harsh gaze landed on him. "Are you saying you do no want this honor? That you would wish to forfeit it?" Her voice sang through the air, her English clear and lovely.

"No! God, no, you misunderstood me."

Of course I want to do this. It's important. I need to do this.

The speakers' eyes all raised, and Todd softened his tone. "I'm sorry. I'm not very good at this." His body shifted again. "After the terrorist attack and losing Jerry, we all thought you were going to leave or, worse, strike back at us."

Mirtoff's eyes narrowed on General Gahumed as Mi'ko fussed with his tieback, his hands shaking.

"I know it was discussed, and I know how close you came to attacking...potentially destroying our world." Todd bit his lower lip, trying to get back on point. "I understand it won't be easy and that I have a difficult challenge ahead of me. One I don't take lightly." The timepiece ticked, reminding him of why he was here. He was here to represent not only himself but everyone, seven billion people. He took a breath.

No small task.

"Please realize I'm going to do everything I can to make sure that both our species appreciate one another, whatever that takes. I may not be exactly what my government wants, and I might not even be what you want, but—" His gaze fixed on Mi'ko and a smile crawled over his lips. "—sometimes we don't get to pick what we want. Sometimes what is needed gets picked for us, by some higher power that no one fully understands until everything plays out."

Mi'ko offered Todd a small bow and smile.

Todd exhaled.

"Well said, Special Envoy Todd Landon. The clan Altraee welcome Todd Landon with no future question or recourse." General Vi-Kamu stood up, offered a stiff bow to Mi'ko and Mirtoff. "Let us all hope the faith we put in you and this endeavor lead us to peace and understanding." She bowed and outstretched her arm.

General Gahumed La-Enn remained seated, studying the others. Her face was stone. "To imagine this interview ceremony almost didn't happen, but I insisted," she said in Nentraee and turned to the speaker general and the vice speaker.

Todd picked up on her Nentraee, and he watched them, unsure what to say or do. It was clear she didn't want him to understand the exchange. However, thanks to a great deal of work on his part and the help of Mi'cin, he was able to understand Nentraee better than he could speak it.

"The two of you aren't the only ones who can use historical laws to get what you want," Gahumed said. "I can keep him here all day, but I don't need to. I made my point by insisting on this meeting. It's a small victory." She glared at Mirtoff, a cruel smile twisting her face.

"We agreed, Speaker Gahumed, to conduct this meet in English so my special envoy can understand," Mi'ko responded in English. The tips of his ears started to puff up and turn a pale blue.

Todd swiveled his head as if watching a tennis match.

What is this? Some kind of power play? What's going on here? Mi'ko is clearly angry.

"Very well." She waved a dismissive hand his way.

Gahumed leaned forward and rested her flat chin on her raised hands. Several strands of her light-brown hair fell just off to the side of her face. One wisp hit her oddly shaped nose. "You have spoke a great deal about the honor and about you concern." Her eyes narrowed on him. "You have mention how you may not be best person for post. And yet, here you be, while others are no. What of the one that died during the attack. Do you value their death less than you sacrifice?"

Todd started to open his mouth.

"It is almost impressive for one with much doubt," Gahumed said. "You seem to have so much weakness. A weak male." The word *male* sounding like a curse to Todd's ear.

Todd's hands balled up. "I'm not a weak man."

"Then prove it," Gahumed spat. "I suspect you would like to flee, go home, and forgot about this. Go back to world more familiar to you. One that is easy. One without Nentraee." She stopped. "Is you a coward?"

Todd's shoulders tensed, and his face contorted into a frown.

What a bitch.

She held up a hand. "I think you want a place where you no be challenge or force to grow. Why you no go home and forget about all this? Forget all pain and hide back in office somewhere on Earth while we force to continue to live with the suffering caused by humans. Tell me, Todd, would you like? We no need a weak male like you."

"General Gahumed, that is out of line," Mirtoff barked, her ears double their normal size and the tips an angry blue. "You have—"

"Me only son killed by people like him. Weak cowards. He only here because of luck. I have every right, you—"

"Enough! You will no disgrace me or me special envoy," Mi'ko snapped, his own ears matching Mirtoff's and Gahumed's.

Several of the speakers fidgeted, not sure where to focus. Everyone fell silent. All eyes were on him.

"We have all suffered loss, some more recent than others," Mi'ko said. "There is no need to bring up the ugliness of *our* past."

Todd was frozen in place, unsure what to say or do. What was happening here? This wasn't just about him. It couldn't be.

"General, before we agreed on Special Envoy Landon, you want to go to war and take what is not ours." Mi'ko massaged his ears. "You want blood for blood. We said no. Now you have us here for this ceremony, and you insult my special envoy. General Gahumed, do you have questions for my special envoy, or are you just going to berate him?"

General Gahumed's eyes blazed on Todd. He was pretty sure her ears were going to pop right off her head.

"You could leave," Gahumed said. "You free to go at any time. You are no bound to us like a cádo to its provider." She waved her hands as if shooing him away. "History would no consider you weak or coward for leaving. You action in saving the vice speaker would see to that. Even though I no agree. Tell me, would you like leave? Go home, allow someone more qualified to do this? Go back to you pathetic life?"

He took this job to honor those who died, to honor Jerry. He sure as hell wasn't going to let her get away with insulting the speaker general. So what if her son died? Jerry died too. A lot of people died, and it wasn't going to be easy, but they had to move on.

"I have doubts, but doesn't everyone? Don't you?" Todd pointed at Gahumed. "I can't imagine what it would be like to lose a child. I'm here to honor those who died, so their deaths have meaning. With all due respect, General Gahumed La-Enn, I have no intention of going anywhere, and I doubt you have the authority to say otherwise." He crossed his arms over his chest. "And, for the record, my life isn't average. God knows, it's not perfect, but everything I've—"

"Very well." General Gahumed cut him off. Her voice rang louder to overcome his. "Now you mention a higher power, tell me, Todd, do you believe in the higher power you race call God? I understand you of a faith, Christian." She picked up a datapad and studied. "Catholic, I understand."

His hands balled into fists. He lowered his arms to his side, trying to relax his body.

She's a bully. Nothing more.

He nodded. "Yes, I'm Catholic, and of course, I believe in a higher power. I may not understand Him, but I believe that God is watching over us. All of us. Whether we believe in Him or not." He zeroed in on her. "There is much about religion that is good and wonderful. It brings out the good in people. How can there not be a God?"

His shoulders straightened. "And, yes, there is a lot about religion that can be mean and cruel. That's part of the balance. You can't have the good without the evil." He glanced around the chamber, meeting each of the speakers' eyes, thinking about what to say next. "I probably sound ridiculous. I'm no religious scholar, and I don't go to church, but I believe in God, and it's His hand at work here. All of this is part of some plan He has for both of our races. The good and the bad. We're just not meant to see it yet."

"Even the death of you mate and my own son? Is that part of J'Veesa's, or you God, plan?"

Was this all part of God's plan? Jerry blown up, General Gahumed's son dying? All the religious protests. Did Todd truly believe that?

I have to be brave. If not for me, then for the ones who died in the attack.

"I...I don't know. I don't want... No one should have died that day, but if anything good can come from it, then I suppose it is."

Tears tickled his eyes, but he held them back.

I will not show weakness to this woman.

"Very well, I learn all I need." Gahumed's face hardened. "I pushed you all I can, and you did not break. You a strong male, after all. I believe Denes, me son, would respect you despite what you government may said." She turned to the other members of the Speaker's House and stood. "The Dentraee clan will accept Todd Landon, but I watch you and reserve full judgment. See if you truly worthy or if we need bring you before us again."

She stopped and turned to Mi'ko. "If you pick well, there may be future for both human and Nentraee, Jealug Bravisa willing, assume Todd no fail us."

"Todd Landon, by acceptance of this Speaker's House, I official welcome you as the special envoy to Mi'ko Soemu for Terran Affairs." Mirtoff bowed. "What lay in front of us is unknown, what lay behind us is the past. Let us learn from where we come so it help us prepare for what come next."

Each member of the Speaker's House bowed toward Todd and left the stage. The light that illuminated them during the session dimming. Mirtoff stood alone on the stage, facing Todd. A smile crossed her face and she bowed a final time before leaving. The ceremony over, Todd was left alone, standing there.

"You did well." Vi-Narm moved next to him, her tone seemed astonished. "Even General Gahumed came around. I did not consider that would happen."

"Well, good." Todd quickly wiped at his eyes. "All I wanted was to answer her questions to the best of my ability."

"General Gahumed La-Enn may be overfilling her boat to spite the speaker general, but she is a fair female and represent our clan well," Vi-narm said. "The speaker general Mirtoff is first of her clan to be in this position and is determine to be the best she can. Her and General Gahumed do no always agree. General Gahumed hope she would fail this day." Her voice lowered. "She wait for her to fail, so she...can point out her weakness and get her remove as speaker general, but that no happen. Not today." Vi-Narm's lips broke into a slight smile. "In part, she owe it to you. You did better than any have imagined."

Todd took a shaky breath.

"Your answers to her were direct and perfect. She no like weakness, chiefly in males. Her son was strong, and you remind her of him." She started to leave the chamber. "Come. We have much to do before tonight."

"Wait a minute." Todd grabbed her arm. "You knew she was going to do this. You knew she had every intention of making me look foolish." He wanted to reach out and slap the braids off her head. "You might have warned me or given me a heads-up? You know, to have helped me prepare. Why are you making this so difficult on me?"

"My duty." She stopped and glared at his hand.

Todd kept his hand in place.

Screw you and your no-touching culture.

"My duty is to this council and to protection of vice speaker, not to you. I will assist you with your position as instructed by Mi'ko and Speaker's House. Do not confuse my duty to them with caring for your comfort or making sure you do not fail. That is for you. Just like it is for the speaker general." She shrugged off his hand and proceeded toward the doors. "Are you come?"

"Unbelievable." He was angry with her and all of them, but mostly himself. He should have been better prepared. "Is there a choice?"

"There always a choice, Todd," General Gahumed said. "So, what yous?"

Four: After the Ceremony

TODD'S HANDS SHOOK with frustration. Gahumed's words haunted him, not because she was wrong, but because she might have been right. His conversation with Vi-Narm after the ceremony didn't help.

"You realize she intentionally didn't give me any warning about the vote." He sat back in his office chair, facing the monitor where his brother Brad sat, drumming his fingers on the desk. "I'm glad it wasn't with the House of the People—that would've been a nightmare, there are over two hundred of them. I don't get it. I've never been anything but nice to Vi-Narm and she—"

"Toddy, who cares?" Brad interjected. "You're not going to make everyone happy. You've only been up there a couple of weeks. Just do your job, write your reports, and play tour guide." He paused. "It sounds to me like you impressed them, even that Speaker Gummy La-Ann. Well, impressed her enough to pass you, or whatever."

"It's Speaker Gahumed La-Enn. She's a general in the military." He closed his eyes, his head pounding from the meeting. "You know, and that's another thing."

"What?"

"Why the hell does everyone care who I slept with or share my life with? Is that the most interesting thing about me?" Todd massaged his temples. "First, the bitchy secretary of state and her snide remarks about Jerry. Then the media. Do you know some of those bastards contacted my ex-boyfriends and interviewed them? Now General Gahumed..." He huffed. "What the hell? You know it wouldn't surprise me one bit if she were gay. Her and that fugly ass nose."

"Come on. It's not that bad."

"What her nose? It's hideous," Todd said.

Brad crossed his arms over his chest.

"May it be you race no approve of matings of same sexes?" Todd impersonated General Gahumed's voice. "She actually said that. Why the hell do they care what I do with my—"

"Hold up." Brad waved his hands in front of his face. "Listen, you know some people see being gay as a weakness. It's possible the Nentraee do too. Like you're not a real man 'cause you're not sleeping with a bunch of women."

Todd glared at him.

"Don't be mad at me. That's how some people view it. It's reality."

"And what about you?"

"I never saw you as weak." Brad shook his head. "I've always known you to be a tough SOB. I was stupid and couldn't get past the icky factor. And I came from a conservative family that didn't understand."

"I came from the same family, dumbass."

"I never said they were good excuses, now did I?"

"I can't believe it's only been six months since you showed up on my front porch." Todd glanced at the photo on his desk of Jerry and him in front of the house when they bought it.

"Never again, little brother." Brad flashed him a roguish grin.

"You know she can pull me back in front of the Speaker's House? I checked. I didn't think she could, but she can." Todd's temples throbbed again. "Now both her and Vi-Narm are gonna be watching me."

"Stop. Enough about them. You'll be fine," Brad said. "More importantly, how do I get into those restricted drive sections of their ships?"

"Um. Never. There is no reason to go in there, and the Nentraee are clear as to what humans—what we can and can't access. It hasn't been decided what drive technology they are willing to share. Even I'm not allowed in certain areas of the ship, so quit asking."

Brad frowned.

The left side of Todd's screen blinked as ten additional requests popped up. He had no idea there would be so much information to go over and sort out. The Nentraee had been allowing more people to come to visit the ships, which was great, but it created a lot more work for him. Especially with all the various winter holidays coming.

"Hey, Brad." Todd leaned back in his chair. "I want to invite Mi'ko and his family down to Earth for Thanksgiving. What do you think?"

"I thought you were mad at him?"

"Nah, it's not his fault, and he did confront General Gahumed at the meeting so..." He shrugged.

Brad fell quiet.

"Hello?" Todd waved at the monitor. "What do you think?"

"Mom will freak out... You may work with Nentraee every day, but most people don't see them as much as you do. What about security? Are you sure the Nentraee will even like it? Can we even eat the same things? I read that some of them are allergic to peas...*peas*, I mean, come on, who has a pea allergy?"

"Fine. We won't serve peas," Todd said. It would be a good opportunity for all of them. He could arrange security, and the press wouldn't be an issue with them hovering around the speaker general in Washington, DC. Still, he could issue a standard press release and go from there. It would be a small social experiment, his social experiment, on how well both cultures mixed in a closed setting. It'd be fun.

"I'm gonna do it." Todd leaned forward, pulled up another window on his monitor, and started to compose a message. "You tell Mom. We'll do it at my house. I'll take care of all the details, just make sure you tell the family." He paused and focused back on Brad. "Oh, and for God's sake, tell them I don't want to deal with our family bullshit with Mi'ko and his family there."

"Great, thanks." Brad frowned, shaking his head. "Leave me with the hard part. You realize it's not the holidays until someone goes off to their room in a crying fit. I hope it's not Mom."

"Okay." Todd's head filled with the images of his family and the Nentraee at his house for Thanksgiving and how perfect it would be. Everyone sitting around the sparkling table, chatting and enjoying a meal. They could share stories. Everyone learning more about one another in a neutral setting. Each group gaining insights into one another's culture that they would never have been able to do otherwise. It would be perfect, as it should be. "I need to head off. I'll talk to you in a few days."

"But...wait, Todd..."

Todd closed the communication. He stretched his leg to ensure the muscles were as loose as possible. He glanced out the window to Earth off in the distance. Several shuttle-class ships came and went from the larger ships.

Watching the ships is amazing, particularly from here.
The chime of his door pulled him from the view.

"Come in," Todd said.

The door swished open.

"Hello, Todd," Mi'cin said, datapad in hand.

Mi'cin scanned Todd's desk, and a frown crossed his lips.

"I know, I know. All that paper is wasteful." Todd's desk had two notepads and a couple of folders with hardcopy reports in them. It had gotten much better.

"It has improved," Mi'cin said.

"What can I help you with?"

"The vice speaker wanted to be advised if you had a chance to review the upcoming human events for the rest of November." Mi'cin sat in the chair in front of Todd's desk.

"This is everything." Todd picked up one of the datapads, tapping the upload button a couple of times. An ugly buzz sounded. "Dang it." He cleared the error message, tapped on the files, then entered the save command. "It's not all entered into the system yet, but I've marked the events that he'll need to make special note of, since those are the countries he has pending deals with. The others can be farmed out..." He stopped, noticing Mi'cin's confused expression to the phrase he used. "Um, some of the members of the Speaker's House or the House of the People can attend those events, or even some of their aides."

"Good. Please send the information to me."

Todd pursed his lips, glancing at the datapad and the small stack of paper on his desk.

"Um..."

"Very well, please get it entered into the network system for uploading to the vice speaker. It can forgo my review."

"Fine. Fine, he'll have it this afternoon. You'll be happy that this is the last of it." Todd pointed to the binders and paper. "After these couple stacks are inputted, I'll be off paper."

"Good," Mi'cin said. "You will be gone from work how long for this *Thanks for giving*?"

"It's called Thanksgiving, and I'll be out three days."

"Special Envoy," a polite computer voice said with perfect English. "There is an incoming call from White House Chief of Staff Greg McNeil. Do you wish to accept it?"

"One minute please, Mi'cin." He turned the terminal so they could both view it. "I accept."

The screen cleared, and Greg's image appeared.

"Todd. I'm sorry to bother you, but I had..." He started in a businesslike tone, then stopped. "My apologies," he added. "Hello, Mi'cin."

Mi'cin bowed.

Greg's eyes darted back and forth off-screen. "You're busy. I was hoping I could run an idea by you. I have some information that doesn't make any sense."

Todd glanced at Mi'cin, then back to the monitor.

A knock came over the monitor and Greg turned his head. He frowned and his eyes narrowed. "I'm getting called to a meeting. It'll have to wait," Greg said before Todd could reply. "Please extend my hello to the vice speaker."

Todd raised his brows.

Odd, Greg doesn't seem himself.

"Oh, and, Todd, if I don't speak to you before then, Happy Thanksgiving." He ended the transmission.

"That was strange." Todd touched the monitor as the screen filled with the Nentraee government seal.

"Several things your race does are strange." Mi'cin picked up his datapad. "I should leave so you can contact

Mister McNeil and find out what he needs. Many humans aren't comfortable dealing with us directly, and it would seem Mister McNeil is one of them."

"It's not that. You heard him. He got called out to a meeting. If it's so important, then he would've said." Todd took the datapad and plugged it into its docking station. "Plus, as far as I know, he has no issues with the Nentraee, especially your father. So, that's not the case." Todd tapped the monitor to close down his system. "Are you going to the vice speaker?"

"Yes, he's expecting a status update."

"Good." Todd grabbed his suit jacket. "Do you mind if I come with you? I've got a question for him. And for you, for that matter."

Five: Thanksgiving

"BE CAREFUL," TODD yelped. "That's the bone china Jerry picked out." He hadn't used it since before Jerry's death.

"Bitch, please. I got this." Dan swirled the plate in his hands, then placed it on the table. "I don't know why you thought this was such a great idea. Seriously?" He surveyed his work.

A gold damask tablecloth lay under gold chargers. Jerry's cream-colored bone china edged in gold and turquoise trim sat on top. Three different-sized crystal goblets next to each place setting. Polished silver utensils were lined up like soldiers gathered for inspection. Yellow orchids and white and yellow roses had been arranged to complement the china and crystal, while allowing for unobstructed conversation.

What was he thinking? Parties were a Jerry thing. He hadn't hosted anything in their home since way before Jerry died. Now he was not only having his family here, but his boss, who also happens to be a leading figure with an alien species.

I can do this. I have to do this. God, I wish Jerry was here.

"It'll be fun." Todd tried to sound convincing. He flicked his hands in the kitchen sink, then picked up the towel off the counter to dry them. "I've been looking forward to it, and I'm pretty sure Mi'ko has too. Plus, you're the one who wants to meet the Nentraee."

Dan shrugged.

Todd grabbed the mits off the counter and pulled the tray of stuffed mushrooms out of the oven. He stepped back, nudging Bianca as she ran past. The tray landed hard on the granite counter as he almost fell.

I've missed you, puss, but you're trying to kill me. I wonder what Faa would think of you?

"Sounds like you're the one who needs to be careful," Dan teased.

"Whatever." Todd checked the datapad he was using to keep track of the dinner.

"How do you like that gadget anyway?" Dan pointed.

"I like it." Todd pursed his lips, tapping the enter button. "Well, I'm getting used to it." As he pulled up his notes on cooking turkey, a light flashed on the datapad. A holographic, three-dimensional view of his house appeared. With an unpleasant buzz, the image vanished.

A knock came from the front. "Crap!" Todd jumped. "They're here." Todd felt the pit of his stomach sink as the images of his perfect Thanksgiving flashed into his head. "I had to do backflips to make this all happen."

"I'd like to see that."

"Screw you. Trust me, some government officials and Nentraee weren't too happy about it."

"Toddy...? You home?" Brad called from the entry hall.

"Hey, Brad."

Brad's wife walked in behind him, holding a bottle of wine. "Lori." Todd hugged her, getting a mouthful of dark hair that smelled of strawberries.

Behind Lori, Todd's nephew and niece, Kevin and Michelle, trailed in. Kevin wore khaki pants and a long-sleeve shirt. He held a plastic-wrapped tray. Michelle was dressed in dark pants and a sweater, her head buried in her smartphone.

"Hi, Uncle Todd," they said in tandem.

"Here, let me help you with that." Dan took the bottle of wine from Lori. "Nice pick—Napa Valley 2012 Pinot Noir. You have class."

"Thanks." Lori brushed a few strands of her hair behind her ear. "Oh, Todd, we brought a dessert. I realize you said not to, but..."

"I see that." Noticing the brownies, Todd took the tray from his nephew. "Thanks."

Lori took off her coat and handed it to Kevin. "Go put this in the den, please."

He made the same pouty face Brad made when he was that age, then stalked off with her coat and purse.

She headed toward the kitchen. "Wow. The table is amazing."

"Thank you. Thank you." Dan bowed. "I figured it needed to be amazing today. So, I *Danned* it up." He stuck out his tongue so only Todd could see.

"I love the kitchen. There's so much space. You could hardly tell with all the people at the—" She glanced down to the tile floor.

"It took Jerry and I eighteen months, but it's what we wanted." The memories of the two of them working on this kitchen flooded back. Lori stared at him, and he smiled. "Lori, it's fine. I wish you'd gotten to know him. He would have liked you."

"I'm sure he was wonderful." Lori touched Todd's arm. She turned to Dan. "And you, Mister. You're an angel."

"You got that right." He snapped his fingers. "I want wings and a halo that glitters."

"Hey, Mom and Dad are here," Brad called from the living room. "I'm gonna give them a hand."

"Watch him," Todd told Lori as he pointed at Dan.

Todd headed to the front porch, the sun blinding his vision. As his eyes adjusted, he watched his parents come up the walk with Kati. "Hey there." He kissed his mom's cheek and gave his dad a welcoming hug.

"Good to see you, Button," his dad said.

"Heya, Dad."

"You've been away too long, closed up in those damn ships," his father said. "They treating you good up there?" He pulled Todd's light-green shirt up. "No probes or anything like that, right?"

"Seriously, Dad. Probes?"

"It might happen."

Brad laughed, marching up the front steps.

"Kati, I'm glad you made it," Todd greeted her with a hug and took in her dark hair, gold floor-length skirt, cream-colored sweater, and her signature heels. It always amazed him how breathtaking she was. Despite her often gruff language, she tended to look stunning. She had always been one of the best-dressed people at CRiNE and probably still was. He missed working there with her.

"Hey, Mister Big Shot." She pinched his arm.

"Ouch."

"What? Too good to call me?" She gave him a feisty wink.

"I've been busy getting probed, according to my dad." He pointed at her. "Not a word."

Kati wobbled her eyebrows devilishly.

"Come on. Let's get in the house." Todd ushered the group to the kitchen.

Todd smiled as the kitchen bustled with activity. Everyone chatting and hanging out. It had been eight years since he'd spent a holiday with his family. That wasn't right. This was how a kitchen should buzz on the holidays.

"You sure they can eat everything? What about the turkey?" His mother pointed to the food. "I heard that tryptophan is deadly to them."

"That was some crazy rumor out of Arizona or some other bullshit." Todd chuckled. "I double-checked, and there is no reason they can't enjoy the meal."

"Assuming it's edible," Kati teased.

"So, you get to go all over the ships?" Kevin pushed past Kati and grabbed a stuffed mushroom, then popped it into his mouth before his mother noticed.

"Yep." Todd beamed at his nephew.

"And you're sure they're not giant lizards here to take over?" Kevin asked.

"They're not from one of your dumb movies." Michelle's eyes raised from her cell phone. Her dark hair matched Lori's.

"Okay, cool it, you two." Lori put the rolls in the oven to bake. "You, off the phone." She pointed to Michelle and then turned to Kevin. "And you, enough snacks. We have a big dinner to eat."

"Speaking of the aliens." Brad popped a cracker with cheese in his mouth, then tapped his watch.

"I know, I know. They should be here soon." Todd ran a frantic hand over his forehead to wipe off the sweat. "Mi'ko has all the details. They probably got held up." He wiped his sweaty palms on his pants. "Enjoy the snacks." He pulled out his pocket watch and checked the time.

They should be here.

"Everything smells amazing. Is that chestnut stuffing or sage stuffing?" His dad rolled his glass of wine in his hands.

"Sage," Dan said.

"If they're not here soon, we eat without them." Kati held up her glass of wine, taking a sip. Todd's dad did the same.

"Like there aren't enough snacks." His mother took a bite of the mushrooms. "Honey, these mushrooms are great."

"Thank you, Missus Landon. They're my mot—"

A loud knock at the door called all their attention.

Todd straightened his shoulders and considered his family and friends. "Please, everyone, be nice and everything will be fine." He headed to the dining room. "Oh. Don't shake hands." He glanced back at everyone. "Unless they offer."

Todd's hands shook as he took a breath, the mob of people not more than a foot behind him. Even Bianca sat off to the side, watching.

He took another breath and opened the front door.

Mi'ko, Laina, and Mi'cin stood there, dressed in similar outfits to those worn at the White House dinner. Laina's form-fitting cream-colored gown flowed at the hips. Her soft brown hair was done up in an intricate bun with a few wisps to the sides of her face. A typical gray suit hung clumsily on Mi'ko, his matching tieback slightly lopsided. Mi'cin, in contrast, wore a dark-gray fitted suit with a light-green shirt that made his eye color pop. Mi'cin had a matching gray tieback. Unlike his father's, his was perfect. Each family member was adorned in their ceremonial cloak.

No Hir-Shif and Hir-Ko? What happened?

Todd gulped as he stepped aside to let them in.

"Welcome," Todd said.

The black sedan was parked out front, along with three human guards, all in dark suits and sunglasses. One made his way to the backyard.

"I thought..." Todd pointed to the security.

"I am sorry." Mi'ko shook his head. "Vi-Narm wanted to have our own security, but I convinced her to go with your government-provided personnel."

"Of course." Todd closed the door.

The room fell silent with Todd in the middle of both groups, his family and friends on one side and Mi'ko's family on the other. Both groups stared at one another, the silence deafening. This was nothing like the image he had in his head.

"Dr. Soemu and Vice Speaker, I would like to present my family." His heart beat like a drum in his chest. "This is my mother, Beatrice Landon; my father, Philip Landon; my brother, Brad; his wife, Lori; and their two children, Kevin and Michelle."

"It is a great honor and pleasure to meet you all. I am Laina Soemu." She turned to her husband. "It is my honor to introduce my husband, Mi'ko Soemu, and our son, Mi'cin. Our other two sons, Hir-Shir and Hir-Ko, were not able to attend today. Their work did not allow it. Forgive them, and do not take it as an insult to your offer of hospitality." She bowed.

Crap.

Todd had forgotten to tell his family and friends they should bow back. He bowed, then turned to Kati and Dan. "These are my friends, Katherine Nishimura and Devante—Dan—Rios." When he pointed to them, they both picked up his cue and bowed awkwardly. Kati almost did a curtsy.

"It's an honor to meet you all," Laina said.

Silence.

Todd's manners were quickly replaced by nerves. He mentally stumbled on what to do next. He saw his nephew and niece fidgeting.

This is not how I pictured it.

"Michelle is an honor student," Todd blurted out, focusing on her. "She's interested in becoming a vet, an animal doctor."

Michelle gave him a blank face, turned to the aliens briefly, then stared down at her cell phone.

"Caring for animals is a noble profession," Mi'ko said. "Our animal companions are very particular on who will treat them."

Michelle peeked up and smiled at him, not saying a thing.

Kevin pushed forward and watched each of the Nentraee. "Do you got any pets?"

"No, they are very picky creatures." Mi'ko focused down at him. "We thought we would be selected by one when Mi'cin was young and we were evacuated from our planet, but we were not lucky in that way."

"So, they pick you?" Kevin asked.

"That is correct, but we were not lucky," Mi'ko said.

"Bummer." Kevin nodded and turned back to the kitchen.

The conversation stopped and everyone stared at Todd.
This is bad. Think. What would Jerry do? Oh, God.

Todd needed to get them all to relax. "Well, please come in and grab a seat." He pointed to the living room. "Or, would you like a tour of the house?" He glanced to his mom. "Mom, do you mind? I should check dinner. It's almost done." The words rushed out of his mouth. He wasn't sure what more to say to save this.

Her eyes opened wider as she peeked up at the aliens. They towered over her. "Of course not." She stepped closer, glancing up at them with a welcoming smile on her face. "Mister Vice Speaker, Laina, Mi'cin, please come with me." The polite smile grew larger as they moved. "So, why do the men of your race wear bows in their hair? I've seen them on TV. Is it a fashion thing? And are you all this tall? You didn't seem this tall on TV."

"Yeah, why is your hair so long?" Kevin pointed to Mi'cin. "Isn't that a little girly? And why is that bow in your hair crooked, Mister Vice Speaker, sir?"

"Idiot! A lot of guys have long hair." Michelle smacked him on the back of the head.

"Hey. Mom said no—"

"Enough, you two!" Lori snapped. Red-faced, she turned back to the Nentraee. "Sorry." She wasn't meeting anyone's eyes.

Todd bit down on the inside of his mouth and pushed past Kati and Dan. His face was cold and clammy. He knew somehow his mother would find a way to get everyone talking.

"This isn't awkward at all." Dan reached the kitchen and crossed his arms over his chest.

Todd pulled out the rolls, beating the timer by a few seconds.

"It'll be fine. Drink a little wine." Todd placed the tray on the counter. "I should've brought some e'xin from the ship for them. God, I should've thought of that." He tapped the top of one of the rolls.

"You're kidding, right?" Dan pulled over the bottle of wine. "Getting this group drunk—can they even get drunk?—might cause an intergalactic conflict, or worse, a war. I don't want to say it—"

"Then don't." Todd held up a hand. "This is going to work. It has to work." He frowned at Dan, and his head started to ache. "You say one more word about it, and I swear..." He grabbed the bread bowl. "It's been five minutes."

"Dios mío, is that all?"

"Let's get the food served. Once everyone starts eating, things will smooth out."

"Can we help?" Brad and Lori came into the kitchen.

"Not unless you've got Xanax." Dan shook his head.

"Ignore him." Todd pulled off the oven mitts. "Lori, you and Dan are on potatoes. Brad, remove two place settings from the table since we're down two." Todd froze and gulped, staring at the turkey. "I'll take care of the bird."

"It's not that bad," Todd whispered. "It'll be fine." The turkey sat on the cooling rack, mocking him.

Jerry always cut the turkey. Time to step up.

The rolls waited, covered in their bowl. The potatoes were mashed and piled high with a dollop of butter. The sage stuffing was ready to serve. The brussels sprouts shimmered under the light. Todd set the platter of turkey on the dining table. Dinner was ready. The smells of crispy turkey skin, melted butter, and sage filled his nose. He scanned the table again, making sure everything was all set.

All I'm missing is Jerry.

His mother had everyone talking in the living room. Mi'ko chuckled, as did Todd's father. When he peeked in, they were all picking at the snacks and sipping their drinks.

"It'll be fine, and the bird is great. You did a fantastic job for your first time," a voice from behind him said.

He turned to see Jerry, leaning against the counter by the kitchen, wearing dark jeans and a powder-blue polo shirt. A soft glow all around him. A big bright smile filled his handsome face.

"Everything looks great." Jerry strolled over to Todd and ran a warm familiar hand along the side of his face. "Don't worry."

"Easy for you to say." Todd sighed, wanting to crumple in Jerry's arms. "The tension when they first met was awful." His shoulders dropped.

Jerry reached out and pulled Todd in for a hug. "Nothing's perfect. You know that. I mean, it just takes a minute." The glow around him warmed as Jerry brought him peace.

"I wish you were here." Todd wiped at his eyes. "You could've helped to get everyone talking. You were so good at that. And the turkey."

"Listen. They're talking. That's all that matters." Jerry glanced in the direction of the living room. "You did that. You got two alien species together who never otherwise would've met. I'd say your experiment is working out. Now, call in your guests before the meal gets cold."

"I miss you so much," Todd said.

Jerry kissed him on the forehead and gently stepped back.

The vision of Jerry melted away. "I can do this," he whispered and strolled into the living room, his heart and spirits raised. "Shall we eat?"

The conversation continued as everyone headed into the dining room. Kati reached out and touched Todd's arm. Her eyes narrowed in on him, "You okay? You look like you've seen a ghost."

"I'm fine."

The image of Jerry had reminded him that he could do anything.

TODD TOOK A heavy swallow of his wine. The meal was not how it was supposed to be. They were supposed to have a nice dinner and talk about their cultures, with him as the moderator.

"I do not understand the need to kill a tree and put it in your home." Mi'ko's tone was dry as he rested his clasped hands on the dining table. "Can you not use one that is already dead and ready for disposal?"

"It's not about the tree." Todd's dad leaned over his plate, getting closer to the vice speaker, his voice labored. "Don't you have decorations?"

"What part of the religious ceremony does the tree belong?" Mi'cin put his fork down and a bright smile filled his face. "Plants need trees to create oxygen, and given the amount of pollution in places like Asia and South America, you cannot afford to cut them all down."

Todd's face was hot and his heart pounded in his chest. He wasn't sure how or where to break into the conversation.

"We don't cut them all down." Todd's father clenched his trembling hands. "Christmas trees aren't about the religion—they smell nice." He inhaled, then sipped his wine. "Our trees come from a tree farm. So we're not hurting the environment. They're renewable."

Mi'ko reached up and adjusted his tiebacks.

"It's a tradition." Todd's dad raised his brow and the right side of his upper lip quizzically. "Mi'cin, they're nice and make the house festive."

Todd recognized his dad's expression. It was the same face he made when he talked about hardcore environmentalists.

"Then why do some people not use them," Mi'ko asked. "Or use false or potted trees?" The lines on Mi'ko's face deepened around his eyes and mouth.

"I don't understand those people. They're freaks." Todd's father dropped both hands to the table, hitting the gold charger and causing his plate to almost spill onto the gold damask tablecloth.

"Dad." Todd grimaced at his father.

"Freaks?" Mi'cin's eyes brightened. "I've been studying American slang. In this case, you mean these people perform in a wild and irrational way. So, they are suffering from a mental illness?"

"Yes." Todd's father gave a single firm nod. "I mean no... Sorry, Button—I mean, Todd. I forgot about your fake tree." Todd's dad whipped a hand across his forehead removing the beads of sweat.

"I find it fascinating at how many holidays humans have," Mi'cin said. "All that waste and consumption— amazing." He looked around the table. "Your traditions and customs would never work for our people, not on our ships. Think of how much your nation alone could save. Not to mention all the other nations on this planet."

Kati and Dan glanced at Todd.

Todd groaned and offered a slight shrug. The dinner conversation had been awkward at best and, at the worst, insulting.

"It's like I told my mother," Mi'cin said. "Humans have no appreciation for how lucky they are to have this planet. We didn't understand until we had to leave our world and pay attention to what we used and how we used it. Now look at us. We lost so much, so many Nentraee, and here you sit, wasting your world. Not careful on how you abuse it."

"I don't appreciate that." Brad put his fork down, his eyes narrowing on Mi'cin. "Don't you have holidays that you celebrate?"

"Yes. Of course," Mi'cin said.

"So, by your own admission, you have parties that might not be the best use of resources and materials." Brad's voice raised. "Do you get a chance to spend time together and enjoy each other?"

"They have A' Godá Faoo," Todd offered, his voice meek. "It's the celebration of the rights of fatherhood and quite the event with music and gifts. I believe that's a two-day celebration for the Ultween, your clan, and the Martween, right?"

Laina nodded. "You are correct."

"There's A'Mev," Todd spoke. "It's like our birthdays—"

"Oh, do you get presents?" Kevin interrupted.

Lori shushed him.

"It's the day of naming and presentation of the child to family and friends," Todd said. "I thought that was kind of cool."

Laina's lips played with a smile, and Mi'ko bowed slightly in Todd's direction. Mi'cin stayed quiet, watching Todd while quietly clicking his tongue.

"I think it would be a nice change to hear about one of *these* holidays Todd mentioned." Brad crossed his arms over his chest. "Learn how you celebrate. Maybe, learn how you do it in a *responsible* way."

Mi'cin shifted in his seat. "Of course we have holiday, but not like this."

"Mi'cin, enough." Laina sat taller and her shoulders straightened as she faced him. "You were a child when we left Benzee, and you do not remember the celebrations we once had. They were very much like this." She put her crystal goblet of water down and rested her clasped hands on the edge of the table.

"Our holidays are more reflective and contemplative now," Mi'cin huffed.

"So, no waste?" Todd's dad leaned in.

"That is not complete correct." Mi'ko faced his son. "I apologize for his comments. He still learns."

"I mean no offense. I'm trying to understand." Mi'cin's neck was turning a pale blue. "For us, we may share a large meal. However, we will ensure that everyone has enough." He pointed to the half-eaten food on the plates and serving dishes still full. "This is one day, and you eat all this, while others on your world have nothing and are dying because of it." He pointed toward the large picture window with a view of the houses and the hills behind them. "Even here, in this city, you have people starving or who have next to nothing."

Dan and Kati glanced at the few bites left on their plates. Brad picked up his fork and forced another bite, chewing it slowly. Lori's face grew pink. Both Todd's parents covered their plates with their napkins to hide the rest.

Todd swigged his wine.

I didn't know Hir-Shif and Hir-Ko weren't going to be here. That is why there is so much food.

"What about the leftovers?" Michelle glanced at her plate.

"Michelle." Lori's raised eyebrows.

"I love leftovers." Michelle faced off with her mother. "Turkey sandwiches and your mashed potato cakes."

"Thank you," Lori said.

"You have to understand. Its kind of a presentation of the abundance and the blessing bestowed on us over the course of the year and the hope that it represents the same for the year to come." Todd pointed to the food left on the table. "And Michelle's right. This food won't go to waste. We will continue to eat it over the next few days as leftovers."

"Leftovers?" Mi'cin shrugged. "It's a lot of waste."

This has gone on too long. What can I do?

"All valid points, Mi'cin," Todd said, then tried to sip his wine. He hit the glass on his teeth in his haste. "On our world, there are areas of great abundance, and this day reminds us to be thankful for all that we have and not to forget those in need."

"Leftovers are another human tradition," Todd's mother said.

"I see from your faces, my son remarks have offended you." Laina's expression remained neutral. She folded her napkin and placed it next to her plate. "Despite the image he try to represent of us, we do have celebrations where we indulge. Please forgive us and my son. He does not always think before he speaks."

"If I offended you, I apologize." Mi'cin put down his fork and his shoulders softened. "It was an observation. I only wanted to understand better."

"No, you're right," Lori spoke up. "Like you said, even in San Jose, we have a lot of people who go without their basic needs met."

Todd's mother nodded, while his father crossed his arms over his chest.

"The thing that people don't always see is how many people actually get help and how we try to make sure that we solve those 'sins' of man." Lori sipped her soda. "Millions of people donate money, food, time, and clothing to help. There are hundreds of charities that help people not only on this day but throughout the year."

Todd's shoulders relaxed. Finally, he could breathe. He needed to get better at neutralizing situations like this if he wanted to succeed in his position.

"It's inspiring, and it's not just here. It's worldwide," Lori continued. "I get it doesn't seem like it, but we do try to take care of one another."

"And you and your family are part of this?" Mi'cin asked.

"Of course." Lori's voice rose an octave higher. "Lord knows there needs to be more of it. There is no reason for so many people to go without. Especially here—not anymore, not with our technology and abilities."

"Even on our world, before the Clan War, we had the same issues." Mi'ko faced his son as he spoke. "It only changed after we almost killed ourselves. At one point, our world was home to over two billion people. After the Clan War and the destruction we caused our environment, our population dropped to 425 million."

Todd's parents shared a surprised look.

"I'm sorry," Kati whispered.

"Wow," Dan muttered.

"It was a high price to pay for the lessons we learned." Mi'ko made eye contact with everyone at the table. "Even before our world was destroyed, our population was only 400 million. These *sins* you speak of are universal. If I understand the words correctly."

Todd, his family, and friends nodded.

"I hope that is something we can help you with," Mi'ko said. "Our technology in agriculture alone is much further advanced than yours. We have been working." He turned to Todd. "And Todd knows this to be true—with the Republic of Zimbabwe in Africa. We hope to help them improve their abilities in this area without harming the environment any further."

"It's pretty impressive." Todd leaned in and rested his elbows on the table.

"Elbows, Todd," his mother said.

"Sorry." Todd took his elbows off the table and rested his hands in his lap. "Anyway, they have advanced tech that can pull large amounts of moisture out of the atmosphere, even in the desert, so you don't need to dig wells to water crops, and their hydroponics systems are so much more advanced than anything we have. Their output per square foot is quadruple anything we have. I got a tour of one of their agricultural ships, and their food production is impressive."

"What we've discovered," Mi'ko said, "is that some people on any world, no matter how much you want to help, do not always want to be helped."

"My teachers are saying that with all the technologies and other things you have," Michelle said, "we'll be able to fix some of the things wrong with our world." She fussed with her hands. "Like saving the polar bears and keeping the glaciers from melting and climate change—"

"Assuming you believe in that liberal hysteria," Todd's dad interrupted. "I mean, come on, the sun goes in cycles, there have been how many ice ages, all before we started burning fossil fuels. It's ridiculous. Not to mention the icecaps on Mars have been melting. So how did our CO_2 gasses get there to change that? It's ridiculous."

"Phil, now's not the time." Todd's mother grabbed his hand. "We're having a lovely dinner."

Dan glanced at Todd with wide eyes, using his napkin to cover his mouth.

"Working for a better future, as lame as it may sound, *Mister Landon*, is an ongoing project for us all." Kati shifted on her chair to face Todd's father. "We don't want to end up like the Nentraee, with no home, now do we?"

There were nods of agreement from Todd's mother, Brad, Lori, and Dan.

"Sure, we've had these events in the past." Kati rolled the glass of wine in her hands. "But since we understand that they can happen, why not try to keep them from occurring? I'm not interested in going through an ice age. Are you? And if the Nentraee can help us fix our world, then why not? What can it hurt?"

"I guess I agree with that," Todd's dad said.

Kati raised her wineglass to him and he raised his to her, and then they both took sips.

"And on that note, may I get anyone anything?" Todd offered, hoping the break would reset the conversation. "Don't forget we have dessert too." He'd be making plenty of care packages for everyone to take with them when they left.

Todd started to pick up his plate and wineglass, when a knock came from the front door.

"Excuse me." Todd left his plate and glass, then headed to the entry and opened the door. Vi-Narm stood, meeting his eyes. Her hair was falling out of her braids and her face damp with sweat.

"Vi-Narm," Todd said.

What's going on? Why are you here?

"I apologize for the intrusion." Vi-Narm's breathing was heavy, and her voice strained.

"Of course, please come in." Todd stepped to the side.

"I need to speak with the vice speaker." She rushed in, her cloak disheveled. Todd led the way to the dining room.

"Vi-Narm?" Mi'ko stood, and his face changed from a smile to a frown.

"Many apologies, Vice Speaker." She offered a quick bow. "I must speak with you."

"Todd, is there a place we may talk?" Mi'ko put his napkin on the table and then adjusted his suit jacket.

Todd led them down the hall, all three sets of shoes clapping on the hardwood floors.

"I hope this will work?" Todd pushed open the door to the den, revealing an oak desk and desk chair, oak bookcases filled with trinkets, photos, and books as well as a small love seat with coats and purses draped over it.

"This will be fine." Mi'ko entered and closed the door.

Todd heard muffled noises from behind the door as Mi'ko and Vi-Narm spoke in their native language. He stretched his shoulders, trying to release the tension.

"I'm not going to panic," he mumbled.

"Is everything all right?" his mother asked.

"I'm sure it'll be fine. Vi-Narm is the vice speaker's aide, and sometimes there are things that can't always wait," Todd offered as he picked up the finished plates from the table.

Dan jumped up and grabbed some, too, then headed to the kitchen.

"So what's that all about?" Dan whispered, stacking the plates in the sink.

"No clue," Todd said. "I should start the coffee and tea and get dessert ready." The tension in his neck and shoulders built up again.

"You sure it's all right?" Dan knocked the datapad on the counter with his arm.

"There's nothing we can do about it, so I'm choosing not to worry."

"Do you wish to contact Greg McNeil?" The pleasant voice from the datapad asked.

"Crap. Sorry." Dan jumped to the side, away from the noise.

"Cancel action," Todd said to the device and took the whipped topping out of the refrigerator.

"You okay?" Dan peeked over his shoulder.

"Yep," Todd lied as his hands shook. "Now help me with the pumpkin pie."

Todd and Dan made their way back to the dining room. Todd held the pies and Dan carried in the dessert plates, whipped topping, and forks.

"I hope you all have some room left," Todd said. "These are homemade pumpkin pies, and we also have triple-fudge brownies, if you don't want pie."

"It's nothing special." Lori's face lit up. "I'll get 'em."

Brad let go of her hand.

"This has been very nice." Laina bowed from her seat. "Especially considering the extra work you have gone through to include us in this meal." Her head tilted as she watched him cut the pie. "I'm always amazed at how you males go through all this trouble to ensure that everything is perfect."

Todd's mother raised her eyebrows.

"Well, it's your first Thanksgiving, and I wanted it to be nice," Todd said. "My hope was to show you what an American does on this day." He passed the plated pie to Dan, who added the whipped topping.

Lori returned with the platter of brownies. Kevin snatched one as she walked by.

"Kevin!" Lori barked.

Kevin stuffed the whole brownie in his mouth and smiled. "But they're good."

"Pig," Michelle said.

"Cool it," Brad said. "Both of you."

Lori forced a smile and placed the tray on the table, and then took her seat next to Brad.

"You cook?" Laina glanced at the tray. "I would have thought Brad takes care of such matters for you and the children, particularly with you working."

"I can't even boil water." Brad reached for a brownie.

"How unfortunate for you, Lori. I am sorry." Laina wrinkled her nose at the brownies. "If you both work, who raises your children?"

"Well, Lori takes them to school in the morning, and then they come home after school, and we meet them after work." Brad shrugged.

"I see." Laina adjusted the braids of her hair. "Then you have the children care for themselves? Alone with no parent to ensure their safety?"

"Um...Kevin's eleven and Michelle's almost thirteen, so they do their homework, and we all cook when we get home." Brad explained.

"It's all right," Lori said. "We share duties around the house. I cook. Brad cleans and does laundry. And the kids have their chores to do. It works out. Both Brad and I take care of the kids equally." Lori took the piece of pie offered to her.

"Like we really need looking after." Michelle rolled her eyes.

"Oh, I forget. You're so independent, Michelle." Lori made almost the exact same expression.

"I see parent-child relationships are similar to each species." Mi'cin chuckled.

Kati handed him a piece of pie. "Another universal truth."

"My dad wasn't around when I was a kid," Dan said. "My mom raised me and my sister alone. And I turned out okay."

Todd and Kati chuckled.

"Todd," his mother chided.

"Sorry." Todd cleared his throat to stifle his laugh.

"How very strange." Laina picked up her fork and poked at the pie. "There is much that we need to learn about one another. Your interpretation on raising children is another item to add to the list." Her tone remained relaxed and friendly. She faced Todd. "I am happy you invited us. I have learned...no, I should say I had a wonderful time."

Todd served the last of the pie as Mi'ko and Vi-Narm returned. Mi'ko's frown had deepened as had the crinkles around his eyes. Both he and Vi-Narm stood taller and their shoulders tight and rigid.

"I apologies, but I must return to the ship." Mi'ko's voice was tense. "Todd, please forgive me, Laina, Mi'cin."

"Do you mind if I stay?" Mi'cin asked. "I've enjoyed the meal and the conversation more than I thought. I would like to continue. If that's all right with you, Mother? Father?" He glanced quickly to Todd.

"If you wish, you may stay," Mi'ko agreed and picked up his cloak off the chair. "Assuming it is all right with our host."

"Of course." Todd crossed over to Mi'ko, Laina, and Vi-Narm. "Is there anything I can do?"

"Not tonight, but when you return." Mi'ko's voice was strained. "Enjoy the time with your loved ones. Again, my apologies."

Todd's parents, Brad and Lori, Dan, and Kati all stood.

"Thank you for the honor of sharing a meal with us," Mi'ko said. "I apologize that we must leave before the night comes to an end, and for any offense we caused. My hope is Todd will continue to assist us, particularly Mi'cin, in socially appropriate conversations."

"I, as well, wish to apologies for any offense we have caused." Laina slipped on her cloak. "I hope to share more meals with you in the future and learn more about your family and your culture." She bowed to the group. "Perhaps, we could have you to our home so you can experience one of our celebrations. It would be pleasant to share it with non-Nentraee. I have so many questions."

"Wow!" Kevin said, his face stuffed with brownies. "You mean we would get to go to one of the ships...cool." He swallowed and picked up his glass of milk, then gulped it. "Wait. That doesn't mean I have to wear a stupid bow in my hair, does it?"

"Kevin." Brad's shook his head.

"Of course not." Mi'ko's expression softened as his frown cracked into a hint of a smile. "That is our tradition."

"Again, my apologies for the intrusion. Vice Speaker, we should leave," Vi-Narm chided, taking several steps to the front door. "We shall leave you human security and vehicle, Mi'cin. I come in my own." She led them out of the room and quickly from the house. The door closed loudly behind them.

"Well, that was strange." Brad sat back down, and then picked up his goblet of water and took a sip.

"Vi-Narm would not have interrupted my father were it not important." Mi'cin took his fork and poked the pumpkin pie and the whipped topping.

"Your parents seem lovely." Todd's mom put her napkin back on her lap. "I hope everything is all right."

"They would have not allowed Todd or I to stay should it have been an emergency." Mi'cin prodded at his pie again, sliding it around his plate. "Shall we have *pie*? It has quite a unique scent."

"Um...sure." Todd took his seat.

Six: After Dinner

TODD STOOD WITH Dan and Kati at the end of the walkway to his house. The late fall sun was hidden behind the roofline of the house across the street, casting them in a cool shadow.

"Thanks for all your help." Todd hugged Dan. "I really appreciate it. You, too, Kati. You guys are the best." He handed Kati her purse, coat, and a bag filled with containers of leftovers.

"Well, you know, what can we say? We're total rock stars like that." Kati put her free hand on her hip and flung her head back. "Now, call me. So we can do lunch or dinner, or a movie." She gave Todd a peck on the cheek, then whispered, "I hope not all the Nentraee feel like Mi'cin, or they might just take our world and wipe us out."

"That's not gonna happen," Todd whispered back.

"Right." She adjusted her purse. "Well, anyway, the PoorHouse Bistro isn't the same without you."

"I promise we'll go out." Todd chuckled. "How about dinner and a movie over the weekend? That'll work better for me."

"And you're treating, cause I ain't cheap." She snapped her fingers and winked.

"Later, girly girl," Dan said.

"Have fun with the family, my little pooky-oochy." Kati waved, and her heels clicked down the sidewalk as she sauntered to her car.

"Ugh. Well, ho," Dan said, "I'll see you later."

Hugging Todd, Dan barely spoke loud enough to hear. "Chica, Mi'cin may be hot as hell with a killer ass, but watch him 'cause he's a piece of work."

"Yes...thank you." Todd flushed and stole a glance to Mi'cin, who stood on the front porch, watching them.

I'm going to need to do some damage control here if this is what they think about the Nentraee.

Dan pulled back and rushed off toward his car. The vehicle started and he quickly passed the black sedan and driver left by Vi-Narm to take Mi'cin back to the airport.

With a wave goodbye to both Dan and Kati, Todd took a deep breath, enjoying the fall air and the music from the neighbor's house. After a moment, he headed back up to Mi'cin.

"I appreciate you allowing me stay." Mi'cin bowed. "I'm sorry if I came across poorly. It was not my intention."

"It's fine." Todd watched as one of the neighbor's cars slowed down and then sped up once they passed Todd's home. "It was the free flow of ideas so..." Todd faced Mi'cin.

How am I going to fix this for both sides?

"I guess I didn't expect it to get so heated," Todd said.

"Your family and friends are—" He paused and his tongue clucked before speaking. "—colorful." Mi'cin's voice had a questioning tone.

Colorful. Well, that's a word for it. I can't say they would say the same about you.

"They are unique." Todd stretched his arms over his head, trying to get his shoulders to relax. "I guess we all have a lot to learn."

"I believe if you don't ask questions, then you will be left with only false assumptions and no understanding, and that causes fear." Mi'cin leaned against the railing of the front porch. "That is why I say and ask things that can be seen as inappropriate. Next time, I will be cautious of my words."

Considering how things went today, I'm not sure how that's going to go.

"It can only get better," Todd said.

"Of course." Mi'cin's tone shifted, becoming professional and tight.

Todd pointed back to the front door. "Would you like to go inside and sit down?"

Mi'cin bowed his head. "Assuming my mother gets her way," he said as they walked back into the house. "She will insist that my family host your family for a meal."

"That should be interesting." Todd closed and latched the door. "Did you want some coffee or something else to drink or eat? There's plenty."

Mi'cin's expressions were difficult to read. He always seemed to analyze Todd. He was always focused on him when he spoke and when he moved. Not even Vi-Narm watched him like this.

"No, thank you."

Todd strolled over to the sofa and sat. The couch absorbed his body and his stress along with it.

Mi'cin continued to study Todd as he sat. "Was this a typical Thanksgiving for you?" Mi'cin leaned forward in the side chair.

"God, no." Todd paused, Mi'cin's large frame and height made the chair appear a size too small. "I mean, aside from you and your family being here. This was the first Thanksgiving I've spent with my family in years. Normally, I'd spend it with Jerry and his family in Utah. Thanksgivings with them were much more—" He struggled to find the right word. "—sedate."

He made a mental note to call the Bakers and see how they were doing. He hadn't spoken to them in a month.

"It must be difficult to lose someone you love so much." Mi'cin picked cat hair off his jacket, but more stuck to the fabric. "I remember my father was sick and in the hospital when I was young. My mother, she was worried about him. The doctors did not identify the illness right away." He fussed with his shirtsleeves as he spoke. "It was right before the evacuation of our world. Many had already left or were making preparation to leave. I do not remember being that fearful before, not until the day you saved him. Seeing the explosion and realizing there was nothing I could do. I cannot imagine what you went through, and I am both sorry for it and glad."

Todd's neck grew warm, and he shifted in the couch, tension climbing up his back.

"Both times. he was fine." Mi'cin adjusted on the seat.

He's kind of being awkward here. It's nice to see him like this. It's almost human.

"I can't imagine losing my parents," Todd said.

Silence filled the space between Todd and Mi'cin. Bianca ran from the dining room into the living room and jumped up onto the windowsill to look out into the yard and foothills. The sounds of birds captured her attention.

Todd smiled at his cat. "Don't get me wrong, they can drive me insane sometimes. But I love them."

"Another universal truth." Mi'cin glanced around the living room. "It's quiet here. There is no hum. It makes sense that you do not...don't?"

Todd smiled at the use of the contraction.

"Thank you," Mi'cin said. "It makes sense you don't want to give it up. Plus, all the space."

Must seem like a waste of space to him.

"Before we had to leave our world, we had a big house with a large yard and several trees. I remember playing in the backyard." Mi'cin's hands tapped on his leg. "My father keeping a watchful eye on me and my brothers. This home would be small in comparison."

"Do you have many memories of your home and your world? Your parents made it sound like you were too young." Todd leaned forward. Mi'cin couldn't have been more than five or six when they left their home twenty years ago.

"Yes, despite what my parents said at dinner, I do remember."

"I've read so much about your world, and I've seen the pictures," Todd said. "It was beautiful."

"From what I remember, but the memories of a child are very different than that of an adult. Much like your niece and nephew. They will remember this day and picture it completely different in their minds. Children view things through a cloud of love and innocence."

"Always the poet, Mi'cin."

Mi'cin's brilliant green eyes pierced Todd's.

"Sorry, I don't understand," Mi'cin's said.

"Um...well, I thought your words were eloquent." Todd pulled his gaze away from Mi'cin.

He seems so different here now. It's a nice change from how stiff he normally is. He's really an attractive man...for his species.

Bianca jumped off the windowsill and stared at both Mi'cin and Todd. Todd missed having her around, but she wouldn't be happy in his quarters on the ship. At least that's what he told himself, so he had accepted he wouldn't have her with him for a while.

He turned back to Mi'cin, noting the raised brow and the tilt of his chin. It was such an intense look. "Do you suppose things are okay with Mi'ko? Should we be worried?"

"I don't believe so. I am...I'm curious what Vi-Narm wanted. It is odd that she would interrupt him like this."

Probably just wanted to ruin the dinner.

Todd shook his head slightly. Why'd he allow Vi-Narm to get to him? He did his best to leave her alone and stay out of her way. And really all the other Nentraee were nice, especially Mi'cin...well now.

"Does it have to do with the Dentree clan? General Gahumed seems abrupt and intense like that as well. I'm not sure I trust either of them."

"No. She is a good person, Todd. She has been with my father a long time." Mi'cin adjusted the way he sat, his hips and thighs grinding against the soft fabric of the chair. The side chair didn't seem to fit him. "You should trust her. You don't know her, and you have not spent time together that I'm aware of."

"Oh, I trust her to eject me from the nearest airlock." Todd half smiled.

Mi'cin tilted his head and narrowed his eyes.

"I shouldn't have said that. I'm sorry. It's impolite and a poor attempt at humor." He covered how awkward he felt by stretching out his bad leg and flexing his foot to release the muscles. He leaned back on the couch and rubbed his at the soreness.

"Is your leg all right?"

Todd rubbed where he had just stretched again.

With luck, he'll forget my remark. Mi'cin has known her longer than me.

"It's fine."

"Good," Mi'cin said. "Vi-Narm is a hard person to get to understand, even for us. It's her nature to be suspicious of everyone and everything."

Ugh.

"Since the attack, she has become even more careful. You should try to get to know her." Mi'cin paused, and then his voice softened as he continued. "She wasn't able to protect my father or get him to safety. She failed him when he needed her the most, and that is difficult for her. You remind her of that failure."

"I suppose, but she didn't fail. She was hurt," Todd said. "We all were." He paused, thinking back; there wasn't anything she could have done. She was stuck in the car when the suicide bomber attacked.

The timer on the living-room light clicked on, filling the room with a warm, yellow glow.

"It is getting late, and I should say goodbye." Mi'cin slowly stood. "I will leave you to enjoy the quiet of your house."

"I hope you won't have to go through decontamination." He pointed to the cat hair on Mi'cin's clothes.

Mi'cin dusted his pants. "No. It will be fine."

"You don't have to rush off." Todd wasn't sure he wanted to be alone so soon after everyone had left. "It's early. Plus, I've enjoyed the company and it's given us a chance to talk."

"I don't want to—" Mi'cin thought a moment. "—overstay my welcome."

"No, trust me. You're not." Todd glanced over his shoulder at the door. "If you have to go, of course, I don't want to keep you, but don't leave on my account. It's nice having the company." He paused, suddenly becoming self-conscious. Was he being pushy and desperate? His cheeks burned. Mi'cin's green eyes dug deeper into him.

"All right." Mi'cin glanced back at the chair, then looked at the sofa. He chose to sit on the sofa.

"Can I get you something? Water? Soda? Wine?" Todd offered since he was standing and not sure what more to say.

"As I said before, I'm fine." Mi'cin pointed to the couch.

"Oh, right. Sorry." Todd sat back down, pulling out his pocket watch and placing it on the coffee table. "So, what was it like growing up on the ships?"

"Is that a human timepiece?" Mi'cin leaned forward.

Todd glanced at the watch. "Yep. It's a gift from my prior boss."

"I've seen several pictures of these, but never one in person. It's much small than I thought it would be. May I?" Mi'cin leaned in to pick it up, but Bianca jumped up on his lap. Her fluffy white head tilted left then right. After watching him a moment longer, she curled up and lay down.

"Bianca." Todd snapped his fingers and pointed to the floor.

"It is fine." Mi'cin gently scratched her head. "I don't mind. Earth animals are interesting. They have intelligence. It's unfortunate they don't speak like the cádo."

"Are you kidding?" Todd relaxed. "I don't want to know what she has to say. I doubt it would be very nice sometimes." He chuckled.

Bianca lifted her head and stared at him.

"It seems she heard you."

"Oh, I'm sure she did," Todd said. "I'll pay for it later. If you want her to get down, just push her off and she'll be fine."

I miss having someone here. I miss having someone to talk to and be real with. I miss this.

They both fell silent as Bianca kneaded Mi'cin's lap, her purrs a comfortable addition to the quiet.

Seven: Accusations

"YOU PULLED ME from dinner because agricultural equipment went missing two days ago?" Mi'ko's raised voice focused on Vi-Narm.

Vi-Narm dropped her shoulders and her brows squished together. She adjusted her position in the chair across from Mi'ko. She had refused to tell him anything until they were on the ship, citing security concerns.

And for what?

"Vice Speaker, this equipment was to be the first of many sent to the African continent." Vi-Narm straightened her shoulders. "And Todd was involved in selecting the country." She swiped the reports on the missing industrial atmospheric condensers and hydroponics systems over to the vice speaker's device. "With it missing, we don't know where or who may have it. Not to mention what they might learn from it. For all we know, Todd planned this."

Mi'ko transferred the information to the larger screen. "It was supposed to go to the Republic of Zimbabwe, was it not?"

She gave a stiff nod.

Mi'ko fussed with his tieback as he reviewed the information. It was possible there might be a security issue. One that needed to be tended to, but that was why he had her.

This is absurd.

Todd's involvement consisted of providing Mi'ko and Speaker Rosta an overview of the country, not selecting it. Todd even suggested it might not be the best option, considering the tyrannical history of the country and its former leader.

Since the attempt on his life, he had seen Vi-Narm become overly vigilant, almost to the point of annoyance.

Mi'ko cleared the thoughts from his mind and focused again on the reports. "The agricultural equipment is to be the beginning of trade with Zimbabwe, correct?"

Vi-Narm bowed her agreement.

"For platinum and industrial diamonds?" He checked the information again. "They require better ways to manage food production and distribution for their people?"

"Correct," Vi-Narm replied. "The country and much of the continent has problems with food and water production and distribution, so this seemed a good way to make a positive change and gain goodwill."

The country had once been called the Bread Basket of Africa, the report said. Mi'ko quickly checked the meaning of the term. They had once produced enough food, and now they couldn't.

"The equipment never arrived?"

"Correct."

With this new technology, Zimbabwe might regain the title of Bread Basket.

Mi'ko shook his head.

Rosta should be handling this, not me.

"It never reached the Midlands Province, and our consul in Harare has no explanation." Vi-Narm pulled up a three-dimensional map that highlighted the area. She expanded the image on her datapad so they could both see it.

"We're sure our transport shipped it, and this is not an issue we caused?"

"Correct," Vi-Narm said through pursed lips.

"From my understanding, that part of the country is not stable and is known for conflict." Mi'ko tapped the image, expanding it farther. "Might it be one of the factions there who have stolen the equipment?"

"According to our most recent report and our consul, the situation has improved greatly since our arrival to Earth," Vi-Narm said.

"How so?"

"Many of the elite in that country pulled together, including members of the government and its rebel groups. With the assistance of their military, they removed their former president, Gabriel Manangagwa. In the span of three human months, the current transitional government has been working on improving all areas of life for its people. They want to present themselves well so we will help them and work with them," Vi-Narm reported. "Speaker Gonu has made it clear she will only work with stable countries that want to improve the lives of their citizens and will support change in that regard."

Vi-Narm pushed the holographic map to the side and pulled up the details on the new leadership of Zimbabwe. "The new government met her requirements, which is why Speaker Gonu chose to work with them."

"Moments ago, you told me this was all Todd's doing." Mi'ko's ears started to warm.

She sat, motionless.

"Rosta isn't known to make the most logical of choices at times." Mi'ko leaned back, studying the provided reports.

It's only been three human months, hardly enough to see true change.

"She can be too idealistic. It's possible that our reports were misleading or overstated." He only half believed the words leaving his mouth. Rosta had staff as capable as Vi-Narm. There would have been nothing missed. Rosta was a good woman and a strong leader, one he respected, despite her idealism.

"She was first to approve Todd," Vi-Narm said.

"A wise choice on her part, or do I need to remind you of that?" Mi'ko shook his head.

"Of course not, Vice Speaker."

"Good." Mi'ko dusted off his sleeve, not interested in meeting Vi-Narm's gaze right now. He needed her reflection and focus on his words, not his reaction. "I'll have Todd work with Rosta's aides to find out what happened to the missing equipment."

Vi-Narm's body shifted on the chair, but he refused to look at her, glancing at his datapad instead. "None of the technology is restricted. I'm sure it will turn up, and even if it falls into the wrong hands, nothing will be learned from it. They would need our technicians to help them understand it."

"Are you sure? The humans are very ingenious," Vi-Narm said. "Vice Speaker, I think it would be best not to involve Todd. Humans may be responsible for the missing equipment, and we do not know if he is involved or not."

"Unless you have a river that connects Todd to the government"—Mi'ko's voice slowly raised as he spoke, and he could feel his ears bloat—"or the former opposition groups in the Republic of Zimbabwe, he will work with Speaker Rosta's aides and find the missing equipment."

"Vice Speaker, how do we know?" Vi-Narm leaned in, almost touching him.

Vi-Narm's proximity caught Mi'ko's attention and he sat back, his tight gaze meeting her.

"He had all the access and clearance to do such a thing before he conveniently left for his holiday." Vi-Narm retracted her hand and straightened in her seat. "Inviting you and your family to join him. It's only because of my diligence that I discovered this."

Mi'ko's ears pounded. He grew tired of her constant berating of Todd.

"You give him too much autonomy. It is impossible for us to know to what depths these humans will go to get our technology." She crossed her arms in front of her. "I've studied their tactics in espionage. It is possible he's a spy. His country and many other countries are known for using these types of people. They befriend you, get close to you, and then turn on you."

Mi'ko forced a level tone. "You have no proof."

"He has received numerous communications from several government officials including Greg McNeil just prior to the equipment going missing. "

"Todd speaks with many officials as part of his duties."

"Giving him perfect opportunity to accomplish this."

"You're gathering fruit in a basket with no bottom."

The tips of Vi-Narm's ears were turning an angry blue. If she wasn't one of his best aides, Mi'ko wouldn't have tolerated this.

He pulled his thoughts together and massaged his ears. "Tell me, Vi-Narm, did he plan to blow up his city, kill loved ones, and almost himself for this elaborate trick? Did the humans manage to break into our archive and learn about the special envoy post we gave him?"

Vi-Narm huffed not moving.

"All this work to plant a human onto our ship, so he could appropriate agricultural equipment destined for a country not his own?" His voice hardened. "That is an impressive plan...one that would have taken years to design." He leaned in to drive his point.

Vi-Narm pulled back in her seat.

"Tell me, how did one male human manage to do all this without the support of his government? A government which I had to threaten with our departure to ensure that Mister Landon was given this post. And to what end, Vi-Narm?" The tips of his ears were aching as he struggled to keep his tone professional.

She adjusted as if to speak, but he cut her off with a raised hand before she said more.

"To me, this sounds similar to some of the human novels you've been reading. Might I suggest their literary works, rather than their espionage?"

Vi-Narm sat, stone-faced.

"You've insulted Todd, almost to the point of insubordination." Mi'ko struggled for vocal control. "You've tried to make him appear foolish at every opportunity. Do not think I've been blind. I didn't understand why Todd was so calm about the ceremony and never mentioned it to me. Then I checked the records. You were selective on what you sent him."

Her ears grew large.

"You sent him key documents the day prior to the ceremony, intermixing them with other general reports." He glared at her. "For a female of such high morals of faith, where is that faith now? Or are you the spy? Are you working within our government, perhaps working with General Gahumed? Sabotage Todd to make me and the speaker general appear unfit?"

Vi-Narm's shoulders sank and her head dropped.

"I suggest you stop with these false accusations and accept the fact that Todd saved my life when you failed."

The room froze with silence. Mi'ko had even surprised himself by his comment. He hated talking to anyone in this manner, chiefly Vi-Narm; she was like family to him, but her attitude had gone on long enough.

Mi'ko's voice softened. "He performed a duty that was supposed to be yours and yours alone. It was not the responsibility of an alien. If it wasn't for him, we both would be dead, and that is something you need to accept. What has he done to warrant your treatment?"

"I do not believe Todd is capable of this honor, and your dealings with him has clouded your judgment. He lacks self-confidence and avoids conflict. It was only because of the good fortune of J'Veesa that he saved us, and I do not believe, given a similar situation, he would react the same. He is a weak male who should—"

"Enough!" Mi'ko slammed both hands on his desk, his ears burning on fire with a throbbing to match.

"No," Vi-Narm said. "This is not enough. You asked to know and I shall speak."

Mi'ko balled his hands into a fist but was quiet.

"These humans are barbaric. They will be the end to us, and you are trusting one of them. A weak male. Why? Because he pulled you from a vehicle in an explosion caused by other humans. It was J'Veesa's hand at work that day, not his." Her ear tips burned and appeared ready to explode. "They will attack us again, and he will cower like a...*vak yép*."

"End this now!" Mi'ko stood and moved past his desk to meet her angry gaze. "My patience is gone. Am I making myself clear?"

"Who will protect you and save you for yourself if not me?"

"Are you sure it's me you want to protect and not your pride?" Mi'ko narrowed his eyes on her. "I'm sure your mother would be proud."

Vi-Narm faltered, gasping, then took a step toward the door. "Yes, Vice Speaker," Vi-Narm whispered.

"Good. Now please excuse me." Mi'ko stood and faced the door. "We both have much to do, and I have no more time for this pettiness."

Vi-Narm bowed and rushed to leave his office.

"And Vi-Narm, I'm serious about reading their literature. I've found many of their stories fascinating, revealing much about them and who they are as a people. I suggest their classic literature."

She bowed again and left his office.

His face fell as the door slid closed. Sorrow ached in his heart, but this had to stop. He could not afford her continuing on this path. She and Todd had to work together, because even if an eighth of the people thought the way she did or General Gahumed did, then there was no hope for any of them.

He adjusted his tieback again, his arm and shoulder stiff. He glanced out the window at the stars in the distance and, of course, Earth. He had thought he had seen the last of discrimination from his people. Still, was he the one being naïve, given how Vi-Narm and Gahumed perceived the humans? Before the Clan War, Vi-Narm would have told him as much. Probably calling him a silly emotional male who should be home, caring for his children, and leave the important decisions to the female Nentraee.

Prior to the Clan War, he wouldn't have held a position such as vice speaker. If anything, he'd probably be the aide and Vi-Narm the vice speaker.

Eight: Proposals

"WHAT ARE YOUR thoughts?" Mirtoff called Mi'ko's attention back to the holographic images with the human proposals for their settlement. They had sat quietly around her conference table long enough. The soft lights from the room cast a warm glow around Mi'ko, but she thought the shadows from the light made his face appear older than he was.

Clearly, he was troubled.

Mi'ko read the heading of one of the new human proposals. "A domed city with amazing views of the Pacific Ocean and all it has to offer." He turned to Mirtoff, his hair barely held back by his loosening tieback.

"Dubai, as well as other developers, have completed smaller-scale projects for hotels off their shores. With our environmental control systems and our material stabilization technology, it is feasible." Mirtoff took a heavy sip of her tuma. "At least the drawing is attractive."

Faa looked at the design on the tabletop screen and then up at her. "Yuck, Faa no like."

She stifled a smile.

Faa turned his head to Mi'ko, climbed down, padded over to the sofa, and jumped up. He curled himself into a tight ball. From there, he watched while he flicked his fluffy gray tail.

"I agree with Faa," Mi'ko finally said. "The idea of living in a domed city next to or in the ocean has no appeal for me."

He tapped the holographic image of the underwater city and pulled up a file. He selected the tubular points of entry that extended to the shore of the Phoenix Island chain, expanding them for a more detailed inspection. "It would limit access, so our security wouldn't be as much of an issue, which is a positive. However, I don't like the plan. It's too limiting."

"The domed city is one of a few proposals to seriously consider." Mirtoff was disappointed with all the proposals. "We would want our own territory. We've been assured that as long as we follow their global environmental laws and protection acts, we could develop it as we see fit, with no interference."

Mi'ko maneuvered his fingers around the image, adding additional domes and checking structural integrity specifications.

Mirtoff frowned. He only fidgeted this much when he was upset.

Perhaps the idea of relocation is weighing on him?

Nothing being proposed was ideal, but sacrifices had to be made, and she and her people understood that. "It would allow us growth and the potential for prosperity." She tried to sound upbeat. Leaning forward, she dodged the look on Mi'ko's face. She pulled up another option and changed out the holographic images. "An orbiting city with majestic views of Earth."

"The design is too human and lacks any of our style." Mi'ko shook his head. "Where are the large openings to allow for light? Do they think all those tiny holes will be enough? And why does it appear like a wheel? And the top as a giant bubble..." He frowned. "Life in space for our people." He sighed. "We already have that."

"I know, but no country is willing to give up usable territory and control no matter what we offer them. Our options are few and ideas in short supply." Mirtoff tapped the desk. "Unless we want to invade New Zealand like General Gahumed wants."

"I thought she gave up that idea?" Mi'ko asked. "She didn't factor in terrorism and the willingness of humans to kill themselves for military gain even if we relocate them all to Australia."

"Officially. Yes. However, Danu has caught whispers of this idea from members of the military." She reached up and adjusted the braids in her hair.

"Do you think anything will come of it?"

"No, but I can't be sure. Danu is watching her."

Mi'ko pinched the bridge of his nose. Mirtoff watched the images of the orbital city as it rotated and circled Earth. "It would be like Calda."

"That was a failing of the government." Mi'ko glared at the image, his voice sharp. "Those platforms might've been saved. We could've saved an additional one hundred thousand people or more." His eyes closed. "The Speaker's House at the time did nothing."

"I know. We both know," Mirtoff said. "What's done cannot be changed."

Was this what bothered him? Mi'ko had become involved in the government to keep things like that from happening again. It was this drive that made him such an amazing vice speaker. "There were a lot of mistakes made. People were terrified and doing the best they could," Mirtoff said.

"No, they had the time and did nothing." His brows drew together. "The other two orbital cities were too old, but Calda...Calda was the newest. It was built to last and to be upgraded, and they left it. They were foolish, and it cost us." His hands began to tremble on the table. "Fear is not a defense. They failed people who relied on them. They chose to strip it and use it to build more colony ships, which remained unfinished during the final days." His hands banged the desk. "It could have been towed; it could have been converted to other uses by the fleet. It's just like now. People are shortsighted." He massaged his ears. "The people of Calda never stopped trying, and the government failed them. I worry we are failing our people just like they did back then."

"Mi'ko." She shared his pain at the loss. The Speaker's House at that time paid in the end, and justice was done. "We won't make the same mistakes. We won't have another Calda. You have my word."

"Are you sure?" he said. "How can you be certain? Gahumed wants to invade. The humans attacked us. My own head security aide..." He waved his hand in front of his face.

"What bothers Vi-Narm?" Mirtoff asked.

"Stubbornness and foolishness." Mi'ko cleared the view of the orbiting colony design.

"So, it's not about the missing equipment?" she asked.

"No. I'll have Todd work with Rosta on that. Vi-Narm is..." He picked up his datapad and typed commands. A new holographic image raised from his device, an overlay of both the human orbital *wheel* and of Calda with its domed forest center and spoked-out habitation zones. "If we combine them..."

"If you wish to speak about it." Mirtoff tapped the image, opening up a file on the mass power consumption, biological capacity, and other details. She squinted as she examined the information.

"No, thank you. I dealt with it." Mi'ko frowned as he fussed with the combined design, adding a second central park zone with more habitation zones extending from it, giving it a layered appearance. "I don't blame the humans," he said. "Their world is crowded, and even though there are little more than two million of us, they can't face the idea of giving up land so we can colonize a part of their world." He paused. "I can't blame them."

Mirtoff leaned back in her chair.

"Even with changes and modification, there would be no point to an orbital station." Mi'ko waved his hand, clearing the holo-image.

"The idea of an island city-state is doable," Mirtoff said. "There would be little room for growth and expansion on land, but if we combined that with a domed underwater city, it would give us greater flexibility and more options for our people." She pulled up both the Phoenix Island chain idea, the domed city plan, and the Cocos Island chain. "We could buy or trade for the islands, and then we would be granted the territory as a sovereign nation. The United Nations has provided a list of additional islands that we could acquire."

"Well, it's better than trying to take territory by force or incorporate our society into one of theirs," Mi'ko said.

"Becoming a Chinese citizen," Mirtoff said, "living under their form of government would not work for our people, even though they have said they would make several concessions. Treat us like Hong Kong."

"Nor would becoming Americans or Germans or Australians." Mi'ko's voice was resolute. "If we had to pick—"

"The death of our culture and who we are as Nentraee," Mirtoff interrupted. "No, that is a heavy blow to our people, and all I see is bitterness and anger if we do such a thing."

They both fell silent.

Mirtoff pulled up the proposed plans for integration into various human societies. "Being a minority in one of these cultures with our people spread apart, how long before the novelty of having us as one of their citizens ends and the bigotry begins?" She set it on the table.

"Provider, Todd good. He not mean. Human like Todd?" Faa asked.

She turned to him. "No, little one, not all the humans are like Todd. Some like to hurt people, including us," Mirtoff said.

Faa shivered and his eyes drooped.

"The United Nations did offer us the only continent on their planet that had very few people." Mi'ko pulled up the information and a new holographic image filled the space next to them.

"A glacial paradise waiting to be tamed, long days during the summer, and long nights during the winter." Mirtoff reached for her datapad and pulled up another concept for a domed city and let out a flustered sigh. "At least the tuma will always be chilled." She paused. "Two million of our people starting over on a giant ice block that could be in complete darkness or full sun for days and weeks." This option was quite possibly the worst she had heard. She believed there was a reason this part of their world was void of people. Not to mention the environmental impact such colonization would cause.

"Nentraee City, your home on the moon." Mi'ko read from his device. "This plan would have amazing views of their world, reminding our people daily that we were not fully welcome."

"There are Mars and Venus." Mirtoff pulled up the reports on both worlds. "Neither is ideal. Venus would be next to impossible for us to colonize and claim as our own due to atmospheric pressures."

The image of the frozen white tundra vanished and a photo of Mars appeared, featuring detailed information from both the humans and their own scans. Next to the image of Mars were photos of Phobos and Deimos, along with their orbital information and material makeup.

"Of the two, Mars would be best. Close enough to conduct trade with Earth and transport between the two worlds would be relatively quick. There are pockets of water, making terraforming possible under a dome. But again, we're talking about separation of our two peoples." She went to take a sip of her tuma, only to find it empty.

I need to stop drinking so much.

"But is separation such a bad thing?" Mi'ko asked. "We have been trying to come to some kind of integrated solution. We need to at least consider other ideas."

"It's not what I nor the Speaker's House wants," Mirtoff said. "There has to be a middle ground, a way for us all to share their world. To be a part of it. Or else, who knows what damage that will incur on future generations. Distance did not help our people. It only fostered a lack of trust and war. We will be the minority here, and humans do not always treat minorities well, even in their more advanced cultures." She played with the empty cup. "I think the more we can be among them and part of their world, the less some of them will see us as any kind of threat."

"That may not be practical, Madam Speaker. As you said, we would be a minority on their world, so the distance may serve us better."

"Faa want to walk on green and taste sky." Faa picked up his head and gazed at Mi'ko, then Mirtoff.

"I know, little one. That is what we all want."

"So, then we have three earthbound proposals to consider," Mi'ko said. "None of which are ideal, but they are better than a life in space or on harsh worlds not intended to support life."

Mirtoff nodded.

"The ocean life on Earth is amazing," Mi'ko said. "It would give us an economic boost for tourism. There are great financial benefits to that, given the human propensity for leisure time. Plus, resources under the ocean can be utilized. We could design and build our community in such a way to maximize those effects. Help in minimizing the impact of the environment. It would also be a closed system, to avoid contamination."

Mirtoff retrieved the information and called up the three-dimensional image so they could examine the plan closer. She pulled up different concepts and island locations. Islands the human governments would be willing to sell off for a very large price and trade agreements yet to be negotiated.

"Speaking of environmental impacts, what is being done about our ecology and theirs? Are they going to be compatible enough?" she asked.

"Rosta and her staff are working on those aspects in conjunction with human scientists and botanists." Mi'ko pulled up the detailed status report and swiped it over to Mirtoff. "They will have their studies completed before any decisions are finalized."

"That's good to hear," Mirtoff said.

One less thing for me to worry about.

"With luck, all the reports will be positive. I'm sure they will require us to keep our ecologies separate, and that is easily managed with our environmental controls and resource reclamation."

Mi'ko got up and stretched his arm. After crossing to the sofa, he rested his hand on the little cádo's head, scratching Faa behind the ears. He turned to Mirtoff. "How are the preparations coming for your upcoming December engagements in London?"

"I believe they are going well," she said. "Downing Street and Buckingham Palace have yet to confirm all who will be in attendance." She sighed. " I do not understand them or their social customs at times. Regardless, Danu and Tun'ae are working on the security procedures with both Downing Street and the White House." She leaned back in her chair. "I may ask for Vi-Narm's assistance, given the nature of the event and the number of threats."

"Is there anything that Todd can assist with?"

"No," Mirtoff said. "Not unless you want to have him pick a location for us to live?"

Nine: Countdown to Christmas

"GREG, YOU'RE THE only one I'm getting any answers from." Todd frowned at the monitor. "I talk to one office, and they brush me off. I talk to another agency, and they tell me to call the office I just talked to."

Something has to give.

Todd tapped his fingers on the desk. "What the hell is going on down there?"

"I'm sorry, but you know what I know." Greg's tone was tense, his normal smile gone from his face. "Plus, people are still getting used to dealing with you. You've only been in the position a few weeks."

Todd scanned the information on his datapad again. "According to the ship's manifest, the agricultural equipment never left the Nentraee cargo shuttle." He raised his gaze to Greg. "Now you're telling me it actually arrived after it was diverted from Zimbabwe to one of the joint French/US air bases in Iraq." He ran a hand through his hair. "Why? And, more to the point, under whose authority? Clearly not the Nentraee. Was it on the authority of France, the US, or Zimbabwe? Who has the ability to mess with the Nentraee shipments?"

"Are you sure the Nentraee didn't authorize the location shift because of security concerns?"

Todd had as much trouble with Vi-Narm and General Gahumed's staff as he was having with his people back on Earth, but this time, he was certain that the problem wasn't on this end.

At least I hope.

"Like I said, it was mismarked and bounced around Africa and the Middle East, ending up in Iraq. Have you talked to the people at the FAO? Ana Luiza's staff are easy to work with. They may have more information." Greg shook his head. "Look, once the mistake was found, it was sent to the correct location. I don't understand why or by who, and our diplomats in Zimbabwe have no idea where the breakdown happened." He rubbed his chin. "Our chief diplomat there is having a difficult enough time explaining this to the new Zimbabwe government, let alone you and anyone else who's asking."

"Fine, whatever, just...you know what?" Todd interlaced his fingers and rested them on his desk. "I'll let the Nentraee handle it from this point. We've found where it is. I'll leave the rest to Speaker Rosta Gonu's aide." He picked up the datapad and made a few notes, then sent the files. "Gonu's office can follow up with the respective governments and the UN if they want. I'll put it all in my report and send you a copy."

A smile crept over Greg's face. "At least you found it."

Todd frowned.

But I don't know how it all happened and why.

"I wish there was more I could do." Greg's image flickered.

"What was that?" Todd tapped the channel button on his monitor.

I swear their technology hates me.

"What was what?"

"A stupid flicker. I've been having issues all day."

"The interference with our systems here on Earth, maybe?" Greg shrugged. "Look, Todd, we have our hands full here with all the new security measures and trying to accommodate international security concerns regarding the Nentraee. I wish I could be more help."

Todd wanted to scream at him, but it wasn't Greg's fault. The industrial atmospheric condensers and hydroponics systems were found and on the way to Zimbabwe. It was a clusterfuck, and no one person was to blame. He might continue to research it and see if there was anything else he could learn.

"I understand." Todd leaned back in his chair. "I watched a couple news reports regarding the security concerns for the tree-lighting ceremony. Is the threat level negligible?"

"At this point," Greg huffed. "We're watching things. After San Jose, no one wants to take chances, and you know how all the nuts come out around the holidays."

Todd nodded. "Which is why I don't understand the lack of attention on what happened in San Jose. It's been five months. People act like they don't care anymore."

Since he started, he had hoped to get more information on the attack, but there was nothing. "Promise me that if you hear anything, no matter how crazy, you will let me know. I've been having problems getting a straight answer from Secretary Webster's people. I'm hitting the same roadblocks here with Vi-Narm. She..." He wasn't going to get into this.

"I'll do my best." Greg shook his head. "I hope you understand you're not the only one having issues getting information these days." He offered a halfhearted smile.

"Well, it's nice I'm not alone." Todd was glad he had at least one person down on Earth he could work *with*.

"Take care, Todd. Talk to you soon." Greg offered a small wave.

"Bye." Todd tapped the bottom of the monitor.

The Nentraee government seal filled the screen. Todd picked up the datapad again and typed in a few commands. He pulled up some photos from CRiNE and their staff picnic and holiday party. He ran a hand over the image.

The device chirped with a reminder, and he pulled up his calendar. He had a meet-and-greet later with people from Belize. It was their first time on the ship, and they asked for the human liaison.

"Ugh." He cracked his neck and closed the calendar.

At least the folks from Earth are always excited and enjoyable to be around. So that will be fun.

His stomach growling, Todd checked his watch. A short break would give him a chance to clear his head. He crossed to the window, not sure how anyone got used to this view. Several transport vessels, colony ships and military vehicles, including the Rádo, orbited the planet. *That ship looks scary even without its three plasma cannons.* In the distance, Earth had the moon peeking out behind it.

"THE TREE-LIGHTING ceremony dates back to 1947, right after their last major global conflict," Mi'ko said. The event was relatable to him and most Nentraee understood, a day to pay respect to the past and bring people together. He and Mirtoff were reviewing the reports from Todd over lunch in the Speaker's House private dining hall. None of the other speakers were there, which made for a nice change.

The dining hall could be used by any member of the Speaker's House whenever they wished. However, it was only typically used when they were in session and they needed to break for a meal. The hall was well appointed with comfortable chairs and tables. There were no windows, but a mural of the first meeting of the original Speaker's House shone brightly on the largest wall. Each of the clans were represented by their newly elected speaker. Even though males were not included at the time, Mi'ko always found it inspiring.

They were brave females, and if it wasn't for them and the courage it took to create the Speaker's House, none us would be here now.

Faa was curled up in one of the chairs, peeking his head over the armrest now and then, making a content sound from the back of his throat. He had quickly gone through his own meal and only the bowls remained.

Mirtoff put her *Lagus and Té* down, nodding. "The people of Norway have given the people of London a Christmas tree every year, with several of their local political figures in attendance."

Mi'ko sipped his E'xin. "With your confirmed attendance, we can expect not only the mayors of both London and Oslo, but the Lord Mayor of Westminster, the prime minister, her husband, and representatives of the royal family. Possibly the Queen, but she has not confirmed yet." He rubbed his shoulder, working out the tension. "There will also be the government officials from Norway as well as other invited dignitaries."

"Assuming they attend," Mirtoff said.

"I thought all the concerns had been addressed and planned for?" Mi'ko asked. "Vi-Narm informed me there were no actionable threats."

"Dealing with the humans is proving complicated. Their information continues to change, and threats continue to be an issue. There are worries that one of these new xenophobic groups may attack." Mirtoff picked up her utensils and took a bite of her *Damus with Mī.*

"My understanding is they are scattered and unorganized. I'm sure Danu, Vi-Narm, and Tun'ae will have it all worked out." Mi'ko offered a firm nod. "This event will be an amazing moment for everyone."

"I like the idea of two countries showing cooperation and mutual respect and support, even after such a difficult time in human history," Mirtoff said.

"It's very impressive."

"The fact that the tradition has lasted over seventy human years also impresses me, considering the humans tend to forget the meaning behind events of this nature." Mirtoff reviewed all the data.

Faa stood up, stretched, and padded over. Then he nudged Mi'ko's leg for a head rub.

"He seems more content lately," Mi'ko said.

"Yes, he is. The idea of finally finding a home has done a lot to calm him." She peeked down at Faa. "Isn't that right, little one?"

"Faa happy." Faa's back foot thumped as Mi'ko scratched his head.

"Are you happy that I agreed to go?" Mirtoff reached for her cup of tuma.

"I am." Mi'ko straightened back up in his chair. "The potential for us to support such an event shows that we're willing to work with all countries. That we want to embrace their customs. It shows us as prepared to learn about all of them and respect all their beliefs. It's a good example." He picked up his Lagus and Té and took another bite of his *Sagvarwa and Kumnas*.

Faa nudged him.

Mi'ko put down his utensils, then scratched Faa's head again.

"The reports about our favoritism." She leaned back and fussed with the braids in her hair. "Your visit with Todd and his family at Thanksgiving did not go unnoticed by many of the people of his world; several believe we are picking favorites. The press release Todd sent out prior to the event didn't have the desired effect of keeping the human media happy."

"We realized that would occur." Mi'ko sat up again. He wiped his hands on his napkin. "Todd is my special envoy and a member of my staff and—"

Mirtoff held up her hand. "We both expected it," she said. "It's not a matter that we need to revisit. We won't make them all happy, and it is foolish to think otherwise." Her datapad chirped, then made an ugly buzzing sound.

Faa sniffed at the device and walked over to the small chair. He climbed up, resting his head on the armrest, watching them.

"What happened?" Mi'ko leaned forward and glanced down at the device.

"No. I must have triggered a wrong input." She checked the datapad. "By attending this event in London, it will go a long way to show our neutrality. As will going to the People's Republic of China for their Lunar New Year celebration." She ran a single finger over the device. "With the future of our people to consider, we're going to need the support of their full security council."

"These humans are so fractured. So many different ideologies and forms of government; communism, monarchies, republics, theocracies, it's too much." Mi'ko massaged the tips of his ears. "It's no wonder they bicker and fight. I hope they will appreciate all our efforts."

"It's more than that," Mirtoff said. "Some of them truly hate one another, and with that hate, they have the weapons to destroy one another and their world." She sighed. "I wonder, at times, if they realize just how unique their world is? What will they do when their planet can't support them anymore?"

"I don't think it would ever come to that," Mi'ko said. "I believe they can grow and change."

"Even with the attack on your life?" Mirtoff raised a brow.

Mi'ko nodded.

"Much has changed since then." Mirtoff glanced down at her Damus with Mī, then picked up her utensils and took another bite. "Over the next several weeks, I want to make every effort possible to go to as many cultural and national events as we can. Security is going to have a lot to do. We'll include all members of the Speaker's House."

Mi'ko raised his gaze.

She wants to include all members of the Speaker's House.

"Including General Gahumed." Mirtoff smiled. "I'm sending her to meet with the various members of the Vatican." She chuckled. "I'm curious at how their religious leaders handle a woman of Gahumed's faith."

Mi'ko bit back a chuckle.

"Gahumed offered." Mirtoff placed a hand over her heart. "Regardless, I want all high-ranking members of the House of the People and any prominent civilians, like your wife, to attend events. I want to ensure we have more representation worldwide."

"Laina will be honored. What about Todd?"

"We have to be very careful and make sure that we present ourselves well. We won't send Todd to anything. We'll keep him in the background until the humans get used to him working for us."

Mi'ko glanced down at his half-eaten meal.

"Even though Todd is a member of your staff, he is not seen that way. Humans of other countries continue to see him as a member of the United States of America."

Mi'ko pursed his lips and glanced to the mural. "I wonder if our past leaders had such difficulties?"

"I wish I knew." She sighed and her shoulders relaxed. "We can't afford to show favoritism, especially while we're trying to find a place to settle."

"New home! Faa want a new home." Faa's voice was high and sharp. He flopped his head back down and crossed his front legs.

"We're working on it, little one." Mirtoff bit back a smile.

Mi'ko rubbed his mouth, hiding his grin.

Everyone is getting impatient, not just the cádo.

Faa jumped off the chair and padded over to her. "Faa love his provider." He rested his head in her lap and glanced up at her. She rubbed under his chin.

"You will need to thank Todd for his due diligence, not only to go through the lists of human events, but also for his work on finding our lost agricultural equipment. I'm sure none of it was easy for him," Mirtoff said.

"I'm sure he'll be pleased that you're happy," Mi'ko said. "I wish his people would see that." He shook his head. "They don't seem to realize that, if he chose, he could have us only support places and events that would favor his country." He chuckled. "I imagine it's making things more challenging for him."

"Faa like Todd, want to see Todd again. Todd friends with Faa." Faa's tail swished.

Mi'ko smiled at him. The cádo had such an honesty about them that it was impossible not to take what they say as absolute truth.

Maybe we should include using our cádo in all our dealings with the humans.

Ten: Warning

TODD ROCKED BACK in his office chair, reading the encrypted report in disbelief. He checked the sender's name again. Greg. Verifying the data, he realized the information couldn't be right—not with all the security reports refuting the threat.

Checking the calendar, he noted there was only one day before the Christmas tree-lighting ceremony in London.

Why didn't anyone bring this up before?

The door to his office chirped, then slid open, startling him.

"Todd?" Mi'ko stepped through the entrance. "My apologies, I didn't mean to surprise you. I came as soon as I got your message."

"Mister Vice Speaker." Todd stood. "We have a problem." This wasn't a conversation he wanted to have with the vice speaker, especially since security wasn't his area of expertise. He checked his datapad and handed it to Mi'ko.

Mi'ko read the report.

Todd licked his dry lips.

"Thank you." Mi'ko handed the datapad back. "Vi-Narm and Danu are aware. Danu has been working with Downing Street and the London police. Currently there is nothing to prove that this threat is credible."

It wasn't the reaction Todd had expected.

"Threats come in continually," Mi'ko said. "Not only to us, but to every political leader on your planet. Sadly, this is nothing new for either people. We've taken additional precautions, so you have nothing to worry about."

"But, Mister Vice Speak—" Todd caught himself. "Mi'ko, what if we're wrong? Terrorists only have to be right once." He scrutinized Mi'ko, images of all the death and destruction from the attack on San Jose rushing back—he shuddered. "This is a huge event. Thousands, hell, possibly even a million people all crammed into a small area." His heart banged in his chest as he shook his head. "With Mirtoff going, who knows how many people will actually attend? Not to mention all the government officials. It's going to be a media circus, the kind of event that terrorists love. Just like in San Jose! How many people will die this time, because we did nothing?"

Security wasn't his job, a fact made abundantly clear by Vi-Narm. He'd given her the same report. She had moved it to her terminal without reading it and excused him.

I probably insulted her somehow.

"Todd." Mi'ko's tone softened. "Vi-Narm and Danu are aware of all the threats. I assure you, Mirtoff will be fine."

"Mister Vice Speaker, this comes from Greg McNeil." Todd uploaded the incident report to his console, turning it so Mi'ko might see it better. "He's the chief of staff. That is a rather high posting in my government. He wouldn't have sent this if he didn't believe it."

He was getting a headache from all this. He typed in several commands to his system and pulled up a set of different security reports. "All these people said your visit to San Jose was going to be safe. What happened? I'm not inclined to brush it off so easily. Particularly since my government claims not to have all the details of what happened and why."

"The incident in your home city was different," Mi'ko said. "We all learned a great deal from that event." He broke into a warm smile. "I appreciate your emotions are strong on the subject, but you have to master them. Please, do not let them cloud your judgment." He stepped closer to Todd. "You are doing an admirable job and should be very proud of how you serve." His shoulders stiffened. "Now, you need to let our security professionals handle it."

So many people had died that day. The smell of death and destruction haunted him.

How can I let it go? People died because we thought we knew it all, and I lost Jerry because of it.

Since then, he'd learned that odd reports had existed, warning of an attack in San Jose. But no one had taken them seriously, and now this report said the same thing about London.

I'm not crazy. There is going to be a attack at the ceremony tomorrow. I know it.

"We thought we learned a great deal after nine-eleven, too, but that didn't mean the terrorists didn't keep at us; shoe bombs, underwear bombs, train bombings, mass shootings—they just got more inventive. We had to look harder!"

"That was before we arrived," Mi'ko said. "Things are changing. Your world is cooperating in ways not seen before."

Not everything.

"They attacked our embassies and nightclubs," Todd said. "They didn't give up. They waited. Please, Mister Vice Speaker, talk to the speaker general."

Mi'ko settled his gaze on Todd.

"Can't we send someone else? What about more security or having her shuttle land at the event site instead of at the airport?" Todd tapped his monitor, bringing up more reports, maps of London and Trafalgar Square. "She could land here on Ducannon Street. It should be wide enough." He pointed. "What about using scanners? There must be more we can do? What about a body double?"

Body double? Really, Todd?

"A what?"

"Nothing, never mind." Todd cringed. "Don't you agree it's odd that the report on the planned attack is so detailed?" He cleared all the data and only focused on the report from Greg. "Everything is there, number of human and Nentraee security personnel, where the checkpoints will be, the timeline of the event—"

"The locations of all the dignitaries," Mi'ko finished. "Todd, I assure you Vi-Narm and Danu have been through this."

"Doesn't any of this worry you?" Todd frowned, shaking his head. "What do I have to do? Quit? Leave my position in protest, so someone will take this seriously?"

Mi'ko's shoulders stiffened. He picked up the device again, reviewing it. "I do not wish for you to resign over this. If it will put you at ease, I will speak with Danu and Mirtoff. I will ask Vi-Narm to check into this again and suggest she implement a few of your suggestions."

Todd frowned at the mention of Vi-Narm's name but remained quiet.

"There is much depending on this visit. To fail to attend at this time would not be possible."

"I understand, just..." Todd stopped and met Mi'ko's eyes. Todd's jaw was set. "Please, do what you can. I have a bad feeling about tomorrow." He exhaled. "I doubt Greg would have risked sending me this report if he wasn't worried." He thought of Jerry. "I don't want another incident."

"As I said, I will speak with both Danu and Mirtoff." Mi'ko held Todd's datapad. An angry buzzing sound and blue flashes came from the device.

"I'm sorry." Todd took the datapad. "I must have hit the wrong key or some combination of keys."

"At least you are getting better with our technology and using it."

"Thank you, Mister Vice Speaker." Todd bowed.

"Be well, Todd." Mi'ko returned the bow.

Todd tossed the datapad on his desk as soon as Mi'ko left his office. "Stupid pad," he grumbled, then studied Earth before him. "What are you idiots doing down there?"

Not able to sit in his office any longer, Todd closed down his terminal and left. What he wanted to do was go back to Earth and curl up with Bianca and a movie. Forget the day. But that wasn't going to happen.

He headed down the large corridor, making his way back to his living quarters, passing several Nentraee on the way. Some of the faces he recognized, others he didn't, but the Nentraee recognized him and many bowed in greetings. He did his best to respond, but his mind was awash with disaster…

A bright flash followed by complete silence. He turned in the direction of the flash in time to see a mushroom cloud off in the distance. Turning away and glancing down to his hands, he watched as they turned gray and flaked away…

Todd stumbled and leaned against one of the walls. He closed his eyes and took a breath. He cleared the awful image from his mind.

Not again. I can't let this can't happen again. Enough. Mi'ko will talk to Mirtoff.

Todd decided to stop by the gardens and try to relax and clear his head. He opened his eyes and moved on. He headed to the ship's largest park, needing to lose himself among the flora and the sounds of nature, even if they weren't the sounds of Earth.

Stepping out into the open air, Todd was greeted with warmth. The artificial sunlight was pleasant on his face, and with a few deep breaths, he recognized the scent of fresh water. He wandered around the various plants and tall trees, taking it all in. He was amazed at the height of *Nabutimaba* trees and the bridges that allowed people to cross through the park at different levels.

I wonder if I can see my apartment from here?

Todd looked past the small creek and up the side of the wall. The view from inside the park was nothing like the view from his quarters. The exteriors of the walls could have been generic, but the Nentraee had made the façades resemble buildings. From down there, it had a Central Park kind of feel.

Musical voices of the Nentraee filled the air. Nentraee families milled around and even a few with their cádo. He found a place to sit in the shadow of the large trees, in relative privacy, and tried not to listen to their conversation. His Nentraee was improving, but it was a difficult language to master. Understanding the musical undertones was his biggest hurdle. It was like knowing the words to a song, but not the melody. The rolled *r*'s had one connotation and clipped another. Even the drawn-out *m*'s didn't always mean the same thing. It was all about melody.

Tomorrow, the speaker general would go to the tree-lighting ceremony in London, and whatever happened would happen. Todd would be stuck on the ship, waiting and watching, like everyone else. Perhaps they were right. It was nothing. Jerry always said he was a big worrywart.

What do I know about security?

He leaned his head back and inhaled deeply. Something tickled his throat and he coughed.

"Hello, Todd," a familiar voice said.

Through his cough-induced tears, Todd recognized Mi'cin standing in front of him. "Oh, hello." He tried to fight back another cough; there were some scents he wasn't used to.

"Do you require medical assistance?" Mi'cin asked. "I can summon a doctor or medical technician."

Some water would be nice.

Todd shook his head, holding up his hand in a stop motion. His face grew hot. "No no, I'm fine. Just a tickle in my throat." He forced himself to keep from coughing again. Mi'cin had his typical quizzical look—brow raised and one side of his mouth lifted.

"All right." Mi'cin's face relaxed. "I understand you had a difficult day today."

The light around Mi'cin cast him in a glow like a Greek statue.

Why don't you just sit down already and talk to me like a normal person? Like we did on Thanksgiving.

Mi'cin was so much more formal here on the ship.

"My father mentioned you had a difference of opinions," Mi'cin offered.

"I suppose." Todd finally got his voice under control.

"It is none of my concern, but if you would like to talk about it, I would be willing to listen," Mi'cin offered. "My father can be difficult when he wants to be." He sat next to Todd on the bench, leaving little space between them. Todd's heart skipped a beat. "I know it's hard for you, being so far from your family and friends." He fumbled with his hands. "That's why I came. I thought you might need someone."

"Oh, it wasn't anything like that. It wasn't a fight or anything..." Todd paused. "Wait. You came looking for me?"

Mi'cin nodded.

"That's nice." *I can't believe he came looking for me.* Todd smiled. "Thank you."

"Of course," Mi'cin said. "What troubles you?" Blue tinges appeared around his neck.

Todd examined his feet, and then the trees blowing in the breeze. "I'm worried about tomorrow, and your father— I mean the vice speaker isn't." He kicked at the ground cover. It wasn't quite grass, but that was the closest comparison he had, especially since it was dark green and looked like thin strands of hair. "I should leave the worrying to those who have the experience and the knowledge. But after..." He sighed. "I'm overly sensitive."

Mi'cin blinked and almost reached out, but he placed his hand on his own leg instead.

Todd sat up and cleared his throat. "I gave the information to the people who need it, and that's the best I can do. Whatever happens, happens, and there is nothing more I can do about it." He wasn't sure he totally believed himself; was there more he might've done? Was this another form of running away? Or hiding? He pushed those thoughts aside and turned to Mi'cin. "Have you eaten dinner yet?"

"No." Mi'cin tilted his head, hints of a smile blooming.

"Well, then, how about we get something to eat. You pick." Todd relaxed. "I'll try anything as long as it's dead and cooked and not tuma. I don't like the sweet-spicy flavor. It reminds me of chocolate covered in chili pepper."

Mi'cin was quiet for several moments. "All right. Have you had *Colo Oc Mo*?"

Todd raised his eyebrows at the name. It sounded familiar, but he was pretty sure he hadn't had it. "Um, no. Can't say that I have."

"Excellent. I shall tell my family I won't be at dinner tonight, and we will go." Mi'cin gave him a large smile. "I'm sure you'll like it. It's a special treat to have, but considering your difficult day and your level of worry, it's appropriate."

"Then lead the way, my good man." Todd and Mi'cin stood. Todd caught the quick odd expression on Mi'cin's face before they headed off walking, side by side.

Eleven: Colo Co Mo

TODD THOUGHT HE understood the size of the spaceship. However, walking with Mi'cin, he found there were entire sections of the ship that were still foreign to him. The speaker general's ship was the largest civilian vessel in the Nentraee fleet, and he expected it to be huge, but not this big.

It's a floating city.

Todd reflected on his last five weeks on board. He tended to stay in the government areas where he felt secure and wasn't on display. He hadn't gone out exploring. Now, feeling lost as Mi'cin navigated them, Todd took in the surroundings and tried to enjoy the stroll. He easily kept in step with Mi'cin, despite his sore leg.

"You've not been out here much?" Mi'cin asked.

"Not really," Todd said. "Not since you took me out the day I arrived."

Mi'cin nodded.

"It's like being a fish in a fishbowl when I'm here on my own," Todd said.

"If I understand the reference, I can appreciate that," Mi'cin said. "You are a celebrity among my people. Even though they may not approach you, out of respect, they are curious about you."

They passed several manufacturing sections, then crossed into a more commercial area. This one was larger and more open with plenty of green space, reminiscent of a giant mall with the grand promenades leading to living quarters and other sectors of the ship.

Todd stopped at a large window showing part of the mammoth hangar deck. A pair of maintenance craft were leaving the bay as a small transport shuttle landed and two large transport shuttles disembarked its passengers. Shuttles were positioned on lifts, so storage was easy and they could be rotated as needed. Large hanger doors, off to the side, had the Nentraee government seal on it. He wasn't exactly sure what was housed there. However, he presumed it to be an auxiliary bay available for additional capacity as needed.

"Amazing."

The efficient hangar design incorporated seamless lines and elegant finishes so passengers couldn't detect where aesthetics ended and function began. It incorporated a multifunction station for both maintenance and control. The space was intended to process several hundred ships a day.

Continuing down the walkway, Todd and Mi'cin entered an impressive open space, similar to a city center where the Nentraee conducted their daily business, shopping, and dining. None of them appeared to be shabbily dressed. They reminded him of the pictures he'd seen of how people dressed in the forties; slacks, buttoned shirts, jackets, long skirts, all polished and elegant. The space had expansive green areas with tall trees covered in green, purple, and yellow leaves. Under them were lush red and orange flowering plants. It was less like being on a spaceship and more like being at Alum Rock Park back in San Jose. He gazed up and, instead of a ceiling, a deep blue sky gleamed over him with white puffy clouds floating by.

This is what the Nentraee planet of Benzee must have looked like.

"I need to get down here more often. I've been missing out," Todd said.

Mi'cin's eyes sparkled in the evening sun, and his lips curled up in a smile. "It would be good for you to come here and explore. If you would like, we could come here again." His shoulders stiffened. "So, you are not alone."

Mi'cin led them down one of the pedestrian boulevards to a Nentraee café, across from a magnificent plaza with trees covered in yellow leaves that rustled in the breeze, more red and orange flower-filled planting beds, and stone-and-steel benches, which laced the walkway for seating. Several Nentraee stopped and glanced over at Todd, then quickly went back to their meals and conversations. The place could've been a café on Earth if it wasn't for the aliens and aromas. The scents of spices filled the air. He tried to place them, but his nose wasn't familiar with them yet.

Those scents. Salt, maybe. Possibly chocolate. It may be curry. Ah, that is tuma. I recognize that smell.

"I come here with friends. They have the best colo co mo in the fleet." Mi'cin pointed to an empty table. "When it's available for purchase."

Todd held back his surprise.

Of course Mi'cin has friends. Why wouldn't he? He probably dates and does things just like a normal person would.

Todd sighed.

I remember doing all that. It's been too long. I need to stop hiding from the world. Both worlds.

"It's nice." Todd rested his hands on the firm back of his chair, using it to support him as he stood.

Why was it an odd thought to picture Mi'cin out with friends, drinking, dancing, and doing whatever it was that Nentraee did on their off hours?

When was the last time I did anything like that? Before I moved here. When I was recovering, Dan and Kati made me go out as much as possible, even if I didn't want to. I have to make more of an effort with them. With everyone.

A soft squeak from above caught his attention, and he looked up as a group of five blue-birdlike creatures flew overhead.

"Are those *Xĩmé?*" Todd struggled with the pronunciation, making the *x* sound next to the *ees* sound tripped up his tongue.

Mi'cin nodded.

I have to bring Kati and Dan here to spend a weekend so we can hang out and be together.

"What troubles you?" Mi'cin asked, already seated.

"No. Sorry. Thinking about home. Missing my friends and family." Todd glanced around the café. Mi'cin and he were the only ones speaking English.

"You've been busy and there has been a lot for you to adjust to." Mi'cin's bright green eyes met Todd's.

"I suppose. It's still no excuse. I know it's only been a few weeks, but I can't stay locked away up here or back home," Todd said. The distraction from the day's worries was a nice change. "There is so much I've missed out on. Look at this place, I mean. Parts of it are like a small city on solid ground. You wouldn't imagine we were floating in space."

Mi'cin scanned the buildings and the plaza. "I'm glad you like it. I wasn't sure if it would make you sad for home."

"No. It's very cool. Is it a re-creation of someplace particular on your world?"

"This ship was one of the first built during the evacuation preparations," Mi'cin said.

"How long did you have to prepare before your world was destroyed?"

"Eight years officially. However, some had known longer that our neighboring star would go supernova. But records are hard to come by and those involved in the deception no longer live."

"How awful." Todd shook his head.

"Not long to evacuate a planet, I know." Mi'cin frowned. "It was important that all ships were as much like home as possible. With a population of forty-five thousand, we hold the largest number and enjoy the most comforts." He glanced down and flattened the wrinkles in his shirt.

Todd saw a slight tremble in both hands.

"However, over the years, several other colony ships have been upgraded with larger family units and more open space, even some of the converted short-range vessels, what you would understand as luxury craft, have been outfitted with larger quarters for the long journey."

"Wait. Forty-five thousand people?" Todd said. "I thought it was only designed for thirty-five thousand?"

Mi'cin raised the sides of his mouth in a half smile. "The original design, yes, but over the years, with additional advancement in our technology and resources we were able to obtain on our journey, our usage of space improved. We expanded the vessel's capacity to hold more people by converting areas that were used as storage or were not fully completed when we launched. Those sections could be modified and used as we need."

"That's impressive."

"I'm not sure what information we shared with your people." Mi'cin tapped the table and it came to life.

Graphics and words raised from the table and floated around both Mi'cin and Todd. The images and Nentraee words came into focus as Todd watched, similar to the holographic functions of the datapad.

"There is much to learn." He maneuvered his hands around the holographic interface, tapping on some images and expanding them and swiping away other images. "Do you trust me?"

"Um... Yes."

"Excellent."

Mi'cin changed over to Nentraee as he placed the order. The Nentraee language when spoken by Mi'cin was magical. Todd heard the words, understanding some. The syllables coming from Mi'cin's lips floated on the air like a leaf blown by a soft breeze. The consonants drifted over the vowels, painting pictures of a vast landscape that Todd was slowly starting to learn to see and appreciate.

"I've not visited a human eatery. Is it different?" Mi'cin leaned in, giving Todd his full attention.

"It's pretty much the same, except we have servers who manually take our orders and greet us." Todd caught sight of a server, carrying a tray with multiple plates and mugs on it. Once at the table he was serving, he lowered the tray, allowing it to hover off the side of the table so he could unload it.

"Not too different." Mi'cin shifted back in his chair, adjusting his collar.

"Nope. I guess not," Todd said. "This place...your people created something special."

"I don't know about special. It was out of necessity. We took all that we could of our world. This place is a re-creation of part of our capital city, Oraibi Raee. Not all of it, of course, but enough of the city so it has similar feel." Mi'cin pointed across the plaza. "Those buildings were moved from the capital and installed here. They are over one thousand years old. They were part of the original city, all made of various stones and lumber, the columns are all handcrafted and the window panes are made from..." Mi'cin paused. "I'm not sure what a human comparison would be. It's not glass, but I suppose it's close enough."

"Wow."

"I would offer to show you the interiors, but they are used for offices or living quarters for some of the merchants who work in this district."

"No worries."

Mi'cin nodded. "Most of the colony ships were created in this fashion. We took several of our most beautiful cities and relocated or reconstructed them so they wouldn't be lost."

"Like a living museum."

"Yes. I suppose," Mi'cin said. "I was young, of course, so I didn't fully understand what was happening. My parents tried to shelter me and my brothers from the reality as much as possible." He shifted on his chair. "Once we moved to the ship, they spoke very little of our home." He was quiet a moment. "At least not to us."

"I can't imagine what that was like." Todd ran his hand over the table. It was smooth but not glossy or reflective. He tapped the table. "But having all this must help."

"It's not the same." Mi'cin focused down on his hands. "None of it is. It will never make up for what we lost."

"I'm sorry," Todd whispered. Hearing Mi'cin speak of his home and his people's loss made Todd ashamed for all the troubles and problems they'd experienced since coming to Earth.

"You have nothing to be sorry for." Mi'cin reached out to Todd but quickly pulled back, resting his hand instead on the edge of the table. "Please do not misunderstand me." A gentle smile crossed his lips. "Everyone is grateful for all that we have. We are the lucky ones. It is I who should be sorry. I brought you here to take your mind off your troubles. I'm afraid I've added to them. That was not my intent."

They both grew silent.

Breaking the awkwardness, a female server brought over a tray with their meals. She was a pretty member of the Za'entra clan, with braided and pinned-up auburn hair showing off her expanded forehead and a smooth tan complexion. A silver-colored laced ear cuff accentuated her already-pointed ear. She bowed to Mi'cin and then to Todd.

"Me human English not good. Please enjoy. Summon if more need," she said.

Todd bowed, and she left.

"That was kind of her." Todd sniffed, smelling citrus, spice, and...possibly almond. "I liked the ear cuff. I haven't seen that before."

"It's a fashion accessory that some of the Za'entra wear. It's called a *karoo*. Back after the Clan War, many Za'entra wore the karoo to remember those that died and to remind the Dentraee that they were the cause of the war." Mi'cin shook his head. "Anyway, that was long ago." He peeked back over at the female server. "I'm sure she practiced her English before she brought the food." He inhaled the scents. "What I ordered is the colo co mo, and I took the liberty of ordering us e'xin. The e'xin is best served warm, so please be careful." Mi'cin held his mug, waiting for Todd. "Enjoy."

Picking up the steaming cup of e'xin, smelling the rose-chocolaty scent, Todd remembered the drink from when he'd had dinner with Mi'ko and his family. "I'm glad we got to go out. Thank you."

Mi'cin grinned, then sipped his drink. "You are welcome."

Todd experienced the warmth of the drink lingering in his mouth and throat even after his first sip was gone. "It's like our wine, right?"

"That is correct." Mi'cin took another sip.

"The meal looks like pad Thai." Todd examined his utensils; a slightly sharp-edged spoon called a *té* and what were essentially chopsticks, called *lagu,* were brought with the meal.

I can do this.

The Nentraee were experts at using both these devices at the same time.

Thank God I know how to use the chopsticks. The spoon thing not so much.

He grabbed the chopsticks.

"I'm glad you approve. I was worried you might not find it appealing." Mi'cin grinned and his body relaxed. "I see you are getting better with our utensils."

One of the lagu helping to hold the vegetables slipped out of Todd's grip. He quickly managed to nab it before it dropped to the table and he lost part of his meal to his lap.

Mi'cin focused on his meal, but Todd saw the whisper of a grin.

"I need to look up what this pad Thai is." Mi'cin took the chopsticks in his left hand and the spoon thing in his right. "It pleases me that you enjoyed the e'xin." He cut the colo co mo with both his té and lagu. One of the larger pieces burst and something akin to a yolk spilled out. "Yes, it's similar to your human wine or other alcoholic drinks. Do not drink too much of it, or you will find yourself unwell in the morning."

"So, definitely like our alcohol."

Mi'cin gently tossed the food to mix it together. "I hope you enjoy."

Todd watched him, taking in how to mix the food together so he could duplicate it with his own meal.

"It has only been within the last five years that we've started making colo co mo again as our agricultural ships improved production." Mi'cin swirled some of the leafy vegetables and noodles onto his lagu. He took a bite.

"Thank you, Mi'cin, for all of this. You made my day." For the first time in a long while, Todd felt like his old self.

Twelve: One Bullet Point at a Time

THE DINNER WITH Mi'cin had been a nice distraction. The food had been tasty, and the e'xin left Todd with a warm, comfortable sensation for the rest of the night. But mostly he was happy to have gotten to know Mi'cin better.

This morning, in the light of day and with the effects of the e'xin long gone, Todd reviewed the updated report sent to him from Vi-Narm. The tree-lighting ceremony was still a go. Scotland Yard, MI6, and Nentraee security teams were satisfied that all appropriate precautions for the event were taken. The week-old threat of a dirty bomb or small-yield nuclear device were overstated and not credible, nothing actionable; however, additional precautions would be implemented.

Additional security won't be enough.

Todd hustled out of his office and down the hall, hoping to catch the vice speaker to find out what additional security measures the Nentraee had finally decided on. Perhaps, the shuttles could scan for nuclear material and neutralize it. Maybe, that was why they didn't seem overly concerned about the threats. When Todd reached the office, the door opened, revealing Mi'ko and Vi-Narm both dressed in their ceremonial cloaks.

"Mister Vice Speaker?" Todd took a step back.

Vi-Narm narrowed her eyes, the tips of her ears turning blue.

Crap. This can't be good.

"Todd, what can I help you with?" Mi'ko fixed his tieback.

"I wanted to see if you had more information on the new security reports from this morning."

"I had hoped dinner with Mi'cin distracted you from the topic."

"Per your request and your worry"—Vi-Narm's voice was professional but cold—"the speaker general will not be attending the tree-lighting ceremony in London."

"Oh, thank Christ." Todd didn't let her sour expression affect him; he would have hugged them if it weren't for their custom of no physical contact. This was the best news he'd gotten since all these stupid threats had come to light a few weeks ago. "I get that there are threats all the time, but this seems different—"

"Instead," Vi-Narm interrupted, "the vice speaker will be attending. I will be accompanying him to ensure nothing goes wrong."

Each word crashed down on Todd like an avalanche.

He leaned against the wall for support. "No." He tried to come up with new arguments to stop them from going, but his head pounded, preventing the words from leaving his mouth.

"Todd, we must send someone." The wrinkles around Mi'ko's eyes and mouth softened. His tone grew gentle. "I'm the vice speaker. That duty falls to me. It would be inappropriate to send an aide or a member of the House of the People."

"No," Todd said.

Mi'ko took a step closer to Todd and met his eyes. "Vi-Narm and I discussed your ideas about the shuttle landing onsite, and it seems wise, as does your suggestion to scan the area again. It was all in the report Vi-Narm sent you. We shall do both. All precautions are being met. Vi-Narm, Danu, and representatives from Downing Street met for several hours, after we talked, to ensure that our security concerns were addressed."

"Mi'ko, you can't," Todd continued. "It's not safe. The report from Greg yesterday claimed there will be a bomb larger than the one in San Jose. It could even be nuclear."

"I doubt even your people are that irresponsible." Vi-Narm's ears were blue and puffy. "Plus, we have ways to counter such a threat."

Todd stood in a way to block the walkway. "This can't be happening again. You can't go!"

I sound like a child.

This would not win his argument. He needed good, solid points to bring up.

None came.

"Todd, it is my duty," Mi'ko said.

"There is nothing to concern yourself with, Todd." Vi-Narm's shoulders straightened. "We have been through this." Her tone hardened. "I would suspect that the updated security reports I sent you today would please you. In addition to deferring to your own government and your secretary of state for approval."

Given how beautiful the Nentraee language was and how the beauty tended to translate when they spoke English, it amazed Todd how ugly those words sounded coming from her.

Don't let her distract you.

"That's not good enough," Todd said. "What did Scotland Yard have to say? Did you tell Downing Street and the Secret Service everything? That possibly a device will be hand carried into the event, so security sweeps beforehand won't pick anything up until it's too late? This was part of the information we got yesterday."

"I know how to do my job." Vi-Narm's ears looked about ready to pop off her head. "We have addressed all scenarios, plus the reports from Greg you mentioned have come under question."

"Vi-Narm." Mi'ko held up a hand. "Do not make matters worse."

"Under question?" Todd asked.

"It is nothing for you to worry about." Mi'ko's voice remained calm. "Please, trust Vi-Narm and Danu. They know what they are doing."

"But..."

"Did you know that there were reports of a potential chemical attack for today?" Mi'ko asked.

"No, but..."

"What about a full-on assault by armed personnel hiding in the sewage system, coming up from one of the subterranean transit hubs?"

Todd shook his head.

"There have been numerous reports, coming in hourly for weeks now, and not all the reports made it to you. But our security personnel have them and have reviewed them for credibility. I wouldn't have even seen them if I didn't ask for them," Mi'ko said. "Todd, we are all worried. I am worried as well. However, I have faith in my staff to do their jobs. Now, please, you're doing well and I appreciate your efforts."

"Precautions are being taken," Vi-Narm added. "I'm more than satisfied." She took a step forward. "We received cooperation from Washington and Oslo as well. Now if you'll excuse us, we need to be going." She brushed by Todd, causing him to finally move out of the way.

Todd reached out and grabbed Mi'ko's arm.

To hell with your customs. This is too important.

"Mi'ko, you can't go," he begged. "Please call this event off. Make up an excuse. Anything, just please don't go! Don't do this. Don't put yourself at risk, please, not again."

"Todd." Mi'ko's voice raised as Todd held his arm taut. "I appreciate your worry." He tried to remove his arm from Todd's grip. "This is not your concern. I've done as you asked; I convinced the speaker general to not attend the event. It was not an easy conversation with her. You will not interfere further." The last word ended the conversation, and Mi'ko snatched his arm free. "Now, I suggest you focus on your duties and allow me to focus on mine."

Mi'ko squeezed past Todd and headed down the corridor.

"Learn your responsibilities and your place, Mister Landon," Vi-Narm said in a harsh whisper. "Perhaps, when I return, we can discuss this in greater detail." She followed the vice speaker, her dress cloak billowing like flames behind her.

This wasn't what he wanted. Why were they being so stubborn? Every fiber of his being told him something horrible was going to happen, and he was powerless to do anything about it. He placed his hand on the wall for support as he stared at the empty hall in front of him.

I have to try. Greg and the others can't be wrong. I'm not making up some grand conspiracy theory; the threat is real.

Running back to his office, Todd understood how much more trouble he could get in with the vice speaker. "In for a penny; in for a pound," he mumbled as he pulled out his datapad, then called up *all* the reports on the security threats for the tree-lighting ceremony. As the files opened, he tapped the monitor, waiting for the one person he thought might be able to help him to appear on screen.

"Mi'cin, I need your help. Can you come to my office?" Todd asked.

"Todd, what's wrong?"

"Your father. He's heading to Earth with Vi-Narm for the ceremony." Todd only paid Mi'cin half attention as he scanned details on how to conceal bombs on the other half of his screen.

"He was not pleased. He and my mother discussed it this morning." Mi'cin paused. "You put him in a difficult situation."

"Well, he might end up dead, along with a whole lot of other people." Todd's voice was harsher than he intended. He faced the image of Mi'cin on the screen. "I'm sorry. Please, we need to act. I need your help, please."

"I'll be right there."

The screen went blank, and the Nentraee government seal appeared.

Todd continued scanning the information on dirty bombs, opening up new military reports and cross-checking them to the others.

Who could hide making a dirty bomb? How could one get smuggled into Trafalgar Square? What would it take to do this? Who could do this?

He needed to find a way to stop an attack. He looked for a link of some kind, maybe there was more in the reports from the CIA, MI6, or the Nentraee that had been missed or they weren't seeing.

"What can I do?" Mi'cin said as he pushed past the half-open door. Once in the office, he pulled out his datapad and sat.

"Help me find a link that I can use to stop your father." He swiped his hand toward Mi'cin. "I'm transferring the files from Scotland Yard and the diplomatic protection group to you right now."

"Todd?"

"Something about Greg's report. I know these reports say there is 'nothing actionable,' but I don't believe them."

Todd finally raised his head from the screen. He focused on the Nentraee's full lips and beautiful green eyes.

You've lost so much. I'm not going to let you lose any more.

"I need you to help me," Todd said. "To believe me. One report from MI6 a week and a half ago says that trace nuclear materials have been found at Heathrow Airport. The next day, a report from the security at Heathrow says that no trace elements were found; it was a malfunctioning X-ray machine. There is another report out of Germany, two weeks ago, that says some material from a nuclear reactor went missing, but here's a report a day later saying the first report is wrong and all materials are accounted for. It doesn't make sense."

"I believe Vi-Narm has been through all this with Downing Street," Mi'cin said.

"It's just like San Jose. High-profile, a huge event with the general public invited. There is no way to secure it all. The original reports from October and November even say that. They're not closing the subway and people aren't being searched." He swiped these reports and timelines over to his monitor and pointed at the screen. "They limited security to bomb-sniffing dogs because no one in authority thinks the threat is credible."

"That does not mean—"

"Mi'cin," Todd interrupted. "London is one of the most monitored cities on Earth, and three days ago, Scotland Yard took down some of the CCTV feeds in the city for a software upgrade. No. That's stupid. I don't care if the report says that it's not in Trafalgar Square, that the cameras there will be working. Things like this don't happen." He raked his hand through his hair. "Look, I can't explain it, but please, I need your help. We can't let what happened before—" He paused, images from Jerry's funeral filling his head. He wiped his eyes. "We can't let more people die."

Mi'cin leaned into the monitor. "Are you all right? You know this won't change the past? You can't bring back the dead."

Todd's heart stopped, and he turned to Mi'cin.

Is that what I'm trying to do?

"I'm sorry," Todd said. "I... It's possible I'm wrong, that I'm being paranoid, but what if I'm right? Can we risk that? Can you risk losing your father?"

Mi'cin was quiet. He focused on his device and started to go over the new information. "I hope you're wrong."

"Me too." Todd continued to search backward through the list of reports, trying to find who sent the first security reports and what it said. There had to be a clue, or a link, or this was quite possibly the end of his career with the Nentraee.

TODD AND MI'CIN had taken more time to research than Todd had hoped when Mi'cin made the suggestion to stop and go to the speaker general.

They arrived at the speaker general's office. Todd reached out and tapped the panel by the door. They hadn't found anything new, but Mi'cin told him they shouldn't waste any more time trying to find a clue that might or might not be there. This was their last effort. They both waited until they were invited to enter.

"Hello, Todd." Tun'ae offered a small bow to Mi'cin. "The speaker general is busy at the moment. Please, sit." He pointed to the tan couch and gray chairs.

Todd didn't deal with Tun'ae, but he always seemed pleasant enough for the second-in-charge of security for the speaker general. He was from the clan Martween, so his facial features were much softer than Mi'cin or Mi'ko, and his eyes were a deep, dark blue.

Focus.

"We need to see her as soon as we can," Todd said as politely as possible.

"I sorry. You need to wait." Tun'ae turned back to his datapad, then checked the monitor on his desk again.

Todd tapped his foot, dusting off imaginary lint from his sleeve.

"Patience," Mi'cin said.

Todd reached into his pocket, pulled out his watch, and then checked the time. Doing the math. He shook his head. Time was running out. He got up to knock on the door, but it slid open before he could. Danu and Mirtoff stood in the doorway, speaking.

Danu spoke too quickly for Todd to understand, then typed on his datapad.

"Todd, Mi'cin." Mirtoff switched to English. "What can I help you with? Please, come in." The wrinkles around her eyes and mouth seemed deeper.

She turned to Danu. "Thank you. I'll await your report."

Danu bowed.

Whenever Todd had seen Danu and Mirtoff interact, he got the impression that Danu had more than a professional interest in her. It had to do with the way he watched her and how his gaze always seemed to linger a second longer than need be.

Don't get distracted.

"Speaker General, please recall Mi'ko." Todd rushed the words out, barely waiting for the door to slide shut.

"Mister Landon, you have no idea the trouble you have caused." Mirtoff's polite grin faded to a scowl. "Mi'cin, I'm sorry you are involved." There was disappointment in her voice.

Mi'cin bowed briefly. "Madame Speaker, if you—"

Mirtoff's eyes raised and her lips pursed together.

Mi'cin went silent.

"What's going on?" Todd demanded. "I showed the vice speaker the security report that I received from Mister McNeil yesterday, which pulled all the information together. We've cross-checked it to all the other security threats, and every report that mentions a bomb or other danger is countered by another report the next day, or sometimes later on the same day, saying the first was mistaken. How can reports from Scotland Yard, MI6, Germany, France, and Homeland Security all be wrong, or proven wrong so quickly? We don't have a smoking gun, but there is a lot of information that isn't right. Nuclear material missing from Germany, but then suddenly accounted for. Trace amounts of nuclear materials found at Heathrow Airport, and then poof." Todd made an explosive gesture with his hands. "Nope, it wasn't trace after all. Scotland Yard is taking down the CCTV cameras in London for an upgrade. Look at all the inconsistencies. I don't understand what's happening here."

Mirtoff watched him. "The McNeil report." She slowly inhaled. "Ah yes, the report from the ex-chief of staff, Mister McNeil."

"Wait. What?" Todd froze. "The *ex*-chief of staff?"

"Apparently, Mister McNeil announced his resignation early this morning due to suspicions of him providing false information to us, the White House, and Downing Street about today's ceremony. Every report you mention—" She exhaled. "—was falsified."

"Why?" Todd shook his head as his glance fell to the floor.

"We don't hold you personally accountable for the information you provided us, but..." Her face softened. "People in your government suggested it. And they are also questioning your mental condition. It is bad, for all of us— you and Mister McNeil, most of all."

"No, that's bullshit. Why would Greg do this?" Todd's hands started to tremble.

"It would seem Greg isn't the male you think he is," Mirtoff said. "Your government claims he belongs to one of the new xenophobic groups that have appeared on Earth recently. He and some others have been found out. Others who provided some of these reports you and he referenced."

I'm gonna throw up.

Mi'cin's face dropped. "Todd." He said. "I'm sorry. I had no knowledge of this."

"Greg's only trying to help. Yes, he pulled all the information together, but..." Todd turned to Mi'cin, then back to Mirtoff, his heart ready to burst from his chest. "He's trying to help you and trying to keep people from getting hurt."

This can't be happening! None of this is real. Why is this happening?

Mi'cin reached out and gently touched Todd's arm. Startling him from his thoughts.

Mirtoff glanced at Mi'cin's hand. "A conversation I had ad nauseam, to use a human phrase, with my vice speaker. Which is why I am here now instead of heading to London."

"But if you don't believe—"

"Because he insisted, to appease you," Mirtoff interrupted. "He felt it was the least he could do, given the circumstance with Mister McNeil." The tips of her ears grew blue and started to enlarge. "He threatened to resign his post if I did not arrange an illness that would keep me from attending." Her voice started to rise, but it quickly lowered. "A position I do not like to be in, but I like the idea of being without him as my vice speaker even less." She sat heavily in her chair. "So, here I am, on the ship, instead of representing my people, where I belong. Once people find out, they will not be pleased."

Mi'cin removed his hand from Todd's arm. "Madam Speaker, that doesn't change the fact that my father is in danger, as are all those people in London." He took out his datapad. "The security data does not make sense. Please examine the notes. There are many items, detailed items, that appear odd."

Mirtoff held up her hand, not taking it. "According to Ms. Webster, the information has been proven false. Regardless, all actionable threats have been considered. Even you can't be that blind." She massaged her ears. "There is no reason for me to be here. It was to be an opportunity for my people to be shown as supportive of all your cultures and neutral to all the countries of your world." She glanced up at Todd. "You should understand this. You helped in the selection of these events."

Todd couldn't meet her gaze.

"You do not understand the potential diplomatic damage it would cause should no one from this government attend." Mirtoff reached up and adjusted one of her braids. "I should be there, not Mi'ko. He is acting emotionally and without thought in order to protect you." Her eyes narrowed. "And you seem to be just as emotionally driven."

"I'm sorry." Todd took a step back. He wanted to curl up and hide in Faa's corner.

This is why I don't confront people. It's easier to pretend everything is fine and not make waves. Who knows what kind of trouble I've caused? I'm so damn stupid.

"As I said, it's not your fault," Mirtoff said. "It was Mister McNeil's. It would seem he used your friendship and your personal loss to put us all in this difficult place." Her shoulders relaxed. "Your secretary of state informed us of his involvement this morning prior to the vice speaker leaving and apologized. They will be conducting a full investigation of his actions. He's been under investigation for some time."

"Wait," Todd said. "She provided the information contradicting Greg's report?"

"Correct. The Secretary of State, Martha Webster," Mirtoff said. "Ms. Webster was able to stop him." She grinned. "A resourceful female."

Todd internally rolled his eyes.

"Your government will be investigating him fully and bringing him up on charges," Mirtoff said. "That is all they would tell us. If you wish, look into it. It may help you heal."

Todd tapped his hand on his leg. Greg had mentioned he was having issues within the White House, having trouble getting information and being kept in the loop.

Todd took out his datapad and called up his files on Trafalgar Square and San Jose. "Madam Speaker, most of the information we've obtained comes from the secretary of state's office." He hit the expand button and a holographic image with various reports lifted from his device. "I'm not sure if that's normal or not, but if you look at all the reports on security, they all come from her office, including the security reports for the event in San Jose." He worked the device more quickly. "The data is not from Homeland Security or the CIA or the FBI."

Mirtoff and Mi'cin watched him with interest as the images came into focus.

"All of this, but why? It's not a US event," Todd said. "Why would Greg lie about a planned attack on your life in a foreign country? What would he gain? If you didn't show up to the tree lighting, really, who would that hurt? Not the United States. Diplomatically, it might be awkward, but it wasn't life or death..." He paused, trying to work out the logic. "Even if it was an embarrassing incident, there wouldn't be anything for the White House to gain, or Greg for that matter."

It doesn't make sense.

"We don't understand a great many things your people do," Mirtoff said. "We are continuing to learn, but we must accept the information they provide us. Ms. Webster speaks for your president and your country."

A loud buzz came from Todd's datapad, making him jump. The reports and maps flashed, then faded away.

Everyone looked at the device.

"I see you're having trouble with your datapad as well," Mirtoff said.

"We've had communication interference as well the last few days," Mi'cin said. "I'll report this disruption to maintenance and repairs."

"So, it's not just me?" Todd asked.

"No," Mi'cin said. "We've been having technical issues the last several days. Right after your Thanksgiving celebration."

"Madam Speaker, does anyone know you're not attending?" Todd asked.

"Of course not, we told no one." Mirtoff stood. "It's an internal matter of state. If the speaker general is ill, the vice speaker takes her place. There is no need to tell anyone.

Nothing changes, and in the case of internal turmoil, it keeps a continuity of power. It would keep others from gaining a power position, as was done before the Clan War." She stopped, and her eyes narrowed on Todd. "Why? Should we notify them? We do not want to breach any more human etiquette."

"In our culture, a head of state would notify their host if they were sending an alternate, or unable to attend."

Both Mi'cin and Mirtoff observed Todd.

"So, no one will know that Mi'ko is coming until he arrives? And the shuttles all look the same on the outside." His voice hushed, and he sat on the couch, rubbing his temple.

"Are you all right?" Mi'cin crossed over to him.

"It can't be." A shiver ran up Todd's back. "There is nothing to be gained by you not showing up, but what if I'm right?" He turned to Mirtoff. "What if they are planning an attack and these minor issues with the datapads and communications network are part of it. Hacking your systems, or trying to. They assume you're coming and they've discredited Greg, so there's no reason for you not to go." It was a rhetorical question. "Why would all the information be filtered through the secretary of state's office? Why not the UN, Downing Street, Scotland Yard, or MI6?" His leg began to shake. "The information is wrong. You shouldn't be getting security reports from the secretary of state, not for an event in a foreign country. That information comes from Homeland Security, not her. It would be like your House of the People telling your Speaker's House what to do. It isn't done. Someone might be planning an attack."

"What are you talking about?" Mi'cin asked. "None of this makes any sense." He sat and put his hand on Todd's arm.

"No," Todd said. "That's where you're wrong. It makes perfect sense! Everyone is so worried about who the Nentraee will support. Where the Nentraee go. What countries the Nentraee have contracted with. Worried about how you're going to treat them, so they are blinded by their own wants and needs." He licked his lips. "No one is questioning whether or not people want you here. You've seen the news about the groups calling for you to leave Earth, I'm sure. The threat report on them says they are small and unorganized, but what if they aren't? And why is that a report from the office of the secretary of state and not Homeland Security? If there is another attack, and if say, the speaker general is killed, what would happen?"

Mirtoff and Mi'cin were quiet.

"You would leave," Todd replied to his own question. "Wouldn't you? I know I would. Why stay somewhere you're not wanted. You would leave our world. You've had time to repair your ships and could travel another five or ten years, probably more."

Mirtoff nodded hesitantly; she appeared to be agreeing with him.

"After the first attack." Todd stopped. "Of course." He snapped his fingers. "That's the real reason why you brought me here. I'm the reason you're still here, some ancient tradition brought back right after the attack on San Jose. I was your internal compromise. That's why some of the Speaker's House didn't want me. They wanted to leave."

"That is part of it," Mirtoff said.

Todd put his hand on Mi'cin's. "Look, if you leave our world, then everything goes back to how it was before. People, human people, are afraid of change, and that's what you bring. It throws everything into question, our beliefs in the universe, and in our God. You being here changes everything for us, and that might be too much for some people."

"Your people have an understanding of the universe. They know there are more races out there," Mi'cin said.

Todd chuckled. "No. Not before you got here. It was all theory and a few kooks on the internet. But here you are. If you leave, then it all goes away."

"You suspect Greg was correct, and he is being hushed?" Mirtoff asked.

Todd pointed to her window with the image of Earth. "Someone down on Earth doesn't want you here. It's possible they might be getting help from Nentraee who want to leave but, because of you, are forced to stay. That could explain the sudden issues we've been having with the communication links and the datapads. Someone up here is helping them." He glanced back over his shoulder. "The enemy of my enemy is my friend."

"Our own people working against us?" Mi'cin asked.

Mirtoff fussed with her hands as a scowl filled her face, but she said nothing.

"They tried to kill Mi'ko in San Jose," Todd said. "Forcing you to leave, but when that didn't work, they had to change tactics. They had to wait, continue to hide. The vice speaker wasn't a big enough fish, so they're going after you. The head of your government, as well as the heads of government from England and Norway."

"Think about it." Todd talked faster. "We find out this morning there will be no representation from Buckingham Palace? The Queen of England isn't sending anyone to an event that is happening in the capital of her country. That doesn't make sense, does it? It's an event that only the American ambassador to England will be at, not the secretary of state. Why? What's her reason for not being there? She is the highest-ranking diplomatic officer in our country, and she's not there to support our strongest ally. Why? Was she invited? If not, why? Someone in her office doesn't want her there. They're protecting her because they know what's going to happen. Like when the president and vice president weren't in San Jose. They left it to the governor of California. Now, he's dead, and they are both safe."

"Why would anyone in your government do that?" Mi'cin's voice was soft and calm. "They have nothing to gain, and they've been the most supportive and helpful to us."

"No, it's not my government. It may be staff in the government. Before you arrived, the United States was the one superpower on the planet, or so we liked to think. We've been losing that status over the years to China, and there are a number of other countries coming into play. Russia and Brazil. India. Now, with you here, we're losing even more of our influence."

Todd nabbed his temperamental datapad, typing frantically, pulling up historical records about Earth. "Madam Speaker, please." He rushed over to her desk.

Mirtoff read the details and some of his historical references.

"Think of it in terms of the times before your Clan War." He paused, glanced back to Mi'cin for reassurance. Seeing him nod, he continued. "Our first World War was started by the assassination of Archduke Ferdinand of Austria. One man. One event. That's all it took to launch our entire planet into war..."

She continued to view the information he provided.
How long has it been since Mi'ko and Vi-Narm left?

Finally, Mirtoff put down the datapad and tapped the monitor. "Danu, please contact the vice speaker. I need to speak with him at once, and I want to talk with General Gahumed. Please join me once they are on secure lines." The wrinkles around her eyes increased as the her frown grew. "If you're wrong…"

"If I'm wrong, then you can remove me as an enemy of state. A collaborator in a huge hoax," Todd said. "Hell, you can shoot me out an airlock. It won't matter, but if I'm right?" There was a quiver in his voice.

"Madam Speaker," Mi'ko said, and she tapped a few buttons on her display. The screen's image moved to the main wall-mounted monitor by her small conference table. "Mi'ko, Mi'cin and Mister Landon are in my office."

There was another chirp.

"Madam Speaker," a rough female voice said.

"Good. General Gahumed." Mirtoff added the general's image to the other half of the screen.

General Gahumed bowed.

"Mister Landon has an interesting theory I would like him to share. How long before you arrive to the event, Mister Vice Speaker?"

"We are in a holding pattern, waiting to be cleared in London," Mi'ko replied. "We requested a vertical landing close to the venue instead of going to the airport and driving over." He looked offscreen.

Danu entered the room and joined everyone at Mirtoff's large conference table.

"Maintain the holding pattern until you hear everything that Mister Landon has to say. Please, ask Vi-Narm to join the conversation. I want to hear her thoughts as well as Danu's." Mirtoff nodded to Todd.

All eyes were on him. He took a deep breath and stood. A familiar voice and familiar grin came from behind him.

"No more hiding, Mister Man." Jerry's voice was soft and sweet. "Take it one bullet point at a time."

Todd sensed the ticking of his pocket watch. He took a breath.

Thirteen: Tree Lighting Ceremony

THE BROADCASTS WERE alive with different faces and different languages, human languages.

She edged forward, picking one of the faces and stations. Nodding, she increased the volume. A smile played across her lips. The time was now. This was the day she had worked for, all the planning and the negotiations, the manipulation of former friends and allies.

I have glorious plans.

These deaths are a small price to pay. Her goal wasn't to kill and destroy but, more importantly, to gain possession of those demons' technology.

I can pray for the dead later.

The atmosphere on the television buzzed with excitement, alive with activity and eager people. The image zoomed in on the brightly lit stage where four people stood, all in long jackets and scarves. Behind them a hundred-foot-tall unlit Christmas tree. A choir dressed in red robes and white bibs stood waiting. Everything was framed by the National Gallery, all lit in bright white lights. The image turned to a man holding a microphone. In the background, the UK flag flapped, alongside the Norwegian and the Nentraee flags.

"This is Gabriel Jones for the BBC, reporting live from Trafalgar Square on this most auspicious occasion. Not since the end of World War II and the first historic presentation of the tree have Londoners been this excited."

Gabriel, like everyone there, was dressed for the cold London weather, in a heavy coat and scarf. He walked among the crowd as he spoke. "This strictly London event is being shown live, not only here at home but around the world and on the Nentraee media channel." The image shifted and showed all the various reporters and camera operators. "Not since London hosted the summer Olympics has the atmosphere been this electric.

"People started lining the streets early yesterday morning." Gabriel adjusted his mic. "Some choosing to camp overnight to make sure they had a spot for the festivities."

Cheering people held Welcome Nentraee signs.

From a world away, she leaned back in her chair, watching. "Oh, isn't that sweet." Her words were harsh. "So pathetic."

Gabriel strolled over to a man holding a little girl on his shoulders. "And how long have you been here?"

"We've been here since yesterday morning. My wife and I took turns. This is an important event. I want my little girl to remember this day for the rest of her life." The man smiled; his daughter waved a UK flag.

"Not only have all the onlookers been here all day, the St. Martin-in-the-Fields choir has been here preparing for tonight. They will take the stage at the start of the ceremony. We understand there are other special events planned to welcome the Nentraee Speaker General."

She laughed, quickly covering her mouth. "Oh, Gabriel, you have no idea."

Gabriel's free hand moved to his earpiece. "We're getting reports that the Nentraee ship is in its holding pattern, waiting for clearance from British control." He turned to the sky, then back to the camera. "As we've reported earlier, the landing is going to be a challenge, considering the location and the crowds."

He scanned the crowd. "There are scattered rumors that the Nentraee are holding up the landing on purpose, though for an unknown reason. A potential problem with the ship or its landing apparatus, maybe." The camera panned up toward the ship. "What a ship it is." The image zoomed in on the sleek jet-shaped Nentraee vessel. Warm lights glowed from all the windows as it hovered in position. There was a small hum emitting from the ship and a bright purple glow from the back where the engines were.

She leaned closer to the monitors around her and tapped her lips. "It would be nice to be able to study that ship, really get a look at that tech, like we did with their agricultural equipment."

Gabriel continued. "Prime Minister Wilson and her husband Clancy are ready to greet Speaker General Mirtoff Esmi, along with the Prime Minister of Norway and his wife." Gabriel's bright white teeth reflected the light. The picture changed to a close-up of the stage, zooming in on the dignitaries set to greet the Nentraee.

"This is the first time in many years that both prime ministers are attending, making it that much more special for everyone," Gabriel said. "Sadly, we received word from Buckingham Palace that the queen, who it had been speculated may attend, will not be making an appearance tonight. There are reports of ill health, but no confirmation has come from Buckingham Palace." He turned back to the camera. "I can't begin to explain the feeling in the air. This marks only the third visit to the UK by a high-ranking Nentraee official. The last was a brief visit with the queen in a welcoming event orchestrated by Buckingham Place and Downing Street."

Gabriel craned his neck for a better view as several security personnel rushed to the stage and spoke with the delegation. "We're getting word that there seems to be some sort of incident or activity with the Nentraee ship. It is moving off or repositioning itself. It looks to be…" He stopped and glanced around at the crowd. People were cheering and waving flags.

The image zoomed in on the prime minister and her delegation. Security pointed to the Nentraee ship and then to the crowds of people. The prime minister glanced up.

"No," she snapped and leaned back to scan all the monitors. "Now, do it now," she commanded to the empty room. She continued to watch as all the reporters were in a fit, putting hands to their ears, not sure where to look.

"The Nentraee ship is finally coming in closer. Maybe, to land," Gabriel said. "Samantha, I don't know what you're hearing in the studio, but we're not sure what is happening. There is clearly activity as the choir is leaving the stage, and more security is arriving." He peered at the camera, confused, no longer talking to it but to someone offscreen. "Yes, all right, The prime minister is being ushered off the stage by the security forces and police. Something appears to be wrong, whether with the Nentraee ship or the delegation itself. A potential illness or some sort of emergency we haven't been made aware of yet." His voice took a more serious tone as he watched the stage, holding a hand to his earpiece for any news or updates. "Samantha, we don't know what is happening. We're seeing several police move in. They are starting to push people out. The Nentraee ship appears to be coming in for a landing. We're being told that we need to…"

A quick, white flash blinded the screen, and then the camera went dead.

"Praise the Lord. We did it." Her voice filled with relief and excitement. It took a moment for the stations to switch back. She kept all the other monitors muted, except for the BBC. "Why not stay with the local news?"

From the television, the BBC anchor started. "It would seem we've lost our live feed from Gabriel." Samantha glanced at her own camera from behind her desk. "We're trying to get video from Trafalgar Square. It appears there was either a sudden illness or maybe a problem with the Nentraee ship." She paused, looking offscreen. "I'm being told that there is no live feed from any of our cameras there at Trafalgar Square and that the power in the area is down.

"We're trying to pull feeds from the other media on location— They're not?" Samantha frowned. "It would seem there are no feeds coming out of the area."

Samantha's face drained of color. "There was an explosion at the tree-lighting ceremony. A possible malfunction. We are currently trying to reestablish contact." She stopped and turned to the monitor behind her, waiting for an image to appear.

"Nope. No malfunction, Princess." She crossed her arms and leaned into the monitor, forgetting the other screens.

Samantha's face was calm, but her voice shuddered as she spoke. "We've lost all contact with Gabriel Jones at the ceremony, and all other media outlets are out. We are unsure of the details at this time." The color in Samantha's face continued to drain. "We are in the process of sending out another team from the BBC to the location for an update."

Samantha fell silent. Her eyes grew large. The bottom banner ran across the screen, reading, "Blast at tree-lighting ceremony."

She took several breaths before she spoke. "It would seem there was some kind of explosion at the ceremony." Her tone was flat and her face devoid of expression. "We are reporting the information to you as we get it." She inhaled a shaky breath. "There is no official word, but we are getting conflicting information of various explosions or perhaps one, large explosion. The reason for this is unclear. We don't know if there is a malfunction with the Nentraee ship at this point or not. There is also a report that it may be a gas leak."

"Ha! Gas leak! Nice try, Samantha," she said with a bright, white smile.

There were several loud voices off camera in the studio as Samantha sat silently. She reached up and covered her ear as the voices around her continued in a low rumble.

Samantha swallowed and found her camera, her eyes filling with tears and her voice shaking. "We are being advised now, and are getting confirmation by various sources, that an explosion of unconfirmed size just occurred at the ceremony. The status of the prime minister and her party are unknown at this time. An emergency meeting at Downing Street is being called with the Joint Intelligence Committee, and we understand that the royal family has been advised and is monitoring the situation. The status of the Nentraee ship or of the speaker general is unknown. Please stay with us as we continue to report live from the BBC studios on this horrific, developing news story." Her face had gone to the color of ash before the screen went to an emergency placeholder.

She stood and clicked off the monitors.

Phase one complete. Time to get my team in position.

"THERE IS NO question," Gahumed said, her attention on Todd. "You chose Special Envoy Landon for his conviction, and I see no need to no be trusting him now. If we trust him, now is time for that trust."

"Alert the security for the prime minister and her party. We need to get them and the others out of there," Mi'ko said to Vi-Narm.

She nodded, before moving off to talk to the pilot.

"Madam Speaker, I suggest you contact the governments of both countries and alert them to the situation," Mi'ko said as he ran his fingers over the console.

"I will put the Rádo to alert-ready status, Madam Speaker," Gahumed said. "We can be ready to act on you command."

"Thank you, General Gahumed," Mirtoff said. "Please work with General Yee. He will want to put all our security on Earth on alert."

Gahumed bowed to the speaker general.

Todd kept his attention on the monitor as the inside of the vice speaker's ship shuddered and shifted to the the side. However, Mi'ko didn't seemed concerned.

"What can I do?" Todd asked, his heart starting to race, his face getting cold. Things didn't seem to be moving fast enough. They had to move faster. Why weren't things moving faster? He needed to act. He couldn't just stand there. His heart pounded. He rubbed his hands on his pants.

The lines around Mi'ko's eyes were soft as was his expression. "You've done enough for now. Thank you."

"Special Envoy Landon," Gahumed said. "Thank you. The Nentraee people are in your debt once more." She bowed toward him.

"Why would anyone do such things?" Mi'cin's eyes caught Todd's as he spoke. His voice was distant and soft.

The room filled with a sudden explosion of white light from the screens.

Mi'cin jumped up and rushed to the screen with his father's image on it.

Mirtoff did the same.

The images on screen fluctuated from complete black to what was actually happening on the ship. Smoke filled the screen as the static image showed the inside of the vessel listed side to side. Lights flashed and alarms echoed. As Mi'ko held onto the workstation before falling offscreen.

"Father!" Mi'cin called as the image went to static. He ran his hands over the panel, working the controls and pulling up various menus to try to regain the signal.

"Did you alert their people?" Mirtoff demanded as her face drained of color.

Danu hurried back from the door after calling Tun'ae to join them. An anxious expression on his face. "We did, but we too late? What of our ship? All people on the ground, Madam Speaker, there were no way to get word to them all."

Mirtoff turned back from the monitor, glancing from Mi'cin to Todd. The monitor went dark, and finally the speaker general's seal appeared. The connection lost.

Todd wasn't sure how, but he found himself sitting on the couch. Everything seemed to be in slow motion. They were no longer speaking in English, but in Nentraee. Mi'cin, Mirtoff, Danu, and Tun'ae all rushed about him, using their datapads, tabletop displays, and the speaker general's various wall monitors. Images pulled up with Nentraee faces—some Todd knew, some he didn't. He felt like a witness to a car accident, unable to leave but unable to do anything more than watch.

Mi'cin was frantically working, trying to raise his father again on the screen.

Todd scrutinized the blank monitor, willing it to come to life and show a safe Mi'ko and Vi-Narm.

"Mi'cin, what can I do?"

None of the Nentraee responded to Todd.

How many people died this time? How many lives were lost? Todd had been too late and too slow. He'd failed again. He watched as Mirtoff addressed Danu and Tun'ae, as they rushed between monitors and spoke in frenzied tones. Suddenly very small, Todd was unable to do anything to change what they witnessed.

Just like before. Powerless.

Fourteen: Fall Out

MIRTOFF LEANED FORWARD. "Mister President, Mister Deputy Prime Minister, it's clear this wasn't just an attack on us. It was an attack on your people as well." She swiped a tired hand across her face, pushing a wisp of hair back over her ear. "People in countries who have been supportive of the Nentraee. England and Norway were among the first countries to greet and welcome us."

During the initial moments of the attack, everyone, including herself, had panicked. Finally, Mirtoff reclaimed her office from Danu, Tun'ae, Mi'cin, and Todd, allowing her to focus on dealing with the attack and its aftermath. Decisions had to be made, despite the lack of answers. She had to work with these humans, no matter how difficult they were being and how much she wanted to retrieve Mi'ko and the others.

Neither the English nor the Norwegian prime minister's parties had been found yet. Search and rescue wasn't easy, and much of the area was in ruin, according to initial reports. The human device had done its job, but the damage was reduced, thanks to the Nentraee ship and shield technology, which neutralized much of the radiation and absorbed most of the blast force as it put itself between the people and the blast.

Thank J'Veesa the ship's shielding held.

However, neither the Nentraee nor the humans could make contact with the vice speaker's ship. The death count would, unfortunately, be large, but not as large as those who would be claiming responsibility would like.

She glanced at the estimates for loss of life. It was in the thousands. Her jaw clenched. *Unacceptable.*

"I would like to send down our security personnel to help in the search." She studied both males' expressions to see how far she could push them.

The deputy prime minister's brow was red and beaded with sweat. "We called the cabinet into an emergency session to elect a new prime minister to present to the Queen as soon as possible. Your request must wait for—"

"I'm sorry, Deputy Hague, but that is unacceptable." Mirtoff tried to remain calm, but it taxed her.

"We're doing everything we can," Anthony Hague said. "The radiation is too high. We can't ensure the safety of your people, given the current crisis, not to mention the safety concerns for our own people, as well as, evacuate survivors and the surrounding areas."

"I will assume any and all responsibility for my people." Mirtoff's ears were aching and the warmth started to climb to the tips. "We are in possession of technology you are not, and we are better equipped to help both your people and ours. Or was that not evident in the lessened effects of the blast radius and the lessened radiation spread?"

"All right." He sighed. "President Zachary, I appreciate your offer of support as well."

Mirtoff turned to Danu. "You will coordinate with the Rádo and send down as many of our shuttles and medical personnel as required for assistance and cleanup. We need to ensure the vice speaker and his party are safe."

"Yes, Madam Speaker." Danu bowed, picked up a datapad, and ran his fingers over the controls.

"I'm having my personal head of security and General Gahumed oversee the operation on our end."

Both males offered stiff nods but no additional comments.

There's too much work ahead of us, and we can't waste time on who does what and how to get things done. Not when so many lives are at stake.

"I'M SORRY, AMBASSADOR. I don't have any more information." Todd exhaled. The ambassador was working his last nerve. It wasn't her fault completely. He was worried and flustered. He forced a smile before speaking. "Now, if you'll excuse me, I have to go." He closed the channel and raked a hand through his hair before leaning back in his chair.

I should have stayed at the office.

He pulled up the Nentraee status reports. All shuttles were grounded, stranding 300 humans on various ships throughout the fleet. This included the new ambassador from the Republic of Zimbabwe, who was in a meeting with Speaker Rosta and not pleased to be stuck on the speaker general's ship.

At least she's not stuck on one of the mining ships.

Todd contacted all the human groups and ensured them that everything that could be done was being done. As soon as the situation returned to normal, they could return to Earth. In the meantime, they were to stay where they were and do their best to relax.

Updating the groups took him hours.

He told both the humans and their Nentraee hosts to contact him should there be any issues. This was the fourth call from the ambassador.

He closed his eyes longer, than he thought, but was jolted as the chair leaned back, snapping him to attention. After standing and stretching, Todd paced. Waiting for any word. If he were at home, he would have at least had Bianca to keep him occupied. He was alone with little more to do but wait. After seeing the same images of the vice speaker's shuttle coming in close to the stage with the government delegations, then the explosion, and dead air, over and over, he refused to watch any more of the newsfeed. So, instead, he paced and checked his timepiece.

He tried contacting Greg back on Earth, but he was unavailable. Once the attack happened, Greg was immediately recalled to the White House. At least that's what CNN and Fox News reported as they scrambled for answers, before Todd shut it off.

As for London... He shook his head. It had only been a couple of hours, and reports were sketchy at best. The government, the media, the people were all reacting, just like after San Jose. No one seemed to understand what happened or how, but here they were with a second attack.

Todd checked the computer terminal, calling up Greg's contact information and placing a call. Greg's office line went unanswered. He tried the White House switchboard and was directed back to Greg's office where the line remained unanswered.

I can't sit here.

Todd pulled up all the original reports on the potential attack and these mysterious xenophobic groups. Reviewing them, he made notes, hoping that anything he came up with might be useful for all four governments: US, Nentraee, Norway, and Britain. Even with this task, he lost focus and found he was reading the same paragraph over and over.

Finally, he gave up, went to the kitchen, and made a cup of tea. He missed Bianca. She had a way of realizing when things weren't right. She would jump on his lap and bump her head on his chin.

He sat, letting the chair absorb him and sipping his tea as he watched the gardens below, and inhaling the woody scent. A chirp came from his monitor, causing him to almost drop his tea. He rushed over, put down his cup, and touched the panel.

"Oh my God, Todd!" Dan's voice squealed, and his worried face appeared. "Are you all right?" His eyes were wide with dark circles underneath. "What the hell happened? I've been trying to reach you since we got the news. All communication with the Nentraee has been limited. Official use only." He leaned back and sighed. "London is a nightmare. No one knows what happened to the speaker general's ship. They don't know what happened to the prime minister and her husband." He massaged his temples. "Vaporized, I guess?"

"I don't know what happened. I didn't think a dirty bomb could do that."

"It can't. That was different." Dan rubbed his lips. "They're calling it a dirty bomb, but I've never seen or heard of anything like this before."

"Great." Todd's gaze dropped to the floor.

"Oh, no. No, no."

Todd glanced at the monitor.

"You listen to me." Dan crossed his arms. "None of this is your fault. I don't know what happened up there, but based on what the news is saying, you're not taking the heat for this. You're not military and you're not security. It wasn't your job. It's the job of those MI6 people. Hell, maybe even Interpol, but not you." He pointed at Todd. "If Greg tried to warn people and they didn't listen, that wasn't your fault. Even our media here has said the same thing. You should see what Fox News has been saying, not to mention CNN. They are all calling it the largest failing of the White House, Downing Street, and the intelligence community ever." Both his hands shook on the screen. "Todd, *ever*. Don't you even think for a minute this is because you didn't have a crystal ball."

"I know, I know." Todd's voice was tired. "But the vice speaker was on that ship."

Dan watched him, frowning.

"What if he's hurt or worse?"

"Listen to me—whoever planned this, they understood what they were doing. No way is this some little terrorist group. It's bigger than any of them. Has to be."

"Then who?"

"I don't know. I don't care. I don't care about any of that right now, and it's not your responsibility. What I'm more worried about is you and who actually did this."

Todd chewed at the side of his cheek, Dan was right. Plus, Mirtoff had instructed him not to say anything before he left her office. He couldn't mention any of his suspicions because it would only cause the Nentraee and humans more trouble and might start an actual war.

"Can you come home?" Dan asked.

"I am home."

"No, I mean come back to Earth, to your real home?"

Todd looked around his apartment. He had hardly gotten settled, and it had the same sterile feel as when he first moved in.

Is this really my home?

"I don't think so." He glanced back at the monitor. "Now might not be the best time."

"You need to get on one of their shuttle things and come home and separate yourself from all this," Dan said. "The break will do you a world of good."

Todd had a nagging feeling that something was wrong back on Earth, and somehow it didn't feel like a safe place for him to be. Plus, it felt like running away and hiding.

"I need to stay here and face this. There are over three hundred folks stuck up here with the Nentraee shuttles grounded. I have to be here for them. Plus, the Nentraee need me."

"All right. Call me." Dan ran a hand through his hair. "Call your family. Let them know you're safe."

Todd nodded.

Dan forced a smile. "Bianca says meow." He waved. "Take care."

"Yep." He tapped the screen, ending the transmission.

Todd picked up his tea and walked back to the window. Maybe Dan was right, perhaps going home for a few days would be a good idea.

No, I have work to do and people are counting on me.

He wasn't sure what time it was or how long he had been sitting when the door buzzed. He hurried over. "Mi'cin." Without thought, he reached out and hugged him. "I'm so sorry." Todd held the young Nentraee close to his chest for a long moment and felt a tight, uncomfortable hug back. "Come in."

"They found my father's shuttle." Mi'cin's voice was soft. "Communication is out. We only have a visual of it right now." His voice was calm, but his face seemed drawn and tired. "There is debate among the human governments and the speaker general as how to best to handle the matter. It hasn't been released to the media yet, and it is doubtful we will allow anyone other than our own personnel to retrieve our ship."

"How's the vice speaker's ship?" Todd took a seat. "They say it blocked a lot of the blast, saving a bunch of people? How is that possible?"

"There is extensive damage. Whoever did this meant to blow up the shuttle and kill the thousands of people there." Mi'cin's voice was tight.

"Oh God." Todd closed his eyes.

"I thought you should know." Mi'cin headed back to the door.

Todd had not seen him this tense and distant before. He could only imagine how hard this was on him and the rest of Mi'ko's family.

"Wait." Todd reached out and took Mi'cin's arm.

Mi'cin looked at the hand on his arm and faced Todd. Moisture hovered around Mi'cin's eyes, his shoulders rigid.

"I'm sorry. I'm so sorry. I wish to God there was more I could say or do," Todd said.

"You tried to warn us." Mi'cin's voice cracked. "You tried to warn him. There is nothing more that can be expected from you. Whatever is meant to happen, will happen. It's all in J'Veesa's hands now."

There was only so much a person could hide behind their mask.

Mi'cin shifted his stance and glanced to the floor. "I need to return to my family and wait for news."

"Of course. I understand." Todd wanted to pull him in for another hug and not let him go. "Thank you for coming, I appreciate it."

"Would you like to wait with us?" Mi'cin's voice was soft.

"If it wouldn't be an intrusion."

"You have saved my father once, and you may have saved him again. It would be no intrusion." Mi'cin's gaze darted over Todd's face.

Todd bowed. "I'd be honored."

MI'KO TRIED TO stand, pushing the smoldering chair out of his way. The awkward angle of the ship and the burned equipment made it a challenge. The typically clean, fresh, cream-colored space was no more. Replaced with smoke and blinking lights and broken monitors.

They had been at the zero mark of the explosion, and this was the aftermath. He scanned the interior of the shuttle as the emergency lights cast the cabin in a cool-blue light.

Mi'ko made a quick mental check of his condition: a few bumps and bruises but nothing major. He checked the rest of the sealed cabin and observed various people who needed some form of help. His help. If they had been one second slower, they would all be dead, but J'Veesa clearly had different plans.

Sparks from the console next to him pulled his attention. He needed to act. He rushed over to one of the emergency-equipment lockers and pulled down the medical bag. They weren't as equipped for humans as they were for Nentraee, but some of the devices would work just as well. Or so he hoped.

Inspecting the contents quickly, he rummaged through various items. Pulling out a bio scanner, he fidgeted with it before activating the device. It had been a while since he needed to use anything like this. Luckily, it was all straightforward, and he had been through several courses on basic first aid.

Through the haze, Mi'ko caught sight of Vi-Narm, already tending to the wounded. "How many?"

"Eleven." Vi-Narm's normally tightly braided hair, which was held in a bun, had now fallen past her shoulders. Her dress robes were tattered and torn.

I'm sure I look just as bad.

"We didn't make it out in time." Mi'ko knelt near the Prime Minister of Norway's wife, Nina, who was leaning against a bulkhead.

"If we wanted to save them and shield people from the blast, that was never going to be an option," Vi-Narm responded. "At least the emergency transfer portal worked."

Mi'ko nodded. They'd had to use the ship to its full ability, which meant they would be in the middle of the explosion. He pulled out several compresses and inspected the woman.

Alive. At least they are all alive, and that is what matters. Everything else can wait.

Mi'ko tended to her cut forehead. "I'm not that familiar with human anatomy. Will our clotting agents work on them?"

"No, basic first aid only. We need to assess them and go from there." Vi-Narm wrapped a bandage around the Lord Mayor's skull. Vi-Narm gave Mi'ko a firm nod, and he turned back to Nina.

Mi'ko worked quickly to stop any bleeding and check for broken bones. When the woman stirred, he forced a smile. "You alive. Are you badly hurt?" he asked, being as gentle as possible.

"No. I don't think so." Nina touched her arms and then her legs. "What happened?" She watched him. "We were being ushered off the stage. Where am I?"

"We are on our ship," Mi'ko replied. "We used an emergency device to evacuate you. I need you to stay still until we check on the others."

"Thank you," she said with a nod.

Mi'ko picked up his emergency kit and rose, seeing the others that needed help. He wished they had the power to save all the people, but they didn't. Even with their advanced technology, there was only so much they could do. *He* could do.

Todd was right, and we did not listen. That will never happen again.

"Our pilot is dead. We are on lockdown protocol," Vi-Narm reported.

Mi'ko nodded.

"Only us here in the cabin survived." She leaned over the unconscious Prime Minister of Norway. "He seems stable."

Mi'ko would mourn later for the dead pilot. He moved over to Prime Minister Hillary Wilson.

"How's my husband? And the others? How many did you save?" Prime Minister Wilson demanded as she shifted from where she sat, trying to sit taller.

Mi'ko checked her husband, running a hand over one leg then the other and visually inspecting him for cuts.

"I'm fine," Clancy Wilson coughed out.

Mi'ko found blood on his arm and tore the jacket and shirt so he could inspect the wound and clean it out.

Not bad.

"Our medical equipment isn't set up for human biology." Mi'ko glanced over his shoulder to the prime minister.

"Do what you can. How many were you able to get out?" The prime minister waved her hand in front of her face, clearing away the smoke.

"Not enough," Mi'ko replied. "I'm sorry, Prime Minister Wilson."

"My security started to pull us off the stage and then there was your ship. Then lights. Then I blacked out for a moment." Prime Minister Wilson viewed the interior of the cabin, then pinched the bridge of her nose. "Now we're here." She stopped. "Where is Speaker General Esmi?"

"She had fallen ill, and I was sent in her place. She is safe on our ship." Mi'ko wrapped Clancy's arm.

"It's probably the same illness the queen had," Prime Minister Wilson said through tight lips.

Mi'ko met her gaze, and he understood at that moment that the British government had been suspicious as well.

"I need to contact Downing Street. They'll be going into emergency session." She tried to stand but quickly sat back down again.

Mi'ko recognized many qualities in her that he'd seen in both Mirtoff and Laina. Strength and stubbornness. "The explosion killed our pilot and knocked out our communications, as well as our engines. We're on emergency power, and we are sealed in. We cannot determine the level of contamination outside, so leaving the safety of this secured cabin is not advised." He ran a hand over his bandaging work, then added, "There is nothing for you to do at this time but wait for rescue."

"Nonsense, there is always something. A cell phone?" the prime minister asked, checking for her bag, then turning to her husband.

"The signal would be blocked by the hull of our ship," Mi'ko said. "Without our communications array, nothing comes in or gets out. Now, please, Prime Minister, it's more important for you to rest for the moment." He reached out and touched her arm. It was a breach in protocol, but humans responded well to touch. "We all want to get out of here, and I assure you our governments are doing what they can. We are fine, but right now, we can't do anything. We must rely on those in charge and trust they will do their jobs."

"We could signal them through a window," Hillary said.

"Prime Minister, they were sealed to protect the cabin," Mi'ko said.

Clancy reached up and took her hand. "Hillary, relax. Everything that can be done is being done. You'll have to trust your cabinet to do their jobs." He shifted and pulled her closer. "They won't stop until you're back at Downing Street."

She rested her hand on the top of his head, then ran it through his hair.

Mi'ko left them and got up to figure out who was next. Vi-Narm worked on one of the human guards who was badly injured.

"We were lucky they underestimated our technology." Keeping our military capability, both offensive and defensive, private was one of the best decisions they had ever made.

Vi-Narm smiled.

"How did you manage to get us out of there, Mister Vice Speaker?" Hillary asked.

"A conversation for another time, Madam Prime Minister." Mi'ko had no intention of sharing these details with the humans—not at this point.

"Fine. Then why would anyone do this?" Prime Minister Wilson rubbed her shoulder.

"Todd believes fear of change." Mi'ko worked on the burned and bloodied arm of a human guard.

She scowled.

IT HAD BEEN almost a full day. The news came in as quickly as the official notifications. "Ship found in one piece...shielding the majority of the blast...fewer deaths than anticipated...mystery technology neutralized fallout..."

"No," she growled.

She glared at the reports, fiddling with the gold crucifix that hung around her neck. It had been several long months of planning, and today had felt even longer.

And for what?

Her companion watched his own video link. His red face and sour frown grew even redder and more sour. The video monitors were ablaze with smiling faces. Words in different languages hit her ears, the air of relief and elation filled all those talking heads.

Those sheep! Those idiots. How can they not see the obvious?

"A bright light of hope on this dark day," one of the talking heads said.

"What we thought was the speaker general's shuttle was actually that of the vice speaker," another said.

"The Nentraee confirmed that Speaker Esmi was struck down with a bout of food poisoning. She apparently had a bad reaction to peas," an infuriatingly bright-eyed reporter said. "At the last minute, she was unable to attend and sent the vice speaker in her place.

"The Nentraee have further confirmed the shuttle has been secured and most of its party are alive and well. We're also getting reports that they were able to save Prime Minister Hillary Wilson and her party with minimal injuries. It continues to be a bright spot in an otherwise tragic event," the pretty, young thing said, filled with a pride and enthusiasm.

"Food poisoning, because of peas," she sneered. Whatever the reason for the speaker general's absence, it certainly wasn't caused by some Nentraee pea allergy.

"It's not possible; they don't possess that kind of technology," the angry, sour-faced man said. "That shuttle should've been blown to bits, along with that whole section of London. Tens of thousands should be dead."

She glanced at the monitor, his heavy accent grabbing her attention. He would need to keep calm, or he'd have a heart attack, and she needed him if the plan was to work. The world needed a change, and with the help of the Nentraee technology, she was going to bring that change about.

Use the devil's tools against him.

"Well, clearly they do," she said. "They haven't been forthcoming with any military technology, now, have they?" She tapped her fingers on her desk. "Even our mullah friend's inspection and study of that agriculture equipment provided little. Who knows what kind of technology these demons possess?"

"We've seen nothing of technology like this before," her counterpart insisted.

"Not to fear, my friend. We'll continue to test their datanet. We've had more success with that. Plus, there are other things our friends in Silicon Valley are working on."

"How did the ship survive that? It was right under them."

"The devil has supplied his angels of darkness well," she said through gritted teeth.

"We should have used a full-tactical nuclear bomb." His accented words assaulted her ears.

"Hmm. Perhaps. But our friends in Israel and Pakistan aren't in positions to get us such tools." She tapped her lips. "Not yet." Everything had led them to this point. After all she had done, and now this. She was sure the devil was protecting them, but a tactical nuke was too risky; she didn't want to totally destroy the shuttle. She needed it intact for study.

The first attack, she believed, was luck. There was hope at that time the Nentraee would leave. She and her group wouldn't need to do anything more. The minions of hell would leave the Garden of Eden. The reports had even said as much. The Nentraee were leery. They were contemplating leaving. Isn't that what all the government officials had said? Not to mention the rumors and whispers she had heard from her people on the inside. The technology wasn't the goal then, but God's plan changed, and now she wanted their equipment.

She focused back on the monitors. The media ate this "miracle" up. They loved blood and destruction almost as much as they loved political scandal. All the special reports played out, all the victim's families paraded around like prizes, each one clamoring for their fifteen minutes of fame.

She prayed the Nentraee wouldn't make any more of these "Special Whatevers" like they did with Todd Landon. These demons surprised her at each step, and she didn't like being surprised. Like after the attack on San Jose. Landon, oh how the media loved him. She was sure he was behind stopping the Nentraee, keeping them safe. There was nothing mentioned about him right now because McNeil was the boy of the hour. They were both a thorn in her side. Both of them would pay for their sins against God.

She felt the gold crucifix around her neck for comfort. This time, she and her people had taken everything into account, all the misdirection, the misinformation, the months of planning, and for what? A few stupid civilians dead, a few more city blocks damaged. That was nothing. A few drops of blood paid.

Didn't these sheep know that the fabric of humanity was at stake? Of course not; they were stupid sheep needing to be told what to think. What did that annoying radio show host call them? Sheeple? She hated him but loved the term. It was perfect. He was a blustering idiot, but she loved his colorful metaphors.

"Sheeple," she said out loud. They just followed along.

Not her followers. They knew the truth. Well...the truth she shared with them to keep them by her side. These Nentraee were little more than animals. They didn't have a soul; they weren't human. She walked in the "Light of God" and turned her back on all the sinners. Humankind was promised dominion over this kingdom, and that didn't include these Nentraee devils. She would lead humanity into the Light, even if she had to drag it behind her.

"Now what?" the wide-eyed man asked.

She clicked her fingernails together. "We try again at the UN meeting, with the announcement of the treaty and their new home."

"How? We barely pulled this off. You were supposed to take care of the McNeil problem, and look how that backfired."

She narrowed her eyes at him, and he fell silent. Many people were scared of her—that was why she was so good in her career. That was why she was in charge. She smiled. He was so easy to control.

"Maybe it's time to give this new enemy a name," she said. "Perhaps, it's time to step out of the shadows and reclaim what God has given to us and us alone."

"Praise Him," he said.

"*Liberi Dei*," she said, and the man repeated.

"It's time for God's children to stop hiding and take on the demons, no matter the form they're in. Our next move will be at the UN assembly. It will be a glorious day for humanity. They will see the truth, all of them, and they will praise us and the Lord."

Movement on her outside monitor caught her eye. She inhaled, knowing it was time to show her work face.

She closed the secure line, ending the conversation with her key ally, one of her people. She didn't need to worry about being exposed. None of them did. They had allies everywhere, in every faith and every nation. Stopping hell's minions was what united them. They were no longer single faiths divided against one another. They were united against the messengers of the devil, coming here to take paradise away from them.

I'll bring back paradise.

She stood up as the door opened, the small gold crucifix falling beneath the neckline of her ivory blouse. "Mister President, I was on my way to see you. The news... " she said in her most hopeful voice.

"It's amazing news about the vice speaker and the others," President Zachary said.

She nodded.

"I don't know what we would've done without your work, Martha," President Zachary said. "To think we were going to hang Greg out to dry when he was the only one who saw it, as plain as day."

"It's a small miracle," Martha said.

"We can't have this type of thing biting us in the ass in New York," President Zachary said.

Martha had been with him for years, working together since she was a congresswoman in Mississippi and him a congressman from Ohio. She knew he considered her his political rock, and he needed her now more than ever to get out of this. If anyone could put a spin on it, it was her.

Martha's gaze calmly met his. "God willing, sir, everything that is meant to happen will happen with no glitches." She rested a hand on the desk. "Now, what can I do to help with this? We're going to have a lot to clean up, and we're going to have a lot to account for. Some of it, we might be able to address at the UN meeting, but not all." She glanced at the monitors again, seeing a replay of the explosion. "I've got my staff checking into where we failed on the intelligence. We're working with Homeland Security as well. Someone screwed up and we need to figure out who."

She stepped away from the bank of monitors as talking heads continued their babble. She glanced at the president, standing there, waiting for her. There was so much work to do, and this time, she fully realized what God had in store. She was and would always be Liberi Dei, one of "God's Children."

Fifteen: Liberi Dei

"LIBERI DEI." TODD checked the report.

Mi'cin, Vi-Narm, and Todd sat in Todd's office, going over the recently released material on the terrorist group. The additional information loaded to his datapad from the monitor on his desk. Todd sighed, seeing how little information there was. Vi-Narm sat with her stiff shoulders and typical expression of disapproval. Mi'cin hovered by the window, staring out into space.

Liberi Dei were all over the news and online. Twitter and Facebook were abuzz as everyone searched for answers and information about this terrorist group. What they found was minimal, only appearing within the public's perception within the last week, much like Al-Qaeda and ISIS when they appeared on the scene.

"Children God," Vi-Narm said.

"That's the literal translation, I think," Todd said. "I imagine they mean God's Children or Children of God." He read the translations and the variations that were being presented on his device since Latin wasn't his strong suit.

"There were no known groups with that name." Mi'cin crossed back to the desk and sat.

"Well, nothing that I know about or ever even heard of," Todd said. "They seem to be responsible for many of the religious protests, and they have some links to the xenophobic groups that started popping up when you got here."

Perfect. Just what we need—another hate group hijacking religion.

Vi-Narm leaned back in her chair. "According to your Homeland Security, MI6, and other intelligence agencies, they are global and claim supporters from many of your religions. They provided details of the attacks that only the ones who did it would know."

"And no one identified them before?" Todd chucked his datapad on his desk. He didn't understand how that was even possible; someone had to know about them.

"Perhaps they did and were keeping it quiet." Vi-Narm's gaze narrowed.

"Really?" Todd caught her point, but that didn't mean she wasn't partially right. It was possible someone from this ship might be working with them. A Nentraee, possibly.

Mi'cin glanced at her with a heavy frown. "I doubt very much that Todd had anything to do with any of this, Vi-Narm." He rested his hands on the desk. "If you recall, he was the one who tried to stop everyone. The only one, for that matter. He has no experience in security." He pointed at her. "Not even you saw anything with all your experience."

Wow! Mi'cin's standing up to her.

Vi-Narm switched to Nentraee, addressing Mi'cin. Her accent was too thick and she spoke so quickly that Todd didn't understand. The tips of her ears were blue and they were starting to puff up. She stopped and sneered at Mi'cin.

"Who I choose to spend my time with is none of your concern." Mi'cin glared at her, his English as cold as ice. "I don't report to you, nor will I ever."

Vi-Narm returned to English. "Your father may be the vice speaker, but you are not, nor will you ever be." She stood. Her ears blazing, she walked to the door as it slid open. "I suggest you both continue checking into this group and find out what you can, so we do not suffer another incident." She glanced at Todd. "Remember, Special Envoy, I will be watching you."

The door swished closed behind her.

"I'm sorry." Mi'cin exhaled. "You should not be subjected to that. My father will not be pleased."

Todd noticed Mi'cin's hands shaking, and Mi'cin's ears were a dark-bluish hue similar to his shirt.

"You should...um...not say anything, Mi'cin," Todd said in Nentraee. His pronunciation was getting better but still rough. "I am used to it. There is no reason...to...um...get in trouble with her. Perhaps, I...um...talk to your father and see about step...um...down." He spoke slowly and carefully. "There...um...no shame in leaving the post. I...um...check. It is rare but has been done." It was difficult, but his words came out pretty well, he thought.

"You're getting better." Mi'cin offered a small charming smile in spite of his anger. "I actually understood you." He switched back to English and continued. "Don't be ridiculous. Her accusations are baseless, and you understand how bad that would look for everyone, including you."

Todd hadn't thought of that.

"You don't want to be seen as a weak or soft male, especially by her. You need to stand your ground with her, show her you are her equal," Mi'cin said. "These are old biases, ones that we thought were long since dead, but people are scared, and fear..." He paused and picked up Todd's datapad, placing it in front of Todd. "They are afraid of change and want to hide in what is comfortable and safe, even if it's wrong. Do not let them frighten you off." He smiled, his tone light. "My father won't entertain such a notion of you leaving. He selected you for a valid reason."

"I know, but with all that has happened..." Todd shrugged.

"It is up to you to serve and represent your people well." He met Todd's gaze. "There is no other option in his mind. A position like this is permanent, despite what you may have found." A tight chuckle escaped him. His mood seemed to be improving. "Our clan is very stubborn when it comes to these things."

"Thank you, Mi'cin." Todd rubbed his chin.

Mi'cin stood and quietly watched Todd for another moment.

"Was there more?"

"I'm sorry to leave, but I must go to check on the shuttle's examination. If you need me, please contact me."

Todd bowed.

As the door swished closed behind Mi'cin, Todd called up reports on how the world was reacting to these Liberi Dei. Several governments were coming out and stating that this group would be stopped and that there was no place on our world for these kinds of fear tactics. The US was one of the first to say they were against the terrorists, along with China, Russia, Pakistan, and Saudi Arabia. President Zachary had promised to work hand in hand with the Nentraee and the UN to find out who was behind this. He also pledged whatever support England needed to help with their recovery.

"Contact Mister Greg McNeil, Washington, DC." He put down the datapad and watched the monitor as it processed his request.

Within moments, Greg's face appeared on the screen.

"Hello, Greg."

"Todd, how's the vice speaker?" Greg had dark circles and bags under his eyes.

"He's fine. They're going over the shuttle, examining all the data from the explosion. They should have a report down to Earth in a day or two."

"I'm glad. We're all glad. The Nentraee… " Greg paused. "The Nentraee managed to score themselves a lot of points by saving both prime ministers and their spouses. Even if the Nentraee won't say how they did it."

Todd nodded.

"What can I help you with?" Greg asked.

"What can you tell me about this group?" Todd asked. "You must know more than the intelligence agencies are willing to share. You're the one who warned me." He leaned in toward the monitor. "Do you suppose it's someone from inside a government, or governments, down there? This had to be an inside job, right? My friend Dan says there's no way this could have been done, otherwise."

It took Greg several moments to respond. His face became tight, and he sat taller in his seat. "I'm sorry, Todd. I don't know any more than you do at this point." He looked to either side. "And even if I did, I couldn't say anything *officially*. You know that. I wish there was more I could say."

Todd rapped his fingers on his desk. "Thanks. It was worth a shot." This was why he hated politics. One never got a straight answer.

He waited for Greg to say goodbye and then ended the transmission.

"Officially." He sat up straight.

Greg said "officially."

WASHINGTON'S UNION STATION was impressive. The building wasn't only a hub of transportation but a mall with specialty stores. It was a tourist attraction in its own right.

The architectural design echoed much of Washington, DC, with a lot of white granite and neoclassical lines. Pillars and arches gave the whole building a Roman feel.

After checking his pocket watch, Todd made his way down to the lower level, to Häagen-Dazs. Despite the cold outside, he ordered an ice cream. Todd chose a table and started to eat, waiting for his date while chuckling at the idea of how ridiculous this all was.

Engrossed in his ice cream, Todd wasn't focused on all the activity around him until the chair next to him scraped as it moved. He turned and laughed.

"Really," Todd said.

Greg sat and put his tray down. He adjusted his heavy overcoat and his blue scarf.

"I mean—" Todd glanced around. "—all this cloak-and-dagger-mystery meeting at Union Station in Washington, DC. Seriously?" He took another bite of his ice cream.

"This is serious." Greg frowned. "And it's all off record."

"What's that?" Todd pointed to the tray.

"Lunch," Greg replied.

"Lunch at four p.m.?"

"It's been a busy day." Greg arranged his food and put the tray on the empty table next to them.

"All right, so you got me here." Todd waved. "I'm here." He paused, seeing the scowl on Greg's face. "Now what's the deal? What was so important that we couldn't talk on the video link?" He took another bite of his ice cream. "Sorry, man, but this is pretty cliché."

"Cliché or not, this is how it has to be." Greg's frown and stern gaze reminded Todd how serious this situation was.

"I'm sorry. It's just nerves. I guess. It doesn't feel real."

"Well, it is." Greg picked up his wrap and took a bite.

Todd watched and waited for Greg to speak.

"Isn't it odd that it took us so long to hear from this Liberi Dei group?" Greg finally asked.

"Of course," Todd agreed. "Now, it's all the media is talking about. Not just in the US, but global media as well. I even asked that guy from the White House about it back when we went to that big dinner." He finished the last of his ice cream, dropping the plastic spoon in the cup.

"I've been digging into this, pulling what strings I can." Greg lowered his voice. "Calling the friends I can trust. This new group is working within our government. Not only ours, but other governments as well."

Todd blinked a couple of times. This was exactly what Vi-Narm and he had suggested only a few days ago. Finally, he found his voice. "The president?"

"Thank God, no." Greg paused. "Not him or the vice president, but..." He sighed. "I don't honestly know. I have my suspicions, but no proof." He stopped to take another bite of his wrap. "There are so many things that don't make sense, and like you, this isn't exactly my area of expertise. It's got a lot of people stumped, people who work on this for a living."

"Why?" Todd frowned. "Just to make the Nentraee leave? It's stupid." He shook his head. "It's hard to imagine they were able to do this. It doesn't seem possible."

"You're right," Greg said. "The only way that the attack in San Jose stayed so well covered up would be if it was an inside job with a lot of inside help, both military and government help—same with London." He took another bite of his wrap. "Neither of these events were easy targets, and attacks like this take years to plan out, but they were both done in next to no time. Maybe a few months to plan." He sighed. "No known terrorist group could have done it that quickly. The other oddity is, what happened to Al-Qaeda and ISIS? Where are they, and how do they fit into this?"

Todd's shoulders slumped.

"I suppose that's what's got everyone so worried," Greg said. "This group has got to be unlike anything we've ever had to deal with before."

"Duh! So who's behind this?" Todd asked.

"I'm guessing someone close to the White House or UN, but..." Greg pursed his lips.

"Well, if it's not the president or vice president, then who has that kind of power?"

Greg was silent.

"A general or someone in the military, but they don't have power at the UN..." Todd looked around the food court, running a list of people through his head. The UN secretary general wouldn't have power in the US, or the secretary of Homeland Security, but she wouldn't have power at the UN. At least he didn't think so.

"Martha?" Todd whispered.

Okay, it's a random guess, but why not?

Greg's face grew pale. "You're about to play a very dangerous game." He sighed. "Are you sure you want to suggest such things?"

Todd swallowed hard and wished for a drink. "She's the only one with that kind of power, isn't she? I mean, who else? Could it really be her?"

"No." Greg broke eye contact with Todd to focus on the table. "It can't be her."

"I suppose not." Todd sank deeper in his seat.

Greg shook his head. "She's been with the president for too many years. They grew up in politics together. She's too smart and hardworking. I can't imagine her betraying him or our country."

"Are you sure? It's not hard to fake a friendship." Todd leaned in and whispered. "I've never liked her; she's two-faced and can be cruel." Their one-on-one conversation before he started with the Nentraee came to mind, how she'd called Jerry by the wrong name. Pretended it was a mistake, but he saw her eyes... They were filled with nothing but malice.

Greg watched Todd.

"Didn't Mi'ko have to threaten her, and you, to ensure that I got my post with the Nentraee?" Todd asked. "That doesn't sound like someone who is easy to work with, no matter how well she knows the president."

"If it is her, then she's covered her tracks so well that we'll never be able to touch her. She would have to come out and tell the world, and even that wouldn't be enough to do anything. It's too risky. She's too powerful," Greg said.

Todd needed some water. "I appreciate you talking to me about this off the record." He felt like he was going to throw up. "I do, but Greg, what am I supposed to do with this information now? Specifically if it's someone that high up in the White House and the UN. Is there someone on the ship?"

Greg shrugged, returning to his wrap and taking a bite.

Todd ran a hand over his face. "You know I can't keep this quiet. I'm going to tell Vi-Narm and Mi'ko, at the very least." He covered his dislike of Vi-Narm by speaking in a neutral tone.

"That's why I'm telling you," Greg said. "I can't do anything here, and the..." He stopped. "Anyway, it's important that they know this may not be some outside group. It could be people from within, not only ours, but other governments and the UN, as well. I'm not sure who you can trust here."

"All right, I'll see what I can do." Todd exhaled. "Greg, is the president in danger?"

"Let me worry about that. I'll talk to you soon." Greg stood and tossed his meal in the trash. "Oh and, Todd, be careful. This isn't a game."

Sixteen: Who to Trust

TODD SAT IN the back of the pristine sedan, the soft leather forming to his body as people rushed around, turning the white snow to a muddy slush.

The meeting with Greg had scared him. If people in the government were willing to commit these acts of violence, then what else were they willing to do? Why not hire assassins and be done with it? What could keep them from launching nuclear weapons? He kept asking himself who to talk to, who to trust. Finally, he pulled out his cell phone and dialed.

"Hello," Brad said.

"Hey, Brad." Todd forced a smile, so it would reflect in his voice.

"Toddy, how goes it? Everything all right? You're not letting all this news get you down, are you?"

"Nah, I wanted to talk to you. I'm in DC, and I thought I would jump on a flight home." He kept his voice as pleasant as possible. "I thought we might meet up, or...something, tomorrow."

"Does someone miss their big brother?" Brad laughed. "It's only been a few weeks since Turkey Day." He paused. "Oh, wait. Am I finally off family probation?"

"Har-har. Look, dumbass. I'm not down here a lot these days, and I thought it would be nice. Plus, I like the weather on the West Coast better. This cold shit sucks, and I miss Bianca."

And there's not a chance of me getting killed in my own home.

"All right, all right. Don't get your jock in a knot. When will you be here—what time?"

"I need to check flights, but tomorrow, with any luck. I'll get a hotel room here for the night, and fly out."

"What? Can't you use the Nentraee's shuttle? Then you'll be here in a few hours, and we can go to dinner. And you get to sleep in your own bed...save you some money, or isn't that a worry anymore?"

Todd's shoulders dropped. He didn't want to deal with Vi-Narm and Mi'ko right now. Having to tell them what Greg said, it was too much. But Brad was right. It would be easier.

"I'll call you when I get to San Jose. Bye." He hung up, not waiting for a response.

I didn't think this out.

Todd looked out the window, watching the buildings slowly pass by. If he wanted to get home, he would need the shuttle, which meant having his babysitters with him the entire time. It was a safety precaution, one that Mi'ko had insisted upon and, much to his surprise, Vi-Narm as well. He was sure her reasons were different to Mi'ko's.

It was a short trip to the airport. Once on board the shuttle, he moved to the desk with the monitor and called Mi'ko.

"Hello, Todd." Mi'ko's warm face greeted him.

Todd spoke in Nentraee; he wanted to get some practice in. "I want...um...let you know I...um...heading to San Jose. I...um...be back on the ship tomorrow. I want to see my family and check in on my pet. I hope that not...um, problem."

"I don't see a problem with that," Mi'ko responded. "Your Nentraee is getting better."

"Thank you," Todd said. "Would it be possible to not have security tonight? I...dinner with family and I...not want to worry them."

"I'm sorry, Todd. We can't afford to lose you. I'm sure you're a target as well."

Why anyone would want to come after me boggles my mind.

"All right." He frowned at the thought of the guard sitting with him at dinner.

Mi'ko switched back to English. "Did you learn anything from your visit with Mister McNeil?"

"It would be better to talk about it in private tomorrow." Todd shifted to English as well. "I need time to process what he said."

"Of course," Mi'ko said. "It's always wise to reflect on information first. Enjoy your family."

The Nentraee government seal appeared on the screen.

Todd pulled out his cell phone, choosing not to use the monitor or his datapad—he preferred to use human technology; it made him feel closer to home—and texted his brother, letting him know he would be there in the evening. After the message was sent, he put all the electronic gadgets away and stared out the shuttle window, taking this time to relax and enjoy the view of the blue sky and the clouds.

What am I doing?

THE SHUTTLE TRIP was quiet, and Todd was grateful for the mental break. As he was ready to depart the craft, he turned to his security aide, BarMa Rus-Mor, who was short for a Nentraee, about five-foot-eight, and heavier too. He didn't think she was fat, but bigger, *probably all muscle.* Considering the other Martween Todd had seen, she was, by far, the most hard looking with her more angular facial features and her short, braided hair bun.

Todd cleared his throat and spoke in Nentraee. "Thank you for allow me time with my family."

BarMa bowed, the tight-braided bun unmoved. "Of course, Special Envoy, family is importantly." Her English was much better than his Nentraee.

"Thanks." He shrugged on his coat as the door to the shuttle opened. He walked out into the rain. "Sunny California," he mumbled to BarMa, who opened an umbrella for him as they quickly made their way to the waiting car.

At least, it's better than the bitter cold of DC.

I'm here, Todd texted Brad from inside the waiting car.

Really? Wow! I'll meet you at Lupita's around 5:30. Brad texted back.

Todd put his cell away and directed the driver to Lupita's. The rain came down in sheets.

They passed offices and apartments, almost all decorated for the holiday.

Is it really only mid-December?

The car pulled up to the Mexican restaurant that Brad and Todd had come to when they were younger, before all the family drama. It had also been a favorite location for him and Jerry. Seeing the one-story building with all the small shops, he realized he hadn't been here since before Jerry died and the Nentraee arrived. It was completely unchanged, with the flashing neon open sign and the fenced-off section for dining outside. It was comforting.

The rain pounded harder, and Todd raced for the door. Inside, he removed his coat as BarMa did a quick check of the space, datapad in hand. Todd walked past observing eyes to a table away from the windows but near enough to the exit should they have to leave in a hurry.

"I'll be at the bar, Special Envoy." BarMa pointed to the seat far enough away to give Todd privacy but close enough to her should she need to act.

Todd sighed and nodded.

I wish she could have stayed in the car. So much for going unnoticed.

They were playing a Mexican soap opera on the TV. Todd pulled out his pocket watch and ran his hand over the piece. *Home.* He checked the time.

A waitress brought over a menu, a basket of chips, and a bowl of salsa. He inhaled the smell of the freshly fried chips and the roasted garlic and tomatoes in the salsa.

This is home.

"Can I get a Coke and another menu, please?" he asked.

The door opened and Brad sloshed in, shaking off the rain. His hair was dripping, as was his jacket. He trudged up to the table and dumped his wet coat in the chair next to him.

"It's so good to see you." Todd stood and gave him a big hug.

"Good to see you, Toddy." Brad hugged him back. "Must be nice to be able to travel all over the world in a matter of hours, you spoiled brat."

Brad sat and asked for a beer.

"It does have its perks," Todd said.

It took them a few minutes to settle and review the menus.

"I don't know why I bother. I always get the same thing," Todd said.

Brad's beer arrived, and they both ordered.

"All right, so what's wrong?" Brad leaned in. "And no bullshit!"

"Nothing." Todd pursed his lips. "I missed home and seeing you guys. I didn't want to make a fuss about it. You know how it is." He took a chip and dipped it in the salsa.

"I call bullshit," Brad said. "You're avoiding something. I can tell. Not guy trouble, I hope. 'Cause I'm no good at that. Ask Lori. I'm nothing but a pain in her ass. And I'd like to get off family probation at some point." He chuckled.

"You're a pain in everyone's ass," Todd said. "And enough with the probation cracks already." He played with a chip, circling the bowl of salsa. "It's nothing like that. I'm just... " He ate the chip. "I'm just... Things are complicated and I'm feeling lost and I don't know what to do." He fiddled with his soda glass. "With Jerry gone, I don't have anyone to talk to. Dan and Kati are helpful, and I love them, but there are some things that they don't get. You know?" He sipped his soda.

"Not like working for that high-tech company of yours, is it?" Brad grabbed a couple chips and popped them in his mouth, followed by a pull off his beer.

"Trust me. You have no idea."

"No. Not at all," Brad teased. "First, the attempt on the vice speaker, and now this bullshit in London, where they almost got him again, but it was the speaker general or whatever they were after."

Todd's eyes narrowed on Brad.

"I couldn't possibly understand that kind of shit. Not like being under house arrest for days while our president figures out what the hell to do when the Nentraee first arrived."

Todd played with his food quietly as Brad spoke.

"Oh, stop. I understand," Brad said. "You're up to your eyes in all this political crap." He took another drink of his beer.

"It's not like that."

"Oh right, and the Nentraee woman at the bar is here to try the guacamole," Brad quipped. "I know. We'll order her some and see if she goes away." He wiggled his eyebrows.

"You're an ass."

"And you can't be that clueless, or in that deep denial. You're a big deal. I'm surprised they only have one security aide here." Brad took another sip of his beer.

Why do I even bother? This was a bad idea. I should have gone home and not said anything to anyone.

"Because, Todd, this is exactly what you needed and wanted," Jerry's voice said. "Why else would you call Brad? You realized he wouldn't pull any punches."

Todd peeked over to the table next to him, his heart feeling lighter. Jerry sat, holding a margarita and smiling at him. "Too bad I don't have a sombrero. I could be Dan." He raised his glass. "Now, cut the bull and talk to your brother. Oh, and get a margarita." He took a sip. "They're amazing."

Todd's face softened, and he glanced back at Brad. "It's been a difficult few days, and I'm not sure who to talk to. I thought it would be nice to come home and see a friendly face and sleep in my own bed." He cast a look where Jerry had been. "It all seems crazy to me."

"Duh. Of course it is, so get used to it."

The waitress brought over two plates, one with a wet burrito and the other filled with cheese enchiladas. She left them with a warning that the plates were hot.

"Listen, remember when I showed up on your doorstep?" Brad started. "I told you everything was going to change, and it has. For good or for bad, the world will never be the same again. Even if something happens and the Nentraee leave because of all the crazy shit down here. Whether you like it or not, you're part of it now." He shifted his plate so the small side salad was in front of him. "More so than any other human, including in our government. You have a voice and you need to accept that. You can't hide in your comfortable little world." He picked up his fork and took a bite of his burrito, then looked at Todd as he swallowed. "If that means you suck it up and do shit you don't like, then so be it. It's your responsibility now."

"Trust me. I've been dealing with it." Todd's voice was more harsh than it needed to be. He wasn't a kid anymore. He was a grown man, who had been through a lot, more than most people. "I'm worried—"

"Listen, Toddy, whatever is going on..." Brad waved his hand in front of Todd and bits of his chicken sauce flung off the fork, hitting the plate. "I don't need you to explain. Not because I don't care—I do—but because it wouldn't be appropriate. I'm sure it's secret or confidential or whatever."

There was so much Todd wished he could tell him, but he was thankful Brad didn't ask.

It's nice that he understands.

"Let me ask you this," Brad said between bites. "Whatever the problems are, are you doing everything in your power to fix them?"

Todd nodded.

"Are you trusting the people around you, who can help you the most?"

Todd frowned. He made a point of avoiding Vi-Narm unless he needed to talk to her.

"Maybe that's the place you need to start." Brad pointed his full fork at Todd.

"But I..." Todd stopped.

But I don't like her, and she hates me. Why would I want to put myself in that position?

"Why are you here, hiding?" Brad asked. "Spending the night at home locked away from the world isn't how you need to proceed." He took another bite of his dinner, then put the fork down, letting the words sit in the air while he chewed.

"Toddy, I... You're my little brother, and I was stupid for a long time, and during all that time, I knew the right thing to do. It ate at the back of my brain every day. But I didn't do it, because I was so caught up in my own head that—" He chuckled. "That I wasn't thinking." He leaned back in his chair. "Anyway, you, my little brother, you avoid things, bury them deep and hope they'll go away. And if they don't, you hang on to that grudge. But this problem isn't going to work that way, and you know it. Things are moving too fast to let it sit and fester."

Todd slowly ate and mulled over Brad's words. *I hate that he's right.* Finally, when too much time had passed without him saying anything, Brad focused on him harder.

"I suggest you finish dinner and you go back up there and do what you know is the right thing," Brad said. "Trust the people you know you can trust, and don't put your head in the sand or, worse, up your own ass."

"When did you get so smart?" Todd took a full bite of his enchilada.

"When did you get so dumb?" Brad took another hit off his beer.

BARMA OPENED THE door to the car as the rain stopped. Todd shrugged up the collar of his jacket and headed for the shuttle.

"Brad's right. You know what you have to do?" Jerry sat in one of the shuttle swivel chairs, watching Todd walk on board.

"Yes," Todd replied, not happy with what he had to do but knowing it was for the best.

"Good." Jerry turned around and around in the chair, then stopped and smiled at him. "Because, you two need to work together, and even if you don't tell her tonight, taking this step is important for the both of you."

"I know."

Why is this so damn hard?

"She's gonna respect you for it."

"Or blast me out an airlock." Todd leaned his head back, studying the roof of the shuttle. "I'm going mad, aren't I?"

"What?"

"Seeing you. You're dead, but here you are." Todd faced Jerry. "Don't get me wrong. I'm happy to see you, but I'm going insane. That's the only thing that explains this."

"You're not going insane."

Todd crossed his arms.

"Sweetie, talk to her. No more hiding." Jerry took his hand and kissed it. "Face this head-on and build that bridge."

Todd smiled. "Yes, dear."

Todd tapped a few things on his datapad and a holographic image of the speaker general's ship raised from the screen. He typed in where he was going upon arrival. The locations blinked on the image of the ship. He saved it and closed the file.

He turned to where Jerry had been and sighed. *Gone again.* He cleared the holographic ship, flipped through the screen, and pulled up Kati's contact.

"Hey, sexy buns." Kati grinned. "You're lucky you caught me. I was on my way out. Gots me an appointment for my toes and nails." She held up her hand and checked her nails. "What's up?"

"I just had dinner with Brad and I needed to talk," Todd said.

"What the hell?" She crossed her arms in front of her. "You're here and you didn't call me? You suck. You so owe me. I haven't seen you in forever." She pursed her lips.

"Sorry." He shrugged. "I think I'm losing my mind."

Kati laughed.

"It's not funny. I've..." He glanced at the empty seat where Jerry had been. "I've been seeing Jerry. It's nothing bad, but he appears."

I'm insane. At least BarMa is up flying the shuttle and not back here.

"He's been talking to me, keeping me from freaking out and helping me work through stuff."

Kati silently watched him, to the point were Todd was about to speak.

"You're not insane," Kati said.

"Really?"

"Listen, Todd, if you can ask the question and you understand he's dead and not real, then you're not going insane."

"I'm not so sure."

"It sounds like a *tennin* my *soba* used to tell me stories of when I was little."

"A what?"

"It's a Japanese angel, kind of. Anyway, maybe that's what you see. I don't think it makes you crazy."

"I don't know."

"God, Todd! You need to get laid. You're flipping unbelievable." Kati shook her head. "So, you see Jerry and you talk. You loved him, you were married, and the two of you were prepared to share your lives together. It's all normal. We all talk to people we've lost."

Todd was quiet.

"I loved Jerry, and I loved the two of you together. If he's helping you deal with stuff, great, but Todd..." She licked her lips. "You can't hide in his shadow. You need to move on and live your life. That's what he would want for you." Her face softened. "I, however, want a really expensive dinner, and if I miss my appointment, a full day at the spa."

"I'm not hiding."

"Good."

"You're sure I'm not nuts?"

Kati chuckled. "You're no more nuts than me or Dan."

"Great."

"I don't suppose you're around and want to get a drink? Your treat, of course. I could meet you after I get my beauty treatment."

"I would love to, but I'm heading back to the ship to *not hide*."

Kati nodded. "Fine. Whatever. You owe me."

"Thanks, Kati."

"Anytime, sugar bear," she said with a wave before the transmission ended.

Todd leaned back in his chair, closed his eyes, and rested. The hum of the shuttle filled his ears.

When they reached the speaker general's ship, Todd watched as other shuttles landed. It brought a smile to his face. As he stood up, his knees wobbled. He was tired. It had been a long day. But he had to go see her before he headed to his quarters. Before he lost his nerve.

Todd used his datapad as a map. Once he was there, he recognized the location. He pushed the panel on the side of her door and waited, then took a deep cleansing breath; he hated confrontation. It was late for a chat, but how much more could she hate him? Plus, they needed each other.

The familiar swish of the door caused him to straighten up as it revealed her standing there, watching him. Her usual scowl greeted him. She was dressed in a light-green free-flowing gown, not her usual business attire, and her hair was in a loose braid, cascading down her back.

"We weren't expecting you back until the morning," Vi-Narm said.

"I know. May I come in, please?" Todd asked.

She stepped clear of the door, giving him access.

Vi-Narm's more casual appearance surprised him. She didn't seem as hard and stiff as he expected. In fact, it gave her a more delicate air. It was a nice change.

Her quarters, too, were a bit of a surprise. They were much smaller than his, but she had a view of one of the ship's many gardens. The view of the gardens gave all their quarters the impression of space, giving them a more homey feel. He noted the dark colors on the walls were not unpleasing, and they somehow reflected her. Not that he understood her, but it seemed right.

There were a couple of objects mounted on the walls. One was the infinity circle, a religious artifact he recognized from his background information on their customs and cultures. Seeing her faith so clearly prominent in her quarters made him pause. Clearly there was more to her than he had ever tried to learn about.

He wasn't sure about the other object on the wall, whether it was a piece of art or some other artifact. It had several long rounded pieces, each in an ascending order by size, and there were straps holding them all together. Each cylinder was a different color with a metallic shine. Perhaps it reminded her of her home or a family she might no longer have.

Everything seemed neat and orderly, which didn't surprise him. On the coffee table were several books, both Nentraee and human.

"You may sit if you like." Vi-Narm's voice was crisp and slightly cold but polite.

He walked over and sat on the sofa. On one of the chairs, an open book had been flipped upside down to hold the page.

"My Ántonia," he said.

That's an odd choice.

She pursed her lips.

"I remember reading that in high school. It was one of my favorite books. I always found it to be a tragic love story of sorts, missed opportunities reminding us that there are no second chances in life."

She walked over, picked up the book, closed it, and put it on the coffee table with the others.

"What is it you need?" Her face remained hard.

He had practiced everything he wanted to say in the shuttle. But now, sitting here under her scowl, it was quickly slipping from his mind.

"Vi-Narm—" Todd's voice cracked. "I know you and I don't exactly see eye to eye. And...well, I suppose that I've done nothing to help the situation. Even now..."

I'm doing this all wrong.

His palms were damp, and he rubbed them on his pant legs.

The way she was standing there, her arms crossed in front of her—everything about her was closed off. He wasn't even sure she was listening, but he had to try. "But of everyone here on this ship, I know you most of all want to keep the Nentraee people and Mi'ko safe." He licked his lips. "To help him to the best of your ability. And...that is great. That is something I can...I um...respect. I can respect that.

But I can't make you trust me, and I can't change what has happened."

He forced himself to keep eye contact with her. He needed to show her strength. "I'm sorry you looked bad back during the first attack. That I made you look bad. That wasn't my intention. It really wasn't." He was feeling light-headed.

Breathe. I need to breathe and keep looking at her.

"I need you and your help because I honestly don't know who to trust back home." He leaned forward. "I promise you I don't have anything to do with what has happened. Whether you accept that or not is up to you, but for what it's worth, I offer you my word of honor that I'm not lying to you."

She was a statue.

"You may not trust me." He stood. "You may not even like me. Trust, like friendship, is earned, not awarded. Seeing you here now, in your quarters, I see there are a lot of things I don't know about you. I never bothered to learn. I'm sorry. I never took the time to get to know you, but I need to." His head dropped and his shoulders followed. "Perhaps, that has led us to where we are now. Tomorrow, when we talk with the vice speaker, I'm going to need your help. Or at some point. I don't know. But...sorry." He stopped meeting her eyes and went to the door.

Say something. Say anything.

Vi-Narm said nothing, continuing to watch him.

Todd didn't move.

"I will reflect on your words," she finally said.

Todd bowed. He could feel Vi-Narm's eyes on him as he stepped through the door. He waited for it to close and let out a sigh of relief. He had done what he came to do.

I need her as a friend. We're all going to need each other to deal with the Liberi Dei.

Seventeen: Tolerance

"THANK YOU, TODD." Mi'ko leaned back in his office chair as Todd finished the overview of his conversation with Greg.

Mi'ko faced Vi-Narm and Mi'cin. They were both quiet. Vi-Narm sat motionless, and Mi'cin tapped a finger on the side of his face. Both seemed distracted and offered no additional remarks.

"It was as we feared." Mi'ko waited no longer for comment. "We have much to figure out. Continue to see what you can learn from Mister McNeil. If it is helpful, provide him with whatever additional information we have. Here is my clearance." Mi'ko swiped his clearance information to Todd.

"You got it," Todd replied. "I'll do my best." He stood and bowed. "I'll be in my office if you need me."

"Unless there is anything else?" Mi'cin stood, focused on his father.

Mi'ko shook his head.

Mi'cin offered a bow and headed to the door.

Mi'ko's lips pinched together as he tried not to give away his thoughts.

I hope he's going to talk to Todd about tonight. Perhaps I should have offered to speak to Todd for him.

Vi-Narm waited for Todd and Mi'cin to leave. Mi'ko noticed her disapproving frown. "Do you have anything more?"

"He confirmed what we have suspected," Vi-Narm said. "There was nothing new, but I suppose it will be helpful."

"I hope so." Mi'ko glanced back at the reports on the two attacks as they populated his device. He grew more and more disappointed with recent human events. There was such great potential on Earth if they all worked for the greater good. However, these problems caused by Liberi Dei stopped them from moving forward and offered support to the doubters in both the Speaker's House and the House of the People.

"Will we stay here or try to go elsewhere?" Vi-Narm's tone was cautious.

"Where? How?" Mi'ko put down his datapad. "Our ships are old. The years in space have not been easy on them. The Speaker's House has been meeting over this matter, and the consensus is that we stay. Even General Gahumed agrees, which is a small miracle." He sighed. "Even with all the repairs we've been making in orbit, we can't wander space indefinitely."

"We've suffered two attacks by that group," Vi-Narm said. "We've not responded with force, even though we could. We've allowed the humans to lead the investigation, instead of searching out these barbarians ourselves and getting retribution."

"We don't know who's involved." Mi'ko huffed. "We haven't tracked down the leaders. We can't punish an entire planet."

"Our numbers are so limited. Can we afford to stay here and risk extinction by these beings?"

"Mirtoff has been working within the confines of their United Nations for solutions and options." Mi'ko pinched the bridge of his nose. "They are getting close to a deal. One that will help us and keep our people safe. It won't be easy, but considering the alternative...we must try."

She's worried. I'm worried. Mirtoff's worried. Our civilization is at stake. We have to be more vigilant. But the humans have to see us among them. Change how they view us, not as monsters or outsiders but as equal beings. There has to be a way.

"Todd came to my apartment last night." Vi-Narm's words pulled him from his thoughts.

The bringer of peace is never an easy step to take. I wish it had been her.

"And yet he lives." Mi'ko bit back his smile. "What did he have to say?" He rested back in his chair, feeling for the tieback in his hair.

"He trusts me. Wants to mend our relationship."

"Sounds promising."

"He gave his word of honor that he has nothing to do with any of these attacks."

"And you don't believe him?"

"I'm unsure." She paused. "However, he could not do this on his own, so perhaps I've misjudged him."

Mi'ko's smile broadened.

"He showed a level of courage by coming to me." Vi-Narm's tone held begrudging gratitude. "He also said he respects me. All pretty words, but I don't judge him to be lying." She crossed her legs. "It took a lot of strength for him to come to me and speak as he did. Males are not known to share respect and fear so freely, especially Todd. He prefers to avoid it, much like a coward."

A weight lifted off Mi'ko's shoulders. "I'm glad it went well." He noted the thinning around her eyes as she licked her lips. "What are you thinking about?"

"Many things, Vice Speaker." She let the silence fill the room. "I'm worried."

"How so?"

"He is becoming too familiar with your son, and it is possible he is still involved with the attackers *unknowingly*, which puts you and Mi'cin at risk. I can't deny that he was correct about what happened in London and that his connection with Mister McNeil has proven beneficial to us."

These were things Mi'ko had considered himself, but unlike her, he had faith in Todd. And his son, for that matter. "I wonder if it is possible that Todd may feel the same way. As if he's being used or manipulated. You should talk to him."

Her head snapped in his direction.

"Perhaps arrange a private conversation for the two of you. He reached out to you. Now you should return the kindness," Mi'ko said.

"It...may be worth the effort, see what more I can learn." Vi-Narm nodded.

"Did he say anything else in your conversation last night?"

"He was surprised to see me reading a book he read back in school. He said it was one of his favorites."

"That sounds like an additional connection. It may help build up your relationship."

She stood from the small conference table. "As to the other matter with your son—"

"Mi'cin is of *Emisaration*." Mi'ko watched her clench her fists. "Who he chooses to spend time with is not my concern."

"You're his father. Of course, it's your concern. Raising him correctly is your—"

Mi'ko waved off the rest of her comments.

"I'm proud of how I raised my sons, as is Laina, or I'm sure she would have taken away my Rights of Fatherhood long ago." He appreciated her concern, but when it came to his children, Laina and he would intervene when needed. Vi-Narm had no business offering him advice. No matter how long they had known each other. Plus, he liked Todd. "I trust their choices, as does Laina. I don't see any harm in them having a friendship. It's good for the two of them and our people."

"Is it friendship? Are you sure?"

He inhaled deeply. She was moving close to a boat she should not dare take. He respected her a great deal, but this was a family matter, and he would not allow this female, or any female, to undermine Laina's authority.

"That is none of your concern."

She bowed. "Of course not, but he's human."

"And a good male. An intelligent male." Mi'ko put all his focus on her. "I've witnessed worse among our own people. Or need I remind you of some of your former potential mates? If Mi'cin and Todd choose each other, then I count myself lucky." The tips of her ears started to turn blue and enlarge as she took a small step back.

"I only worry about what kind of message this will send to our people," she finally said with a small bow.

"One of continued tolerance. Mutual trust and respect, something both Nentraee and humans have in short supply these days." Mi'ko's words hung gently in the air.

She bowed.

"Thank you, Vi-Narm, for your concern and your continued support of this office, even when we don't always agree." He turned back to the blank screen of the datapad, ending the conversation. Once the door closed, he put down the device.

"A Nentraee-and-human relationship might be what our two people need to break down the barriers," he muttered as he tapped his fingers on the table.

And Mi'cin could do much worse than Todd and, in fact, has.

TODD HEADED DOWN the hall back to his office, exhausted. His body wasn't sure what time it was after being both on the East Coast and the West Coast over the course of a few hours. He was finding it especially challenging to concentrate. Glad his meeting was over, he wanted to go back to his office and focus on his visitor reports and updates.

"Todd." Mi'cin caught up to him.

"What's up?" Todd stopped by one of the large windows that had a view of the ship's central business district. Somehow Mi'cin seemed different today. He kept tapping his hands on the sides of his legs and seemed to look everywhere but at Todd. Todd leaned against the wall.

Mi'cin shifted on his feet and checked up and down the corridor. "I was curious if you would be interested in having a meal together again?"

"Sure." Todd tried to focus, but his brain demanded sleep. Still, he didn't want to be rude. "What did you have in mind?"

"Something different. Are you open tonight?" Mi'cin's brilliant green eyes narrowed in on Todd's face.

Todd wanted a quiet night in his quarters, with his feet up and sweats on, watching a movie or maybe checking on the game boards. Dinner with Mi'cin, however pleasant, would be better tomorrow, when he was fresh.

"How about tomorrow night? If you don't mind, I want to relax tonight. I didn't sleep well last night and I'm exhausted."

Mi'cin took several long seconds to respond. "All right. That'll be fine." His hands stopped tapping his legs.

"I need to head back to my office and go through these reports from the Speaker's House and the House of the People." Todd peeled himself off the wall. "I'll talk to you later."

"Yes." Mi'cin stiffened up his shoulders. "I need to follow up on the damage analysis from the shuttle." He turned on his heel and headed off in the opposite direction.

Mi'cin was so dedicated to his position and the Speaker's House. He was truly a brilliant man. That aside, Todd couldn't help but appreciate the way Mi'cin filled out his trousers, particularly from this angle.

Wish I looked that good.

The door to Todd's office opened as he approached. The lights brightened automatically to his preferred setting, which had taken him two weeks to figure out.

His office was more settled now. He'd spent time unpacking his "office box" and putting up a few of his knickknacks. Trying to explain a replica Star Trek Phaser to the Nentraee had not been easy. They couldn't understand why he kept an antiquated nonoperational weapon that lit up and made noise. Finally, he gave up and told them that it was a toy that was given to him. That ended the questions.

Todd pulled out his timepiece and set it on the desk. He sat heavily, not bothering to remove his suit jacket and downloaded the reports from his meeting with Greg and the information on human visitors to his desktop.

"He likes you," Jerry said. He was playing with the phaser.

"He's a nice guy."

Jerry put down the phaser and peeked out at Earth. "This view. I'm so jealous." He pulled himself away from the window. "He asked you out, and you blew him off."

Todd wanted to focus on his work but was unable to. "I'm tired. I don't want to be sitting there and suddenly nod off. Plus, he's just a friend."

Even if I check out his ass. I'm not blind.

"It may have started out as friends, but he crossed that line a long time ago. You didn't see it." Jerry turned back from the window. "That's why he looks at you the way he does and why he acted the way he did when Vi-Narm was cross with you. He's being protective, and it's sweet."

"I doubt it."

Why would he be interested in me?

"Come on." Jerry laughed. "Where is your self-esteem? There is nothing wrong with someone finding you attractive. Even him. God knows I fell for you the minute I saw you."

"You always did have problems with your eyes." Todd wanted to reach out to him, but Jerry wasn't there. He liked the illusion and didn't want to mess it up. "You're the only one for me. Plus, I doubt he even likes men."

"You're an idiot. These beings aren't anything like us. I'm sure, to them, gay, straight, bi, or whatever doesn't matter." His smile grew wider. "Look at Vi-Narm. She's a total Princess Leia lesbian if I've ever seen one."

Todd laughed.

Jerry sat on the end of Todd's desk. "We're not in some religious land of denial. Sweetheart, I'm dead, and I'm not coming back. It's been five months. You're alive and you're going to be alive for a long time. I don't want you to be alone. I want you to be happy and take advantage of everything the universe sends your way."

"Don't say that." Todd glanced down to his desk. "I'm not alone. I have friends. My family and work. Our cat. Well, Bianca's back on Earth, but she's still there kind of. I'm even spending Christmas with my folks and brother and his family."

"That isn't living, Todd, and you know it." Jerry crossed his arms. "You're hiding."

Todd shrugged.

"Listen, I never wanted you to pine away for me after I died," Jerry said. "I wanted you to go on and live and be happy. Nothing would please me more than if you met someone nice and started to date." He lifted Todd's chin with his hand. "Mi'cin is nice. And we both know you think he has a great butt. You've stared at it enough."

It was so hard for Todd to hear Jerry and have him this close. It hurt.

"I think you like him, too, and that's okay. Really, it is. Please don't worry about me."

Todd swallowed hard and gazed at Jerry's face.

The door chirped.

"Come in." Todd wiped at his eyes quickly.

The door swished open, and Danu stood there, datapad in hand. "I have the updated damage figures and human casualties from the London attack. I thought we might review it."

Todd nodded, forcing a smile as he spoke. "Thank you, Danu. I appreciate it."

"IS EVERYTHING SET for Mi'cin and Todd tonight?" Mirtoff smiled the moment her office door shut and Mi'ko stepped in.

"I believe Mi'cin is speaking to Todd now."

"Excellent. Are you sure you shouldn't have talked to Todd about it first, considering how important this is to Mi'cin?"

"I don't believe so. Mi'cin said he would ask." Mi'ko bowed. "Thank you again for your support."

"Of course. I hope it goes well for him. Humans are quite strange on these matters." Mirtoff called up the reports on the various scientific and engineering contracts they had been working on. "Now, how are the negotiations going?"

"Surprisingly well." Mi'ko sat, the tie in his hair lopsided as ever. "Boeing, Space X, Bigelow Aerospace, and Airbus are eager for their engineers to work on our propulsion technology. You know, it's odd. They moved so quickly with vast improvements in flight and aerospace, and then they stopped and stagnated. They even had civilian airships that traveled faster than the speed of sound, but they stopped them." His face was a mix of excitement and confusion. "A shame."

"I suppose it happens with a great many things," Mirtoff said. "I can't say what motivates them. Since the last attack, many of them are more willing to work with us, to show that they're not like this group of terrorists. Even their governments seem easier to work with."

Mi'ko crossed one leg over the other. "Even with the tighter security, the human scientists and engineers continue coming in large numbers, spending time with our engineers and studying the larger applications for the drive technology with great enthusiasm."

"Whatever it takes to foster good relations." Mirtoff viewed the updated reports. "Including opening up more of the ships for the general human population to come and visit. We suffered greatly from being so guarded, two attacks on our people and for what?" She didn't wait for Mi'ko to respond. "Because we've been too closed off. This has to stop."

Mi'ko nodded.

Making us less mysterious is key. We need to do more of this if we're going to be able to work and live together.

"How goes the latest work on the colonization proposal?" Mi'ko asked.

Mirtoff leaned back in her chair. "With the current proposal from the UN, I think it'll provide the barrier we need until we build a much stronger relationship."

It's a shame, really. I had hoped for so much more, but we had too many missteps and now this is our best hope.

"That is the current hope." Mi'ko sighed. "Giving us and them a neutral zone of sorts?"

Mirtoff's gaze narrowed on Mi'ko. She was confused by the reference.

"Todd is fond of an entertainment genre called science fiction, and in one particular series, they refer to a neutral zone," Mi'ko explained. "It keeps the humans and their allies buffered from this other species to ensure that they don't go to war again. It's an interesting concept."

Mirtoff wasn't fully understanding, especially since they weren't at war with the humans. "Let us hope it never comes to that." She pulled up the list of trade items to review. "Considering events, are there any concerns with the technologies we're willing to sell and trade with?"

"General Gahumed has reviewed all the items and is content." Mi'ko rested his hands on her desk. "We are trading technology already deemed possible in theory by the humans. Such as our drive systems and our gravitational fields. We're only giving them the application to make them work, to fill in some of their missing pieces."

"Then you're pleased with the trade deals?" she asked. There were some in the Speaker's House and the House of the People that felt they should go slower with trading technology with the humans. They had valid concerns. However, she needed the humans to trust them and want to work with them, and this was the best approach.

"I wouldn't recommend them if I wasn't. Anything we give them can have military applications, but that can't be helped. It's a risk we're willing to take."

"I'm pleased General Gahumed supports this," Mirtoff said.

Mi'ko nodded.

"She appears to be impressed with Todd," Mirtoff said. "The way he handled himself during the attack in London made an impact."

"I've noticed that as well."

"Let us hope that remains the case." Mirtoff quickly checked the provided trade contracts from Mi'ko for her approval. She turned to face him. "I don't know why I bother checking your work, Mister Vice Speaker."

"Thank you, Madam Speaker."

She put down the datapad, picked up her cup of tuma, and took a deep swallow, savoring the spicy-sweet taste. She had been weighing her thoughts for a long time on what she was about to say.

"Do you remember when we first got here?"

"Of course. It was a turning point for all our people."

"And yet not all our people have seen that," Mirtoff said. "Because of the first attack and our customs, we've kept our people away. Protected. Limiting their contact with the humans. Giving them time to adapt and learn, and for our people, it has gone well. But for the humans..."

Mi'ko frowned.

"We need to expand our policies on human contact. Allow more of our people to go to Earth. We must encourage more humans to come here to our ships, all our ships, not just the cultural ones. To interact with our people to see how we live and work, much like we experience with Mister Landon."

"If that is the course you wish to take, that is your right." Mi'ko made several notes on his device.

"They need to understand that we are like them. We talked about our cultural celebration and sharing them with the humans. I want that to happen." Mi'ko nodded as Mirtoff continued. "We'll, of course, take the needed steps to protect our people and theirs, but I want to encourage friendships and mutual cooperation. Like Todd and Mi'cin. I want more of that."

"That may be a challenge. Not everyone is as open—"

"I want our people to go to Earth to experience their world and their culture. I want the humans to witness us on their planet, not on television or in crowds at a protected distance. Ask Todd to work on this. The humans are coming here, but I want our people to go there, tour their world, see what makes the humans a unique and interesting people."

"Do you think this is wise, considering the recent attack? And what about these Liberi Dei?" Mi'ko frowned at the name.

"We face risks every day, and if we show the humans how similar we are, then these Liberi Dei will be weakened. Especially as the humans realize we're all equals." She picked up her tuma and sipped. "This is long overdue. I'm troubled by my conversation with the human driver after my first speech at the UN. They don't trust us, and now some of them fear us. We have to change and I can't think of another way."

"I'll speak with Todd." Mi'ko stood and bowed. "Have a peaceful rest, Madam Speaker."

"And you, my friend." Mirtoff rolled her cup of tuma in her hands as the door closed behind Mi'ko. "We can do this. We need to do this," she mumbled, then finished off her tuma.

Eighteen: The Sky's the Limit

"I'M NOT SURE what we need to do," Todd said. Mi'ko had just explained Mirtoff's idea about encouraging more of the Nentraee people to travel in groups to various places on Earth. In theory, it didn't sound too hard to do, but he had learned nothing was ever easy. Bureaucracy and logistics were beasts not easily tamed.

Mi'ko had come to Todd's office first thing. Todd had overslept and rushed so as not to be late.

"I have a friend in the travel industry. He worked mostly in Europe, but had to travel all over the world," Todd said. "I can talk to him. Invite him to the ship. I can show him around, introduce him to your culture, and we can put together a proposal. Your people will need some kind of passport and possibly travel visas."

"We've already worked out the details for our people's travel documentation to coincide with what is required by a majority of your world's countries."

"If I may, Mister Vice Speaker? I'm confused." Todd leaned forward in his chair. "What about security concerns and making sure we keep the Nentraee people out of harm's way? Plus, I thought your people wanted more time to understand us?"

"Security is the important issue," Mi'ko replied. "But we need your people to see us. Isolation was a miscalculation."

"And you figure now, with everything happening, it's the right time?"

"We do not want to give the impression to those people causing harm that we intend to leave or hide." Mi'ko's voice was determined. "But mostly we want your people to see we are the same as you, and we can't do that if we don't let our people go to Earth."

"Let me talk to Dan and put together a plan," Todd said. "He's been itching to come to the ship anyway. That won't be a problem, will it?" He opened up a link on his datapad and pulled up Dan's contact information so he could get it sent to security.

"Of course not. You can make arrangements for him to stay in temporary guest quarters, or he can stay with you." Mi'ko's datapad chirped, and he checked it. "I need to go meet with the full Speaker's House. Please inform Vi-Narm, and she will work out the security details."

"I'll do that. Thank you, Mister Vice Speaker." Todd sent the files and information on Dan to Vi-Narm.

Mi'ko tightened the bow tying his hair back. The poor guy always seemed to have issues with it, unlike most of the other Nentraee males he had met. It might be a nice idea to find him a hair tie that would be easy to use, like a clip-on.

Todd stood.

"I understand you and Mi'cin will be having dinner tonight?" Mi'ko fussed with the bow.

"Yes." Todd's heart beat faster, both out of nerves for the dinner and having this conversation with Mi'ko. "We had dinner some time ago." He responded in Nentraee. "He took pity on me when I was in the ship's gardens. I guess he figured I needed a friend."

Mi'ko took a deep breath and a slight scowl crossed his lips.

Todd hesitated. Had he misspoke? He changed back to English. "I'm sorry. Did I missspeak? I thought I used all the correct words."

"Your Nentraee is fine," Mi'ko said.

"Oh, well...um...if you would prefer I don't go, Mister Vice Speaker, that's okay. I'm sure he was being nice. I don't want our socializing to cause any trouble for you or your family."

"The speaker general wants to encourage more friendships among our two people." Mi'ko's voice was much more crisp as he spoke. "She views the friendship between you and Mi'cin as an example of how we can all get past our differences in appearance and culture."

Not since Todd had first met him had he seen Mi'ko's body this stiff. His shoulders were straight, and his posture was impossibly perfect. Todd's heart pounded in his chest.

Am I being hypersensitive?

"You don't approve." Todd deflated. He was looking forward to the dinner. Now, possibly, he would need to cancel.

"I had expected and hoped for something different," Mi'ko replied. "See what help your friend can be and keep me informed. We want to start encouraging more of our people to experience Earth and her people as soon as they can." He bowed. "Enjoy your dinner with *my son*." He walked out of Todd's office.

Todd gulped as the door slid closed.

I should call Mi'cin. Perhaps cancel dinner. I don't want to offend anyone, chiefly Mi'ko. This is silly, especially with how important this idea of building friendships between the Nentraee and the humans was. Mi'ko did tell me to enjoy the dinner.

"Stop," Todd mumbled.

I'm reading way too much into this. There is a lot about their family dynamics I don't understand. Maybe that's it.

Todd sat, tapped a few buttons, and waited for the line to be picked up. "Hello, Dan."

"Oh, hey there." Dan waved on the screen. "What can I do you for?"

"Believe it or not, I need your help."

"Oh, dear." Dan's hand covered his mouth. "Tell me, please. Dear God, you're not trying to wear spandex workout shorts again? I've told you that it's a bad look for you. Well, for anyone, except for me, of course." He shook his head. "Honey, you know you don't fill them out in the places that count."

"Ass!" Todd laughed. "No, you sick queen. And for the record, I've never gotten a single complaint about how I fill out a pair of shorts. Thank you." He gave Dan a firm nod. "God, you're a mess."

"Says you. I'm fabulous."

"Anyway, listen, Dan. The Nentraee want to bring more of their people down to Earth. You know, to explore and experience our culture and our world. I told Mi'ko that you would be willing to help."

"Cool."

"Dan, they want to move on this quickly. So, I'd like you to come up to the ship to meet and talk. I want to put together some kind of plan and proposal. Are you interested?"

There was silence, and Dan's expression didn't change much. "Are you kidding? Of course, I'm interested." Dan bounced up and down, grinning at the screen. "I get to come up there and work on alien travel. Oh, honey, this is what the doctor ordered. I can be ready for beam up by tomorrow morning." He fussed with his hair. "I would've said today, but I need time to pack and get a facial, a haircut, and if there's time, a pedi and mani."

"They don't beam people up."

"Right!" Dan raised an eyebrow at Todd. "Then how do you explain that rescue of the prime ministers? They magically appeared in the shuttle? Chica, please. They beam you up. I know they do."

Todd ignored his remarks and continued. "I've scheduled a car and driver to meet you at the house tomorrow morning. We can meet as soon as you get here. Bring your passport too."

"Seriously? You're sending a car and a driver. Wow. And why do I need my passport? I'm going into space, not to Mexico."

"Come on, of course you need it. It's like traveling to another country. This is their home, and they have rules."

"Gotcha. Passport, check. I should pack my speedo. God, I hope they have a pool, where I can lay out and show all this sexiness off." Dan pulled back in his chair and ran his hands down the sides of his chest.

Todd rolled his eyes.

"So, what else is happening up there, Mister Man who comes to San Jo for dinner, then bails on me and Kati?" The frown on Dan's face was a complete contradiction of his sexy pose.

"Sorry about all that. It's been crazy, and of course, there is all this drama going on. You have no idea what it's like dealing with government officials and bureaucracies day in and day out."

Dan crossed his arms and huffed.

"Honestly, I don't understand how people get anything done," Todd said. "It drives me nuts."

"I know, hon. Anything I can do?"

"Well, I do have a question. It's probably stupid."

"Oh dish. Gotta love it. Who is he?" Dan squealed and clapped his hands together.

"Messy-ass queen," Todd said. "So, Mi'cin asked me to dinner tonight, and I'm not sure if it's a date. Kind of like the dinner we had right before the London attack. Then Mi'ko seemed strange when he asked me about it today, and I'm not sure what to think. Maybe, I should cancel or postpone it? Change it to a lunch? Am I overthinking it?" He shrugged.

"Hell no!" Dan said. "Don't you dare cancel. That fine slab of spaceman meat asked you to dinner, not once, but twice. Oh, honey, you better jump on that. He's fine with a capital F-I-N-E. And that amazing butt of his—I bet you can bounce quarters off it. Now listen, chica, I did some checking on the government webpage about them, and biologically, their naughty bits and ours are the same...so yum-and-ee. I want all the details."

"Of course, you did. Anyway, he probably didn't mean it to be a date."

"Listen." Dan's voice became serious and softer. "I don't care if it's a date or not. That boy is fine. Go out. Enjoy. It's dinner. It's not like it'll cause the world to blow up. If that's all it takes, then we're in a world of hurt. It'll be fun. Don't be a wimp. You need it."

"And what about Mi'ko?"

"What about him? Is he going to be there?"

Todd shook his head.

"Then don't you worry about him." Dan picked at his fingernails, shaking his head. "Man, I need a mani. Anyway, he knew about Jerry, and he knows you. If he has a problem with it, then that's his issue and he'll have to learn to deal with it. Hon, this is a whole new world. The sky's no longer the limit. Don't you forget that."

"He's my boss and the vice speaker, and I don't want to cause any trouble," Todd said. "Truthfully, this is all ridiculous. He's being nice. Especially since he's finally seen how Vi-Narm treats me." He sighed. "Which, by the way, that's why I didn't stay home after dinner with Brad. I wanted to get back up here and talk to her. I'm pretty sure it went well."

"Okay, hold up." Dan held his hand to the screen. "First off, if he's your friend, then don't worry about it. It's all good. At the very worst, you get to sit across from him and those brilliant green eyes. Second, if he goes out of his way to check in on you, then you definitely need to try and tap that. Third, who cares what the nasty-ass evil alien has to say?"

"Dan!" Todd glared at him.

"Whatever. Stop being so PC. It's you and me, and you know what I mean." Dan crossed his arms in front of his chest. "Anyway, I suppose as long as you're the bigger person and you talked to her and cleared the air, then good for you." His lips pursed. "The most important thing—and I can't stress this enough—is that you still owe Kati and I."

Todd laughed.

"I'm serious, bitch," Dan said.

"Fine, fine." Todd chuckled. "Vi-Narm's a tough nut to crack, but I'm working on it." He leaned back on his chair. "He really does have nice eyes." He sighed. "They are so green. I swear, sometimes, it's like Mi'cin's drilling into my soul with those eyes when he looks at me."

"Mmm, he has 'nice' lots of things," Dan said, "and being 'drilled' by that is not such a bad thing."

"You're such a ho." Todd grinned. "All right, I'm done worrying about it. Dinner it is, but there won't be any drilling..."

"Attaboy. Have some fun, perhaps a close encounter of the sexy kind." Dan beamed.

"And on that note, I'll talk to you tomorrow." Todd waved. "You might be here for a few days, so make sure Kati can watch Bianca and please remember to dress appropriately."

"Oh, I know just the thing. I own this glitter halter top that will go perfect with my shorty shorts."

"Goodbye, Dan." Todd ended the call.

It was insanity, but he was happy that Dan was coming to the ship. It would be good to have his positive energy around. He should take Dan to that café where he and Mi'cin went. The colo co mo was good, and he thought Dan might enjoy it.

Nineteen: Earth, Moon, and Stars

TODD SPENT THE rest of the afternoon running around from various meetings and going over Nentraee population statistics, potential cost analysis, and Nentraee cultural information for his meeting with Dan. He also needed to ensure he forwarded everything to Vi-Narm. To his surprise, she responded quickly. She assured him everything would be set for Dan's arrival and thanked him for the information.

It was the first time that she had actually thanked him, and it felt good.

While working, he tried not to focus on his upcoming dinner with Mi'cin. Chance was not on his side. Todd and Mi'cin encountered each other several times during the afternoon in the corridor as they both finished out their workday. He didn't know what Mi'cin thought, and during work was not the time to talk about personal matters. To call it awkward was an understatement.

Todd was wrapping up the last of his reports when a chirp came from the door. "Come in."

The door swished open, and he caught sight of Vi-Narm. The hard lines of her work clothes kept her posture perfect. He tapped his datapad, closing out the files, and gave her his full attention.

"Vi-Narm! Welcome. What can I help you with? Please have a seat."

She bowed and sat directly across the desk from him.

She didn't speak, only stared at him.

This was odd. She rarely came to his office and never sat. Well, not unless they had a scheduled meeting. He was starting to worry. "What happened? There hasn't been another attack, has there?" He spoke in English to make sure there was no additional confusion on his part.

Vi-Narm's face relaxed. "No, Todd, nothing like that." She inhaled deeply. "After spending some time thinking about our conversation in my quarters, I wanted to thank you for coming to see me." Her gaze remained focused on his. "I appreciate the effort and did not want to let too much time pass before I acknowledged it."

Holy shit! Did Hell freeze over?

Todd bowed, trying to hide his smile. "You're welcome."

"I shall let you get back to work." She stood, then bowed. "Thank you for sending me the information on your friend's visit to the ship. I understand he is to assist you with planning tours for our people to go to Earth." Her posture was stiff, but her face had softened somehow. "I look forward to meeting him, and I shall ensure that there are no problems with his entry to the ship."

She's being incredibly pleasant. What's wrong with her? Why is she acting this way?

"Thank you."

"Will you be meeting him at the docking station, or should I provide him an escort to your office?"

"I thought it would be best for me to meet him there. This ship is huge and can be intimidating, particularly when you first get here. Plus, I'd like to show him around." He huffed out a breath of air, smiling. "I remember my first day here. I walked around in a complete haze."

"Very good. Are there going to be any accommodations needed?" Vi-Narm asked.

"No, thank you. Dan will be staying with me in my quarters."

She bowed.

Todd was further amazed.

"You know, you don't have to do any of that." Todd wanted to make sure she saw how much he appreciated all this.

"I'm aware," she said. Her tone was tight, and Todd realized she wanted to be helpful and friendly with him.

"Of course, thank you." This time, Todd bowed. When he straightened up, she wore an almost pleased expression. "How are you enjoying the book?"

Vi-Narm was quiet, and her jaw worked back and forth. "I am finding it interesting. Maybe once I am finished, we can talk about it. I have questions about some of the use of language and cultural references. I do not fully understand. Perhaps, we can meet for a cup of tuma or warm e'xin, if you prefer."

Yay! I actually got through to her, at least a little. There is no way I'm going to screw this up. I need her as an ally, if not a friend.

"I'd like that."

She stepped out into the hall without another word. When the door closed behind her, he dropped into his office chair, grinning.

TODD WANTED TO shower and shave before dinner. He'd gotten used to no longer having the goatee and thought he appeared younger without the facial hair. It was a plus. Not that thirty was old. At least he would fit in with the Nentraee males. And he wasn't comfortable growing out his hair, especially with how unruly it could be. Not even a hair scrunchie could keep it under control.

Todd found that he enjoyed the idea of dinner more when he imagined it as a date. Even if it wasn't, the thought was fun. He hadn't been on a date since he and Jerry had started going out, and that had been almost nine years ago.

Together with Jerry for nine years, and it seemed like it was only yesterday that I was getting ready for my first dinner out with him. Am I ready for this?

Walking into his living room, Todd rolled up the sleeves of his shirt. He had no intention of wearing a suit and tie, not for this. Even though the Nentraee occasionally wore formal dress, he wanted to be comfortable. He dusted off the front of his shirt, giving himself a final nod.

This is as good as it's going to get.

His apartment door chimed, and he pulled out the pocket watch Varick gave him. "Right on time."

He took a deep breath, headed to the door, and tapped the entry button. *No backing out now.* The door swished open.

Wow.

Mi'cin was dressed in what Todd had come to call Nentraee casual wear. Less formal form-fitting tan dress pants and a light-green, long-sleeve shirt that complemented his deep-tan coloring and soft-brown hair. His hair was back in a perfect tie that matched his pants. The top two buttons on Mi'cin's shirt were open, revealing hints of what was sure to be an amazing chest.

How is it possible for anyone, of any species, to look this amazing in clothes? It's like he has an entire hair and wardrobe team.

"Hello, Todd." The musicality in his speech and voice filled Todd's ears. It was one of the things he adored about their language.

"Greetings," Todd said. "Do you wish to come in for a minute? Or do we need to go?"

Mi'cin grinned and bowed. "We can sit if you'd like, or we can go. We have plenty of time." He scanned over Todd. "You look very comfortable tonight."

"Um...thank you." Todd stepped to the side.

"What I mean is you look very nice." Mi'cin walked into Todd's quarters and looked around. "Your quarters are becoming much more like your home. They look peaceful."

"I figured I should make it—" Todd stopped. He didn't know the Nentraee word for what he wanted to say. "Um...homelike." He switched back to English. "Sorry, I don't know the right way to say that in Nentraee." He took a breath, finding himself suddenly nervous. His practicing of the Nentraee language had kept his mind busy; now it was lost on him. "Would you like something to drink? I have some white wine, soda, or water. I don't have any tuma or e'xin. Sorry."

"No, thank you." Mi'cin chuckled. "It's entertaining to me when you're so nervous or unsure what to say or do that you become a waiter, like at Thanksgiving," he said in English. "Is that normal for everyone, or is it just you?"

"I...well, I've never thought of it that way," Todd replied. "Yes, I'm a little nervous, but my mother raised me to be a gracious host."

I haven't had a first date in nine years, and back then we met for dinner. Jerry didn't come to pick me up like this. Ugh...Jerry. I shouldn't...

"I wasn't trying to insult you. I am sorry," Mi'cin said. "All Nentraee children are raised in a strict manner. My mother could be particularly harsh if we misbehaved or acted inappropriately." He chuckled and rubbed his cheek. "My brothers and I often believed you could see the imprint of her hand in our cheeks. Even now, she will reprimand us if we...um...I believe you say cross a line."

Todd didn't know what to say. He had no idea.

She slapped them? That's awful.

Mi'cin clucked his tongue, the color in his cheeks flushing blue. "I believe I misspoke again." He rubbed his neck. "Our parents did not harm us. It was more to shock us and to alter our poor behavior. Greatly harming a child or beating them to wound them is publishable by law, and fathers can lose their Rights of Fatherhood if great physical harm occurs to a child."

Todd stood silent.

"This is not a conversation I thought we would have." Mi'cin paused. "I would very much like a drink. Water would be nice. I have no taste for your wine, I'm afraid." He took a shallow breath and sat down.

Todd walked into the kitchen and filled two glasses.

I knew Nentraee justice was strict, but to spank or slap children. That doesn't seem right. Of course, my dad spanked both Brad and I when we got out of line.

"I understand you're going to work on getting more of my people down to Earth to explore your world," Mi'cin said from the living room. "That is a good idea. Several of my friends want to visit and learn more about your people."

"Excellent." Todd turned off the tap and took a deep breath.

I can do this.

"I've told them what I know, but they are curious and jealous," Mi'cin continued. "They are particularly interested in one of your amusement centers. Disneyland."

Todd laughed and walked back from the kitchen. He handed Mi'cin a full glass and sat in the chair off to the side of the couch where Mi'cin was sitting. "Disneyland is a special place. Your people will enjoy it." He took a sip of the cool water.

"There are other places, of course, not only in your home territory." Mi'cin rolled the cup of water in his hands before sipping it.

"It's going to be a lot of work, but I'm pretty sure it'll be fun for everyone," Todd said. "I have my friend Dan." He stopped. "You met him at Thanksgiving dinner. He's coming up tomorrow to help with a proposal, to share his ideas. He works in the travel industry."

"I remember him." Mi'cin stifled a laugh. "He was interesting." He finished off the water in one large gulp.

"I'm sure he'll be helpful," Todd said.

If I can see that Mi'cin is nervous, what about me? Does he know I'm worried about tonight?

"If you need the help," Mi'cin said, "I'm willing to assist." He shifted around in his seat. "It might prove helpful to have the opinion of a Nentraee."

Todd finished his water and put the glass on the table next to him.

"I'm curious about a great many of your customs and cultural places." Mi'cin placed his empty glass near Todd's. "For example, in the city you're from, there is a place called the Winchester Mystery House. I would love to find out why it is such a mystery. From what I've read, it is a house of beauty but a poorly designed space."

Todd chuckled. "It's not easy to explain. Ghosts and American mysticism are involved."

Mi'cin's head tilted.

"Who knows? We might go there. It's beautiful. I've been there a couple of times," Todd said.

The room fell quiet. Mi'cin glanced at the wall in front of him and tapped his leg. "You should paint that wall. Bring in color."

Todd glanced at the big blank wall. "I could do that. Can I get you some more water, or should we head out?" He stood.

Mi'cin quickly got up, his smile growing. "We can go."

Todd picked up the glasses and took them to the kitchen. "What's the plan? You've been vague about this dinner. Is there another café that you want me to try? Or are you planning on keeping me guessing?"

"Curious." Mi'cin smiled. "I want to keep you curious; that was my intent."

"Alrighty then. Shall we go?"

I can do this.

As they began their walk down the corridor, Mi'cin occasionally turned to Todd but said nothing. Mi'cin led them away from the governmental living areas, passing the open spaces, recreational centers, shops, and eateries that made up much of the ship's interior.

By the time they stopped, they were at the docking bay.

"The docking bay?"

"You'll see." Mi'cin beamed.

They moved away from the main lobby area and through two large double doors. Todd was amazed to see an extra-large shuttle sitting there, a shuttle unlike the ones he'd been on. This one was new. There were no signs of wear and tear. The height from floor to ceiling had to be one hundred fifty feet. The length of the shuttle was easily four or five hundred feet long, and like all the Nentraee shuttles, it had an organic, smooth silhouette. On what appeared to be the second level, several large windows melded seamlessly into the roof of the craft. There were also inlays of what Todd thought were gold and silver in intricately designed patterns.

The ship wasn't the only unique thing about this place. The hanger bay also had a completely different design than the one next door.

"This location is not a place for general use but for dignitaries and special guests of the speaker general," Mi'cin said.

Todd noted that the finishes and the murals painted on the walls were similar to the ones in the council chambers where the Speaker's House met. The only difference being that these showed the Benzee planet and her moons, along with the various ships of the fleet, and not the past leaders of the Speaker's House.

"My father had it designed to showcase our people and our world. It used up a lot of resources, but it's worth it." Mi'cin pointed out the display cases.

Todd walked along the cases. They were filled with Nentraee statues, dress cloaks, a small Za'entra ear cuff, an infinity circle similar to the one he had seen in Vi-Narm's quarters, and other artifacts he didn't recognize.

"We have to use the elevator to get to the entry point. Unless you want to climb up a maintenance hatch," Mi'cin said, with a playful smile.

"We get to go in?"

"Of course. I wouldn't have brought you here, otherwise."

"Amazing. It's so beautiful."

"So, the elevator will be fine?" Mi'cin pointed.

Todd nodded and walked to the elevator. Mi'cin went to the panel, which scanned his hand. The doors opened, and he stepped in. "Don't worry about our using the ship. My father approved the use, mainly because his shuttle is being repaired and this one sits empty."

Todd entered, and the doors closed without a sound. On the inside of the elevator, the closed access point created the seal of the Nentraee people. The design was comprised of seven gold patterns, each a symbol for one of the clans.

This is unbelievable. Mi'cin is amazing, and we're alone. He smells so good. Like sandalwood.

Todd's hands were sweating and trembling, and he put them in his pockets so Mi'cin wouldn't see how anxious he was.

Mi'cin stepped out and crossed over to the main entry. On the large doors was the seal for the Nentraee government. It had been engraved, then accented with gold and silver leafing, reflecting each of the clans. The craftsmanship was stunning. Todd was floored by the amount of work that must have gone into the design.

The entry point opened, and Todd followed Mi'cin.

The ship's foyer spilled opened to a large reception space with floor-to-ceiling windows. They had a curve that melded perfectly into the ship's roof and floor. The floor was soft carpet, and the walls extended their simple, elegant lines and warm-toned colors.

"It was thought that it would provide neutral space for our people to meet," Mi'cin said. "Giving your people a comfortable view of your planet. The design was based on what we anticipated to be appropriate needs." He walked around a bit. "This space can be used as a reception hall or large meeting room. There are three smaller conference rooms to the back, with a crew area for service, maintenance, and a galley. Down the main stairs in the center are additional meeting spaces about half this size. Several small suites, a communications center for the media, small interview rooms, an emergency medical facility, the flight deck and crew quarters, as well as service shafts, and an overflow galley with elevator to the main galley."

"It's a giant space cruise ship," Todd said. "I thought the shuttles were nice, but this... Wow!" He ran his hand over the detailed walls and windows.

"It's impressive even by our standards." Mi'cin walked over to where Todd stood. "I know my father is proud of it. Sadly, it wasn't used once we arrived. It would not work as we had hoped, another miscalculation on our part. We didn't expect your world to be so fractured. We thought your United Nations was a worldwide governing body."

"I'm sure there will be opportunity to use it at some point. People will be clamoring to view the planet from here." Todd walked along the outer wall, running his hands over the carvings. "It's got to be the most luxurious space I've ever seen."

"I hope so." Mi'cin went over to one of the panels on the wall, pulled out the portable datapad, and tapped it. "Vi-un, we're on board and ready to go."

His Nentraee is always so beautiful. So is he. My God, could he look any better? Stop. Don't go there.

"We're at station, Mi'cin. We'll be underway shortly," Vi-un responded. His Nentraee didn't sound nearly as nice to Todd's ear as Mi'cin's.

"Wait. Are you?" Todd stopped, understanding them. "Are we? If we're going to Earth for dinner, can't we just take one of the other shuttles? We don't need to go in this. Plus, can it land at the airports?"

"Todd?"

"Not to mention, people haven't seen this class of ship before. Aren't you worried about what people will do?" Todd's face was suddenly warm.

"We're not going down to Earth." Mi'cin grinned. "The engines on this ship are more suited to where we're going." He put the datapad back, and then he turned back to Todd. "I can't wait for you to see this." He moved over to one of the windows, and Todd joined him as the docking bay doors opened, revealing Earth in front of them.

As with all the Nentraee ships, the liftoff was smooth. Todd didn't feel a thing. The inertia-dampening systems and gravitational fields left him feeling like he was on solid ground. He was nowhere near as nervous as he had been for his first trip in a Nentraee vessel. The ship moved out of the special hanger bay, entering the darkness of space. Several smaller shuttles and maintenance craft moved about them but gave them a wide birth. They moved closer to Earth, giving an inspired view of Africa and Europe.

"I asked Vi-un, our pilot, to circle Earth so you can see it fully. Your planet is amazing." Mi'cin glanced to the large windows. "So much beauty."

Todd watched the Earth go by. "Incredible. I mean, I've seen the planet from the ship, but to see it like this...with a clear view." Todd took several steps toward Mi'cin.

Mi'cin bowed, pleased.

The white clouds swirled around as the blues of the oceans peeked through below. Todd sighed. There were no borders—it was all one planet. It was so small, so fragile.

If more people saw the world like this, we wouldn't have all the wars and violence we have.

"How am I ever to thank you for this wonderful treat?" Todd said after several quiet minutes.

"I hope you don't mind, but I took the liberty of picking out several Benzee dishes for our dinner tonight," Mi'cin said. "You enjoyed the colo co mo, so we'll have that and a few other selections."

Todd nodded his approval.

"I have to be honest, my father helped me plan the meal," Mi'cin said. "I'm not the planner he is, but I'm improving. He wanted to invite you to this meal for me, but after studying your culture, I knew it would be best for me to ask you. He and my mother don't fully understand these things yet."

I'm confused.

"We get to eat here?" Todd turned to him. "In this ship?"

"Of course."

"I guess I can fill you in on the rest of the dinner plans now that we're here." Mi'cin chuckled. "I thought it would be nice to orbit your moon for dinner."

"Wait, what? How is that even possible?" Todd shook his head. "Doesn't it take days to get to the moon?"

"Not with this ship's advanced propulsion." Mi'cin stepped closer to Todd and lowered his voice. "Even your people have vehicles that have made it in less time than that."

"How long will it take?" Todd cleared his throat as the distance between he and Mi'cin became surprisingly close. Not that he minded.

"We can be there and back in about four standard hours." Mi'cin's brilliant green eyes met Todd's. "Longer if we choose to take longer."

Todd stepped away from the window and explored the empty reception area in wonder. His mind was a mass of thoughts, but at the forefront was the word *date*. Was this a dinner date?

He turned and faced Mi'cin. "I have to ask, and I'm sorry if I'm misinterpreting all your kindness, but"—his skin warmed up—"is this a date?"

Mi'cin stared at Todd.

"I mean, you know, a mating ritual or something?" Todd added quickly. "Between us..." He frowned the minute the words came out of his mouth. His whole head was on fire. He hoped it didn't sound as dumb as he thought it did.

Mi'cin was quiet. His gaze left Todd's face.

Oh God. I blew it. He assumes I'm nuts. I knew this wasn't a date. How stupid could I be? I mean, Jerry is the love of my life and this is just...what?

If he knew the Nentraee term for dating, he would have used it, but instead he used the words he knew and that left him unclear. "Oh God, I think I... Mi'cin, I'm sorry I... You have to understand, I—"

"You need to stop talking for a moment." Mi'cin walked closer to Todd. The smile did not fade.

Todd took a breath. His face was burning hot with embarrassment.

Oh God. Now I'm gonna get it.

Mi'cin stood less than an arm's length from him, staring right into his eyes. Earth continued to shrink outside the ship's windows behind them.

"When I met you, I was curious about you," Mi'cin started. "I wasn't sure I liked humans, but you were different from the others. When I asked you about your former mate, Jerry, you seemed ashamed. I thought I had embarrassed you or insulted his memory. Or, like my father said, I had chosen a poor time to talk of such things, which was not my intent. But I was interested—curious—and so I continued to watch you. I wanted to understand you better."

Todd shifted his stance and started to open his mouth to speak. To tell Mi'cin that he wasn't sure how to talk about Jerry and his relationship, given the setting they were in.

Mi'cin held up his hand. "My father insisted I work with you, which was not what I wanted. I wanted to watch humans from afar, study and learn. At that time, I did not even realize I liked you. My father didn't understand my intentions at the time either. Or maybe he did. He never said. My father can be..." He paused, staring out the window, then continued. "I suppose the word is sneaky."

"I would say canny," Todd said, unable to keep silent. Mi'cin had spent all this time learning about him to see if he liked him. Not even Jerry had gone through that much trouble before they started dating.

"Please, I must finish," Mi'cin resumed. "Either way, my father knows now, of course. I wasn't completely sure what I thought of you. I figured you would have been proud of your relationship with Jerry and your human marriage to him. We are very proud of our relationships and the people we choose to share our lives with. We celebrate such things." Mi'cin paused. "I suppose you would not notice because we do not show affection in the same manner, but it is clear to us, perhaps too alien for you."

"I've seen people together, but no one touches. So..." The Nentraee seemed so emotionally stiff to Todd. How could anyone tell who was a couple and who wasn't?

Mi'cin nodded. "Touching is intimate and personal, not done in public, as you know." He frowned. "I do not want to get off topic. I thought you would have celebrated Jerry and his life, but you rarely spoke of him, leaving me even more confused and curious."

Todd focused on the floor. It wasn't that he was embarrassed by his relationship with Jerry. It was hard to talk about. Maybe, he did hide a bit and lock that part of him away, but that was how he tried to manage the grief.

"However, then as I got more familiar with you, I found you intriguing and strangely charming, particularly for a human." Mi'cin reached out and lifted Todd's face gently with a finger under his chin. "I learned, to my surprise, that it was your sadness that kept you from talking about him, not shame. It was the emptiness in your heart."

Mi'cin offered a brief, warm smile. "The loss of your mate." He shook his head. "I can't imagine. If I'm breaching a human custom or insulting his memory, please accept my apology. I don't fully understand your rituals around death and grieving. Again, that is not my intent, but I must get this all out."

Todd remained quiet. He wanted to tell Mi'cin it was fine, that he knew how to talk about Jerry now and that it didn't hurt as much as it did then.

Mi'cin continued. "I researched as much as I could about human relationships. You meet, you get to know each other, you see if there is attraction, you decide if you wish to spend your lives together, and then you bond or marry. Your race is very complicated when it comes to those matters. There are many things I don't understand, and I wish to talk about, but later."

I can only imagine. Arranged marriages, multiple marriages, multiple partners...

Mi'cin stared out the window a moment. "After your Thanksgiving dinner when we talked, I thought you might have found me appealing. I wasn't sure. You share intimacy with a great many of your friends. It's hard to recognize what is attraction and what is not. And your words contradict what your true meaning and intent is. Then when I saw you in the garden, alone that night two months back, appearing defeated, I thought I would ask you for a meal."

Mi'cin fussed with his collar, taking a breath. "You surprised me by asking me out for a meal instead. I wasn't sure what your intentions were."

"I was..."

In need of a friend, but maybe even then, I wanted more.

Mi'cin held up his hand. "Please, Todd."

Todd's heart beat a mile a minute. He wanted to reach out and hug Mi'cin. Tell him how he was sorry for being so mysterious, but was he really being mysterious or was it a cultural difference? It was probably a chunk of both.

"I was even more unsure what your opinion of me was. I was getting more flustered. I didn't want to embarrass you further, so I said nothing at the time. I didn't consider it appropriate to bring it up." Mi'cin met Todd's gaze.

The bright blue planet had become even smaller.

I had no idea, or maybe I ignored it. I'm so flipping clueless.

"When all the watching, listening, and researching failed me—" Mi'cin sighed. "—and you seemed unfazed when I touched your arm the day of the attack on London, I thought I would try this." He moved his arm to indicate the space. The rest of the Nentraee ships were only small dots now. "Be more direct, my last attempt. My intention was to speak to you about this and see if my attempts were for nothing. I'm grateful you brought up the subject." He walked back over to Todd. His stance stiffened and his shoulders became straighter. "To answer your question as simply and directly as I can now, yes, this is a date, if you would like it to be so."

Their eyes locked.

There was a lot to process, and Todd was dumbfounded. He had been blind. "I'm sorry. I misunderstood your efforts.

I'm such an idiot. I can't imagine how frustrating it must have been for you." He started to reach out, then stopped. Keeping his hand by his side instead, not sure what to do.

Mi'cin nodded his agreement, his shoulders stiff.

"Mainly the touching, I didn't pay attention to it," Todd said. "Touching is common among us humans—well, Americans—and I never thought about it."

"I understand that now," Mi'cin said.

"Mi'cin, I would like this to be a date," Todd said.

Mi'cin's body relaxed. His posture and his shoulders loosened. He took a step forward, reached out, and touched the side of Todd's face gently, holding it there. "I'm very pleased." He started to laugh. It was the first time Todd had seen him laugh so fully. "J'Vessa be praised. You have no idea how nervous you make me and how hard it was for me to say all that, Todd Landon."

"Me? Making you nervous? You're joking, right?"

"Yes, you. Even my friends have teased me about this. Calling me a *vak yép*."

"A troublemaker?" Todd asked, not understanding the reference.

"It means something less polite in this context. Please don't use that phrase. My mother would not be happy with me if she knew I taught you such things, and I have not felt her hand in many years."

Todd laughed. "All right. I won't use it."

Of course, now the word is etched into my memory.

"You have no idea how challenging a male you are to figure out. You are nothing like the other males I've known or spent time with romantically. That is part of the charm I see in you." There was a bright twinkle in his eyes. "The waiter at the café we went to is a good friend, Luvan, and you can't imagine the teasing I received after we ate.

Watching me suffer made him happy. If I understand your slang, you would call him a 'bitch' for how I was treated."

Todd laughed. "Please don't use that phrase. My mother would not be happy..."

Mi'cin chuckled. "Apologies."

All this time, Mi'cin was nervous and intimidated by me.

"You did all this for me, to get my attention." Todd watched the Earth. "I don't know what to say."

I suppose it worked out for the best, but still, shouldn't I be healing and coming to terms with Jerry's death?

"We have both said enough for now. Now we enjoy our time together, nothing more," Mi'cin said.

Should I even be here tonight on this date? Just stop.

They watched the Earth together.

The ship moved on to the moon with effortless grace. Mi'cin had used the datapad from the wall to set up an internal wall viewer, so they were able to view the Earth behind and the moon in front of them. As they moved closer to the moon, it grew larger in size with the Earth there in the background. Finally, as the ship got to a comfortable distance, it slowed down and began its orbit. Mi'cin took Todd on a tour of the rest of the ship, showing him all its features and introducing him to Vi-un and the five other crew who were on duty for the night.

After the tour and introductions, they came back to the main reception and observation area, which had been transformed. There were elaborate, living floral displays all around the eating area. The lighting had been changed to make the room warmer, and in the middle of it all was a table set for two. Even though the space was huge and the setup simple and small, it drew the eye to the window and the view of the moon.

"Impressive." Todd walked around the table and examined the plants. "Vi-un and the others did all this while we were on the tour? Wow."

"Yes." Mi'cin bowed. "Despite their teasing, they are good friends. They did all this for us to enjoy so we might get to know each other better. However, I'm going to owe Vi-un and the others a great many favors for all their work tonight." He stepped forward. "We had planned it for last night so Luvan could be here, but he had to work at the café today."

"Sorry about that." Todd frowned.

"Don't be. I was being impatient. It worked out much better for tonight. I had more time to plan and prepare."

"It's like a dream."

"I can't take all the credit. My father did help," Mi'cin said. "I hope you enjoy the dinner."

"If it's anything like the rest of this night, I'm sure it'll be amazing." How would Todd ever be able to thank Mi'cin for this, or plan anything as wonderful? "You know, there is no way I can ever beat this on a second date. I mean, this has got to be the date of all dates." He crossed to the table and the arrangements.

"This isn't a competition," Mi'cin said. "I'm sure whatever you come up with will be equally as nice." His smile grew. "It pleases me to hear that you want to continue on this path together." He pulled out a chair for Todd. "A human custom I like."

Todd sat down.

The rest of the evening meandered as they ate and talked. Mi'cin's friends served them without a single word, to Todd's surprise. Mi'cin explained that their English wasn't as strong as his and that it would have been considered rude for them to speak unless spoken to at such a dinner. Todd found it old-fashioned, like staff out of the late 1800s, where servants were to serve and not speak unless spoken to. Regardless, everything else was perfect. The views from the ship were incredible, and seeing the moon this close was surreal.

Todd realized that he was one of only a handful of humans who had seen the moon and the Earth like this. That would be changing now that the Nentraee were here. Everything was changing. He found it difficult to keep his eyes from the windows and the views. Mi'cin didn't seem to mind, even when he had to repeat a question or wait for Todd to turn back to him.

After the dinner, as they returned to the Nentraee ships, they had fallen into comfortable silence, enjoying the view and the company. Mi'cin was having a cup of chilled tuma at the cleared table, and Todd a cup of warmed e'xin. They were getting closer to Earth, bringing their dinner to an end.

After returning to the docking bay and leaving the shuttle, a big part of Todd didn't want the night to end.

I wonder what Mi'cin would say if I asked him to spend the night?

"Thank you again for this amazing evening." Todd gazed at Mi'cin. They were standing outside his quarters. He didn't even remember walking back to his apartment, but here he was.

What time is it, anyway? Who cares?

"It was pleasing that you were there with me." Mi'cin bowed. He reached out gently and touched the side of Todd's face. "I look forward to doing this again."

Todd's cheeks grew warm under Mi'cin's touch. His body stirred. It had been a long time. He smiled and leaned in, kissing Mi'cin softly on the lips. It only took Mi'cin a second to respond, returning the kiss.

Mi'cin's hand moved from Todd's face to his shoulder, then down, joining his other hand at Todd's waist, holding him closer. Todd did the same, feeling how strong Mi'cin's body was as the kiss deepened.

Todd's heart was pounding in his chest. The way Mi'cin kissed him was soft and gentle. His smooth skin was a complete contrast to the facial stubble he was used to. As tender as the kiss was, Mi'cin held him firm, his hands planted at Todd's waist. He inhaled more of Mi'cin's scent: sandalwood. It was intoxicating. He could stay like this all night. Todd noted the rougher texture of Mi'cin's tongue, but it wasn't unpleasant.

They were close enough for Todd to feel Mi'cin's body start to respond.

Todd pulled away, taking a breath. "Would you like to come in? To talk or..." He paused.

Mi'cin inhaled. "What I would like and what would be appropriate at this time are very different things."

Mi'cin's gaze scanned Todd's body up and down, a wanting look on his face. He understood what Mi'cin was talking about.

"I should say good night and thank you for this evening." Mi'cin stepped back.

"All right." Todd tried to hide the disappointment in his voice. The logical part of his brain understood. The rest of his body did not. "Good night, then."

"Sleep well, Todd Landon." Mi'cin raised his hand to Todd's cheek resting it there for a moment. He pulled his hand away, then slowly turned to walk down the corridor.

Todd watched every step Mi'cin took until he was out of sight. What an amazing night.

Twenty: Travel

TODD WAITED IN the lobby area of the landing bay for Dan to arrive. He checked his timepiece out of habit, in spite of knowing Dan would be there momentarily. The landing bay was busy with all the traffic coming and going. It was nice to see humans and Nentraee mix into a friendly crowd.

It's good for both groups. They seem to be trying.

Todd rubbed his eyes as he faced the large doors that led to the VIP shuttle bay. He couldn't believe that eight hours ago he and Mi'cin were returning from their dinner date among the stars.

He was tired, but it didn't matter; the date was remarkable. So was the kiss. It made his heart race. The thought of seeing Mi'cin again and spending time with him was exciting.

Still, a part of him ached.

Am I rushing things?

Todd remembered his and Jerry's first real date. How they had met up for dinner and talked about movies until the closing hours of the restaurant.

A sad smile brushed over his lips.

Hearing the vice speaker's shuttle land jolted Todd away from his thoughts. Dan exited the shuttle down the small enclosed ramp, his mouth open and his head twisting around so he could see all the shuttles and people.

"Holy shit," Dan said once he met Todd in the lobby.

"Impressive, right?"

"Now I understand why people are climbing all over one another to come up here on tours."

"And you, my friend, get to see more than they ever will." Todd beamed. "Well, for now. I thought we could do a quick tour. There's a lot to see, but this will give you a flavor of the ship and its people. So you have a point of reference for the travel talks."

"Lead away."

Todd decided to show Dan all the places he was familiar with. The main plaza area, where he and Mi'cin had had dinner. The speaker's chamber, where he had his interview. And the garden that he could view from his quarters.

Todd walked too fast for Dan and found he had to slow down as they started their tour of the ship.

Just like Mi'cin did with me that first day.

Todd pointed out the garden, trying to remember the names of the plants and trees. But his mind was on the kiss and his date with Mi'cin. It was hard to focus on Dan.

Should I have invited Mi'cin in last night? Was that the right thing to do? I can't believe I did that.

They passed several Nentraee going about their daily routines. A few of them bowed out of respect. He navigated to a gallery—a bridge linking two different districts—that gave everyone a chance to walk among the tops of the trees. It was a remarkable feeling. A few of the brightly colored trees reached up, obscuring parts of the overlook from view.

"I've never seen blue and purple leaves." Dan pulled out his cell phone and snapped a few pictures. Then he took a selfie with Todd before putting his cell phone away.

"Yep, it takes a bit of getting used to." Todd paused. "This is the largest garden on the ship. It was designed after a garden on one of their moons. Smaller but an exact duplicate, or so Mi'cin told me."

Dan rested his hands on the railing and peered out. "This is abso-freaking-lutely beautiful."

"I spent the first week I was here walking everywhere and getting oriented," Todd said. "It's hard to imagine I've been here for over a month now. I'm getting used to it, but..." He stopped. "Hey, you wanna go to the council chamber where the Speaker's House meets? It's really beautiful."

"Sure. How many of us come up here usually?" Dan asked.

"On a normal day, about three hundred or so. Most go to the cultural affairs ship, kind of like the Nentraee's version of the Smithsonian." Todd started walking. "People also come here to tour around the life science ship. Mi'ko's wife, Laina, loves showing off her bionanotechnology research." He chuckled. "She's pretty funny. I like her. She's brilliant. Anyway, right now, mainly scientist and medical folks from Earth go to those ships. They are trying to make sure that the Nentraee don't have any bugs that can kill us or the other way around."

"Well, you look healthy."

"I still have to get checked out." Todd stopped. "I don't know if you noticed the decontamination you went through when you left the shuttle. It's pretty seamless. I didn't even realize it happened until someone told me."

Dan turned away from the large window with a view into one of the small central plaza districts, which had a few shops and eateries.

"Anyway, we mainly get a few small tour groups as part of the shuttle rides, and we get business leaders or diplomats who come here for meetings."

"Has Varick been up here yet?" Dan asked as they started walking again.

"Not yet, but he's been after me to get him up here to meet with Mi'ko." Todd grinned. "Anyway, this is all about getting to know one another."

"Maybe we can start with more specific cultural exchanges, like dining experiences or art exhibits?" Dan glanced around.

"That might work."

"You know, there's a lot they could do if they had the space to open a few hotels on this ship." Dan smiled. "Imagine all the people coming up here and spending time and money. I'm sure it would help them as much as it would help us."

"Space is at a premium here, but it's worth talking about. They want to prove a point by being more open, and the speaker general wants to ensure they won't be scared off. It's funny. They are doing a one-eighty with how they first were guarded and careful. Now they want to put it all on display."

"Works for me," Dan said.

Todd guided Dan down one of the bigger gallery halls. They arrived at two twenty-foot-tall open doors surrounded by a tightly manicured garden of bright trees and orange flowers that framed the entrance perfectly.

Dan stared at them and let out a whistle. "Wow."

There were several other Nentraee inside the arched doors, walking around the chamber hall. A few of them watched Todd and Dan, but most continued to point at the walls of the council chamber. There was also a group of ten humans. Dressed in dark suits, the group was part of the South Korean business delegation, here to meet Speaker Syde.

Todd pointed to the various murals of the past speaker generals on the walls. He called out the craftsmanship, focusing on the detailed painting and how it was a mixed medium of both etchings and paint. He also pointed out how it was embedded into the walls.

"So this is where they meet?" Dan ran his hand over the railing in the center of the room, which blocked off the platform where the speakers sat during their meetings.

"Yep. When they're in session, this is the place." Todd leaned against the platform. "'Course, I've only been here one time, but that was a special event." He frowned at the memory. "Anyway, they also have private meetings, but those are usually held in the speaker general's office."

"Oh, right—the evil vote from hell."

Despite the vote, it wasn't a bad day. I got the idea for inviting Mi'ko and his family to Thanksgiving, and I got to get to know Mi'cin better. Which led to that amazing kiss. So, I can't complain.

There was a pang of guilt in Todd's heart. "Anyway, today is a nonsession day, so it's open to the public. It's a replica of the Speaker's House back on their home world. All the artwork and wall carvings were pulled from there and transferred here when the ship was finished."

"Who are the Nentraee in the paintings?" Dan pulled out his phone and took more pictures.

"They're the past speaker generals. The oldest is over two hundred years old." Todd pointed to the murals.

"Cool." Dan took another picture. "I can't imagine having to leave our home. I mean, how hard would that be?"

"The worst part is how many people they left behind. It's a guilt I can't imagine, picking who will live and who will die. Realizing you can only save so many people."

At least with Jerry, it was sudden. I don't know how I could have handled leaving him behind like that. I don't think I could.

"I thought they said it was a lottery system?" Dan asked.

"That's what the official reports say, but it's not something they talk about, and I don't really want to ask." Todd stopped. It was hard to consider such things. "I hope we never have to experience anything like it."

I wouldn't wish that kind of pain on anyone, and yet the Nentraee deal with it every day. I lost Jerry, one person, but they lost their world and all the people they loved and cared about.

"This is their executive branch, right?" Dan's question pulled Todd out of his thoughts.

"Yep, the House of the People meet in a separate hall and the um...shoot." Todd snapped his fingers, the name of the judicial branch finally coming to him. "The Board of Law. They meet in another location. I haven't been to either building yet. They tend to not be open to the public, since that is where the majority of the governmental work is done, or so I'm told."

"I guess all that studying you did on them paid off." Dan walked past the former speaker generals' portraits.

"More like trial by fire. Come on. I'll take you to my office so we can get started. Then we can have dinner where the locals hang out. It'll be fun. Plus, there is this drink I want you to try."

"As long as there are cute menz, I'm there. Oh, did I tell you? Girl, there was this fine Nentraee boy on the shuttle? He totally wants me."

Todd chuckled as they walked out of the chamber and headed to his office.

By the time they were wrapping up for the day, they had managed to come up with a selection of different travel proposals. They were considering anywhere from one human and one Nentraee guide to groups no larger than thirty-five and, depending on speed and modes of travel, how long each tour should be. They both agreed that trying to visit the whole planet at once was impossible, so they would focus instead on key tourist attractions and recommend that the groups be set up accordingly.

The idea of a cultural exchange kept coming up in their conversation. So, the idea of a youth exchange program, was added to the proposal.

Dan leaned back in his chair, putting down the datapad he used. "All right, I gave you the majority of the day to tell me what happened at your dinner last night, and all we've done is work. And don't think I didn't notice how distracted you've been." He picked up the cup of coffee, inhaled the aroma, then took a sip. "Spill it, Miss Thing. I want the details."

"It was amazing." Todd's face filled with warmth, both from the night with Mi'cin and his lingering guilt over Jerry. "Mi'cin got permission to use their diplomatic shuttle, and we flew out to the moon and had dinner in its orbit."

"Shut the fuck up." Dan put down his coffee.

"I...you have no idea. It was so beautiful. We had a nice talk and a great dinner. He even had his friends there to wait on us. I've never been on a date like it."

"Did you grow a pair of balls and ask him if it was a date?"

"I did." Todd closed the files and put his device back in its storage space.

"About time."

"I felt like an idiot. He laughed, saying how nervous I made him." Todd chuckled. "Can you imagine, me making anyone nervous?"

Dan took a sip of his coffee. "With a date like that, did you have a close encounter of the horizontal kind?" Dan waggled his eyebrows.

"We did not." Todd's face grew hot, and his gaze dropped to his desk. He should have never been so forward. "It was all very nice. We just had dinner and talked. Then he walked me back to my apartment and said good night." He cleared his throat. "Well, we did kiss. He's an extremely good kisser, and he smelled great. I don't know if it was a cologne or him, but he smelled like sandalwood." He rushed out the words and stared at his desk. "I may have invited him in, but he politely declined."

"You did what?" Dan squealed and moved his chair closer. "I knew you were a nasty ho. Dish, chica."

"It was just a kiss, and he put his hand on my cheek. It was sweet. Plus, it was late, so no one saw us." Todd tried to look up but couldn't meet Dan's gaze.

"Hey, what's wrong?" Dan's voice went from high-pitched excitement to normal, and he reached out across the table for Todd's hand.

"It's Jerry. I know he's gone, and I need to move on." Todd frowned. "Last night—I haven't felt like that in a long time and I don't want to disrespect Jerry's memory. I shouldn't have gone to dinner, and I sure as heck shouldn't—"

"Stop right there." Dan lifted Todd's chin so they could look at each other. "You and Jerry loved each other and how Jerry died was...well, was the worst way possible, but he wouldn't want you sitting around, not living. Especially when you have the opportunity to have first contact with a sexy-ass spaceman." Dan took Todd's hands. "He'd want you to move on and find someone new."

Todd nodded. "It was incredible. It was nice to sit and talk to him."

"Good." Dan released Todd's hands and sat back in his chair.

"I'm just—"

Dan held up a hand. "You're allowed to be happy, and if Mi'cin can make you happy, then nothing else matters. You're not disrespecting Jerry or his memory."

Todd raked a hand through his hair. "Thank you."

Dan stood and went to the bookshelf and pulled the photo of Jerry and Todd with the guard at Buckingham Palace. "This was a great trip. I'm glad you guys got to come visit."

"Jerry should have grabbed the guard's butt."

"I'm glad he didn't. They don't take kindly to that." Dan put the photo down and they both fell quiet.

"I still miss him."

"I know you do." Dan brushed at his eyes. "Okay, enough of this." He returned to his seat. "Jerry was one of my best friends and the pity party stops here." He glanced around the room. "You are so flipping lucky. You have an amazing gig with the Nentraee and a hot spaceman flying your sorry old ass to the moon for a romantic dinner. Bitch. I hate you." He crossed his arms in front of his chest.

He's right. I have to move on.

"Watch it. You're older than me, and you're the one with a man in every port, ho."

"Whatever you say, slut." Dan flourished a hand wave. "Are you two lovebirds going to fly off to Mars or Venus for Christmas then, or are you going to come down and spend the time with us lame humans?"

"I don't know." Todd shrugged. "Other than getting everything ordered online and sent out to family, I haven't given it much thought—"

"Bitch, you're on a spaceship surrounded by aliens," Dan interrupted. "You better not have gotten your family stuff from Amazon."

"Of course not." Todd's face warmed, and he made a note to do some shopping in the central district. "Anyway, I might spend it with my folks and brother. But now that I think about it, I might want to spend it here on the ship." He sighed. "It's not a holiday for the Nentraee."

"So, they give you the time off, right?"

"They did."

"You spoiled bitch." Dan sighed. "I hope you got them some nice gifts as thank-yous." He sipped his coffee.

"I did. I have them wrapped in my quarters," Todd said. "You're going to spend it with your family?"

"Yep, I have all the *familia loco* to deal with, so it's going to be crazy good fun." Dan's voice was flat. "You can come to be part of the nuttiness, if you want. My mom and sister would love to see you, plus there'll be homemade tamales. Bring Mi'cin. That would be fun. My mom would faint—or fall to her knees praying."

"You know, maybe I should invite Mi'cin for dinner with my family. It might be nice for him. And for my family too." Todd tapped his fingers on his desk.

"That's a big step."

"Do you think it's too much?"

Dan's eyes narrowed and he shook his head. "Nah. Better they find out now than some other way."

"I suppose."

Todd cleaned up and put the last of their notes together, swiping most of it over to the main terminal on his desk. "Tomorrow, I want to run all this by Mi'cin and get his opinion on what we have."

"Oh, I get to check out the hunk from outer space again." Dan chuckled.

"Come on, you. Let's go get some food, and I'll show you my quarters and the couch you'll be sleeping on." Todd closed down his system for the night.

Dan clucked his tongue. "The couch?"

"And you're lucky to have it."

"I don't suppose there are any single Nentraee security men that need a bunkmate?" Dan winked.

"Nope. Sorry. It's the couch or the airlock. Your choice."

Twenty-One: Book Club

TODD CHECKED HIS pocket watch.

He decided to meet Vi-Narm at the café he and Mi'cin had come to for dinner on his first day. It was comfortable and familiar.

She must be running a little late.

He had hoped to see Luvan, to see what Mi'cin's friends were like. Unfortunately, he hadn't seen Luvan when he and Dan had eaten here a few days ago, and he wasn't seeing him now. He tapped his hands on his leg, checking around for Vi-Narm.

The rhythmic beat of his watch helped him stay relaxed. It was a miracle this meeting was happening at all.

He read the first few pages of *My Ántonia* again on his tablet. It had been years since he'd read it, so he had to refresh his memories.

A cup of what the Nentraee called "human tea" was in front of him. It was black and boring, but he appreciated it. The Nentraee had added a few human items to their menus to give the earthlings options. He didn't envy the person who had to decide what to offer on the menu. He couldn't guess at how many types of foods Earth had.

With his feedback, the Nentraee had programmed public computers and system interface devices for human use.

Todd sipped his tea and viewed the plaza. It was odd not seeing any holiday decorations or anyone running around with bags and boxes. He was going to invite Mi'cin to come down to his family's house for Christmas. It might be interesting to see them interacting again, specifically after how things went at Thanksgiving. Mi'cin didn't seem as blunt anymore, so it might work. He would check with Brad and see what he thought before telling his mother.

"Good morning, Todd." Vi-Narm's voice was cool but surprisingly pleasant. "I hope I did not keep you waiting."

"Not at all. I was enjoying a cup of tea." He put down his tablet.

"Not a datapad?" She took a seat and reached out. "May I?"

Todd handed her his tablet.

"Impressive. They are very much like our datapads." She tapped the device and pulled up information. She pursed her lips. "Not as functional, however. No multiscreen interface, and it only has access to the human datanet. No visual interface either. I assume no three-dimensional interface or display? Can you link up to your office terminal? Does it provide written and verbal translations? At what distance can it scan and sense threats? What about biological functions?"

He chuckled at her eagerness to understand. "It's not quite there yet."

Vi-Narm handed back the device. "I'm sure that will be developed at some point." She glanced down at the table. "You did not bring the book?"

"I brought my tablet," Todd said, pulling up *My Ántonia*. "Do you want lunch? My treat." He ran his hand over the table control and pulled up the digital menus.

"You are becoming familiar with our systems. That's good." Vi-Narm changed her menu back to Nentraee and placed an order.

"With help from Mi'cin and Danu, as well as you." Todd closed the menu and picked up his tablet. "So you liked the book?"

"I did. However, I didn't understood why Jim and Antonia never got together in the end. I was certain that is what should happen, considering the title of the book."

"I'm pretty sure the writer wanted to show that not everything in life is fair and works out the way we hope, but that, in the end, it works out the way it should."

Kind of like what happened with me.

"Anyway, they were both happy with their lives in the end," Todd continued.

"I found it sad," Vi-Narm said. "It reminded me of the great many hardships we have faced. How we have struggled to make our situation work in less than ideal circumstances."

Vi-Narm's shoulder dropped. He knew she carried the loss of her world. It was a pain he witnessed in most of the Nentraee at one time or another. It might have only lasted a moment each time, but it was always there.

"Well, the thing to remember is that this book wasn't so much about them, but about women's rights at that time in American history," Todd said. "Not to mention what it was like for families living in and settling the western half of the United States. For me, it's all about how we make the best of the situations we're forced to live through. We've all suffered some form of hardship that we can kind of relate to in the story." He sipped his tea.

Vi-Narm was quiet.

A server—someone other than Luvan, disappointing Todd further—brought out Vi-Narm's cup of tuma and a plate with what looked like a sandwich on it.

"I do not understand what you mean." Vi-Narm leaned forward. "Humans were always in that part of your country, so why would that be a hardship?" She picked up her utensils, the lagu and té, and cut up her sandwich thing.

"Well, this book was written about a hundred years ago. Things were different back then. At that time, the United States wasn't the country it is now."

"All right." She began eating. "Please, continue."

"Oh, boy." Todd's face heated up.

This is a more complicated conversation than I'm prepared for.

Todd talked about how the United States was settled, how that had impacted the Native Americans, and lastly covered the inequalities of the sexes during that time period and even today. It was an odd thing to try to explain one's culture to someone whose only point of reference was what they've seen in videos and read. Finally, he wrapped up, taking a breath. He impressed himself with how well he did.

"I'm sorry. I'm not the right person to explain all this to you. There is more to it, and I'm sure I'm missing a lot of details." He paused. "The people of our country, sadly, like most countries of our world, haven't always treated one another very well. Even now, as you're well aware, we are struggling."

"A turbulent past is a common thread," Vi-Narm said. "We almost destroyed ourselves for our petty differences. It has only been in the last hundred years that we've gotten better. Like you, we struggle. Even I say and do things that are not appropriate. It is not easy, particularly given my family and how I was raised."

"Really? I'd love to learn about you, if you don't mind."

Vi-Narm sipped her tuma. She put down her cup and adjusted her braids. There was a small tremble in her hands.

"I was raised in a small city called Yaá-Ha. It was the largest city in the Dena island chain. The area was colonized by my clan, the Dentraee." She shifted in her seat, clearly feeling self-conscious. "The city had thirty thousand people and the whole, a group of islands, had maybe a hundred thousand people. That was before we left our world, of course. It was a conservative and traditional area. Everyone, including my family, followed closely to the teachings of J'Veesa. And *Godá Faoo* was taken very seriously."

"Sorry, *Godá Faoo*? I'm not familiar with that phrase."

"Rights of Fatherhood," Vi-Narm offered. "My father stayed home, raising us. My mother didn't allow him to work, nor would he have ever considered it. His duty was raising my sister and me. A job he took seriously and with a heavy hand at times." Her eyes twinkled. "It wasn't that long ago that having a male vice speaker would have been unheard of."

"Really?" Todd said. "Were you and your father close?" He rested his arms on the café table.

"Not really." Vi-Narm shook her head. "As I grew older, I came to respect him and his choices. He did what he thought was right and raised us how he was raised." She stiffened in her seat. "It wasn't until he died that I understood how lucky I was."

"So, he died before your planet..."

"He died about a year before the announcement." Vi-Narm's face tightened. "He didn't have to deal with the heartache or knowledge that our world was ending. Nor did he have to deal with the stupidity of our leaders in how they handled the situation. For that, I am grateful."

I can't imagine.

"Was anyone else from your family selected?" Todd asked carefully, knowing the tender nature of the subject.

There had been a lot of favoritism and bribery involved in that process. They weren't proud of any of it.

"My mother." Vi-Narm straightened her shoulders as she spoke. "She was selected because of her field of work. However, she refused to go, saying her place was with my dead father on Benzee. He was buried at sea per our family tradition. He was one of the last." She sighed out an exhale. "She suggested that her eldest daughter take her place instead."

"So, is your sister here too?" Todd beamed.

At least she has someone here with her. So that's not too bad.

"No." Her tone was sharp. "My mother gave up her place for me. I wasn't selected in the lottery." She sat taller in her chair. "Some Dentraee believed, at the time, not many of us were selected because of our historical part in the Clan War. Feeling we were being punished." Vi-Narm spoke stiffly. "Some think that."

"I'm sorry."

"You had no part in it. There is no need for you to be sorry." Vi-Narm rested her hands on the café table. "My younger sister was not selected either. I don't want to believe that my mother bribed the people she worked within the government selection committee, but a lot of people did. And if she did bribe them, why not for my sister as well?" Vi-Narm turned away.

Todd watched her.

I can't imagine having that weight on my shoulders.

"I'm here for them." Vi-Narm focused on Todd as she turned back. "I live my life to honor them as best I can."

"From everything I've seen, you do it well." Todd's voice was gentle. "I'm sure they are all pleased with the job you're doing."

"That is kind of you," Vi-Narm said. "I try to be worthy of their sacrifice." Her posture grew more rigid. "That was all in the past." Her voice strengthened. "There is nothing that can be done now. We all must live with the mistakes of the past and hope that we do not repeat them."

"Well said," Todd said. "It goes to show that neither race is perfect."

"I suppose we are more similar than different."

I couldn't imagine having gone through what Vi-Narm went through. It made my troubles seem petty.

"Now, if we can get everyone else to understand that, we wouldn't have the issues we're having with those idiot terrorists." He noticed the morning was slowly turning into afternoon. Todd pulled out his watch from his pocket and checked the time. "Oh wow. I didn't think we had been talking for this long. I should let you go."

Vi-Narm went silent.

"It's been nice, thank you," Todd said. "I've appreciated this opportunity to learn about you and to talk about the book. Perhaps, we can do it again." He finished the last of his tea. Then tapped the console to have the charges billed to his account.

"It has been educational getting to know more about your people's history, and thank you for the meal. That was kind of you."

"It was my pleasure." Todd grinned. "The more I learn, the more I've come to realize that my world is like your world was before the Clan War." He paused. "I suppose I should pull up the historical records on them and study them." He stood.

"If you would like"—Vi-Narm stood as well—"I would be happy to talk with you about our history pre-Clan War. It's an area of interest to me."

"I'd like that." Todd bowed. "Have a good afternoon."

"You as well." She bowed.

Todd watched her stroll away.

It's hard to believe she went through all that. Why didn't I make this effort sooner?

Twenty-Two: Christmas Eve

MARTHA TOSSED THE files to her conference table and glared around at all fourteen assembled members. "I've gone to great lengths to ensure that you're all cleared and in place for this meeting." She played with the gold crucifix around her neck. "Every world leader will be there. We can't ask for a better chance."

"About that," one of her agents started. "Killing all the delegates. Are you sure this is such a good idea?"

Martha's eyes narrowed. "We won't be killing all the delegates, but even if we do, they're collaborating with the soulless minions of the devil. Welcoming the Nentraee with open arms. So, a few of delegates and world leaders die. It'll make clear to everyone about what happens to those who work with the devil and his minions. Your blood will be spilled in His name."

The man nodded, glancing at the others in the room. "Once we're in, what do you want us to do?"

"Keep the room secure and stand witness to the power of the Almighty God." Martha raised her hands to the sky. "He has even shown us a way to block their communication and sensor technology." She smiled. "Once we have control, no one will try anything. Our military contacts will see to that. The rest are all cowards, hiding behind suits and ties and saying pretty words with no substance. And behind them, the weak-minded and the weak-spirited. They will quiver and fall on their knees, begging us to save them."

The others nodded or mumbled their agreement.

"The external media is run on a separate, secure network that will keep the cameras rolling. We'll need to knock out their other forms of communication. That won't be too complicated for you, will it?" She turned to the sour-faced man with the heavy accent.

"I have all the access and clearance I'll need," he said, puffing up his chest. "The world will see everything."

"Very good. Then I suggest we adjourn," Martha concluded, and the others gathered up their materials and notes. "Oh, and Merry Christmas to those that are celebrating."

"Same to you," one of them said.

There were a few smiles and nods as one by one they left the room.

The heavy-accented man stepped aside, letting the others clear out. "What about the shuttle?"

Martha's eyes narrowed. "Have your people in place so we can take over the demon's shuttle. We'll take their vice speaker so we can get out, and once we have the shuttle, we'll kill him."

"And if something goes wrong?"

"God has shown me what to do, in that case." She rested a hand on his shoulder. "Have faith in his plan, and we'll bring about paradise on Earth."

The round-faced man nodded. "Of course. Are you and your family going to be joining mine for dinner?"

"Not this year. I think it would be best if we keep our distance, in case things don't go to plan."

He nodded.

Martha's mouth curled into a righteous smile. If everything went to plan, this would be the best Christmas present the world had seen since the birth of their Lord and Savior.

TODD PULLED HIS Jeep up to his parents' house. "Are you sure you want to subject yourself to this?"

Mi'cin removed the tieback from his hair and tucked the bow into an inside pocket of his suit jacket. This was the first time Todd had ever seen Mi'cin with his soft brown hair falling to his shoulders.

He's so handsome even without his hair pulled back. Spending these past two weeks getting to know him have been great.

"You don't have to take the tieback out," Todd said. "Not for them. Not for anyone. You're fine the way you are."

"Thank you." Mi'cin reached out and softly touched Todd's face. "Your family is no more challenging than mine, and I want them to see me, not our differences."

"I like your family, especially your brothers. They're smart and funny."

"When it's the three of us, Ko and Shif can be frustrating and annoying."

Todd took Mi'cin's hand and kissed it softly. "That is a common bond us younger brothers all share."

Todd released Mi'cin's hand. He was glad to drive his car again. It was a small miracle that he had convinced Mi'ko and Vi-Narm they would be all right at his parents' house without security, and he was perfectly capable of driving them in his own car so didn't need a driver.

Todd and Mi'cin went to the back of the car and pulled out bags with presents.

"What's the purpose of the wrapping?" Mi'cin played with a bow on one of the gifts.

"To keep people from figuring out what's inside and to make the package look pretty." Todd grabbed two of the larger bags in one hand and helped Mi'cin with the others.

"Seems like a waste of resources."

"Yes, I know. Everything is a waste of resources."

Mi'cin shrugged.

"If it helps, I only get recycled paper and biodegradable bows and ribbon." Todd grinned. Mi'cin was quiet, only letting a slight sigh escape him. Todd closed the trunk, and they walked up the path.

Christmas lights covered the large suburban-style home. A Christmas wreath—one his folks bought back when they purchased the house—completed the decoration. Todd remembered helping his father climb on the sloped roof to put the lights up.

"Your family has a nice home. Different from yours," Mi'cin said.

"Yep, my folks had the front remodeled a couple years ago to update the style. To me, it's suburban, but I guess it's better than the super homes with no backyards." The Christmas tree stood in the front window. He couldn't keep back a smile. It was so much like when he was a boy. "It hasn't changed a bit."

Todd opened the front door. "Hello!" he called out.

"Well, come in," Todd's mom called before rushing over to them from the dining room. She wrapped her arms around Todd. He hugged her back.

Todd's mom stepped back. "Hello, Mi'cin. Welcome to our home."

Mi'cin bowed, wisps of hair falling to the sides of his face.

There was a buzz from the kitchen. "Brad, come help your brother," Todd's mother called from where they stood, before rushing off deeper into the house. The entry hall led to the open dining room, kitchen, and family room. To the left was a sunken living room. A half wall separated it from the dining room but didn't take away from the open feeling of the space.

Brad waved as he appeared from the hall opposite the dining room and came to greet them. "Toddy!" He grabbed packages and bags from Todd and Mi'cin. "Nice to see you again, Mi'cin." He stepped down into the living room where he unloaded the packages and put them under the tree.

"Where are Kevin and Michelle?"

"Watching movies with Dad." Brad pointed over his shoulder in the direction of the family room. He went back to unloading the gifts.

"Let me guess. *Scrooge.*"

"Yep. Landon family tradition," Brad said.

Todd's father sauntered over to greet them. He had on a bright red-and-green Christmas sweater.

"Interesting." Mi'cin tucked his fallen hair behind his ears.

"There's my boy." Todd's father tugged at the sweater.

"Nice sweater." Todd held back a chuckle.

His dad glared at him and then turned to Mi'cin. "Mi'cin, welcome to our home." He shook the Nentraee's hand. "It's good to see you, especially after Thanksgiving." He glanced to his feet.

"Merry Christ Mass," Mi'cin said.

"And you." Todd's father beamed. He hugged Todd harder than necessary. "This sweater is from your mother, so be good," he whispered in Todd's ear.

"Ouch, Dad." Todd struggled to get free.

"So, what do we have here?" Todd's father caught sight of all the gifts and bags. "Bradley, what the hell are you doing to the packages?"

"Dad, all I did was start to put them—"

"Stop. You'll screw up my system." Todd's father walked over to the tree and knelt down. He pulled out the ones Brad had stacked and started to reorder them.

"Yeah, Bradley." Todd smirked.

Brad crossed his arms in front of his chest.

"Is there significance to how the packages are arranged?" Mi'cin asked. "I thought the purpose was to open them and be surprised by the contents?"

Todd chuckled as his father peeked over his shoulder at him. "Consider it another mystery of us humans." He held up a small gift with Kevin's name on it.

Todd touched Mi'cin's arm gently. "Come on. It's best we leave Dad to it."

Brad shook his head. "Dad has a system."

Mi'cin's eyebrow raised.

"Come on." Todd gestured, and they headed off to the rest of the house.

"Where are you going?" Todd's father said. "You started this mess, Brad. You can stay and help."

Todd waved to Brad, who frowned as he went back to his father and the tree. Todd and Mi'cin moved to the dining room and kitchen.

"So, this is the rest of the house," Todd said.

The table was dressed in a green-and-red tablecloth. Various sizes of nutcrackers and other holiday decorations used as the centerpieces. China, crystal glasses, and polished silverware finished off the look.

"Todd." Lori lifted a tray of rolls from the kitchen oven. "Merry Christmas, Mi'cin." She put the tray down on the counter.

Mi'cin bowed. "Merry Christmas." He no longer emphasized the *Christ* and the *mass*. "I must share with you that my mother is amazed at how you both do all the homemaker work while your husbands' do little to help. If my father tried that with her, she would not be pleased."

"Well, um." Todd's mom glanced around the kitchen at all the food. "I can assure you, you don't want to trust Phil to cook. Unless it's barbecue or Sunday breakfast."

"We were all relieved that your father and his aide weren't hurt in London." Lori changed the topic, clearly deciding to ignore the previous comments. "I don't understand these people. They're nuts." She frowned. "They don't represent us or any religion. I hope your people don't think we're all like these Liberi Dei terrorists."

"No," Mi'cin said. "They are cowards who hide in darkness and are narrow-minded. We understand the majority of humans do not act this way. They are a small radical group, but don't worry, they will be found and put to death." His posture stiffened. "Thank you for your thoughts of my father. We are very pleased he is all right." He bowed and his hair fell around his face. He frowned and pushed it all back behind his ears.

"Toddy," Todd's mom said, starting to chop the rest of the carrots on the cutting board. "Give your friend a tour of the house. It won't be much longer before we can eat."

"All right," Todd said. "You sure you don't need any help?"

"No, honey, we're fine."

"Like she would allow the help," Lori said. "I don't know about how the Nentraee men do it, Mi'cin, but that woman right there won't allow anyone to help her. I'm lucky if I get to help with the dishes and pull things out of the oven."

Some things never change.

"So, that's the kitchen, and you saw the dining room and the living room." Todd moved them over to the family room where Kevin and Michelle were sitting on the couch, watching the movie. "Family room or TV room, with the two lumps. Hey, guys."

Kevin waved.

"Merry Christmas." Michelle didn't look up from her smartphone.

There was a breakfast bar and pass-through into the kitchen with a couple of plates filled with homemade popcorn balls and fudge. The vaulted ceiling emphasized the space to the second floor, where a railing illuminated with Christmas lights and garland filled the room with a fresh pine scent.

Todd turned to the TV. "We used to watch this movie every year on Christmas Eve. It was a lot of fun, all of us sitting around in our pajamas snacking on cookies."

"Sounds nice." Mi'cin ran a hand over the well-worn recliner.

Todd pointed to the second floor and led him to the stairs. They passed several family photos on the wall before reaching the top landing.

Mi'cin pointed. "Is this you?"

Todd froze and checked the photo, then his face heated up. "Oh God." He rubbed his face. "I can't believe she has that photo up." It was a photo of him when he was fourteen, his face full of pimples and braces on his teeth. "Could I lie and say no?"

Mi'cin laughed. "No. I can see the same eyes and kind smile."

"I look awful. That was an awkward time in my life."

"I understand," Mi'cin said. "When I was young, I had to wear braces on my legs. My bones were not fully developed. I was teased for it." Mi'cin reached out and touched Todd's cheek. "Now we are both attractive adult males. Without that past, we would not be who we are now."

Todd's face grew warmer.

He cleared his throat and opened the door. "Guest bedroom. This was my room when we were younger. Brad didn't want it."

"You grew up here?"

"Yep. Not that you can tell. I got rid of a bunch of stuff. Some of it, I moved to my house."

Mi'cin walked in the room and over to the window.

"I'm pretty sure Brad let me have it so I wouldn't sneak out."

Mi'cin glanced down. "I can see the deterrent. That is a long fall." He walked over to the bed and sat. "Did you get into a lot of trouble?"

Todd laughed. "No. Not really."

Mi'cin's brow raised.

"I mean, I got into some trouble, mainly when I started dating."

"Ah, with the other males. I can understand that. My parents didn't always approve of the males I pursued relationships with. They always felt the males were not worthy of me. I suppose that is why they like you."

"Really?"

"Of course. You have impressed them both a great deal. They are very fond of you, and I'm sure they would intervene if they felt our relationship needed it. Much like they have done in the past and with my brothers. Poor Ko, to this day will not date a female without the blessing of both my mother and father."

Todd smiled.

"But even if they were not, I would wish to spend time with you. I appreciate their efforts and their wisdom, but I wish to learn on my own." Mi'cin peeked around the room. "So, tell me, did you have to beat off all the human males who wanted to pursue you?"

Todd almost fell off the bed as he laughed.

Mi'cin's shoulders slumped.

Todd caught his breath. "Sorry, what you said." He laughed again. "You can't say it like that."

"Say what?"

Todd cleared his throat and lowered his voice. "Beat off." He shook his head. "It has a different meaning in this context. I can't explain now, but trust me—do not use that phrase again until I explain it."

Mi'cin's eyes narrowed. "All right."

Todd took a breath and looked around his old room. "Anyway, I didn't date guys in school. I dated girls."

"I'm confused. I thought you preferred males?"

"Oh, I do now." Todd stopped, not sure how to explain this. "I dated girls in school."

"So, you enjoy both males and females?"

Todd shook his head.

"I'm confused."

"So was I," Todd said.

"I see," Mi'cin said. "Is that what caused the trouble with you and your brother?"

"No. That came later, when I told Brad I like guys. Same with my family. Being gay here is, well, it's only become more acceptable recently, I suppose. And my family is very traditional, so..."

"I'm sorry. I still don't fully understand your culture on this matter. We have no stigma of such things. I guess that was what confused me at first." Mi'cin stood. "Shall we continue the tour?"

Todd nodded and stood. He showed off the bathroom, and then they walked down the open hall, which overlooked the family room. There was a wet bar and game table that had a half-completed puzzle on it and a desk with a computer.

"This is the den."

Mi'cin ran his hand on the table with the puzzle. He found a piece and put it into its proper place. "This home is very large."

"Considering the rooms on the ship, I suppose so. We had parties here all the time, both friends and families. This house was made for entertaining, or so Mom would say. I'm pretty sure that's why they bought it. My mom loves having people over."

They walked back down the stairs to the family room.

"Do you want me to hang up your cloak?" Todd's father offered, getting up from the recliner.

"Yes, thank you," Mi'cin replied. He twisted around, unclasped his cloak, and handed it to Todd's dad. "This place reminds me a great deal of the home my family had on Benzee." He turned to Kevin and Michelle. "I was a little younger than Kevin was when we left. You are lucky to have a home and a world."

Todd's dad nodded. "Yes. Yes, we are. After meeting the Nentraee and understanding what happened to you and your people, I'm sure we all have a greater appreciation for what we have."

"Mi'cin, can I borrow my little brother?" Brad smiled.

"Borrow him?" Mi'cin's brows raised.

"Have you ever seen *Scrooge*, Mi'cin?" Todd's father pointed to the TV with a big smile.

"No."

"Excellent, come and watch with us," Todd's father said. "It's a must-see Christmas classic."

Mi'cin bowed and followed Todd's father over to the couches.

"I'll only keep him a minute." Brad pulled Todd down the hall. He opened the bedroom door, and they walked in.

"What's up?" Todd asked as Brad closed the door behind them.

"You tell me. We're all curious, actually."

"What are you talking about?"

"Mi'cin? Mom said you called a couple of days ago and sprang the news of him coming with you for Christmas."

"I tried to call you, but you were busy and didn't get back to me. So, I figured I would call her to give her a heads-up. Plus, it's a good idea for him to see how we celebrate the holidays. They have a lot of questions about our customs and—"

"Bullshit." Brad held up a hand. "Toddy, you like him. That's why he's here. And you want to test the waters with the family."

"Are you saying you don't want us here?" Todd asked. "I thought we were past all this. Is him being here too awkward for everyone?"

"That's not fair and you know it." Brad reached for Todd's arm. "That's not the issue. Todd, he's not human!"

Todd followed Brad's gaze to the door.

"I didn't know that." Todd lowered his voice. "Not like I've been working with them every day, living on their ship, circling our planet in space." He crossed his arms over his chest.

"You know what I mean." Brad shook his head. "What about Jerry? It hasn't even been a year."

Todd took a step back, stunned. He sat on the bed. "That's cruel. I loved Jerry."

Brad's features softened. "I'm sorry. That wasn't how I meant it. It just seems quick."

"You don't think I get that? You don't think I see Jerry's ghost every time I walk into our home? Do you have any idea how hard this has been for me? To realize the people who killed him are out there and no one can seem to find them? Not even our own government."

Brad's whole face was red. He was focused on his hands.

"I can't imagine." Brad's voice was barely above a whisper. "I don't know what I would do if I lost Lori like that."

"Mi'cin has been nothing but nice and sweet to me. He treats me like a real person, a whole person, and not some—" Todd stopped. "He doesn't treat me like an alien or, worse, broken." He sighed. "He treats me like a man, and that feels wonderful."

Brad walked over to the small bed and sat next to him.

"I don't want to be broken, Brad. Not anymore." Todd sniffed.

"Toddy, we worry about you. All of us do." Brad looked to the ceiling. "Up there with them, dealing with God-knows-what. Mi'cin is a nice guy. He must be for you to be interested in him. But he's not human. He's Nentraee, and considering what's going on with these Liberi Dei nutcases, do you think that dating one of the Nentraee is such a smart move?"

"I don't know." Todd faced his brother. "I don't, but I like him. Although he's so different from Jerry. Spending time with him makes me happy. You know, not hiding anymore. Trusting the people I know I can trust. I want to be a real person again, and part of that means dating."

"Well, yeah, but I didn't..." Brad rubbed his temples. "I did say that, didn't I?"

Todd nodded.

Brad sighed softly and stood. "It's going to put you in greater danger than you already are."

"I know."

"Are you sure you're ready for that?"

"I want to be."

"Todd, you need to be," Brad said. "These Liberi Dei are no joke. The news says they are everywhere. They're like a virus. No one knows for sure how deeply they go."

"We've seen the reports, but I was already a target. That's not going to change, no matter who I date."

Brad inhaled. "So, then you're dating an alien?"

"Yep."

"But what about Dan? He's a nice guy, human, and I guess not bad-looking? You could date him. Plus, he's ex-military and can really kick ass if need be."

"You're joking, right?" Todd laughed. "Dan's a friend and nothing more."

"Fine, fine, but..." Brad leaned in. "Are you sure you're compatible? You know...like...well, you know."

Todd leaned back. "Are you kidding me?"

"Look, I just...I mean, you know. These things are important."

"I'm not having this conversation with you, Brad."

Both their faces were beet red.

"I'll take that to be a yes." Brad fanned his face. "Anyway, Mi'cin better treat you good, or I'm gonna kick his extraterrestrial ass." He ran his hands through his hair. "Please, be careful and don't take any unnecessary risks."

"Thanks, Brad." Todd stood.

"So, they have gays too?" Brad headed to the bedroom door.

"It would appear so." Todd smiled.

Brad scratched his head and exhaled. "Well, I guess some biology is universal."

Twenty-Three: Christmas Day

MI'CIN PEEKED OVER at Todd, whose gray suit complemented his blond hair and olive complexion. The necktie he wore was bright red and contrasted his cream-colored shirt. It all showed off his strong frame and masculine features.

Mi'cin felt his neck warm.

Considering all he's been through, he carries himself strong and assured. It's very appealing.

They were outside Mi'cin's family's residence. Todd held boxes wrapped in brightly colored paper. Not one kind of paper, several different types. Todd had asked if he could come to see Mi'cin's family today, but Todd was unaware of the small surprise they had prepared for him.

Mi'cin inhaled Todd's musky scent. It was intoxicating and always made his heart beat faster and his body crave contact. It was one of the first things he'd noticed about Todd. Most humans didn't smell as appealing.

I never thought I could have feelings for an alien.

The door swished opened, and they walked in.

"Is that a Christmas tree?" Todd held the gifts and turned toward the corner of the living room. "What's that on top?"

"It's a gargoyle." Mi'cin's heart skipped a beat with anticipation. They had rearranged the seating area to focus on the tree like in Todd's parents' home. "We liked the human symbolism of scaring off evil and felt that it suited the holiday. It's similar to one of our myths."

Todd's eyes grew larger, and he nodded. "I see."

Mi'cin's chest swelled with pride. He was thrilled he had made the right choice of getting the tree and having his family decorate it. If Todd was going to share this human custom with his family, then they were going to have a Christmas tree for him.

Unfortunately, there was a foul odor coming from the tree that he hadn't noticed in Todd's parents' home.

It's only for the one day, and I can manage the smell for Todd.

A door closed. "Yes, we wanted to surprise you with it," Hir-Ko greeted Todd, coming from the back bedrooms. His shirt was untucked, casually draping over his pants and his hair was tied back in a tight bow.

Mi'cin met his brother and leaned in, whispering to Hir-Ko. "As I recall, you didn't wish to help until Father made you."

Hir-Ko shrugged.

"It was a family effort." Hir-Shif joined them from the kitchen. His shirt the same light-green color as Hir-Ko's, but his was properly tucked in. "It wasn't easy, but it was fun."

"It's festive." Todd glanced at the decorated tree and stepped forward. There was a wrinkle to his nose, but then it vanished.

"Luvan helped me find it."

This is my treat for Todd. My brothers will not be taking any more credit for this. Especially since they complained about the death smell too. Perhaps, I should have found one that wasn't rotting.

"Welcome, Todd." Laina and Mi'ko joined them from the den, and she offered a polite bow. Her cream-colored dress flowed gently from her shoulders and off her hips. "Hello, Mi'cin." She touched the side of his face softly.

Mi'cin held her hand there, beaming back at her.

"You look beautiful as always, Dr. Soemu." As Todd bowed, the gifts shifted and he quickly stood, huffing.

"Merry Christ Mass." Mi'ko offered to shake Todd's hand.

"Merry Christmas." Todd shifted the boxes again.

The gifts. I should help Todd with them. What am I thinking? I must make a better effort.

"Apologies." Mi'cin took several of the unevenly balanced gifts and ushered Todd toward the foul-smelling tree to put them away, eyeing his brothers to assist him.

"No worries." Todd's glistening hazel eyes met Mi'cin's.

Such beautiful eyes. Showing a beautiful spirit. I could watch them forever.

"These are for you and your family." Todd handed a couple of gifts to Mi'cin as he put them next to the tree.

"Gifts were not necessary." Laina stared at the packages. "It is us who should be giving you presents with all you've done."

Mi'cin's eyes grew large, and he slightly shook his head.

She's going to wreck the surprise.

Laina blinked an acknowledgement to Mi'cin but said no more.

"Nonsense," Todd said.

Thank J'Veesa he didn't notice anything.

"I enjoyed shopping for you," Todd said. "I even got to poke around the stores on the ship. It was fun."

Mi'cin held his breath, trying to remember Todd's scent as he continued by the tree. The rancid smell had gotten worse. Thank J'Veesa the window was open to gardens below and the air circulation system was operating.

Mi'cin pointed to two empty seats near the tree for his brothers to sit. Hir-Ko waved him off.

Cowards. It's a small price to pay for Todd.

Mi'cin finished with the packages, covering his mouth with his shoulder so he could take a breath. "It's a complicated ritual. Todd's father was insistent that it be done correctly and to his specifications. I suspect this is what caused the trouble with Todd's nephew and niece. I can't be sure. It could've also been all the sugar they ate."

"You have a culturally rich family, Todd. All these traditions and events." Mi'ko took off his suit jacket and hung it on the back of the chair.

"I don't know about that." Todd cleared his throat. His face had beads of sweat where his hair met his skin.

"Tell us." Hir-Shif met Mi'cin's gaze. "Mi'cin was well behaved. Are you familiar with the term *Yép*? Typically that describes Mi'cin."

Todd covered his mouth. "Mi'cin was a perfect guest and not at all a troublesome child."

"Shif, do not poorly represent our family," Laina said with a warning glance over her shoulder as she and Mi'ko went to the kitchen.

Mi'cin gritted his teeth and stood. "It was an educational experience."

"We looked through the American historical data on Christmas." Hir-Ko adjusted his tieback. "We found that trees of this type are decorated with various kinds of boxes, fruit, little metal strands called tinsel, candy canes, glass balls... The list is rather long, and the area of Earth you are from dictates what you put on it."

"It's beautiful," Todd said.

"We did the best we could, wanting to represent your planet, not only your country." Hir-Ko adjusted the pillow on the sofa and leaned farther away from the tree. "These are not normal things we keep around our home."

Hir-Shif sat forward. "There are some trees that have decorations on them that are very old—"

"Yes, brother," Mi'cin interrupted. "Todd is aware. It is his culture and traditions." He stood taller.

Todd is not unintelligent on these matters. He is a brilliant male as proven by his saving Father twice.

"My mother has an angel on our tree that is my great-grandmother's." Todd turned to the tree. "You did an amazing job. I especially like the sugar skulls." He sat down next to the tree, examining the decorations, holding up one of the small lighted Japanese paper lanterns.

Mi'cin's posture relaxed.

The smell must not bother him.

"I'm glad you both enjoyed the event yesterday." Hir-Shif nudged Mi'cin and went to sit next to his twin.

Todd smiled up at Mi'cin. "They had so many questions for him. It was embarrassing."

"Is your family well?" Mi'ko's firm voice called their attention as he sat down with a warm cup of e'xin.

"They are, thank you." Todd leaned forward. "They asked me to relay how happy they are that you were not injured in London."

"Another debt we owe you." Laina walked in, holding a tray with cups of e'xin and a tuma.

Mi'cin quickly rushed over to assist her. He took the tray, allowing her to take the tuma.

Family duty. Serving. Being the one to assist Mother. I understand I'm the youngest, but Ko and Shif could have assisted me. Especially with Todd here.

Mi'cin put a cup next to Todd, should he want it. "According to Todd's family, before you open the gifts, you must watch a movie called *Scrooge*. It's a musical. Then you eat a meal, and finally you may open the gifts." Mi'cin sipped his e'xin. He needed the warmth to calm his nerves.

"Afterward, you eat sweets and sit and talk. According to Brad, they also play games, but we didn't do that."

"Oh, boy." Todd ran a hand through his hair, causing the waves in it to become more pronounced and fall from their place. "Remember, that's only how my family celebrates Christmas."

Mi'cin grinned.

"Not everyone celebrates in the same way. Dan, for example, went home, and his family goes to church, and they don't open gifts until today, after Santa comes."

"Ah, right, Santa Claus." Mi'cin clapped his hands together. "I almost forgot. He's the fat human who rides around in a red sleigh with flying reindeers, giving gifts to good people and lumps of coal to the bad."

"Yep, that's him." Todd adjusted in his seat, wrinkling his nose again.

"Michelle, Todd's niece," Mi'cin started, "told me about him and how only small children believe in him." He watched his brothers and parents. He had learned so much yesterday, and he was excited to share it. "She confessed to me that she hopes Santa Claus will bring her a new smartphone."

"Amazing," Hir-Shif said. "I'm sure our ships would have picked up a ship like that last night. It would be interesting to see how these reindeers are able to make the altitude and the journey so quickly." He stood up, walked over to the bookshelf, and picked up a datapad.

There was a red flash from the device and an alert sound. Hir-Shif glared down at the pad and ran his fingers over the commands.

Mi'cin was sure he must have entered a wrong command or was doing something to intentionally make the device malfunction and sound the alarm. "Having issues with the datapad?"

Hir-Shif's eyes narrowed. "It appears we are suffering from failures in our systems. I thought our datanet systems were repaired?"

"As did I." Mi'ko reached out and Hir-Shir handed him the device. He tapped a few commands and finally the alarm ended. "I'll speak with Vi-Narm. Clearly, there is more to repair."

Mi'cin noted the odd flicker in his father's eyes and the slight shift of voice. There was more happening, but it was not his position to ask, and this was not the correct environment to bring it up.

"Todd," Hir-Shif said, calling attention back to him. "Why have we not seen anything in your world's zoological information on such creatures? They must travel at incredible speeds, even for us."

"Um...well..." Todd bit the bottom of his lip.

"According to Michelle, Santa Claus is a magic creature, much like our A'Ko Hune," Mi'cin replied. "I plan on researching it more. There are volumes of source material. It's a big human subject and quite controversial too."

"Mi'cin, I wouldn't put too much into this." Todd had a bright smile, similar to what Brad and Kevin had last night. It was more endearing on Todd.

"Wait," Todd said. "When did you and Michelle talk about Santa Claus?"

"When you and Brad went to speak privately," Mi'cin replied.

"It's all very complicated, and there's more to the story," Todd said. "Some adults claim Santa Claus is a myth, something only well-behaved children believe in." He stroked his face, creating a soft scratching sound as the short hairs on Todd's skin rubbed against his hand.

Mi'cin enjoyed that sound. He doubted any human even noticed it, but he and his people easily heard it. It was like when the iz-cus berries released their sweet smell before they dropped.

"I'm making this much more complicated than it needs to be," Todd said.

"Interesting." Hir-Ko sipped at his drink. "Does it work in helping children behave? It might be worth trying here in our classrooms in conjunction with corporal punishment. Help to reinforce the behavior we want."

"Um...it doesn't work all the time." Todd leaned closer to Mi'cin, bumping his leg.

Mi'cin smiled at Todd.

"You must have a rich mythology as well."

"Of course, but nothing as interesting as this." Laina crossed her legs at the knee. "Imagine if the A'Ko Hune could keep children from misbehaving."

"Instead of causing trouble at our É'mawees." Mi'ko nodded.

"Please, Mother. Father." Hir-Shif waved. "We do not wish to hear the story of how an A'Ko Hune almost ruined your wedding day. I'm sure Todd has no interest in this." He leaned in. "I'm very curious to hear more of how human children are keep under control by this Santa Claus."

"A story for another time then." Laina bowed. "Todd, please continue."

Todd cleared his throat. "Um, at best, it only works around Christmas, if at all. When Brad and I were younger, I didn't care about being good until Thanksgiving, and even then, I'm sure I wasn't always that good." He chuckled. "I bet my mom has stories about Brad and I, and how they would threaten us. Tell us they were going to write letters to Santa, informing him we had been naughty."

"That's unfortunate." Hir-Ko put his drink down.

"It would have been nice to have this Santa Claus when our boys were young." Laina sipped her tuma.

"It would be nice even now," Mi'ko added.

Mi'cin and his brother glanced at their parents. Todd covered his mouth with a hand, but his smile peeked through.

"Do you believe in this...mystical Santa Claus?" Laina's eyes sparkled at Todd over her cup of tuma.

"He's kind and good and wonderful, so why would I ever not want to believe in someone like that? The one thing about Santa is he loves everyone. He embodies kindness and reminds us of how we should treat one another. Not just at Christmas, but always."

"I agree." Mi'cin turned to Todd. He had not stopped smiling since they arrived.

"All right, enough about human legends for today." Todd grabbed the gift bag from next to the tree. He walked over to Laina and handed it to her. "This is from my family to yours."

"That is kind." Laina took the offered bag. "They did not need to do this."

"They wanted to," Todd said.

She opened the bag. "Human wine." She read the label and turned the bottle upside down and around.

"It's a Groth Cabernet Reserve '05, made in Napa Valley." Todd sounded proud. "It's actually a nice wine. It's kind of like your e'xin, but this is served at room temperature, and it's best if you open the bottle and let it sit out and breathe, maybe an hour or two before you serve it."

"Breathe?" Laina held the bottle by the top and watched it. "Is it alive?"

Todd's eyes grew large.

"No, Mother, it's a human saying," Mi'cin said. "I thought the same, but the wine needs the air to help release its flavor."

Laina brought the bottle in for a closer inspection. "Please extend our gratitude for this gift." She put the bottle on the table behind her. "We have yet to experience human wine."

Todd went back to the tree, pulled out a gift, and handed it to Hir-Shif.

"Should I rip the paper off?" Hir-Shif put down his cup and held the present in his hands.

Todd nodded, so he obliged.

"I realize you can pull up whatever information you want on us, but I thought you might like these books," Todd said. "They're all about the human animal."

Human psychology books. Todd did well.

"Thank you," Hir-Shif said. "It will be interesting to read them." He bowed. "I'm sure I will learn a great deal about your people." He flipped the first book open. "Good, English. I need more practice."

Todd turned to Hir-Ko and handed him a small box wrapped with a large red-and-gold bow.

"It's a pretty box. It's a shame to rip it apart." Hir-Ko flipped the box over in his hands, examining the wrapping. "May I keep it as it is? I don't want to mess it up. It's too beautiful."

"It's their custom, brother," Mi'cin instructed. "Open it, but save the bow, because it is pretty."

Hir-Ko pulled off the bow and put it aside. "Perhaps I should use it as a tieback?"

"The material doesn't appear strong enough." Hir-Shif picked up the bow and examined it.

"Unfortunate," Hir-Ko said and carefully unfolded the paper, making sure not to rip it. "The Story of America." He held up the box, flipping it over in his hands, a lopsided smile crossing his lips.

"It's only about the United States, but I thought you might find it interesting to see how my country was founded." Todd fussed with his necktie, causing a dimple in the middle of the knot. "There are so many other countries and cultures, but it's about my home, so I'm biased."

Mi'cin bowed at Todd.

Another thoughtful gift. Todd put a great deal of consideration into this.

"Thank you. I'm sure it will be both interesting and educational." Hir-Ko put the gift down.

Todd handed the next gift to Laina. "This is from me."

"You did not need to do all this." Laina took the gift from him, a sudden twinkle in her eyes. "This one doesn't live, does it?"

"Of course not." He chuckled and his cheeks brightened.

She tore the paper and pulled out a frame. Then she turned it so everyone could see it. It was a photo of their family at the White House reception where they all met Todd.

"I wasn't sure what to get for you, and I remembered the dinner in Washington." Todd stood stiff as stone, watching her. "I called the office of the social secretary and asked if I could get a duplicate of the photo for you and your family. I hope you like it."

She ran her hand over the image. She was quiet, and to Mi'cin's surprise, she reached up to Todd and touched his arm. "You are too kind to me and my family. We will never be worthy of all you've given us."

Mi'cin's brows shot up.

She sees him as family. She's never touched another, not in this manner. She approves of him. His kindness and strength of character are clear to everyone, not only me.

"I'm happy you like it." Todd glanced down at her hand on his arm. He smiled, not moving until she removed it. His face was now a bright crimson.

"Todd, you now have proof our mother has a gentle side. Well done." Hir-Ko shared a look with Hir-Shif.

"Ko, that is not suitable conversation," Mi'ko reprimanded.

Hir-Ko bowed.

Mi'cin peeked down to the floor, hiding his smile.

I hope Todd does not judge me by the actions of my brothers. They are much too flippant with him tonight.

Todd cleared his throat and grabbed the second to last gift under the tree. "Well, um, moving on. You are a tough man to shop for." He handed Mi'ko the small box.

Mi'ko glanced at the box and then up to Todd. "Thank you." He opened the box and took out the gift.

Mi'ko held up a narrow leather tieback. "This is a personal gift. Thank you."

"I was worried about making a cultural mistake." Todd's shoulders relaxed and he took a deep breath. "I didn't find anything that said it wasn't appropriate. I asked several people at the shops, and they assured me it would be a nice gift. So when you wear it, you'll remember how much I appreciate all you've done for me."

"Thank you for your kindness and thoughtfulness," Mi'ko said.

Todd fumbled with the last wrapped gift as everyone watched him. "I saved this for last because, honestly, I'm worried about you liking it." Todd handed Mi'cin the small box.

Mi'cin took the gift and removed the wrapping paper.

You have already given me the best possible gift. You have honored my family and me. You have shared time with me. Nothing in this box will compare to that.

He opened the box and uncovered the gift. He turned up to Todd. "One of your human watches."

"Turn it over." There was a small quiver in Todd's voice.

Mi'cin did as instructed, and on the face of the watch was an image engraved in white gold. "It's your moon." Mi'cin's heart beat faster in his chest.

"I wanted you to have something to remind you of our dinner." Todd rubbed his hands on his slacks. He scanned the room. "I hope you'll wear it."

"Mi, you will finally be able to show up when you are requested at a proper time with that device." Hir-Ko pointed to the gift, grinning.

Hir-Shif chuckled.

"This explains why you wanted me to open it when we were alone before we came here. It represents a personal moment between us. I see now that might have been a better idea. I apologize." Mi'cin reached up and touched Todd's cheek softly. "Thank you."

He struggled with the clasp of the watch, and after a couple of seconds, he got it. He moved his hand around, feeling the weight. It wasn't as heavy or as awkward as he thought it would be. It would take time to get used to it, but it would be worth it.

Mi'ko stood and nodded toward Laina. He turned to his sons and then back over to Todd. "If we understand your traditions and based on what we have seen here, today we have a Christ Mass gift for you."

"You didn't need to get me anything." Todd licked his lips. "I wanted to share this with you. I didn't expect—"

Laina raised a hand. "Much like you didn't need to get us anything, but we chose to."

"In that case, thank you."

"I have spoken with a few members of our scientific teams, and based on their results, we are able to grant you permission to bring your animal companion Bianca on board," Mi'ko said. "We weren't sure how a human would present news like this, so I hope me telling you is acceptable."

Todd fell back into the chair, laughing. "Really?"

"She will be limited to your quarters and will need to be fully examined, but we see no reason to keep her from you—"

"But what about her fur?" Todd interrupted. "Won't that cause problems with the air filters, or whatever?"

Mi'cin stifled a laugh.

Such an odd concern, but then he doesn't fully understand our technology.

"No, Todd," Laina said. "Our biofilters are designed for such things. It would be the same with the cells of our skin that fall off our bodies or the hair from the cádo." She smiled. "We wouldn't have lasted in space for long if we hadn't overcome these concerns."

Todd nodded.

"We would also like to ask that you let us insert a small monitoring device in her so we can check for any changes in her biology," Mi'ko said. "We don't want her to get sick if we've missed a bacteria or potential illness. The device won't hurt her. You have my word."

"Thank you." Todd quickly glanced around the room. "You have no idea what this means to me."

"It was not my idea entirely. Mi'cin has witnessed you and her." Mi'ko bowed.

Mi'cin inhaled, blocking out the foul stench of the tree. "They may not have the full intelligence or language abilities of the cádo, but it's not right to keep her from her provider."

Todd chuckled. "Thank you. This means the world to me."

"Plus," Hir-Shif said, "we're all interested in seeing her. Mi'cin has told us a great deal. Even without language, he mentions the two of you understand each other. This sounds fascinating."

"We wish to judge for ourselves if what he told us was correct or not," Hir-Ko said. "Particularly since we were not able to attend your Thanks for Giving day meal."

Mi'cin's eyes narrowed on his brothers, and they both gave him a lopsided smile.

You're both vak yéps.

MIRTOFF LEANED BACK in her chair, enjoying the quiet of the afternoon. She would be having dinner with Ecra and Suloff soon enough. Mi'ko was off with his family and Todd.

Todd was so different from any of the other humans she had dealings with. What was it about this male that was so unique? He was honest, diligent, and intelligent, but she had seen these same traits in others, both human and Nentraee. Still there was more about him. Maybe it was all the pain he had been through and how, despite that, he managed to find moments of happiness and peace. One thing was certain. Todd being around her and the others in the Speaker's House had been impactful, and not because he helped uncover the attack in London.

She examined the gift Todd had brought for her. A coffee press and a bag of coffee.

She had only tried coffee once and didn't care for it. However, she didn't want to insult Todd. Perhaps she would try it again, maybe with Danu.

She picked up the bag of coffee and read the label.

"Kona Coffee. Made in Hawaii." She sniffed at the bag.

It smells like it has been burned.

There was a buzz on her monitor. She put the bag down and tapped the "Receive" button. "Yes."

"Madam Speaker," Tun'ae said. "You asked to be notified when we detected another datanet systems malfunction."

"The system has failed again?" she asked, leaning in toward her monitor.

"Only momentarily, but it would appear so." Tun'ae's dark-blue eyes twinkled with worry. "This time, the signal came directly from Earth, not a satellite or other foreign body. It wasn't powerful enough to do any damage, and the systems have self-corrected."

Mirtoff rubbed her ears. "Liberi Dei?"

"Nothing has been reported yet," Tun'ae said.

"Ensure General Yee is aware and ask him to prepare a report for the meeting with the Speaker's House."

"Of course, Madam Speaker," Tun'ae said. "Also, General Gahumed and Speaker Rosta are on their way to see you. Would you like me to delay them?"

"I'll receive them," Mirtoff said and ended the communication between her and Tun'ae as her door chirped. She tapped the monitor on her desk. "Yes?"

The door swished open, and Gahumed and Rosta walked in.

The military general and the speaker for agriculture and health—not a pair I see together often.

"Ah, General Gahumed and Speaker Rosta, what brings you here today? I hope all is well." She pointed to her small conference table. "Please, let's sit. Would either of you like a tuma?" She peeked down at the coffee on her desk. "Or I have this *coffee* that Todd gave me for Christmas. We could all try it."

"No, thank you, Madam Speaker." Gahumed sat heavily at the conference table. Her shoulders straight and stiff as always.

"Oh, is that the Kona?" Rosta rushed to the coffee and picked it up. "Have you tried it yet? It's strong and a bit bitter, but once you get past that, it's not bad." Her smile brightened and her eyes twinkled. "I suggest you drink it in limited quantities. It had an ill effect on my digestive system."

Mirtoff cleared her throat and glanced at the bag of coffee and the coffee press. "I shall keep that in mind." She pointed to a seat. "Please, Speaker Rosta."

Rosta crossed over and fell into the chair.

Gahumed inhaled and clasped her hands in front of her and resting them on the conference table. "I understand that Mi'ko is with Special Envoy Landon, sharing a meal. I would prefer he were here as well, but I didn't wish to interrupt his time with family."

"Is everything all right?" Mirtoff asked, glancing between Gahumed and Rosta. There had been no reports or any issues. She wished more of her days were like this.

"We'd like to send a series of probes to Benzee," Rosta blurted out, then took a breath and adjusted her blouse.

"I'm sorry?"

Is this some form of joke? There are no resources for such an effort, and even if we did, we must settle our people first.

"Considering we've decided to stay here in this system"—Gahumed's voice was strong—"Speaker Rosta and I talked, and we would like to study the effects of our home system's destruction."

"Madam Speaker, we haven't had a chance to fully research the effects of the supernova—"

"And it would give us the chance to see if anyone, other than us, survived," Mirtoff finished.

"The possibilities are slim, but Rosta and I agree that now is the time to explore that potential truth."

"We left our world so quickly," Rosta said. "It would be good for our people to see that we've not forgotten where we come from."

Mirtoff turned to Gahumed. "And you support this?"

"I do." Gahumed bowed. "We should start making efforts to learn if more of our people live. I realize this will take time and resources, but if we start planning now—"

"We must settle on a location for our people here—"

"I thought that was handled with the human United Nations?" Gahumed interrupted.

"Not as yet." Mirtoff frowned. "There are many details to work out, and with all the human end-of-year holidays, much is being held up." She caught Gahumed's jaw tense. "We need to settle and build our new society. These are our main priorities. I'm sorry, but there are no resources or time to spend on such an endeavor."

"It is possible that others escaped," Rosta said. "No matter how slim the chances."

"And what would we be bringing them to?" Mirtoff shook her head. "A world that is fractured with groups of humans that want nothing more than our deaths and destruction."

"Madam Speaker, we would be bringing the survivors back to their own people." Rosta's voice became louder, filled with passion and fire. "I don't think they are better off scattered around the galaxy, possibly alone and in need. We must find them and offer hope and assistance."

"You are the one reminding us—reminding me—to maintain faith in these humans," Gahumed said. "That it is a small number and the majority of humans accept and welcome us."

"Madam Speaker, we should start planning on the chance, J'Veesa willing, that we find more of our people." Rosta leaned in.

Mirtoff typed on the conference table interface, bringing it to life, and pulled up the final reports on the destruction of their solar system. She swiped it over to the large monitor on the wall for them to view.

"You think it's possible there are more of us out there?"

Rosta typed on the table, pulling up gravitational fluctuations and details of their neighboring star explosion, as well as abnormalities from their former system. "I've had my team working on this question, as time permits. No other Speaker for Agriculture and the Interior has done so." She bowed. "We will never be able to identify what got missed and what might still be out there if we don't continue our research and go back there."

"It's been almost twenty standard years."

Gahumed sighed. "It's a matter we should examine."

"But now is not the time." Mirtoff shook her head.

"Madame Speaker?" Rosta said.

Gahumed was silent. A scowl tightened her face.

Mirtoff held up a hand. "Now is not the time for an expedition. However, we should start planning and examining carefully what such an endeavor would require." She opened a file and began typing her directions. "I won't be the speaker general who passed up on the chance that there might be more of us out there. I give you my full support. Please, provide me updates and inform me what additional resources you might need."

Rosta bowed and Gahumed smiled.

"Speaker Rosta, you will bring this to the full Speaker's House for consideration after we settle our people. General Gahumed will be your second, and I will offer my support."

"Thank you, Madam Speaker." Rosta clapped her hands together.

"Our first priority is to the Nentraee in our care now." Mirtoff eyed Rosta. "Do not forget that."

Rosta bowed.

"There is still much to do with the humans on Earth. If you try to bring this matter before the Speaker's House..." Mirtoff trailed off.

But the chance to see if there are more of us out there. No. I have to focus on those under my care now. My first priority must be to them.

"Of course, Madam Speaker. I—" Gahumed turned to Rosta. "We understand."

"Excellent. Now, what if we find a signal?" Mirtoff focused on Gahumed.

"The Rádo could be sent to investigate," Gahumed said. "Its drive system is the most powerful, but they would still need to be upgraded for faster travel time and that would give us time to upgrade and outfit it for scientific research."

"And you would be willing to let your command ship go?" Mirtoff stifled a laugh. "Ah, you would wish to go with it."

"Assuming the speaker general allows it, and I'm not yet retired." Gahumed bowed. "This process will take years, and as you reminded me, our first priority is to our current population."

"I'm not sure I wish to lose our top general and most opinionated member of the Speaker's House." Mirtoff closed down the files on the screen.

"Of course, Madam Speaker."

"Thank you, Madam Speaker." Rosta stood. "If you decide to try the coffee, please, let me know. I would be interested to hear your thoughts on the drink."

"Yes, of course." Mirtoff turned to her gift.

I'm not sure I'm going to. I wonder what the tradition is for not using a gift. I'll have to research that.

Rosta bowed. "May you rest well, Madam Speaker. Oh, and happy Christ Mass."

Mirtoff returned the bow. Oddly, Gahumed remained at the conference table.

"Was there anything else, General Gahumed?" Mirtoff asked.

"I wanted to..." Gahumed paused and glanced around the office. "Since the attack in London and witnessing firsthand how well the special envoy handled himself. If it wasn't for him..." Her shoulders grew more stiff. "I wanted to tell you I was wrong about him. He has served us and the humans well."

Mirtoff returned to her seat.

Proud General Gahumed humbling herself to apologies. J'Veesa be praised. I never thought this time would come.

"We've never met on the same bridge of thought," Gahumed said. "After witnessing how much Special Envoy Landon has done for us, he is not the weak fragile male I thought he was." She leaned forward. "It calls to question some of the other biases I've had. We can no longer afford to be divided."

"That is kind of you."

"It is the truth." Gahumed reached up and adjusted her hair braid. "I would like to believe I would have done better, but with the death of my son, I quite possibly would have led us to war."

"Neither of us is free of blame." Mirtoff's voice was soft.

"You may be right." She clasped her hands together in front of her. "Nothing is finalized yet. There are many bridges of faith to cross. I'm still haunted by your words, General Gahumed: the arm of peace we extend to them has cost us greatly. You know this cost too well."

"Losing my son has brought sadness to my world." Gahumed's shoulders dropped. "Todd reminds me of my Denes, and since Denes's memorial sculpture only has the offerings for J'Veesa, I have nothing of him. So, I see Denes in Todd. At times, it's been a bitter reminder because of my past words. Seeing Todd Landon and what he has been through and realizing his loss, I find strength in his resolve." Gahumed adjusted her collar and her gaze narrowed slightly on Mirtoff. "I plan on being vocal, and I will not back down from what I think is right, but I will endeavor to honor my son's memory better than I have."

"I would expect nothing less," Mirtoff said.

Gahumed stood. "I do not wish to take more of your time."

"Wait." Mirtoff held up a hand. "I understand why searching for our people is important to you. The Dentraee clan was not treated fairly in the evacuation of our world, and that is a wrong that can never be righted." She joined Gahmued, meeting her gaze. "I will not allow that to happen again. We will search for our people. You have my word." She offered a low deep bow.

Gahumed bowed. "That pleases me to hear. Rest well, Madam Speaker." She walked out the door, her shoulders a bit stronger than they had been only moments ago.

The door closed behind Gahumed. "That took a great deal of strength," Mirtoff whispered as she stared at the sealed entry. *The bringer of peace is never an easy job, especially for one such as Gahumed.*

Twenty-Four: Dating

TODD TOOK A moment outside the vice speaker's office to review his notes on the additional security measures for the New Year's Eve celebration. He checked his suit and grinned at the white hair stuck on it. Bianca had made her presence known in their quarters.

It feels so normal having her here with me. It's more like home.

He tapped the office door button, and with a small chirp, the door swished open.

"Todd, please sit down," Mi'ko greeted him.

Todd took up his customary chair, putting his device on the desk. With a swipe of his fingers, the data filled the screen as his reports transferred over to Mi'ko's desktop terminal.

"You've been busy." Mi'ko watched his terminal screen populate. "I thought you were planning on taking more time off?"

"I did," Todd replied. "Well, with the plans for New Year's, I wanted to make sure I was around. Just in case I was needed." He found another cat hair on his pants. "And I wanted to get Bianca used to her new home."

Todd hadn't wanted to waste any time in bringing Bianca to his ship. Getting her cleared through the quarantine was easier than he thought, so she wasn't without him for too long. Despite being a cat, she didn't like being alone. Now she was in his quarters, becoming familiar with her new setting. She even found a spot to lie and peer out the window, down into the gardens.

"All your extra work is much appreciated," Mi'ko said. "I'm pleased to see you and Vi-Narm working so well together."

"It's not just Vi-Narm. General Gahumed and General Yee have been a great help, chiefly with all the security concerns. That's also part of why I came back sooner. I didn't want them to think I was being lazy." Todd brushed off another piece of Bianca's fur.

An odd expression crossed Mi'ko's face, one that Todd wasn't sure how to read, but then it vanished as he leaned back in his chair. He pointed to the cat hair. "How is Bianca doing?"

"Other than getting hair all over everything, she's doing fine." Todd rested his hand on the table. "Thank you again for letting her come aboard."

"I'm pleased you are no longer separated." Mi'ko tapped his monitor. "I'm sure it has been difficult for her to be away from you."

"I think so." Todd cleared his throat and focused on the task at hand. He gave the vice speaker an item-by-item overview of where his list of cultural events for the new year were, as well as the idea of establishing a human press office here on the ship. He wanted to provide an update on Dan's travel ideas, even though that would probably need to go to Speaker Rosta and Speaker Syde. Todd didn't want there to be any surprises for the vice speaker.

Once the meeting came to an end, Todd cleared the reports. "Mister Vice Speaker, I wanted to talk to you about a personal matter." He put down his datapad.

"As you wish." Mi'ko tapped several commands on his terminal, then clasped his hands in front of him.

"Well, um." Todd stumbled, unsure where and how to start. "All right, as you're aware I, well, um...me and Mi'cin."

"You wish to talk to me about my son and you spending time with each other romantically?" Mi'ko stated. "Human or Nentraee, it's always the same when it comes to matters of the heart." He reached back to adjust his tieback.

"Yes, I wanted to make sure it wasn't a problem." Warmth tickled Todd's cheeks.

"I would not have agreed to help him arrange the dinner if Laina and I thought it was an issue." Mi'ko leaned forward. "I'm happy my son has found someone he's interested in and sees as an equal. If I'm to be honest, you're a better choice than some of his past interests. He refused to listen to us about them. However, I ask that you keep that between us."

"Of course." Todd bowed. "And I appreciate it. But what about me being human?"

"I thought you and Mi'cin would have talked of such matters before." Mi'ko tilted his head as he watched Todd. "Prior to our arrival to Earth, we discussed our respective biologies, and over the last few months, we've researched the issue further. Now, with full access to your physical information, our physiological differences are somewhat minor. Even though reproduction doesn't seem possible between our species, there should be no reason for you and my son not to enjoy your physical encounters. If you are curious about the kinds of intimacy you—"

"Mister Vice Speaker," Todd blurted. "That isn't what...that isn't what I wanted to ask about." His face was burning hot. "What I meant to ask about is us dating, seeing each other, being seen out together. Out in public."

"Oh, I see." Mi'ko nodded. "I don't see a problem. I was upset the day he asked you to dinner and you appeared to not be interested. But understand, he is my youngest son, and I didn't want him hurt, but now...I'm pleased, as is Laina." Mi'ko tapped his desk. "I would be lying if Laina and I were not worried about the current tension with the Liberi Dei."

"If you're worried it will increase tensions—" Todd started.

"No." Mi'ko held up his hand. "Their hatred belongs to them, and nothing will change that. More importantly, neither you nor Mi'cin seem bothered by your differences, so we consider the issue resolved. As long as proper precautions are taken for both your safety."

"My family had a similar concern, but they like Mi'cin and your family."

"I see it as an occasion in which both our peoples can witness the potential for friendship and trust," Mi'ko said. "The speaker general agrees with me as well." He paused. "She seemed almost as pleased as Laina and I. The speaker general mentioned she was witness to the closeness you both shared the day of the London attack. So, she wasn't surprised."

Todd's face felt warm again.

I can't believe I was so clueless about Mi'cin.

"There is no need for you to feel shame or anxiety." Mi'ko pointed at Todd's face. "It is natural for families to worry for one another, no matter the species." He sat forward on his chair. "My family was anxious when Laina and I started our relationship. My parents were concerned she would take advantage of me." He chuckled. "They were there to help us navigate the relationship, and it changed their minds."

I can't imagine anyone taking advantage of Mi'ko. Or Laina.

"I don't want to put you, or anyone, in an awkward position." Todd sighed.

"I understand and I appreciate it." Mi'ko leaned back in his chair. "You humans are apprehensive about matters that are not yours to worry about. Of course, Laina and I will be here to assist you when and if you need it, as I would expect your family to do the same."

I can't control what others think. I have to do what is best for me and not be afraid to take the risks to make it happen.

"Thank you," Todd said.

There was a quiet buzz from Mi'ko's terminal.

Todd stood and headed to the door.

"Oh, Todd," Mi'ko said.

Todd turned around.

"I noticed in your reports, there was nothing more about the Liberi Dei from Mister McNeil. Has he tried to contact you?"

"No, Mister Vice Speaker," Todd said. "I've received reports from Homeland Security regarding the New Year's Eve celebration, but nothing from Greg directly." He paused. "I assumed they would work with Vi-Narm and the other members in security. I can reach out to him if you'd like?"

Mi'ko massaged his ears. "I don't believe that will be needed. Thank you."

TODD SAT AT the café with Mi'cin, savoring the flavors and spices of his meal. "I'm still mortified over how the conversation with your father started." He placed his lagus and té to the side of his plate.

"He said you were rather embarrassed about the incident." Mi'cin sounded amused as he stirred his cup of tuma before sipping it.

"I didn't need a talk about the birds and bees with your dad. That wasn't what I wanted to talk about."

"Birds and bees?

Todd's lips pinched together and he lowered his voice. "The sex talk."

"Ah, yes. He wasn't embarrassed. That's what parents are for." Mi'cin took another sip.

Todd fussed with his collar to loosen it, feeling uncomfortable about the incident. He turned to the small plaza. The early-evening light filled the district. The Nentraee were so creative in the way they simulated their sky, even making it "rain" to filter water and provide moisture for the plants.

"Weren't you curious about such things?" Mi'cin put down his cup. "I was. It was all part of my research before I invited you to dinner. I wanted to find out how two human males engaged in physical and sexual intimacy."

"I— Wait, you did what?" Todd's cheeks grew hot.

"I viewed your planet's source material on human mating. I focused on males, but I also examined female and male, as well as female and female. There were additional combinations, but I didn't feel the need to study further." Mi'cin's voice and tone were neutral.

Does nothing embarrass him?

"I found it's similar to ours, so I wasn't worried. I suppose I could investigate more should the need arise," Mi'cin continued. "There are things that, I admit, I found confusing, such as bondage and pain and pleasure. Some of it holds no appeal for me. The information was much more extensive than I thought it would be, specifically for a race that is so..." He paused and his mouth stood open for a moment. "I don't remember the word for it."

"Prudish?" Todd's face burned for a second time today.

"I suppose." Mi'cin leaned back in his chair, crossing a leg over his knee. "It was astonishing how much male and male performance information there was. To be honest, I'm curious about some of it."

"This conversation is not happening." Todd fanned his face. "I don't know what source material you found. I'm sure it wasn't provided by any of the governments. In which case, you're talking about pornography and that...well, that is nothing like real life." He lowered his voice. "More than ever when it comes to human bodies. The proportions of things that are shown...are not... Well...I don't..." Visions of porn he had watched flashed through his mind.

If that is what Mi'cin is considering source material, then there are going to be some intimacy issues.

"That would explain several things. I thought some of the human proportions seemed exaggerated." Mi'cin clasped his hands and rested them. "But, I don't wish to make you feel uncomfortable; nor should you be. It was simple research. It had its purpose." He smiled. "I assumed you would have done the same thing before agreeing to our date. I can provide you with several images and vignettes for you to watch, showing you our acts of physical intimacy. We don't have the extensive data your race does, but I assure you it will answer any questions you might have. I would be willing to explain it to you if that would be more comfortable." His eyes twinkled.

Todd glanced down at the table, his face burning. "I um...well, I um...no. I mean, I, um, didn't really give it much thought." He took a breath. "What I mean to say is, Dan and I talked about it. Well, Dan talked and I sat there. I mean...well, I do have questions, but I kind of figured it would all work out. I read the reports on our general biological information and all that. So, I know we are similar in regards to—"

"Our reproductive organs," Mi'cin finished.

Todd cleared his throat and whispered, "I figured, if it ever got to that point, it would all be worked out by us. Together."

"Okay." Mi'cin grinned. "I'm very curious about a human physical feature." He lowered his voice and leaned in closer to Todd. "Your race tends to have a lot of body hair, all over, and I'm wondering about you and your body. I've seen it on your arms and I've seen that it grows on your face, but does it grow in other places? And, if it does, do you remove it like the people I saw in the material I viewed? If so, why?"

"Well, that." Todd's attention fell to the table again. "I mean, I, well, yes, I have hair on my arms and legs and my chest...and um." He paused and forced himself to meet Mi'cin's gaze. "This is difficult. We're talking in your language where other people can understand us."

"Are you worried your vocabulary is lacking? Your Nentraee has become strong and natural," Mi'cin said.

Todd raked his hand through his hair. He needed water.

"No. It's not that. I'm...well, I'm not..." He shook his head.

"What is it?" Mi'cin leaned in closer, reaching out to touch Todd's hand.

"I've only been with one person. Jerry. So, I'm not... I mean we...well, it's..." he whispered, barely looking at Mi'cin.

"That is nothing to be worried about, nor should that bother you. I will not judge you for it." Mi'cin continued to hold Todd's gaze. "I cannot say the same about my sexual experience; however, I hope my past is not going to bother you." Mi'cin squeezed Todd's hand a bit more. "I am surprised. I would have thought differently, given your invitation to join you the night of our first date."

Todd's heart jumped to his throat, and he didn't think it was possible for his ears to be pounding any louder. "About that. It was a...well, I wanted...but..."

"You were sexually aroused, and your physical desires superseded your greater mental capacity." Mi'cin's voice was low. "I know that feeling. It was not easy for me to decline your invitation. It made for a strained walk home."

"I'm sorry," Todd mumbled.

"I'm happy you shared this with me. It makes me even more pleased at the choice I made that night."

Todd wanted to look away, but Mi'cin watched him with such a look of tenderness it was impossible to turn away.

Mi'cin placed his hand under Todd's chin and gently raised it. "Thank you for telling me."

Todd forced what he hoped was a smile.

I feel so stupid. I'm an adult. I was married, and Jerry and I had an active sex life. Ugh.

"I don't wish to shame you." Mi'cin removed his hand. "I'm sorry the subject made you uncomfortable. But I must be honest. I'm glad we talked about it. Plus, I find your change in skin tones appealing and endearing."

"It's all right." Todd sat taller in his seat. "It had to be talked about at some point. But, I figured it wouldn't be now or here in a public place or in conjunction with the conversation I had with your father." He wished for more water.

There were so many new things about dating Mi'cin that he hadn't considered. Clearly, Mi'cin had thought long and hard about all this. He, however, was winging it. Todd took a breath. His ears finally no longer pounded, and his face and neck didn't seem to be on fire anymore. At least Mi'cin hadn't asked him which position in bed he preferred. On the plus side, if and when it ever reached that point, one of them would know what they were doing.

Twenty-Five: New Year

MIRTOFF HAD INVITED Ecra and Suloof to her quarters to share a meal. She had become accustomed to cooking and took some pleasure from it, especially for her family. Having family over made her quarters seem less empty and more like her home on Benzee. It was difficult to believe that they had been gone from their world for twenty years.

Perhaps the proposal by Rosta and Gahumed to go back to what was left of their home world's system was a worthy endeavor and one she should move forward with in greater haste. It might help her people adjust to this new world and give them hope.

A thought for another time.

"What was your opinion of the New Year celebration that Todd set up for us?" Mirtoff asked Ecra and Suloof.

"Considering it's the same as *A'Sootee*"—Erca's voice was gentle—"with more fanfare and explosions in the sky, it was acceptable." He pushed his finished plate away. "Re'pia and I appreciated our extra time together." He set his lagus and té diagonally across his plate. "From what I've heard, everyone enjoyed the days of rest. Specifically since we've endured how many recent human holidays? Do these beings ever work?"

"They do indeed work. For some, it's all they do." Mirtoff picked up her chilled tuma. "Todd explained that this is how their calendar works. The last two months of their year are full of these events." She sipped her drink.

"Well, their Gregorian calendar anyway. It would seem there are several calendars used by the humans. However, this is the one that is recognized by their United Nations."

"Auntie, is this the one we'll be changing to now that we are staying?" Suloff scratched Faa's head, causing him to murmur softly.

"Yes, it makes the most sense." Mirtoff put her cup down. "We've already adopted their way of timekeeping. It's a natural step for us to take."

"Another concession to the humans." Ecra crossed his arms over his chest.

"Not a concession." Mirtoff tried to keep her tone level. This wasn't about the calendar. Ecra wasn't the only one showing his discomfort at all they had given up.

Another reason to see what happened to our home world. People need to reach full acceptance.

"It will make working with them easier," Mirtoff said. "Plus, the twenty-four-hour clock is determined by the spin of Earth on its axis—not by the humans." Mirtoff's voice softened as she relaxed. "We cannot ask a world of seven billion to change for us, a race of two million."

Ecra offered a stiff bow in acknowledgement.

"We need to standardize both our calendar and timekeeping to make trade and business easier." Mirtoff savored the flavor of her drink for a moment.

"Our calendar and way of keeping time are better." Suloff pouted. "They should change." She blew a strand of hair off her face.

"Suloff, that is not possible." Mirtoff sighed. "We are in a different solar system. Even if there were no humans, we would have to change these things." Mirtoff leaned closer to her niece. "It is only a way of keeping time. Nothing more."

Faa nudged Suloff to continue the scratching, but her hands stayed still.

"We've come to them, not the other way around," Mirtoff said. "If they came to our world, we would expect them to adapt to us and our way of doing things."

Ecra sipped his own cup of tuma.

Mirtoff glanced between her brother and her niece. "We came to the Sol systems. It is us who must adapt to this place."

Suloff sighed.

"Today, it is a calendar and timekeeping and we moved A'Sootee. Tomorrow will we need to change how we pick a mate? Change our death rituals? What of J'Veesa? Will these Liberi Dei win and force us to convert to their deities? Or will they kill us and steal our technology?" Ecra leaned forward and his gaze focused on Mirtoff. "I've heard mention that the glitches in our datanet are caused by them."

Mirtoff straightened her shoulders but said nothing.

I cannot speak of such things.

"Sister, I'm worried that we might lose ourselves and forget where we came from"—Ecra sat back deeper in the chair—"if we are not careful."

"Of course, it is a valid concern."

"Thank you." A smile broke through Ecra's otherwise neutral expression.

"Why are we the ones changing everything?" Suloff huffed. "Why did we have to move A'Sootee?"

"When Todd brought the idea of having the New Year's celebrations on our ships, the Speaker's House and the House of the People agreed it would be a good way to tie our two cultures together." Mirtoff's expression was stiff. "Moving the day of A'Sootee to coincide with the human New Year made sense." She reached up and adjusted a braid of hair. "Besides, we've changed the date of A'Sootee before.

This is nothing new." She tried to brighten her smile for them. The change of A'Sootee added to the growing list of complaints by the Nentraee traditionalists. "We are doing what we feel is in the best interests of everyone." The tips of her ears were starting to ache and warm. "We are not going to change any of our other cultural events or holidays. There would be no need for that."

If my own family is worried of such matters, I'm going to expedite the plans for our mission to Benzee.

"All right." Suloff's tone was gentler as her gaze dropped from Mirtoff's, and she stared down at Faa.

"Suloff." Mirtoff massaged her ears to cool them off. "I understand these changes have been difficult. However, I believe the humans are excited about celebrating some of our events, particularly *A'da Magina*. Todd seemed to think they would enjoy that one the most, with its week-long festivities and celebrating each of the clans."

"Good." Suloff rubbed Faa's head, messing up the fur. "I wish we had a cádo. Faa is such a love."

"Faa sorry you not been picked. Faa happy he get all the scratches," Faa murmured.

"It's probably for the best, considering cádo don't get along well with one another." Mirtoff watched Faa shake his head and rest it back down, closing his eyes.

I wonder how he will get along with Todd's cat?

TODD GLANCED UP at his office door.

"I've got the approved list: China, Brazil, Japan, England, France, Australia, Germany, Russia, and the US." Dan stood in the doorway, holding up his datapad.

"Excellent." Todd saved the space analysis report he was working on. He was trying to justify the office allocation for a media center as well as a request from NASA for a research office here on the ship. With all these requests from Earth, it wasn't going to be an easy argument. He would need to prioritize.

"The preparations are going to take weeks," Dan said, "if not months, but spring is the best time to travel." He strolled over to Todd's desk and sat. "It'll be ideal, assuming we pull this off."

Todd blinked several times, giving his exhausted eyes a moment to adjust to Dan.

Todd was slammed, putting together the big New Year's events for the Nentraee. Arranging the message from the speaker general and the laser-light shows in all the parks on the various ships had taken a lot to coordinate. He had worked with several of the various eateries on the ships to provide a mix of both Nentraee cuisine and a selection of human foods from around the world. Still, the payoff was worth it. He got to watch the Nentraee, including Mi'cin, dance to Nentraee music. The dancing reminded Todd of swing-based 1950s-style couples dancing. It consisted of most of the couples moving together around the dance floor in perfect timing with lots of quick free-flowing movements. The music sounded like it could have come from 1950s jazz.

The best news was that Liberi Dei had been quiet, which unfortunately posed its own sets of worries.

They must be planning. But what?

Todd leaned back. There was nothing he could do about it at the moment, so he gave Dan his full attention.

"If all goes well and the Nentraee like the trips, more countries will be included." Dan placed the datapad on the desk. "Trust me, there're a bunch of countries who want to be on the list. You were right." Dan pointed to the datapad. "These little doohickeys are pretty cool."

"I'm finding I can't live without my datapad."

Dan nodded.

Todd covered his yawn.

"Anything new in the love department?" Dan wiggled his eyebrows. "You and Mi'cin put any of his research into practice yet? Have you checked out those files I sent you on the Nentraee? I tried to make sure to include the ones with the most pictures. I recommend file number twelve."

"I should have never told you that." Todd's face grew hot.

"Oh please, like I'm going to tell anyone." Dan cracked his neck. "It's just us, and I love to see you get all flustered."

"And to think I was going to tell you what a great job you've done with all this." Todd paused, leaning forward. "Speaker Rosta and Speaker Syde are impressed. They want to employ you full-time."

"Shut the fuck up." Dan clapped his hands. "Would this mean a place on the ship? Would I get to live here? 'Cause, chica, let me tell you, I could get used to it."

"Well, I—"

"I have all kinds of ideas for them." Dan waved his hands, ignoring Todd. "We could do lunch and dinner cruises to the moon. Hell, if they, or we, could make larger ships, the Nentraee could offer cruises of the solar system." He talked faster. "Can you imagine how amazing that would be? In a few years, people could actually tour the rings of Saturn or spend time seeing Jupiter and her moons, all in a luxury space—"

"Hold up," Todd interrupted. "Dan, one thing at a time. We're trying to get them to buy into the idea of a youth exchange, remember?"

Dan crossed his arms.

"Mi'cin told me over dinner that, near the end, when they had to evacuate their world, a lot of families got separated. Children and parents got forgotten." Todd shook his head. "The idea of being separated from their children for extended periods of time isn't nothing they're excited about."

"Well, it's not like they wouldn't come back," Dan said.

"I told him that, but it's still not a popular idea." Todd sighed. "The Rights of Fatherhood are a big deal, and the dads don't want to mess it up."

"But I've already got lists of people who want to either come to the ship as an exchange student or be a host family." Dan picked up the device and tapped the screen, pulling up the lists. "I don't know how they found out, but there are thousands of requests and inquiries. You should see the social media pages." He passed the datapad over to Todd. "See? It's nuts."

"That's good." Todd gave the list a cursory glance. "I guess. It'll be interesting to see what Mi'ko and the others say about that."

"Oh, I've got something to show you." Dan grabbed up the datapad and typed. "Check this out."

"You have the itineraries put together already?" Todd asked. "The polling went well."

"Chica, of course it went well. I dazzled them. They loved me, and, chica, there were quite a few cuties too." Dan winked. "Muy bonito." He waved his free hand infront of his face.

"You're a mess." Todd checked the itineraries; Grand Canyon, Yosemite, New York, Las Vegas, Washington, DC, San Francisco. He stopped and turned to Dan. "Seriously, they want to go to Disney World?"

"Oh please, it's the happiest place on Earth. And they want to go." Dan snapped his fingers. "Plus, what better way to end the trip of our beautiful country?"

"What about Yellowstone?" Todd asked.

Dan shook his head. "Anyway, we'll be doing similar itinerary for other countries. The formula is pretty simple, a few days in each spot and off to the next. They should have fun, but we'll get their feedback and make sure it's what they want and what they are expecting. I even reached out to Disney to see about getting some help from them."

"Wow, cool," Todd said. "So, I guess all this travel stuff will be moved over to its permanent home under the Interior and Education departments. Have Speaker Rosta and Speaker Syde figured out how that is going to work yet?"

"No clue." Dan shrugged. "I suggested they spin it off and create a Human—Nentraee joint private venture, with me as the head, but with their government oversight, but who knows what they'll decide? Just as long as I'm involved; it's my baby, and I'm not willing to give it up. I've made that perfectly clear to them and you know, hell hath no fury like a queen scorned."

"Oh, I'm sure you'll be involved. They like you, and who else is going to push them into doing all this weird stuff? Plus, I don't think I'm the only one who doesn't want to see you pissed off and angry. You can be scary when you want to be." Todd chuckled. "Anyway, you have an interstellar-travel dynasty to build."

"You got that right." Dan snapped his fingers again.

Todd raked his hands through his hair.

"It should make things easier on you once my program has been moved." Dan straightened up. "Free you up to work on your other projects. You know, all that Terran Affairs stuff you do." He paused. "Hey, maybe they'll have you be the oversight. Handle all the large problems. Have someone to blame when things get screwed up. That would work for me. I like blaming you."

"Great, just what I need."

There was a chirp from Todd's office door. He checked his monitor and tapped the door lock command on his screen. The door opened.

"Mi'cin." Todd stood.

"Hello, Todd." Mi'cin stepped in and headed over to Todd but stopped when he saw Dan. "Hello, Dan. I hope I didn't intrude."

"No, not at all." Dan stood and bowed. "In fact, I think we're about done." His voice deepened. He glanced down at Mi'cin's wrist. "Is that the watch Todd got you?"

Mi'cin stuck out his arm a bit for Dan to see.

"Wow. Nice."

Todd cleared his throat. "Thank you."

"Did you need anything else?" Dan spoke to Todd but focused on Mic'in. "I really think file twelve would be amazing." He waggled his eyebrows over his shoulder at Todd.

Mi'cin said nothing, and Todd hoped he wouldn't ask.

"Yes, well anyway, we're good. Thanks. See ya later." It always amazed Todd how Dan could go from a snapping you-go-girl attitude to polished and professional in the blink of an eye.

"In that case, Dan, would you like to join us?" Mi'cin relaxed his arm and adjusted the sleeves of his shirt. "I was going to take Todd to where I took classes, my university, and you are welcome to join."

"Oh fun. Sure, if it won't be a problem."

"Not at all. I'm happy to have you join." Mi'cin's lips grew into a larger smile, and he stood taller.

Todd touched the side of his monitor, putting his system into security mode. "Shall we go?"

Twenty-Six: Allies

TODD WASHED HIS hands as the toilet flushed behind him. It was an amazing perk having his own bathroom off his office. He dried his hands and headed back to his desk. He tapped off the media reports. Everything at the UN was running smoothly, and it was only a bunch of talking heads as they waited for the big vote.

He wanted to get through the budget for all of Dan's plans and review the final numbers of the New Year's event. And today was the perfect time. The vice speaker and speaker general were down on Earth. Mi'cin was on the Rádo, working on some project General Gahumed and Speaker Rosta had going on. He couldn't ask for a better time to get work done.

Todd's monitor chirped. He grinned and accepted the call. "I've been meaning to give you a call. Did you have a—"

"I need to see you. Is there any way you can come down here?" Greg's voice was tight with tension, and he appeared to be sweating. This was not the Greg he knew. Greg was normally calm and professional.

"Greg, what's going on?" Todd leaned in. "Wait, shouldn't you be at the UN?"

"I don't know who is listening, and I don't know who is involved," Greg said. "Todd, we need to meet in person. How quickly can you be down here?" He checked over his shoulder, then faced the monitor.

"All right, I'll be there in about an hour and a half." How could Todd say no, particularly if Greg didn't know who to trust?

"Good, I'll meet you at Reagan National Airport. That should give us enough time." Greg checked his watch, then glanced back at the camera.

"Greg? What is it? What's going on?"

"Something is going to happen at the meeting today. Now, please."

The screen went blank.

"Oh, crap." Todd grabbed his jacket. Another attack, and there was no way he was going to sit around and do nothing. Not after London. He left his office and headed for the hangar bay.

Rushing down the corridor, Todd caught sight of Vi-Narm and headed toward her. "Shouldn't you be down on Earth with the vice speaker?"

"The vice speaker has me here today." Vi-Narm's expression was pulled tight.

Todd knew that look. She wasn't happy.

"The security detail provided by Danu is more than enough for him, the speaker general, and their guests."

Todd frowned. He didn't believe that, and by her expression, she didn't either.

"It was also suggested that it may appear intimidating to the humans if we had too strong a presence." Her frown deepened. "Is everything okay?"

"I don't know." Todd took a breath. "But I need your help. I'm heading to Earth."

"Why are you going to Earth?" Vi-Narm asked. "Your assignments are here today."

"Can we talk in private?" Todd glanced around the corridor, noting the other Nentraee government staff going about their duties.

"Of course."

Todd led them quickly down the hall to one of the private meeting rooms.

"I just received a call from Greg McNeil," Todd said. "I'm on my way to meet him in Washington, DC. Something's wrong. He seemed worried."

"Interesting," Vi-Narm said.

"I suggest you come with me."

Her eyes grew large and a hint of a smile started to cross her lips.

"I'm not sure what Greg's worried about. He didn't appear normal. Nothing about our conversation seemed right, and I can't think of anyone better to handle what might or might not be trouble, other than you." He ran his hand through his hair. Was Greg being threatened by the Liberi Dei? Todd didn't know, but he had to act. Too much had already happened. "I need help. I don't think I can do this on my own."

Vi-Narm offered a tight bow. "I suggest we go."

THE SHUTTLE RIDE to Reagan National Airport was quiet. Todd paced back and forth while Vi-Narm toiled with her datapad. She told him repeatedly to sit down and focus, that they would arrive when they arrived. Pacing was not going to help.

Once the door unlatched, Todd rushed to the exit. Vi-Narm was next to him. She seemed nervous, which made Todd breathe easier but sweat harder.

A black sedan waited inside the security perimeter. Greg stood outside of it. He was pale and looked like he might not have slept for days. It reminded Todd of the day Brad showed up on his doorstep, warning him and Jerry about the Nentraee's arrival.

"We need to head to New York." Greg approached, waving them back aboard the ship.

"Mister McNeil." Vi-Narm held up her hand so as not to be pushed back in the shuttle.

Greg glanced up at Vi-Narm, then frowned at Todd.

"I didn't know what to expect, so I asked Vi-Narm to come along. She can handle anything, and I trust her." Todd had no hesitation in his voice.

"All right, but we need to go." Greg stepped past them, entering the ship.

"Greg, what's going on?" Todd demanded as the shuttle door closed.

"There's going to be an attack on the UN, and we have to stop it," Greg said. "Please, we need to leave now. There isn't any time."

"Impossible, we—"

"I don't—"

"Liberi Dei is going to attack the meeting at the UN," Greg interrupted and sat down on one of the shuttle's seats. "We've been hearing some chatter this week but weren't sure until right before I called you. Todd, there is no way they could do it without the help of staff in the White House, members of the military, Secret Service, local police, the security within the UN, and God knows who else. This is bigger and deeper than anything. I don't know who to trust. You're all we've got. We need to stop this."

"What?" Todd yelped. How was any of this possible? It didn't make sense, but at the same time, it was the only thing that felt right. Every level of government had to be involved. How else could all these attacks have happened and no one see them coming? And now with the biggest announcement ever known to mankind being made at the UN. "Oh God," he whispered.

"How is this possible?" Vi-Narm's voice was her typical calm. None of this seemed to faze her.

"We aren't sure," Greg said. "They've covered their tracks, and we're still trying to sort out the details, but I can't risk it, not again." His stare bore into Todd. "I can feel it, Todd. This is going to be big, especially with all the leaders there. Do you have any idea what would happen if they succeed?" He shook his head. "Why aren't we moving? Please, we need to go."

"A total power vacuum would send the world into chaos." Todd's head ached as he tried to picture what would happen to the world without leadership.

"Then why not alert the security there?" Vi-Narm pulled out her datapad and started running her fingers over the commands.

"Don't you think I tried?" Greg glared at her. "But I can't reach them. Someone is jamming us. No cells and no radios. We can't even reach the security outside the building. We thought it was you, but..." He paused.

Todd had been monitoring the events at the UN. Everything appeared fine. "It all seemed pretty routine to me."

"To the outside world, but it's not," Greg said. "They are receiving help from inside the UN and who knows who else. Ever since the attack on London, I suspected someone from inside the White House, but I couldn't prove anything. I talked to the president and he had me reach out to you in hopes you would talk to the vice speaker and the speaker general. Over the last week, we've had email trouble, server issues, phone lines going down. We thought someone was hacking our systems, but nothing. Then I thought maybe it was being done to cover the tracks from the inside. A couple hours ago, we backtracked the cause of the issues to the secretary of state's office. We've put her staff, quietly, into lockup. We're not sure who's involved and who isn't. But what we found in her office confirmed the attack today." Greg took a breath, looking around. "I understand these ships can travel faster than anything we have, and no one will try to stop a Nentraee ship today. It's our best cover, especially if I'm wrong. We can't have helicopter gunships and National Guard units converge on the UN building, even if it's a rescue. We might alert the Liberi Dei, but your ship, no one would think twice."

Vi-Narm went to the flight deck.

"Who do you suppose is behind this?" Todd asked. He tried to inhale, but his lungs were tight. People in his country were causing this. Why?

"At this point, there's only one person who can manipulate the security and the diplomatic process without question, and she's going to be there with the president and all the other world leaders and dignitaries."

"You mean..."

"We will be there shortly." Vi-Narm returned to Greg and Todd. "We are going to ignore the flight restriction on our vessel. It should go unnoticed. But if not, we can come up with a deception."

Todd glanced at her, curious as to what kind of *deception*. "How so?"

"You will both need to trust me." Vi-Narm ran her hands over the datapad.

"As long as it gets us there without suspicion. We don't want to make it any easier for the Liberi Dei than we already have." Greg took a deep breath and started to fan himself.

Todd peered out the ship's window as they lifted off. Within minutes, the shuttle arrived over New York and moved toward the UN building. The speed was impossibly fast. Everything passed outside of the window in a blur.

"How is this speed even possible? What about sonic booms?" Todd asked.

"There is much about our technology you do not understand," Vi-Narm said.

Todd wasn't sure how they managed it but was grateful they could. Once they'd approached, they landed smoothly next to the speaker general's shuttle.

"Where is everyone? Where is the security?" Todd checked the surroundings.

"I don't know," Greg said. "There is supposed to be security stationed all around the building." Greg visually scanned the area. "Maybe inside. I'm not sure. But that was one of the things that didn't seem right. The plan was to move all the security inside, keeping the exterior with minimal force and relying on street closures and checkpoints, but even that doesn't seem to have happened." He pinched the bridge of his nose. "Homeland Security was pissed, as well as several of our allies, but no one questioned her."

"Not possible." Vi-Narm tapped her datapad. "I can't reach anyone." She frowned.

"What?" Todd and Greg said in tandem.

"I don't know how, but I can't scan the building, and I can't reach Danu. I'm being blocked. The Liberi Dei have been attacking our systems for months since the equipment for the Republic of Zimbabwe went missing, but we've been able to counter their attacks, but now..." Vi-Narm's ears swelled and turned blue in anger.

Todd nodded at Greg and Vi-Narm.

Time to stop these bastards.

Twenty-Seven: God's Plan

THE UN ASSEMBLY hall was occupied by every leader of every member country and their staff. Media and guests filled the gallery. Erca and Ra'pia sat in the gallery with Suloff. Mirtoff had decided they needed to be here for this. It was too important to only be viewed via the live-streaming on the ships, and Mirtoff wanted to share this moment with her family.

This is it. This is the day that all our hard work will come together.

United Nations Secretary General Duck-Hwan Park stood at his green marble desk. This time, neither the undersecretary nor the president of the general assembly were there. The gold wall and the UN seal framed Secretary General Duck-Hwan Park perfectly.

"It is my pleasure to see all one hundred ninety-seven member states here and our permanent observer from the Holy See. It pleases me even more to welcome our new friends, the Nentraee, represented by their Speaker General Mirtoff Esmi, their Vice Speaker Mi'ko Soemu, members of the Speaker's House, and their honored guests." He pointed to the chairs in front of him as Mirtoff stood. "Today, with the full recommendation of the Security Council, we bring forward the petition of membership for the Nentraee."

The crowd applauded.

Mirtoff considered all the delegates. Her cloak draped perfectly off her shoulders. Her braided hair gently grazed the side of her face. This event was for show and the general population. The real work had been done over the last several weeks, operating within the confines of the United Nation's charter to enable today's actions.

She reached the lectern. "I am pleased to stand here before you all. My government and my people welcome this opportunity to join this long-standing organization of peace."

There was more applause.

Mirtoff crossed back to her seat as the room quieted. Duck-Hwan was ready to call for a vote of the full assembly, she had been told passage was assured with well over the needed two-thirds majority.

It took a great deal of negotiation.

"I would like to call for the vote." Duck-Hwan stood tall with his smile bright.

Mirtoff focused on him and the other delegates. The blow to the back of Duck-Hwan's head knocked him to his knees, and he crashed to the floor. Mirtoff sprang to her feet but got pushed out of the way by a human military guard and fell back onto her chair. Gunshots and screams filled the room.

MARTHA CHECKED HER watch. From her spot sitting with the president and the rest of his delegation, she was able to scan the room, making sure all her people were in place as Duck-Hwan blathered on. With subtle nods of confirmation, each entry point was cleared and secured. The guards in their UN colors took their positions. No one would be getting in or out. It was no easy task to ensure that all her followers were the ones in charge of the security and broadcasting. To further safeguard from outside interference, she'd managed to have all her logistical people on the outside, keeping up the appearance of normalcy.

God's will be done.

She smiled up at the glass windows where the translators worked; soon they would be locked down as well. Now her focus could be on the people in this hall—they were the only ones that mattered. She checked over her shoulder as the guards moved up the steps, getting closer to the UN secretary general's desk.

She checked her watch again. It was time.

Her guards quickly moved in and struck down Duck-Hwan with the back of their guns. Others on her team fired their weapons into the ceiling. Four more guards rushed the guest seating and lectern from either side and dropped the Nentraee security like they did with the UN secretary general. They weren't to be killed yet.

So much for their advanced technology.

The confusion and chaos played like music to her ears.

"No one move," Martha shouted over the yells and screams. "The room's been secured."

As if to emphasize her point, several members of the African groups pushed to the exit doors but were unable to open them. Her guards pointed their guns at the group and pushed them back to the center of the hall.

Martha shoved her way to the lectern as the guards moved in to secure the Nentraee and the president. The guards dropped Duck-Hwan next to the group of hostages as several of the delegates tried to flee, finding all their exits secured. It only took a few more shots for people to settle down.

"We've secured the room," shouted one of her guards as he pushed the last of the African group away from the door.

"Excellent." Martha watched over the crowd. "Bring me His Excellency, the Most Reverend Denis Koester, Titular Archbishop of Suacia." The edges of her lips curled into a smile.

Martha scowled down at the body of Duck-Hwan. Her disdain for the man filling every corner of her brain.

Perhaps he's already dead and being judged.

"Martha, what the hell are you doing?" President Zachary hurried over to the fallen UN secretary general.

Zachary disgusted her the most. He might as well have bent over for these devils, as accommodating as he'd been. He was no man of God. He was nothing to her. Another sinner that would suffer the wrath of God.

"Shut him up," Martha barked.

One of the guards backhanded the president, knocking him to the ground.

"Are you insane?" Zachary wiped blood from his mouth. "Martha, you've always detested violence. What're you doing?"

Again, the guard went to backhand him and Martha held up her hand.

"I'm doing what you were too weak to do," Martha spat at him.

"Don't do this," Zachary said.

Martha backhanded the president. "Shut up!"

Two guards brought forward the archbishop and dropped him at Martha's feet. She laughed. "A supposed man of God. You're nothing but a coward. You welcomed these devils to our world—"

The archbishop faced her. "Devils? What are you talking about?"

"Them," she shouted and pointed to the Nentraee. "And now you must pay for your sins." She turned to the guard. "Do it."

"Praise be to God," the guard said, pulled out his gun, and shot the archbishop in the head. His body crumpled to the ground and his blood started to pool.

The room exploded into screams and cries. "Oh, shut up, or one of you will be next," Martha yelled, trying to get control again. "You useless idiots."

People rushed the exit doors again, only to be pushed back by her guards and their guns. From the African group and the Asia-Pacific group, several delegates rushed the secure doors again, this time taking down her security guards and managing to break through the doors. It only took moments for additional guards to come into the area and re-secure the doors, but by then, some people had managed to flee.

Let them go. The chamber hall is secure. Let the cowards flee.

"Settle down! Or I'll blow this whole building." She raised her hands, showing a red blinking light. Everyone froze in place. There was nowhere for people to run. "You're all fools," she yelled, forcing the room to grow quiet. "Allowing these demons here. Welcoming them with open arms, these soulless monsters. We say no! No to this!" She glared at the full assembly. "You're all godless. Nothing but soulless, empty suits, and I'm ashamed to have called some of you friends."

God will judge them. These posturing fools have no idea what I have in store for them, or the world, once I rid them of these demons.

Martha glowered at Richard Zachary. "You're the biggest fool of them all. I tried to warn you. I tried to talk you out of it, but you wouldn't listen." She shook her head. "Why wouldn't you listen? How long have you and I known each other? For you to turn your back on me, and on God?

For shame." She spoke to the room but turned and focused on him. "You're no man of faith." She pointed to the sky. "You'll be judged worst of all. I tried to warn you and save you. Look at them." Martha pointed at Mirtoff, Mi'ko, and the two unconscious Nentraee security guards on the floor.

"Devils, both you and your people. I only wish I could blow up your hellfire ships and rid our solar system of your corruption and filth." She had full control of the situation and wasn't going to give it up. Her voice calmed. "We can avoid all this ugliness, but they have to be dealt with." She pointed to the Nentraee. "Banish them from this place, never to return, like God did to Lucifer. Banishing him to the depths of hell to burn for eternity." She snarled at the world leaders. "For once, you useless nits get to make a change for good. We'll banish those outside this building, sacrifice the ones here to God as our penance for our sins."

Her guards fired their weapons at the ceiling again. In the section that was occupied by the African group and the Asia-Pacific group, the delegation from Zimbabwe seemed to be causing the most trouble: rushing the doors, moving around, yelling, not taking their seats.

I miss Gabriel Mnangagwa; he knew how to keep his people in line. They've gotten this bad in eight months. This can't continue.

They rushed the doors again, trying to flee. "Cowards," she hollered to them. "Get them under control." A few more guards headed over, and the crowd settled down again.

"Martha, this isn't you." The president rubbed the back of his head, sitting up. One of the guards pointed his weapon at him. "I'm sure we can talk about this. No one needs to die or get hurt. Let everyone go, and we can sit down and work through this. Like always. You and me."

"Another teachable moment, Richard, you idiot." Martha chuckled. "God has a plan for us all, Richard, and this is His plan for me. I've realized it since we heard from these demons, and I'm not the only one. There are others. Look around." She smiled. "How do you think I accomplished all this? God sent me soldiers from all over the world—from all His various faiths: Christian, Muslim, Jewish, Hindu, all His true children. His human children. He called us all together for this one cause, to rid His garden of this pestilence." She pointed again at Mirtoff, Mi'ko, and the other Nentraee in attendance.

TODD, VI-NARM, AND Greg continued to check the doors. Locked. All the doors Todd tried were secured from the inside. The chamber hall had been sealed. Shooting and screams came from inside as one of the doors burst open and members from the African groups and the Asia-Pacific group rushed out. Todd nodded at Greg and Vi-Narm and managed to weave through the crowd before Martha's men were able to gain control of the doors and the area. Todd, Greg, and Vi-Narm were beckoned over by the delegates from these groups and were assisted in hiding and keeping Martha's guards from seeing them.

Todd was disgusted by what she was saying. Who did she think she was? She was crazy.

"We need to stop her," Greg whispered.

Todd scanned the delegates who were shielding them from view, thinking of options.

"I have my weapon." Vi-Narm opened up her suit jacket, revealing what appeared to be a small gun. "But I don't know what will happen to the explosives." She kneeled closer to Greg and Todd as a few of the delegates closed in tighter to keep them undetected. "We need to inform our shuttle and any security outside what we are going to try in here. They should be alerted by now and additional security should be on their way. But whatever it is, we need to do it quickly."

"Got it," Greg said. "I can do that, plus they'll be more willing to work with me than either of you."

"Take this. It will provide a three-dimensional view of the assembly hall with the current locations of the terrorist and the hostages. They should also be able to locate the explosives. I believe I now have the frequency of Martha's device." Vi-Narm handed Greg her datapad. "I've been recording everything since we left the ship."

"Why?" Todd asked.

"Now is not the time." Vi-Narm checked around them.

Greg tapped several of the delegates' legs in hopes they would help. They were the new delegates from Zimbabwe. He gestured to the doors, and they nodded.

"Go," she said.

Todd and Vi-Narm watched as several of the delegates rushed the doors and the guards again, providing Greg the cover he needed to get out of the hall with a few others.

The guards waved their weapons, focused on keeping the representatives under control. They moved them away from the side doors once more as Martha continued to talk. Todd couldn't allow this to happen again. The guards were ready to fire at the groups and not up at the ceiling.

"Can you get close enough to stop her?" Todd muttered. His mind raced—they had to stop her.

Oh, God. I have an idea.

"What are you thinking?" Vi-Narm touched his arm.

"A distraction. A big freaking *Dan*-type distraction." Todd forced a nervous smile. The pounding of his heart kept in time with the pounding of his pocket watch.

This is it. This is where I need to be the hero. Oh, God.

"She hates me, and I'm a big-ass sinner in her mind. I'll keep her attention on me."

"Are you sure?"

"No." He wiped his forehead. "But right now, I'm trusting you with my life, so don't mess it up." His mouth was moving, his brain no longer in control. "I'd like to talk to you about the books I gave you for Christmas. I want to learn more about your people and—" He paused. "—and I have a whole lot of things I still want to do. So please don't let me die."

He grinned at her one last time and crawled away as quietly and as quickly as possible. Moving along the half wall, Todd used it as cover. The guards were distracted by both Martha and the crowds of people. Luckily for him and Vi-Narm, several of the delegates and guests in the area were helping them stay hidden. They were standing and shuffling around in place, keeping the guards busy. With all the people in the room, it was impossible for the guards to watch every single person. They were relying on fear and weapons, not numbers.

Good for me. Bad for them.

Todd made his way, slowly, thinking about everything that had happened. The people who died in the attack in San Jose and in London. He thought of Mi'cin, his friends and his family, and saw Jerry's face, watching. As he got closer, the surrounding people continued to keep him blocked from Martha's view and the half wall kept him blocked from the guards at the doors.

Finally, he got as close as he could, and the wall ended. Desks sat in front of him; nowhere left for him to hide. He took a deep breath, glanced at the representative from the Congo, smiled, and stood.

Oh, shit. Oh, shit. Oh, shit. What the hell am I doing? This is stupid. Think Dan.

Martha was speaking, but Todd wasn't hearing her. He had his own agenda. "What about the other causes, Martha?" he shouted at her in his best Dan impersonation, stopping her sermon of hate. "You know, ridding the world of all the other sinners?"

Martha paused and glared in the direction of Todd's voice. "Who's that?"

"Oh, come on, Madam Secretary, Martha, sweetheart. Don't you remember me? Where's the love?" Todd called out, his voice cracking. "I'm probably the worst of the lot. You remember *James's* partner, don't you? The man that you and your friends blew up in San Jose."

I'm gonna barf.

"I was hoping you'd be here," Martha snarled.

"Surprise." He blew her a kiss.

Okay, that was stupid.

"Get him," she called out.

Within seconds, two guards grabbed him.

Where the hell did they come from?

"Anyway, what about us? I mean you religious wackos have hated us gays long before the Nentraee got here." He didn't struggle.

Please, dear God, let Greg and Vi-Narm get to where they need to be. Get the help we need to stop her, or this is going to be the quickest and most useless distraction in the history of the world.

A dark, cruel smile filled her lips. "I was going to send you a special invite as my guest to ensure it. But then I remembered you're a petty little gnat, a nothing, a homosexual sinner in league with the devil." She spat the words at him. "I'm cutting off the head so the rest of the body dies."

"Ah, so you do care," Todd said. The guards pulled him up to the front of the hall. He didn't fight, but still, they pushed him along. "I thought you were a pain in the ass. But I didn't realize what a crazy bitch you are." One of the guards shoved him up to where Mi'ko and Mirtoff were standing.

He landed hard on the ground right next to them.

Mi'ko helped pick him up. "What are you doing here?" he asked in Nentraee.

Todd winked and stood with the guard pressing a gun in his back.

I'm not dead yet. Let's hope I can keep it that way.

"We'll see who's crazy." Martha sneered at him, grabbing his face.

Todd took a breath and peeked over his shoulder at the guard. "Is that a gun or are we both sinners?"

The guard pressed the gun in Todd's back harder.

"Okay, gun." He turned to both Mirtoff and Mi'ko. "We're not perfect, and there are a few bad apples. Like this psycho bitch." He pointed to Martha. "Don't hold that against us."

"Who do you think you are?" Martha snapped.

"I'm the entertainment." *Think Dan. Think Dan.* "The warmup act. I mean, look at this place. No wonder you picked the location. What a stage. A little small. Although, honestly, I'd redecorate. The gold is so last century, don't ya think?" He glanced around, trying to find Vi-Narm, but she was gone.

"You're nothing," Martha said.

"Maybe so, but I'm fabulous, and you're in an ugly pantsuit," Todd said.

She started to turn.

"Wasn't blowing up parts of San Jose and killing all those people enough for you?" Todd scanned the room.

"What about London? Killing the innocent people there. Not grand enough? So, you decided to go big time." He grinned. "Or do you just like all the bling?" He waggled his eyebrows.

"Shut up!"

"Come on. Tell us. Who do you think God hates more—aliens or mass murderers?"

"That was the will of God," Martha bellowed.

Todd saw the president pull the secretary general a few steps back, giving both him and Martha the stage. The president's head twitched slightly to the left, and Todd caught sight of the prime minister of England, who was helping to keep Vi-Narm hidden as she moved to get into position.

Thank God. Now what? Now what? Now what? I need to keep her going.

"No, of course not. Why get your hands dirty?"

"It was God's will," Martha repeated. "God picked them all, and as for your friend in sin, he's rotting in hell right where he belongs."

"Anyplace is better than here."

"Oh, you'll be with him soon enough. An eternity of fire and burnt flesh awaits you." She scowled. "God told me to show the world His true power and that these creatures are soulless monsters, damned to hell."

More time. I have to keep talking. I need more time. Keep talking, you crazy bitch.

"You're such a psycho bitch." Todd laughed.

"Go ahead and laugh, sinner. You'll see what God and I have in store."

"God doesn't want this. Only your corrupt version of Him does." A heavy punch slammed across his face as one of the guards struck him. He tasted copper in his mouth and felt what might be a loose tooth.

Dammit.

"Don't preach to me, sinner," Martha snapped. "You don't know His word, His true word."

"You're right. Who am I to talk about God?" Todd smiled at her with blood dripping down his chin. "Who am I to judge? That's up to Him. Not me."

"We can bring those before Him to be judged." She raised her hands to the heavens.

"These people you're calling devils and demons—they are no such thing." He bowed to Mirtoff and Mi'ko. "They are good and kind and would never do anything as evil as what you've done. Even though it would be easy. You realize they have flipping spaceships, right? With lasers? They could destroy us and never have to land a ship."

"That won't be a problem, for long." Her eyes narrowed, and her face filled with a menacing smile.

What the hell is she talking about?

He shook his head. "No one with any kindness in them could have done what you did."

"Is that what they've filled your head with?" She laughed. "All instruments of the devil, but what can we expect from a weak homosexual sinner? Of course you're in league with them!" She faced the crowd. "Or is it you've fallen for one of them? A certain young son of the vice speaker. The devil comes in all forms. I'm sure his form is very tempting to someone like you," she taunted. "You little fool, falling into the welcoming arms of the devil. Too bad he's not here. That would have been perfect."

How does she know about Mi'cin and what he's doing? Say nothing.

Todd tried to free himself from the grip of the guards.

"Oh, how sweet." Martha beamed and turned to Mi'ko. "Don't look so surprised. I don't live in a cave or under a rock. You can't hide from God. He has eyes everywhere, even in space."

It didn't matter what she said. None of it mattered. He had to keep her engaged. Fixed on what he was doing and saying. Running and hiding from her wasn't an option. It didn't matter what she knew. She was an evil woman, and that's what evil did. It made someone doubt and feel bad about who they are because they couldn't look at themselves without witnessing their own evil.

"Killing people because you're scared of them, is that what your God tells you to do?" Todd tried to search for Vi-Narm but didn't see her. "Just like the other terrorists we've been plagued with. Blowing up planes and buildings, killing thousands of people, all because your twisted and sick view of religion tells you to."

Martha smirked. "You know so little."

Todd gasped.

Oh God, this isn't it. She has bigger plans.

He shot up and quickly glanced around, scanning the assembly members. "Unless you have other plans? What is this actually about, Martha? It's not the Nentraee. That's too easy. What?" he shouted at her.

"Too bad you won't live long enough to find out."

Todd turned to Mirtoff and Mi'ko, then back to Martha. "They're not the devil here. You are!" He spat the words at her as a blinding pain filled his body. Gunfire and screams rose as he fell forward. Vi-Narm came out from behind Martha before Todd hit the ground.

Twenty-Eight: Aftermath

"YOU WERE IMPRESSIVE out there." Jerry rested a hand on top of Todd's head. "You should run for political office. I mean, I knew you had big balls, but wow!"

Todd opened his eyes.

Jerry knelt next to him.

A soft gray haze clouded everything else that should've been in Todd's view. The only person Todd could focus on was Jerry.

"Am I dead?" Todd asked. "Did I get shot?"

"You got the job done, is what you got." Jerry chuckled. "Well, you, Greg, and Vi-Narm, which is inspiring. And, better yet, you did it live on TV. Broadcast to billions of people all around the world and to the Nentraee ships." Jerry kissed Todd's forehead. "You, my dear, are once again thrust into the spotlight and the public eye."

"Ugh." Todd grimaced." I forgot about that."

Jerry pushed a few pieces of hair from Todd's forehead. "You really did a good job channeling Dan. Although, you should have worn a different shirt. Not the best color for TV."

Todd closed his eyes for a long second.

"I'm proud of you," Jerry said.

The words spurred Todd to open his eyes again.

"The Todd I remember wouldn't make that kind of scene, specifically with that passion." His face was surrounded in a soft glow that radiated warmth. "You really do know how to get your point across."

Todd winced at the thought.

I was broadcast all over the world. I think I'd rather be dead.

Jerry patted his arm. "Don't worry about it. You were amazing. You faced her head-on. You didn't back down, and you helped stop what could have been the biggest international and, for that matter, interstellar disaster in history. You saved billions of lives today. It was incredibly brave."

There were so many thoughts running through Todd's head. So much had happened. He inhaled softly. It hurt like the devil, but he managed to take a full breath. "Thanks."

Jerry leaned in and kissed his cheek.

Todd needed to rest for a minute.

"Todd," a soft voice said from beside him.

It took Todd several moments, but he opened his eyes. This time, he was in the vice speaker's shuttle. "What happened?"

Straps held him down on a gurney. It wasn't uncomfortable, but it kept him from moving.

"You don't remember?" Mi'ko examined him carefully. "You distracted Martha Webster and her people long enough so Vi-Narm could stop her from setting off the explosives. We had her, but—"

Todd went to speak, but Mi'ko gently patted him on the shoulder to stop him.

"Yes, Greg managed to alert the authorities to what was happening. They were able to take care of the rest of her people but one." He shook his head. "Her plan, from what we can tell, was ill-conceived and sloppy." He fussed with the blanket that was around Todd. "A good thing for all of us. Not to mention the three of you. I was impressed with how well you all worked together."

Todd tried to lean up on his elbows but was cut off by the straps and his own pain. "Ow."

Mi'ko gently forced him to stay on the gurney. Todd was impressed to see this side of Mi'ko. A nurturing parent and father. "You better rest. My son will not be pleased with me if I don't bring you home in one piece. Your family has also made such inquiries. We are bringing them to the ship so they can see you. They should be there when we arrive."

"Ugh." Todd frowned. His family, Mi'cin, all saw him on TV. *No hiding from this.* He forced his mind to focus. Activity buzzed around the shuttle. "Vi-Narm?" He glanced around the shuttle.

"She's fine. The bullet grazed her arm," Mi'ko replied. "She is much faster than people give her credit for. She has insisted on making sure that our shuttles and our delegation were secure and that your family will be delivered to you once we're back on the ship."

"Why aren't we going to the hospital?" Todd asked.

"After what happened here today"—Mi'ko shook his head—"we are not taking any chances. We don't know who and how deep Martha's group goes; they are still out there." He rested his hand on Todd's arm. "And you are too important to us and to your people. It was not negotiable."

Todd sighed and rested his head back. Every part of him hurt, principally in his head. He caught sight of Mirtoff, walking up to him. A thoughtful smile filled her face.

"Ah, I see you're awake. Good," Mirtoff said. "Thank you again, Todd. You helped us all. You're making this a habit. One I hope you won't need to continue."

"I didn't do anything that anyone else wouldn't do." Todd felt the tick of his timepiece, still in his pants. Maybe it was time he accepted that he was a hero. He wondered exactly how many people watched him and heard all the things he'd said. Why the hell did he say all that stuff? There were other ways to get her attention and keep her focused on him, weren't there?

The kind smile remained on Mi'ko's face. "Rest."

"Be well, Todd." Mirtoff offered him a bow. "My brother and niece asked me to pass along their gratitude. However, they will want to thank you personally." She turned to Mi'ko. "I need to return to the UN chamber hall."

Todd blinked, collecting his thoughts. So many things swam around his mind, it was hard to focus. "Wait. What about the vote and the meeting?"

"Postponed." Mirtoff adjusted her braided hair. "But do not worry yourself. It has been a distressing day for everyone, and you should rest." She turned her attention back to Mi'ko. "I'll be meeting with the UN Security Council momentarily. They are going into an emergency session and asked me to join them. Then, I'll be meeting with President Zachary. He has much to explain."

"I do not believe he realized any of this was happening," Mi'ko said.

"I would not wish to be in his position, the poor male." She shook her head. "There is much to work out."

She glanced back to Todd. "Take care of our special envoy."

Mi'ko bowed as she left the shuttle.

Todd watched her exit with additional security personnel, all Nentraee.

They must have come down from the ship to assist.

"It wasn't the president's fault," Todd said. "She was crazy. I hope they lock her and the rest of those nuts up for life." He sighed. "They don't speak for us. Please, understand, she was crazy as batshit."

"They won't need to," Mi'ko said. "As I started to say, we had her only shortly, before one of her people, we assume, mixed in with the additional human security shot her. She is dead. The area was unsecured and the event was still chaotic, so he or she was able to vanish before anyone understood what happened. I don't suppose she had any intentions of leaving that hall alive." He touched Todd's arm carefully.

"Oh, God."

"I'm afraid—"

"What about what she said? Her plan? This can't be it. She was up to more than this."

"Her secrets and motives may never fully be understood, but we will ensure a proper investigation is done. I will suggest General Gahumed work with your government."

Todd grimaced. *I feel sorry for them.*

"I'm afraid this is far from over." Mi'ko smiled softly. "It won't make any of this easy, but we'll move forward. Things will have to change, but such is the world."

He sounded more determined than Todd had ever seen him.

"It is going to be part of the conversation the speaker will be having with the security council." Mi'ko checked the monitor on the wall. "Ah, you might want to see this." He moved the monitor down.

The news played and Todd watched.

"In a surprise announcement made moments ago by the White House, Chief of Staff Greg McNeil is being named the new secretary of state. Press Secretary Frank Chen cited Mister McNeil's instrumental involvement in preventing the failed assassination attempt of the Nentraee speaker general and other world leaders by former Secretary of State Martha

Webster. Chen continued, speaking of McNeil's lasting support of the White House and his good standing with other world leaders and the Nentraee."

The newscaster turned to face a different camera.

"Meanwhile, support for the Nentraee and outrage over this afternoon's failed attempt at the UN headquarters in New York have been pouring in from every corner of the world. In one of his strongest statements since the arrival of the Nentraee and following the assassination of His Excellency, the Most Reverend Denis Koester, Titular Archbishop of Suacia only hours ago, Pope Pius XIII had this to say: 'Any person claiming to have a standing relationship with Christ could ever do such a thing in His name. God has a place in His heart for all His children, including the Nentraee.' The Pontiff has called on all religious leaders around the world to denounce such hostile acts against all people, human or Nentraee. He concluded by saying, in the eyes of God, we are all equal, and none can judge, but God."

Todd blinked several times.

"You realize that you are partly responsible for this," Mi'ko said. "You should be proud. I knew I made the right choice when I picked you. Now let's get you home."

Todd flushed, leaning back on the gurney, not sure what to say. The ticking of his pocket watch was matching the beating of his heart.

Twenty-Nine: Resolve

TODD ADJUSTED THE blankets on the bed to better cover his legs. The room was a bright white, and the windows had a view into one of the ship's many gardens. Unlike the hospital on Earth, with its antiseptic smell and scratchy sheets, this room smelled fresh and the bedding was soft, like his bed at home.

"You should have come to get me before heading to Earth." Mi'cin sat on the edge of the bed. He checked the digital display behind Todd's head. "Are you in pain?"

On the table in the corner was a small flowering plant. It wasn't from Earth. It was an Iz-Cus, which had large lavender blooms with spiky green leaves and smelled like the ocean. It was beautiful. A balloon floated above the plant with the words *Get Well*.

"Who sent the potted plant and balloon?"

Mi'cin peeked over his shoulder. "General Gahumed."

"Really?"

"She was quite insistent," Mi'cin said. "General Gahumed informed the head medical director that it is a human custom, and since you are the special envoy and human, she would not allow such disrespect."

Todd chuckled, then coughed.

"Are you sure you're not in pain?"

The doctors had run various tests on Todd to ensure he had nothing more than a concussion and two bruised ribs. They wanted to monitor him for the next forty-eight hours.

"I'm fine." Todd offered him a tired glance. "I was in a rush. Plus, you were on the Rádo." He closed his eyes, seeing Martha glowering at him, and shuddered. "I didn't know about Martha. And Greg? I'd never seen him like that before."

"I should have been there," Mi'cin said.

"No." Todd shook his head. *Ow.* "She would have killed you. I know it."

"Instead, it's you who's hurt and I'm to sit by your side and worry." Mi'cin frowned and touched Todd's cheek softly. "Watching you on the broadcast get hurt and fall to the floor was terrifying. I don't want to experience that again."

"I didn't mean to get hit in the head. Next time, I'll be more careful."

"I will send my words to J'Veesa that there will not be a next time." Mi'cin ran a hand through Todd's hair, careful not to hurt him. "What would I do without you, Mister Todd Landon?"

Todd's heart raced at Mi'cin's words. "Well, for now, you are stuck with me."

"And I am lucky for it." Mi'cin leaned in and gently brushed his lips to Todd's. "There are many things I want to explore with you," he whispered.

"I can't wait." Todd leaned forward and kissed Mi'cin again, inhaling his sandalwood scent.

The door swished open. "Oh, thank Christ!" Kati rushed over to his bed.

Mi'cin pulled back, and Todd sat up in the bed as his parents, Brad, and Dan poured in behind her.

Mi'cin stood and bowed. He changed to English. "I'm sorry to have to see you again under such circumstances. Todd is fine, I can assure you." He stepped out of their way.

"I will go. Give you time with Todd. I can check on him later."

Brad reached out, blocking Mi'cin. "No." He straightened his shoulders. "You have as much right to be here as any of us."

Todd's mother bowed to the Nentraee. "Please." Her voice cracked.

Todd was overwhelmed. How had they all been allowed in here? How many Nentraee had they stormed past?

"You scared the hell out of us, Button." His dad walked over and sat on the edge of the bed. "The things you said. Who knows what she could have done to you?"

"That woman was fucking nuts. What the hell were you thinking?" Kati demanded. "The crazy-ass bitch could have fucking killed you." She glanced sideways at Todd's parents. "Um...sorry." Her face reddened.

"No, you're right. She was fucking nuts," Todd's mother said.

The room froze as all eyes turned on Todd's mom.

"Mom." Todd raised a hand to the bridge of his nose as pain twinged behind his eyes.

"Honey, sometimes there are no other words." She adjusted her sweater. "Plus, she threatened my baby. I would..." She wiped at her eyes. "I hate seeing you in a hospital. Promise me you'll be more careful. Let the security and military people handle these things. That's what they're for. Why does it always have to be you?"

"Because they're all flipping incompetent," Dan said.

"Dan's right. Screw that," Brad said. "Promise us you'll take some self-defense classes." He patted Todd's leg. "You need to work on your blocks and definitely your follow-through. All you need is some training, and you could seriously kick some ass."

"We'll work on it." Dan nodded, sitting opposite Todd's father on the bed. "You need to watch your back when you're in those situations." He paused, facing Todd's mom. "Trust me, there is no better self-defense training than what the military provides. Once you're out of this bed, I'll whip your butt into shape. No one will get the drop on you again, not if I can help it."

"You're all talking like this is going to happen again." His mom pursed her lips. "Can't you do your job and leave the dangerous stuff to the others?" She fussed with the blankets on his bed. "Like that sweet Vi-Narm woman. She was the one that met us and got us here without a single word from anyone. She must like you. The poor thing was all bandaged up."

"Vi-Narm brought you here?" Todd asked.

Dan and Kati nodded.

"She even asked where Lori, Michelle, and Kevin were," Brad said. "She has accommodations ready for all of us to stay here until you're better. I'm getting them to come up tonight. They want to see you."

"Honey, I don't want you to have a bigger target on your back than you already do. Please?"

"Mom, too late for that. Todd was all over the TV," Brad said. "Be realistic. He can't just hide." He met Todd's gaze. "Right?"

"Trust me, I'm not going to look for trouble, but considering all that has happened, I think they might be right."

This was his family. Old and new. And this was the reality that lay before him. He had to learn the best ways to protect himself and them. The world was changing, and Mi'ko was right. This wasn't going to end because Martha was dead. It was only the beginning, and he would be damned if he let people like her win.

Thirty: The UN

TODD SAT IN the gallery of the UN assembly hall with the other guests and members of the media. Security, both Nentraee and human, was doubled at every entry point of the building. Everyone, including members of the diplomatic delegations, had to pass through full-body scanners and patdowns. He pulled out his pocket watch and checked the time. A sense of finality filled his mind because, for now, both the humans and the Nentraee were safe and Martha was dead.

Vi-Narm stood with the vice speaker, her arm in a sling but otherwise no worse for wear. She smiled and bowed to him.

His mother was more right about Vi-Narm than she realized. Vi-Narm took the bullet that was meant for him. When he asked her about it, she waved him off and refused to speak any more of it.

I'll watch out for her, and I know she'll watch out for me.

It felt good.

The UN secretary general stood at the same spot he was in two weeks earlier. Considering what he had been through, he had a million-dollar smile. He gave a different speech from the last one. He spoke of building a stronger bond between our two peoples and acknowledged a common enemy. Duck-Hwan Park's speech was drawing to a close.

"No one should take lightly the events of the last several months. The world we once recognized no longer exists. We have to see past our differences and focus on the horizon ahead. Now is an exciting time for the human race. A time to embrace differences and build a future together.

"A special thank you to the three people without whom the future we face may have been completely different...if those who tried to wreak havoc on this organization had succeeded. I am of course speaking of Mister Greg McNeil, secretary of state for the United States of America, Vi-Narm Kapeila of the Nentraee, and lastly, Mister Todd Landon, Special Envoy to Mi'ko Soemu for Terran Affairs and citizen of the United States of America. Their conviction and courage are why we are here today." The room thundered with applause as all three stood up.

Todd glanced at Greg, who was grinning. Vi-Narm smiled at both men. When the applause died down, they all took their seats again, allowing Duck-Hwan to continue.

"Today, we welcome the Nentraee government to the UN as our newest member state." Duck-Hwan shifted his stance and rested his hands on the marble desk. "With a special vote of the UN Security Council, the Nentraee not only will be a full member of this assembly, but they will be joining the UN Security Council as a permanent member." He paused. "It is the hope of this world body that our two peoples will build a lasting peace, ushering in a bright new future for all of us."

"At this time, I welcome Mirtoff Esmi, speaker general of the Nentraee, to say a few words."

Mirtoff walked to the lectern, her cloak hugging her shoulders. She offered a bow. "Thank you, Secretary General Park. It's an honor to be here today. I, too, wish to thank all those who have worked tirelessly these past several months to bring us to this point."

The applause thundered.

"The path ahead of us isn't for one species alone. It's for both our people. We have learned that this path is bumpy and filled with fear of change and prejudice. These are not barriers to halt us, but opportunities to learn and grow. We await this journey of learning and growing."

Mirtoff's dark-brown gaze found Todd's. "It is because of great, brave people, who trusted in one another and believed in the future, that I am able to stand here. They understood they could not make a difference alone, but together. Together, they delivered great change.

"With the approval of this assembly and through private consultation with the security council and all the space-faring nations of this world, we have been given a location to build a new home world for our people. That world is the planet you know as Mars."

An image of Mars filled the large screens on either side of the podium.

"I say here and now, not only to my people, but to the people of Earth, no two worlds, no two species, will be closer than ours. Sharing a bond of loss and a desire to focus on the future. Building a better and stronger tomorrow. This is our first step of a new journey we are all about to take. With our help and with the help and support of this world organization and your space agencies, interplanetary spaceports will be constructed on your moon and on Phobos, the largest orbiting body around Mars. Thus providing our two peoples a link between worlds."

On the screens were both the moon and Phobos, with renderings of what the spaceports would look like. The moon had a large domed city built into the side of a crater with several smaller domes around it. There were animated shuttles, arriving on various landing pads. Phobos spaceport was built underground with large open spaces and picture windows that opened up to views of Mars.

"This undertaking will not happen quickly," Mirtoff continued. "It will take dedication from both humans and Nentraee. We reach out the arm of peace to all of you to ensure a strong and lasting foundation. Finally, I would like to thank the people of Earth personally for myself and my family. Your support and your friendship has proven to us that we have made the right choice in coming here. Thank you." She stood tall with her shoulders in perfect posture.

Applause filled the assembly hall, and like the others, Todd found himself standing and clapping, enthusiastic about the coming future for everyone. It was going to be exciting.

Epilogue

TODD COMPRESSED THE soft grass as he walked. The rain had ended, and the sun peeked out from behind the clouds. The crisp air caused him to zip up his jacket. Eight months. Had it only been eight months?

"And only seven months since Jerry had died," he whispered under his breath as he pushed forward.

"Are you sure you wish me to be here?" Mi'cin glanced over at Todd as they walked.

"Of course," Todd said. "You're important to me, and so was Jerry. I feel it's time for you two to meet."

Mi'cin stopped.

"In a matter of speaking," Todd amended.

They continued wandering until they reached the spot where Jerry's remains were entombed.

"It isn't much, but cremation doesn't leave much." Todd stared at the mausoleum.

"I understand." Mi'cin walked over and touched the marker. "He was twenty-eight. That is young."

"He would've liked you," Todd said.

"Your words are kind." Mi'cin took a step back. "Have you been here often?"

Todd shook his head. He had only been here a few times, which bothered him, but he knew Jerry wasn't here. Jerry was in a far better place.

"We don't keep our dead in large buildings like this," Mi'cin said. "The Martween used to, but no longer. We burn the body with our offerings in a ceremony to help the *nayus* move to be greeted by J'Veesa."

"Is that how all Nentraee memorialize their dead?"

Mi'cin chuckled. "No. It varies by clan. My clan..." He stepped forward. "If you would allow me, I brought a *ta-oolee*, an offering, for Jerry to take with him to meet your God. He was your first mate, and I would like to honor him. It will demonstrate some of what my clan does."

Todd pushed back the tears in his eyes, nodding.

Mi'cin pulled from his cloak the bow and wrapping paper from his Christmas gift.

"You kept that?"

"Of course," Mi'cin said. "It was part of your gift to me. I had hoped to keep it, but a *ta-oolee* must hold great meaning or it is unworthy." He knelt on the ground in front of Jerry's tomb and placed the paper and bow on the ground, finding a small stone to hold it in place. He reached into his pocket and pulled out a small device. "Will you join me?" He peered over his shoulder.

"I don't have anything."

"It doesn't matter," Mi'cin said. "I'm sure you've offered Jerry plenty in your mourning of him." He pointed to the ground next to him. "Please."

Todd kneeled next to Mi'cin as he lit the paper and bow on fire.

Mi'cin bowed and hummed softly until the paper and bow fell to ash and the fire went out. "Jerry Marcus Baker. I will honor your memory and hold Todd dear to me. We never met in life, but I wish for your nayus, your soul, to find your path to God using the smoke from my offering." He raised his head and opened his arms to his side. He turned to Todd. "Thank you for letting me honor Jerry."

Todd wiped at his eyes. "That was lovely. Thank you. What was the song you hummed?"

"An old Ultween death song. I think you would call it a dirge."

Todd shrugged.

"I don't know the words to the song," Mi'cin said. "I doubt there is anyone around who does, but the music is known and used at these ceremonies." He looked at the remains, brushed them into his hands, and stood up.

Todd stood. "Now what?"

Mi'cin thought a moment. "He finds peace. What remains is memory, and you and I will have to honor that memory."

TODD HELD HIS champagne in his hand, watching the bubbles. The space buzzed with conversation and soft music. They couldn't have picked a nicer location for the reception.

The weeks after the UN announcement had been exhilarating and busy. Planning still needed to be done and additional negotiations with the various countries continued. Concerns had to be listened to, and complaints by some of the smaller countries that felt left out. Environmentalists were worried about how the Lunar and Martian environments would be affected, but in the end, everyone seemed to be reaching the agreements necessary. Including changing the mandates from the UN about how the moon and Mars were to be developed. By the end of February, everyone, including Todd, wanted to take a breath and reflect on what had happened.

"What are you talking about?" Todd asked. "When I saw that flash and heard the gunfire, I thought I was dead."

Greg fixed his tie. "I'm sorry I missed it all. Nothing would have made me happier than watching that monster go down."

Todd adjusted his cloak. It had become more familiar. Like everything else. He flexed his hands. They were still sore from his workout. He'd taken Dan up on his offer and was now training in self-defense.

I want to be ready for anything.

"I can't believe you actually took her down without shooting her." Greg beamed at Vi-Narm. "Good thing the media was there. I doubt anyone would've believed it without viewing it all broadcast live."

"It was not much of a challenge." Vi-Narm reached up and pushed a few wisps of hair from her face.

Vi-Narm's being modest. That's an interesting look on her.

"I was pleased it all worked as it did," Vi-Narm continued. "It could have ended badly for everyone. The explosives Martha had in the building could have brought it down and killed everyone inside." She shook her head. "Such a waste of a life."

"Well, what you did was amazing." Todd held up his champagne to her. "I'm glad you were there." He hadn't been aware of how close they had all come to being blown up.

"It was good we were all there." Vi-Narm bowed. "Sadly, there are more of these Liberi Dei out there, hiding."

"I hate the idea of not being able to track down the rest of these people," Greg said. "Martha barely left a trace. I know everyone is searching for them and doing what they can, but I'm worried it won't be enough."

Todd sighed.

"We've managed to find a few of them," Greg said. "The rest are buried deep and quiet for now."

"We will need to be extra vigilant," Vi-Narm said. "I understand you are working with General Gahumed."

"Yes," Greg said. "She's challenging. She doesn't allow for political correctness or care about stepping on people's feelings, which is good. I even got a chance to visit the Rádo. What an impressive ship."

"Scary, right?" Todd asked.

Vi-Narm lifted her shoulders. "It's a battle cruiser. It should be intimidating."

Greg chuckled.

"Well, I'm sure you both will sort it all out." Todd sipped his champagne. "That's why you make the big bucks. As for me, I'm happy to stick with what I do best, running reports and organizing things. My spy days are over."

"I don't believe you were actually a spy," Vi-Narm said.

Todd laughed. "Really?"

Vi-Narm remained quiet.

"Anyway, I had to promise my mom to leave saving the world up to security and the military." Todd tapped his forehead to them.

"Probably for the best." Vi-Narm nursed her e'xin.

"Ouch." Todd held a hand to his heart. "Anyway, I have confidence in both of you." He glanced over the buffet. "Now if you'll excuse me, I have a date with that great-looking food."

He headed toward the table. It was a mix of both human and Nentraee delicacies. He scrutinized the assortment of offerings. He didn't want to hear about that day or the Liberi Dei anymore. A break from it all was what he needed. Yes, they were out there and they would have to be dealt with, but hopefully not by him.

"Mister Landon," a heavily accented voice called out.

Todd turned to meet a short man with a heavy face and a woman. "It's a pleasure to have the opportunity to speak with you. I don't know if you remember, I'm Dr. Dejan Lupu and this is my wife Marya."

"It's a pleasure to see you again, Dr. Lupu," Todd said. "And a pleasure to meet your lovely wife." He rested his champagne glass on the buffet. "You both must be relieved that you weren't in the UN general assembly hall that day."

"I feel as deputy secretary general, I should have been there." Dr. Lupu frowned.

Count yourself lucky. No telling what Martha would have done to you.

"I told my husband that I had to meet the brave man involved in saving so many people." Marya smiled. She had dull eyes and blotchy skin. She had no striking features, but she seemed pleasant enough.

Todd's cheeks warmed at the compliment. Dan and Kati told him his speech went viral, and there were various mixes of it out there. He refused to watch them. That didn't stop Kati. She constantly sent him YouTube links to make sure he saw them. Sometimes he hated technology.

"Well, it's more Vi-Narm and Greg than me."

"Oh, Mister Landon, don't be so modest. You saved the vice speaker during the first attack and then you and Mister McNeil in London. Very brave." Marya's accent was not as thick as her husband's.

"A lot of people still died," Todd said. "So many people lost their loved ones. It's hard to consider it a success with so much loss."

"I'm sure they were all welcomed into the Kingdom of Heaven." Dejan's round face jiggled as he spoke.

"Yes, I'm sure." Todd forced a polite smile. "Sadly, that is little comfort to their families and friends." He spoke as civilly as possible. He understood from experience it was hard to console anyone with those words.

"Much sadness has occurred these past few months, including the loss of Martha Webster." Dejan's expression dropped.

Todd found his accent hard to maneuver. He heard enough and was unable to stop the frown crossing his lips at the mention of Martha's name.

He met Dr. Lupu's gaze. "I'm sorry, but it's because of her that all those people died in the first place. Her and her ilk." His tone had a bite to it.

Dejan shifted from foot to foot. Before he spoke, Marya said, "You misunderstand my husband, Mister Landon. He and Martha worked closely together for many years. She was a family friend. It is a sorrow of losing her to such—" She paused. "—to such darkness."

"Then I'm sorry for your loss." Todd softened his tone, even though the memory of Martha still held bitterness for him.

"Thank you," Dr. Lupu said. "It's a pleasure to speak with you, Todd, and a pleasure to be on such an amazing ship." He glanced around the space.

"A pleasure to meet you, Mister Landon." Marya shook his hand with a warm smile.

He watched them walk off and turned back at the buffet table. It had to be devastating, working so closely with someone only to have them betray you and still manage some form of compassion.

Dr. and Mrs. Lupu are better people than me.

His appetite now gone, Todd moved to the large windows. The coast of Africa sparkled as they floated by with the continued drone of conversation, laughter, and instrumental music behind him. He cleared his mind. He had stood in this exact location for his dinner with Mi'cin. That seemed like a lifetime ago.

"Hello, Todd," Mi'cin said, his voice musical.

Todd turned, meeting Mi'cin's gaze. Those beautiful green eyes—he could stare at them all day. It's hard to believe that green and blue eyes were as common with the Nentraee as brown and hazel were with humans.

Mi'cin reached up and touched Todd's cheek. He noticed the cool graze of the metal from the watch he had bought him.

"I'm glad you're wearing the watch."

"Of course." Mi'cin removed his hand. "Someone close to my heart gave it to me. I could never disrespect him by not wearing it."

Todd had finally asked Mi'cin about the significance of this gesture. Mi'cin had explained it as sign of affection, similar to a human kiss, but this was acceptable in public, where kissing was not. Kissing had been considered too intimate.

"Using this ship was a brilliant idea," Todd said. "Giving everyone a chance to see Earth this way. Seeing how small it is and how small we all are."

Australia now passed by through some of the cloud cover.

"Thank you," Mi'cin said. "My father was pleased with the idea. As too was the speaker general. It made security easier." He stood closer to Todd. "Plus, for me, it has pleasant memories."

"Me too." Todd reached up to touch Mi'cin's cheek softly with the back of his hand. Mi'cin closed his eyes and smiled.

"Please forgive the intrusion, Todd," Mirtoff said.

Todd pulled his attention to Mirtoff and her two companions.

"I would like to introduce you to my brother, Ecra, and niece, Suloff, " Mirtoff said.

Todd bowed.

"I am honored to present Ecra Palmus," Mirtoff said, bowing to Todd.

"It's nice to finally meet you, Mister Landon," Ecra said with a bow. "You have done a great many things for our people, and for my sister. Thank you."

"You honor me." Todd bowed in return. "It's been my pleasure to help in whatever ways I can."

"My niece, Suloff Palmus." Mirtoff bowed.

This is the same formality Mi'ko and Laina showed me at the White House.

"It is a pleasure to meet you, Mister Landon." Suloff bowed. "Thank you for the continued life of my aunt."

Todd said nothing, allowing them their moment of thanks. It was awkward. She was young, maybe a year or two older than his niece Michelle.

I wonder if I should introduce them. Michelle could take her shopping.

Todd bit his lip to keep from smiling. "It was my honor to be of aid. I hope we will never have to endure such a tragedy again."

All three raised their heads.

I'll never get used to that.

"Mi'cin, I apologize for the interruption," Mirtoff said with a polite bow. "We do not wish to keep you from your conversation. However, they insisted on meeting Todd. I'm sure you understand."

"Of course, Madam Speaker." Mi'cin returned her bow.

"It is a pleasure to meet you both." Todd bowed again. "I hope to see you again."

"So do we," Ecra said.

Mirtoff led them off.

Since she was the host, Todd had made sure that she understood the duties humans would expect of her. He didn't want her to accidentally offend anyone. He checked around the group assembled. There were various people on board—a mix of both human and Nentraee.

After the announcement at the UN and the soirée that followed, Todd learned that Mirtoff wanted to have a private reception for those countries that had suffered directly in the attacks—the United States, Great Britain, Norway. A shared pain and memory to build a positive future on. He, of course, had made sure that there were other countries included—all the members of the UN Security Council and Zimbabwe, without whom Todd, Vi-Narm, and Greg would not have been able to stay out of sight when Martha was on her rampage.

Mi'ko bowed, and Todd recognized the perfect knot in the tieback, the one he had given him at Christmas. Laina stood next to him. Todd was certain she had fixed the tieback before they came to the reception, as it wasn't lopsided or loose. She raised her glass to him.

His smile grew larger, and he returned the gesture.

Both Mi'ko and Laina seemed happy that he and Mi'cin were dating. Laina had come to his office and told him she was pleased with the positive effect he had on her son and that if he ever needed her counsel to seek her out.

He returned his attention to Mi'cin and the view outside the window.

"Are you excited about the opportunity to build a new world on Mars?" Todd asked, genuinely curious.

"We will make it work." Mi'cin faced him. "It will be a challenge." He glanced out at Earth. "It is the best option, considering the state of your planet. There isn't anywhere for us to settle."

Todd watched the world pass by.

"Plus, we have the technology to build there. With our propulsion systems, the travel time between worlds will be between ten and fourteen days, giving travelers a chance to enjoy the trip, much like a cruise on one of your oceans."

"I'm excited to see what you and your people come up with," Todd said. "I have no doubt it will be spectacular. It'll be a whole new world for you to build on, giving you the opportunity to recreate the best of Benzee without our interference."

They both turned to the window, Earth slowly rotating in front of them.

Appendix of Terms

A': Day

A'UNA: Benzee holiday, the day the Clan War ended; celebrated by all Benzee but mainly celebrated by the Za'entra.

A'A LUTA: Marks the day the Nentraee world was destroyed; a day to remember all those who died and were left behind.

ACTIONSHIP: A two-seater (pilot and gunner) attack ship.

A'DA MAGINA: Day of hope, celebrated to remind the people that there is always hope.

A' GODÁ FAOO: Celebration after the third right of fatherhood is complete.

A'KO HUNE: Evil little spirits who are known to haunt weddings.

A' MEV: Naming day. This is similar to a birthday. It is the day that the Nentraee are given their name and presented to friends and family. Normally a week after birth.

A'SOOTEE: Rebirth, when the Nentraee calendar begins.

BENZEE: Nentraee home world

A'ZEN: Day the Za'entra celebrate the final winning battle over Dentraee, Martween, and U'Zraee.

CANDRA: First planetoid of Benzee; closest in orbit; similar size to Earth's moon.

CÁDO: Companion animal to the Nentraee. They are a medium-sized animal that has limited intelligence and can communicate on a basic level.

COLO CO MO: A Nentraee dish—a combination of meat and vegetables over a noodle. Very popular but very expensive to make as both meats and vegetables are rationed on the ships. It has an almond and citrus scent but is spicy.

DAMUS WITH MĨ (MEES): A vegetable-based dish with a thick sauce and a flatbread. A common dish among the Za'entra.

DEN A'TAE: Four-day religious event to honor Jealug Bravisa.

DUSAL: Flying water bird that buzzes and can be annoying.

É'BOWUNÁ: Stone unity bowl, used in all Nentraee wedding ceremonies. Each clan uses a different type of stone decorated in various ways.

EMISARATION: All Nentraee children, when they reach the age twenty-four, are considered adults with full rights: voting, É'mawee, etc. At this point, they are no longer considered children and can make all their own life choices.

É'MAWEE: Nentraee wedding. A two-day event where the families and invited guests of the couple come together to witness and speak. It is a celebration of the couple and the family.

É'MAW Po: Family dinner hosted by the families of the couple getting married.

É'MAZEE: Day of joining—the actual day the couple is legally married.

É'MAZ PO: Couple's first dinner—the lunch or dinner hosted by the newly married couple.

É'TOK: Wooden token placed in the É'bowuná by each person in witness of the É'mawee. The token has a unique symbol on it that represents the person in attendance. They will place the token in the bowl as an indication of their support of the couple and the wedding.

E'XIN: A rich Nentraee wine, served warm. Traditionally served at weddings or very special events, now it is enjoyed on other occasions. It has a fruity chocolate flavor.

GĨ (GEES): (1) A flying lizard-type animal; (2) A medium range passenger shuttle holding between ten and fifteen people, used mainly by government personnel.

GODÁ FAOO: Rights of fatherhood, there are three stages. Once the third right is granted, the only way Godá Faoo can be revoked is if the father has a child by another female.

IZ-CUS: A flowering plant. Instead of petals, it has pink sweet-smelling berries. The berries are used as a perfume or deodorant.

IZ-GOOT: A flowering plant with large lavender blooms with spiky green leaves. Smells like ocean mist.

IZ: A flowering plant

Ĩ-TA (EES-TA): Vulgar word used to describe the Za'entra, meaning half blood. Commonly used prior to the Clan War. Now it is considered very offensive by almost everyone.

Ĩ-NO (EES-NO): One of the worst, most vulgar terms in the Nentraee language. The English equivalent would be "Fucking Bitch."

JAREEDAN: A leafy plant that has a strong lavender scent.

JEALUG BRAVISA: Formal reference for the Nentraee deity.

JEKTĨL (JEK-TEESL): A high-level accountant or controller for a dedicated project.

J'VEESA: Common reference for the Nentraee deity.

KAP'ERIN: Ceremonial cloak, dress garb, used by the Nentraee. Often embroidered in gold or silver with the symbols of the seven clans. The military Kap'erin differs in that it will only be embroidered with the signet of the specific branch of the military.

KAROO: Silver-laced ear cuff worn in the left ear by some Za'entra. It started as a way to remember those lost in the Clan War, now it's a fashion accessory. Some were passed down over the years, but most are new with new designs. There is no one single design. They can vary.

KĨ (KEES): Largest class of military ship in the Nentraee fleet.

KUMNAS: An Ultween thick dip. A combination of nuts with oil and spices.

LAGU: Chopsticks used for eating, normally used in the left hand.

LÁOO: A tieback for longer than normal hair, used by males of the Altraee clan to keep their hair in a neat ponytail. The strands are braided around the hair, ending in a standard knot.

OMLANGA: Nentraee dish—a flat noodle and meat dish made like a casserole with the equivalent of cheese and spices. A common dish among the Za'entra Clan. Now, however, after the Clan War, only served on A'una to celebrate. This has a meaty, sweet, spicy scent.

MENTRA: Largest planetoid of Benzee. It also has the farthest orbit.

MÉTKIP: Position or title of a meeting keeper and note taker. Similar to a secretary.

NABUTIMABA: Tallest tree on Benzee, can grow to heights of 200 meters. Most grow between 90 and 120 meters tall. Has a nutty scent.

NAYUS: The Nentraee spirit or soul

NA-TRAEE: The title for the Dentraee spirit finder or talker. This is the priestess the Dentraee use in the event that the body cannot be found or entombed properly.

NENTRAEE: The race of people from the planet Benzee. There are seven clans, each with different physical features. Shared physical features include.

> Noses that continue past the brow line joining their forehead ridges, which vanish into their hairline.

> Pointed ears.

> No body hair except for the hair on the tops of their heads, which both males and females will keep long. Males will wear it tied back and females will create elaborate hair sculptures.

RÁDO: Name of the Kī-class battle cruiser that is the flagship of the Nentraee fleet. It is also home to the General Command offices where military command in maintained—the command center for the fleet and the most heavily protected.

SAGVARWA: An Ultween dish. A sausage filled with meat and various spices and dried fruit. Often served with kumnas for dipping.

SALRA-KÉ: Nentraee dish—meat wrapped in either a leafy vegetable or thin bread with a thick sauce. A common midday meal for the Dentraee.

SEYAS: A baby cádo

TA-OOLEE: Offering for the dead.

TÉ: A large spoon-type device with one very sharp edge used in conjunction with the Lagu—normally used in the right hand.

TIEBACK: A piece of cloth or leather used by Nentraee males as a hair tie to keep their long hair in a ponytail and out of their faces.

TUMA: Nentraee coffee; this drink is traditionally served cold and has a sweet spicy flavor. The scent is similar to chocolate-covered chili peppers.

U'XTRA: Second planetoid of Benzee, smallest, oval shape.

WÁ: Largest water mammal, similar to an Earth dolphin but larger and lacking the long snout. The Wá look like a combination of a shark and a dolphin.

YARUS: Tree, similar in size and color to a Japanese Maple tree, but with purple leaves and bare bark.

YÉP: A term used to describe troublesome children.

VAK YÉP: Slang. A little bastard or a weak little male.

XĨMÉ (XEES-MÉ): Small blue-feathered raven-type bird that flies in groups of five or seven.

Appendix of Clans

ALTRAEE: Benzee clan, race of people whose features are very similar to that of the Martween, but their stature is closer to the U'Ztraee. They have a skin tone that is tan-red. They have dark hair: blacks and deep browns. Their eyes range in the family of greens. They have high cheekbones.

> Some males wear a modified tieback (a Láoo) that braids around their ponytail keeping the hair tight and neat. Normally finished in a tight knot.

CALEEN: Benzee clan, race of people who are one of the most powerful and influential clans on Benzee; much of Nentraee culture is based on the Caleen. Their features, including their hair, tend to be some of the fairest of the clans. The clan typically has blue and green eyes.

DENTRAEE: Benzee clan, race of people who are very religious and conservative. Their features are the closest to the Caleen, sharing many of the same features. Only their skin color and hair color differ, having aqua eyes and skin tones similar to the Utlween.

> Can be very traditional and religious.

> Started the Clan War against the Za'entra. Clans that supported Dentraee at the start of the war were the Martween and U'Ztraee.

MARTWEEN: Benzee clan, race of people, most populous clan on Benzee prior to the evacuation of the planet. The shortest of the clans and they tend to have features that are more delicate than the other clans with midrange coloring. Eyes tend to be darker like the Za'entra as is their hair color.

One of the clans to start the Clan War.

ULTWEEN: Benzee clan, a race of people whose features are much darker than most of the clans with the exception of the U'Ztraee. Their eyes tend to be in shades of aqua and they have mostly brown hair. Their race has the most subtle forehead ridges of all the Nentraee.

U'XTRAEE: Benzee clan, a race of people whose features are the darkest of the clans and their eye color is the lightest. Their hair tends to also be the darkest. They also tend to be the tallest of the clans and have the hardest forehead ridges of the clans.

One of the clans to start the Clan War.

ZA'ENTRA: Benzee clan, race of people whose hair is auburn or darker in color and their features are darker. They also have the darkest-colored eyes. Dark-brown eyes are the rarest. They tend to be an exotic-looking clan. Because of their mixed blood, some of the ridges on their foreheads will be more pronounced than others.

Some males and females wear a silver-laced ear cuff (karoo) in their left ear. It started as a way to remember those lost in the Clan War, and now it's a fashion accessory. Some were passed down over the years, but most are new with new designs. There is no one single design; they can vary.

They are a newly recognized clan. Prior to recognition, they were listed as half-breeds. Neither of their clans wanted to include them. They were outcasts until after the Clan War, where they were recognized as their own clan.

Acknowledgements

As with book one, these novels would not have been possible without the support of my beta readers and writing group. You all have been more help than you know.

A very special shout out to fellow author Barbara Russell—you aren't getting the wedding you want, well not yet, but thank you for continuing to be there. Also, another nod of gratitude to author Randy Krzak—again, your support has been great.

About the Author

M.D. Neu is a LGBTQA fiction writer with a love for writing and travel. Living in the heart of Silicon Valley (San Jose, California) and growing up around technology, he's always been fascinated with what could be. Specifically drawn to sci-fi and paranormal television and novels, M.D. Neu was inspired by the great Gene Roddenberry, George Lucas, Stephen King, Alice Walker, Alfred Hitchcock, Harvey Fierstein, Anne Rice, and Kim Stanley Robinson. An odd combination, but one that has influenced his writing.

Growing up in an accepting family as a gay man, he always wondered why there were never stories reflecting who he was. Constantly surrounded by characters that only reflected heterosexual society, M.D. Neu decided he wanted to change that. So, he took to writing, wanting to tell good stories that reflected our diverse world.

When M.D. Neu isn't writing, he works for a nonprofit and travels with his biggest supporter and his harshest critic, Eric, his husband of nineteen plus years.

Email: info@mdneu.com

Facebook: www.facebook.com/mdneuauthor

Twitter: @Writer_MDNeu

Website: www.mdneu.com

Instagram: www.instagram.com/authormdneu

Blog: www.mdneu.com/blog

Other books by this author

The Calling
The Reunion
A Dragon for Christmas

A New World
Contact, Book One

Also Available from NineStar Press

Connect with NineStar Press

www.ninestarpress.com
www.facebook.com/ninestarpress
www.facebook.com/groups/NineStarNiche
www.twitter.com/ninestarpress
www.tumblr.com/blog/ninestarpress